'Til Death...

Diane E. Lock

Til Death...

ISBN 9781689659079

'Til Death...

For Karen

Til Death...

One

Late again, Catherine thought, letting the Lincoln roll to a stop on the driveway. Late enough, she hoped, turning off the engine. She opened the door but sat for a moment, taking in the big white colonial glowing in the moonlight, with its regimented rows of mullioned windows, all dark at this hour. When she wondered, was the last time she looked forward to coming home? *If it weren't for Alyson...* she might never come back. With a weary sigh she collected her purse and briefcase and took the winding flagstone path to her front door.

Across the road, Janice Kurtz woke from a fitful sleep at the sound of tires crunching slowly up the Moores' driveway. Big car; Catherine's Lincoln. The clock on her dresser glowed a neon green 11:52. Strange hours for a realtor, she thought. Who on earth buys a house at this time of night?

She heard the car door close with a soft, expensive thunk and padded to the bedroom window. Her neighbor, Catherine Moore, tall and slim in a tailored suit, walked to her door, high heels tapping the flagstones. Janice felt a twinge of envy; she'd look like a sack tied in the middle in an outfit that snug.

Janice turned back to the bed she had shared with Gary for the past ten years, empty now. He'd been gone a week, needed to find himself, whatever that meant. There had to be a reason - another woman, something! Tears threatened as she reached for his pillow, but a sudden angry roar in the quiet August night from the house across the road brought her back to her feet; there'd be no sleep now. Grabbing her phone and the old terrycloth robe, Janice hurried down the stairs to the living room and her favorite seat, the wing chair in the bay window.

Barely breathing, she peered through the sheer curtains at the Colonial across the way. She wasn't snooping - heavens, Janice wouldn't be caught dead spying on her neighbors, but the roar had come from the Moores. Something bad was happening over there. Again. They fought an awful lot, Catherine and whatsisname - Frank. Over the years Janice often heard raised voices, slamming doors, one or the other of them driving off down the road in a tearing hurry, but from the sound of it this might be worse than other times.

She wriggled in the seat to get more comfy and rubbed her eyes. On such a warm night a frosty glass of iced tea would help keep her awake, but the kitchen was at the back of the house and she dare not leave her post.

The Moores moved into the neighborhood three, four years ago. At the beginning Janice tried to be friendly, inviting them over for coffee, Ga-- Gary's annual barbeque, her Christmas brunch, but they kept pretty much to themselves. Their little girl, Alyson, seemed to be nice. Kind of shy, but she and Bonnie got on well. Alyson, Bonnie and Brian would be starting Middle School next week. Lordy, how time flew. Janice could hardly believe her twins were old enough.

Yawning, she slipped the heavy robe off her shoulders, imagining the tall glass of iced tea, along with one of the blueberry muffins she'd baked this morning.

Catherine always seemed preoccupied, never a minute to chat, appointments to keep, whatever. Gary—Janice's breath caught every time she thought of her husband - Gary liked her, thought she was a classy woman. And indeed she was, slender and elegant in a way Janice could never hope to be, one of those Boston Brahmins, high society people that Massachusetts was so all-fired proud of. At least she wasn't snooty.

But the husband! What a piece of work. Frank Moore was not a good neighbor, never said hello, not even a wave of the hand as he drove by in his fancy silver Lexus. He behaved as if he was too good for them, like he belonged up on Hillcrest with the really wealthy people like the Wetherbees. He should just move on up there with the rest of the snobs.

A brilliant flash of light flared and died in a bedroom window across the road. The master, Janice knew, their homes were identical. Immediately followed by a bellow of rage, a terrified scream, then dead silence. This was getting scary, like one of those horror movies she couldn't watch. *Oh. My. God.* What to do? Janice grabbed her phone to call the police, but what would she say? Heard a noise in the night? They'd say it was probably some cat caught in a fence. She could call Catherine, see if everything was okay, but then they'd know she'd been listening, and that would be too embarrassing. Better to wait a bit, let things calm down. She settled back into the soft chair...

... and woke with a shock when the mantel clock chimed. The night was quiet again, hopefully her neighbors were at peace. Turning to go back to bed, she spied a car with a tiny flashing blue light on the dash driving erratically up the street toward her house, slowing down at every mailbox, obviously scanning for an address. Janice sank back down into the chair when she saw it turn into the Moores' driveway. Someone *had* called the cops! Quivering, she leaned closer to the window and parted the sheers the tiniest bit.

A man got out and walked up to the Moores' front door. After about a minute the brass coach lamps on each side of the door lit up and Janice recognized Detective Costello, Laura-from-the-church-choir's husband. How exciting! The door opened. He stepped inside. The door closed behind him.

She waited a few more minutes, but it appeared there'd be nothing else to see tonight. Tying the belt on the old terry robe around her middle, Janice waddled to the kitchen, poured herself a glass of iced tea and slathered butter on a pair   of   blueberry   muffins.

Two

This front walk should be longer, Catherine thought, quickly reaching the front door. She stood for a moment, sighed, then tapped Frank's birthdate into the keypad and let herself into the unlit foyer. Slipping off her shoes, she tiptoed across the charcoal and cream checkerboard tiles, but a muffled rumble stopped her mid-stride. Head cocked, she listened hard to the otherwise silent house. Just the ice maker, she realized with a rueful grin as cubes tumbled into the bin in the freezer.

With exaggerated care she placed her keys in the ceramic tray on the narrow hall table, set her worn leather briefcase on the floor, turned and followed a moonlit path up the gracefully curved, thickly carpeted staircase.

Upstairs, peeking into Alyson's softly lit bedroom, she caught the glint of something shiny on the rumpled bed, and crept closer. Max, a life-size stuffed monkey, Aly's bedtime companion and confidante since her third birthday, gazed placidly at the ceiling with his one remaining glass eye. She smiled, remembering the day Alyson saw him in the shop. From her stroller, straining to reach the monkey, calling "Max, Max!" as if he already had a name, quieting down only when she had him snuggled in her arms.

Catherine untangled his ungainly arms and legs from the comforter and tucked him in beside the pillow, marveling as she did at the miracle that was her daughter.

Over the past year the softly rounded child of eleven had turned a lean twelve, with Catherine's long limbs and Frank's copper curls and blue eyes. But no - his eyes were pale blue and cold, Aly's big eyes were a deeper shade, like cornflowers. In a a couple of years she'd be in high school, then off to college, out of the nest. Catherine didn't like to think that far ahead. She straightened the covers, kissed her daughter's firm, soft cheek and crept silently down the hallway to her own dark bedroom.

"Where the *hell* have you been?"

She flinched as though she'd been hit. "Frank! Good heavens, you scared me."

A slight breeze parted the drapes at the open window, and a shaft of moonlight revealed her husband sprawled on the king-size bed, naked except for the bath towel spread across the bulge of his erection.

"It's so late, I thought you'd be asleep." *Hoped and prayed.*

"Well?"

Was it the way he slowly raised himself up on one elbow, a big man appearing even bigger, that intimidated her? Or was it the tone of his voice, stern, like a parent reprimanding a child. Feeling very much like a stubborn child, Catherine folded her arms across her chest. "Where do you think."

"I asked you a question."

"At the office."

"Until midnight?"

"Frank, we've been through this a dozen times." She squared her shoulders and took a step further into the darkened room.

"I'm a realtor, evenings and weekends are part of–"

"Don't you dare lecture me!

"Tonight–"

"Shut–"

"my clients found a house they loved–"

"--the fuck up!"

"Frank, please, you'll wake Alyson." She moved toward her dresser.

"Maybe I want to know more about this 'client'? Just the two of you, cozy dinner, drinks in a bar?"

Oh Lordy, not this crap again. She almost laughed, remembering the sweet elderly couple.

"I took them back to my office to write up an Offer." Turned her back to him. "Which I have to present in the morning. Early."

In the soft moonlight she watched him watching her in the mirror as she took off her pearl necklace and earrings. She knew Frank didn't give a damn about her business, but nerves kept her talking. "Sellers' market, you have to move fast..." She faked a yawn. "I'm wiped."

"Hurry up and get into bed."

Please, not tonight. She crossed the thick Colonial blue carpet to the walk-in closet they shared and flipped on the night light. Shrugged the linen jacket off her shoulders and set it neatly on a padded hanger. Slowly stepped out of her slim tan skirt, hung it with careful precision, smoothing out each little crease. Unbuttoned and slipped out of her cream silk blouse and draped it over the skirt with great care. Dropped her slip into the hamper and reached back to unhook her brassiere.

"What is taking so long?"

Startled, she turned to see Frank's broad frame blocking the doorway, shutting her into the closet. The towel lay in a crumpled heap on the carpet behind him. He grabbed her arm.

"Frank, I'm too tired." Knowing she was asking for trouble.

His punch caught her totally unawares. He'd slapped her before, it seemed to energize him; but a closed fist punch in the face? She saw the shock in his eyes and felt his body sag against the door frame. She shoved past him, stumbled out of the closet and tripped on his discarded towel, diving headlong into her nightstand. Aly's baby picture hit the wall in a shower of shattering glass; the old absurd blue Princess phone jangled to the floor; the lamp wobbled and crashed into the wall; the bulb flared and immediately went dark. Catherine crawled into the corner and crouched there, breathing hard, straining to see in the dark after the brilliant flash of light. The absolute silence was eerie, deafening.

"Cath, Catherine, I'm so—"

Heart thudding, blood pulsing loud in her ears, Catherine saw him grab something off the dresser, looked like a flashlight, and lumber toward her, waving the thing in the air - dear Lord, he was going to hit her with it! Her fingers scrabbled around on the carpet in terror for something to use for protection. A shard of glass stabbed her hand, but she found and clutched the silly little phone with both hands.

Frank steadily closed in on her, whispering. "Catherine?"

But she was not going to let him hurt her again! Raising the phone above her head, she steeled herself to smash his head in with it if he touched her.

Suddenly the light in the hallway blazed and Alyson stood transfixed in the bedroom doorway, Max clutched in her arms, her mouth stretched wide in a soundless scream.

With a roar, Frank turned and lunged for his daughter.

Catherine's horrified shriek filled the room as her trembling fingers punched 911 into the phone.

Three

The shrill of the bedside telephone woke Laura, cruelly wrenching her back from the sparkling white sand and gently lapping waves of Myrtle Beach. She fumbled for the phone, wishing as always that they could get rid of the damned thing, at least get it out of the bedroom. But cops had to have a land line for emergencies.

"Yeah?"

"Mrs. Costello?"

"Mmmph." The digital clock on the nightstand glowed 12:23.

"Stan Jackson here, Mrs. C, at the precinct. Sorry to wake you. I need the boss."

Beside her, Tony was sound asleep, his dark head buried under the pillow.

"He's sleeping, Stan. He just got home."

"I'm real sorry, Laura, but there's nobody else."

Laura poked Tony in the ribs.

"Wha?"

"Stan."

Tony took the phone, instantly awake. "Yeah, sure, Stan. I can be up there in, uh, ten, fifteen minutes." One hand rubbing sleep out of his eyes, the other reaching for the pants he had dropped on the floor half an hour earlier.

"Tony, it's not right, you just got home!" Huddled up against the headboard, Laura watched him pull on his jeans. "You shouldn't have to work both day and night."

"Don's away on vacation and I'm it. That's how it is in a small town." He stood, buckling his belt. "You asked for this, Laura. Remember?"

"Oh sure, it's all my fault." Ever since the move from Boston in June Tony never missed a chance to let her know how miserable he was in the bedroom town of Gilford.

"You're the one begged me to leave the city." He pulled on his shirt. "Woulda made Leut... ah, what's the use!" He swiped the car keys off the dresser. "Domestic call up on the Ridge," he threw back at her from the bedroom doorway, "seems even the rich have their little tiffs."

Laura listened to Tony's SUV back down the driveway and speed away into the quiet night. True, she had pushed for them to move to the suburbs, but she missed the city, hated the dead silence of night out here. In the North End of Boston, where they had both grown up, it never really got dark, all night long there were lights and noise, the rush of traffic, the sounds of people living. She hadn't been too crazy about moving to a small town either, twenty, thirty miles away from friends and family, but she thought it would be safer here for all of them.

The fifteen years Tony worked for the Boston Police Department had turned Laura into a nervous wreck. It was agony, never knowing if he'd end his shift dead or alive, waiting for the phone call, the two apologetic cops at the door.   Laura couldn't relax until he strolled into their apartment, white teeth flashing in a huge grin.   See, I told you I'd be fine, you didn't have to wait up. He'd laugh, call her his little worrywart, but I'm glad you did.   And they'd make love.

But those days on the second level of the triple decker on Hanover Street could have been in another lifetime.   Tony hadn't called her his little anything in years.   And as for making love, they didn't do much of that any more either.

All that aside, though, life was better out here.   For one thing, they had way more space, a family room in the basement; a yard for the kids.   Laura would have loved to live up on the Ridge like her friend Janice Kurtz, but Janice's husband was an airline pilot, everybody knew they made tons of money.   Moving up there was out of the question on Tony's salary, and Laura didn't work 'outside the home', she had chosen to be home for her children instead of out chasing a career.   No, she wasn't crazy about Gilford, but this three-bedroom raised ranch was on a nice street and walking distance to Gina's school.   She still worried about Tony, of course, but angry husbands and teenage vandals were small potatoes compared to the gangs and drugs and crazies with guns that he'd had to deal with in Boston.

Wide awake now, she went in to check on the kids, tucking in each one, kissing them as they slept.   *Madonn'*, how the years flew by.   Anthony's chin dark with fuzz at fifteen.   Gina, going on twelve, light as a feather in her toe shoes, a born ballerina.   And Claudia, nearly seventeen, the same age as Laura when she and Tony started having sex. And getting pregnant.   But they'd been city kids; city kids

12

grew up fast. She crossed herself, sending up a quick little prayer. Please keep my daughters safe from fast-talking good-looking boys out here in the boonies.

She shut the door softly on the girls' room, hugged her bare shoulders against the breeze in the hall as she passed under the attic fan. Tony said she spoiled them but what did he know, the hours he worked. They'd practically grown up without a father; she'd pretty much raised these kids alone.

Shivering a little, Laura went to the kitchen, took a bottle down from the cabinet over the stove and poured a small drink into a water glass. Whenever she got up in the night, especially if Tony had to go out on a call, a shot helped her get back to sleep. She gulped an ounce or so standing at the kitchen counter, shuddering as the whiskey burned her throat, spread warmth across her chest.

They were great kids, everybody said so. She'd done that much right, at least. Laura splashed more scotch into her glass, drank it quickly and carried the bottle to the table. Pulled out a chair. Caught her ghostly reflection in the dark window.

Short brown hair, neatly bobbed, no gray thanks to Lady Clairol®, and still petite. She pulled her nightgown taut over her abdomen and turned sideways to admire her flat tummy. When she married Tony, nobody knew she was three months gone with Claudia. Back then he called her his kewpie doll.

Now, three kids and eighteen years later, she still weighed the same hundred and six pounds, didn't have a wrinkle or a bulge anywhere. People couldn't believe she was thirty-seven years old.

She took another swig of scotch, remembering Tony at

twenty, a dark-haired, dark-eyed sex machine. Tonight, hoping they could make long, slow love, she had worn her sexy black nightie to bed, the one Tony bought her five, six years ago, but he'd stumbled into bed near midnight, she could have been wearing flannel pyjamas for all he noticed.

Mesmerized by her reflection in the window, Laura watched herself push the spaghetti straps off her shoulders, felt the satin gown slip and settle gently around her waist. For an Italian woman she had tiny breasts, something she'd always been proud of. They were still firm with very dark nipples, almost black. Touching one with her fingertips she saw it harden, felt a sexual tug between her legs, heard her breath come faster. Her eyes glazed as her hand slid down the silky smooth fabric to the now throbbing mound-- Trembling, she pulled up the gown, covered her shoulders with a dishtowel left to dry overnight on the oven door handle. God forbid she should start playing with herself here in her own kitchen. Soon, though, she might have to buy one of those vibrators, all the action she was getting. She took another gulp of warm scotch and snickered, imagining Tony coming into the bedroom while she… pleasured herself.

What was wrong with the man? She took good care of her body, she was still crazy in love with him, yet Laura couldn't remember the last time they'd made love. A familiar wave of anxiety gradually replaced the warm sexy feeling. Tony had come in real late again tonight and gone straight to sleep. Double shift, he'd said. The second… no, the third time in two weeks.

It was starting again, just like in Boston, the real reason she'd begged him to leave the city. The unexplained late hours, Tony's short temper, how he went out of his way to avoid looking at her, that hypocritical wide-eyed innocence when she questioned him. It was all happening again! He had to be fooling around! Tony could and did swear 'til he was blue in the face that he never cheated on her - never thought of cheating - but she knew; a wife *knew*. He was messing around again, just like before. And like before, Laura would be more than willing to forgive, but as long as Tony insisted he'd done nothing, what could she do? Unless she could prove it, her hands were tied.

Pazzo. Crazy, he called her. Paranoid. Well he could call her every name under the sun, but she wasn't stupid. All the signs pointed to him tomcatting around. Again.

Laura drained her glass, climbed the footstool and pushed the nearly empty bottle to the back of the cabinet over the stove, hidden among the olive oils and vinegars. Crazy? Maybe, but from now on she'd pay real close attention to his every move. The day she had proof that son of a bitch had a little cupcake on the side, she'd kill him. Or herself.

Four

"Mrs. Moore?" Tony flashed his badge at the door. "Detective Costello."

The woman stepped aside to let him in. Classy lookin'. Thirty-seven, thirty-eight-ish. Long auburn hair hanging loose around her face. With both hands she pushed her hair snug behind her ears. Twice. A tic, Tony figured, probably a nervous gesture she made all the time. The movement revealed her eyes. One puffed-up, half closed. The other green, kinda like the ocean, or maybe blue. Colorblind, Tony couldn't tell the difference between blue and green. But he clearly saw her red hair, his favorite. Five-six or seven, a hundred and fifteen, twenty, pounds. *Very* easy to look at, wasn't for the split lip, the eye that would be black by morning.

"Evenin' Ma'am. Sorry to bother you, but someone here called 911."

She licked her lips, but before she answered Tony heard heavy feet pounding down thickly carpeted steps behind her, sensed her stiffen. A man stopped at the bottom of the curved staircase, arm draped casually around the post, the whatever you call it thingy at the end of the railing with what looked like a pineapple on top. Cool, calm, big guy, mid-forties - maybe the woman was older than she looked - six feet one or two, lean but getting a bit sloppy around the waist. Light brown crinkly curly hair, like Teddy Kennedy, gray at the temples, and pale Husky dog eyes, expressionless, just about the coldest eyes Tony had ever seen in all his years on the force. Lips compressed into a thin, mean line. The bastard looked extremely capable of having given the lady that black eye.

"You would be Mr. Moore?"

Tony watched the man decide to be nice. Saw him put on a smile, come to the door, reach a beefy arm out for Tony's hand. "Frank Moore. Is there a problem?" At the same time the other arm went around his wife's shoulders. Tony saw her flinch.

"The realtor, sir? Casey & Moore?"

"Oh no. My *wife's* the real estate tycoon." Was that a sneer? "*I'm* an executive VP with Merritt, Finch & Thompson."

Tony recognized the name of the investment firm but he kept his face deliberately blank.

"You must know MF&T - we're the largest investment firm in Boston."

"Oh." Tony shrugged. "Oh yeah."

Moore rolled his eyes, now he knew Tony for a complete ignoramus. "So, what can we do for you, officer?" That warm hearty smile didn't reach those cold blue eyes.

"That's Detective, sir. Detective Costello. Someone here called 911 at..." Tony consulted his notepad..."at twelve-thirty-nine this morning. I have to ask you a few questions."

"Certainly, but my wife and I were in bed at that time.

17

We didn't see or hear anything." His arm lay comfortably across his wife's shoulders.

Tony didn't notice any pressure, no warning look, but he saw the spirit flicker and die in the woman's eyes. With this bully around it would be impossible to get anything out of her.

"Trouble somewhere in the neighborhood?"

Cool. Real cool. "No sir. Call came from this house, we have to investigate. You and the wife have an argument?"

"Argument?"

Yes sir, you know, a disagreement." More likely a brawl.

"Well, we did have a bit of a discussion about the charge account bills before we went to bed and I might have raised my voice a tad. You know how women are with money." That cozy smile again, the things we men have to put up with. A shark's grin, all teeth and no warmth. "Did you hear anything, hon?"

'Hon' shook her head.

"Maybe Alyson..."

The wife drew in a quick breath.

Tony turned to her. "Alyson?"

But the jerk was in charge. "Our daughter. She's twelve. Watches TV until all hours, the little minx. All that sex and violence, it's enough to make you want to cancel the cable."

Tony saw a shadow move at the top of the stairs; figured it must be the daughter. Christ, this bozo was slick. Wife standing here with a split lip and an eye turning purple by the second and this asshole babbles about the goddam

18

cable.

"Mrs. Moore, can you tell me what happened here tonight?"

This time Tony saw it, caught the big arm press down into her shoulder. She hung her head. "Nothing, really. Frank and I had a little... argument." Her soft voice seemed lifeless, defeated. "Maybe we scared Aly and she–"

"How did you hurt your face, Mrs. Moore?"

"Oh, this..." She touched her mouth with trembling fingers, rusty with dried blood.

"And your hand, Ma'am? How did–"

She looked down at her bloodied hand like she'd never seen it before. " Uh–"

"You told me it was a paper cut, dear, remember?" Eyes back to Tony. "My wife worked late tonight, came in around midnight. Didn't turn the light on in the bedroom so as not to disturb me. She's thoughtful that way. Walked right into the closet door in the dark, didn't you, love?"

The woman nodded, meek, submissive.

"Yep, that's what we argued about, officer. Catherine tripped and knocked a lamp over, woke me up after all." Big smile, big effin' hug for the wife. "Guess now we'll just *have* to get those new bedroom lamps you've been hankering for."

Son of a bitch is on a roll, Tony thought, listening to the voice dripping with fond indulgence.

"As you can see, things are fine here. Sorry you had to come out at this hour of the night. But it's good to see our men in blue are on the job. Right, sweets?"

Men in blue, thought Tony, disgusted. *Sweets?*

Moore reached around him to open the door, dismissing

him.

Without turning, Tony kicked it shut with his heel. Saw anger flare in the pale blue eyes. Stared the creep down. Wouldn't take much to shove the smug bastard's teeth down his throat.

"We're not quite finished here, sir. I'm sure that's the way it all went down but I need a statement from both you and Mrs. Moore." Tony let his eyes linger on her flushed face. "Separately. Is there somewhere you can wait for a few minutes while I talk with your wife?"

He wanted to argue, Tony could see it in the flashing eyes, the tendons standing out in the bully's neck. "Department regulations, sir." The bastard backed down, apparently not quite ready to take on one of Gilford's *'men in blue'.*

Tony'd grown up with bullies from Southie just like this one, big beefy thugs who liked to pick on the smaller Italian guys from the North End. Probably why he was a cop today, getting back at assholes like this.

Moore's eyes locked on his wife's until hers dropped, a warning, no doubt about it, then he turned and stomped down the tiled hallway toward the back of the house. A light went on, what sounded like the dull thud of a refrigerator door slammed shut. In the heavy silence Tony heard the clink of glass on glass, a liquid gurgle.

"Water." She'd heard it too. "My husband is not a drinker, Detective."

"No ma'am."

She looked pale. "Mrs. Moore, you need to sit down..."

She led him into the dining room. He pulled out a

chair. She stood behind it, hands clenched at her side.

Tony shut the frosted glass French doors. "This the first time your husband's hit you?"

She gave that some thought. Cleared her throat. Raised her chin. "Frank didn't hit me."

"You're saying that lamp up and bashed you in the face?"

Startled, confused, until she remembered the story. Smiled a tiny smile. Which must have hurt, because she put her fingers to her broken lip.

"Mrs. Moore, I think this has happened before."

She shook her head slowly.

"But this time you called the police." Tony tried a different approach. "Something out of the ordinary went down here tonight that..."

Her face crumpled. Her eyes filled, and two fat tears rolled slowly down her cheeks. "Alyson." Her voice was a whisper.

"Your daughter."

A nod.

Son of a– "Did he hurt her too?"

Terror in her eyes. "Oh no, he'd never. But F-Frank turned on her," stuffing her hair behind her ears, "and I got scared."

She'd called it in, of course, he'd known that from the start. But not for herself, women like this took all the shit the goddammed bullies they were married to handed out. No, for her daughter. "Ever think of leaving the bast-- your husband, Mrs. Moore?"

The chin rose again. "I was raised to believe that

marriage is a sacred contract."

Quite a mouthful, for her. "In most domestic cases, Mrs. Moore, the violence escalates. From a little slap across the mouth to a punch in the eye, to who knows... there's been a lot of research into this kind of behavior."

The poor woman was trembling.

"You and your husband need help, Mrs. Moore. Marriage counseling, AA–"

"I told you, Frank doesn't drink."

Didn't have to, the asshole got his rocks off beating up on a woman. "If you've never tried therapy--"

"Detective Costello, Frank and I have been together for fourteen years. Of course we've had the occasional, uh, disagreement, but I was wrong to call you tonight. I swear it won't happen again."

A sound from down the hall. Her eyes wavered, dropped, and she turned away. She was afraid again. Don't push, Costello. Time to go.

Tony held out a card. "If you need to talk to someone, Mrs. Moore, please call me any time, day or night. Now, I just need a minute with your husband."

Following Moore's earlier path Tony went down the elegant hallway, covered here and there with fancy Persian? - what did he know - rugs, modern artwork lined the walls, highlighted by tiny recessed ceiling lights, Laura would go nuts in this place. Tony stopped in front of a pair of dark stained six-panel doors, knocked, waited a few seconds, listening, then pushed them when he heard nothing.

The doors opened onto a big paneled room lined with bookshelves; glass doors at the far end that probably led

22

outdoors to a patio. Dark leather couches and chairs and an antique-looking round table in the center of the room with a vase filled with yellow flowers. The den - or maybe these people would call it a library. Corner shelves held an array of trophies and plaques, awards, but from the doorway Tony couldn't tell what they were for. Frank Moore lay on his back on one of the couches, snoring. Bet the fuckin' coward always slept well after a bout like this. Tony shut the doors. Dream on, scuzzball, I know where to find you.

The wife was still standing by the chair in the dining room when Tony let himself out.

He let the car idle for a few minutes, hit the mic icon on his phone; dictated a brief report. Rubbed at his face, heard the grating sound of the rough stubble on his cheeks, checked his watch. Jesus, one-twenty. What the hell got into people? These two had the best of everything. The car on the drive next to him was a Lincoln, damn sure whatever was inside the garage wouldn't be a broken-down Chevy. And this house! Massive white colonial on half an acre, landscaped flowerbeds, classy black shutters, brass coach lamps - he'd bet there was a pool out back, a world away from the neighborhood he and Laura lived in. Probably had more money than they knew what to do with, and this asshole got his jollies bashing the daylights out of his lovely wife, a woman with blue - or green - eyes, the color of the ocean in South Carolina.

He sank back into his seat, remembering Myrtle Beach, where the water had been bath-water warm, not cold and dark like up here. Back in April, for the first time in nearly eighteen years of marriage, he'd managed to pry Laura away from the kids.   She'd got her mother to stay with them, but she phoned home two, three times a day - obviously her children were more important to her than any husband.

It had not been a great week...   romantic place like that and they'd had nothing to talk about except the kids and the freakin' weather, f'r crissake.   He'd go for a walk on the beach; she'd stay in the room and pour herself a drink. Hard stuff, always a glass in her hand.   Had it always been like that?   Their first real vacation.   Nice oceanfront hotel, cost a fortune!   You'd think they'd've gone at it like rabbits, but no.   The sex used to be great, but lately...   It worried him that in a magical place like Myrtle Beach he'd had virtually no interest in making love.   Laura had made a couple of pitiful advances, but he just couldn't get it up. Gettin' old?   Thirty-nine next birthday, he'd have to check out the little blue pill.   Stress of the job?   *Some*thing.

Stress, he knew, affected people different ways.   Like some guys beat up their wives.   Sitting on the Moores' long driveway in the humid August night, Tony watched the bugs dance in the light of the post lamp and studied the big house.   It would happen again, only worse; always escalated with these fuckers.   And when it did, he'd be back.   Oh yeah, he'd be back.   Sooner, he guessed, than later.

Five

Long after he heard Catherine go upstairs to bed, Frank lay awake on the leather couch in the den, filled with shame.

What had got into him, punching her like that? He'd slapped her before - once, maybe twice, but tonight he'd scared her enough to call the cops! Reminded him of growing up on Shaughnessey Street in South Boston, damned cops showing up at their door at all hours of the night. Christ, they knew his folks by name.

"Again, Mrs. Moore?"

Frank hadn't thought about his parents in years. His Mum, a shadow of a woman with a soft Irish brogue. Soon after his dad died, she took a job at the dress shop down the way and married Joshua Miller, the Jewish widower who owned the place. And six months later blessed him with a half-brother, Benjamin, now in his thirties, a software genius, a fuckin' millionaire! Frank moved out as soon as he turned eighteen, working part-time at the convenience store on the corner while he put himself through college. His mother was gone now, but he'd never been able to forgive her, or accept Ben. Still, he missed her, sometimes.

But the old man! Who could miss the cruel monster

who dragged himself home from the bar night after night to beat up his wife, as if his disgrace was her fault. They lived on welfare, the motherf– couldn't hold down a job, and at the age of forty-nine - blind drunk - lurched into the street and got himself killed by a speeding van in front of O'Malley's, his favorite hangout. Bastard probably never knew what hit him.

Frank swore then that he would never touch a drop of liquor and had never broken that promise.

But aside from that he was turning into his father. Miserable, always pissed at something, a bully. Tonight he had punched his wife, the woman he supposed he loved, the mother of the daughter he cherished above all else, his beloved only child.

Catherine's second pregnancy. He fought the memories of the first, the one that...He didn't want to go down that road, but he couldn't escape the thoughts crowding into his mind...

She had refused him, spun some cockamamy story about her doctor sayin' that sex while pregnant was dangerous for the baby! As if nobody got any for nine months! But he felt shame rise hot as he recalled shoving her down on the floor and assaulting her. And after - oh God, the blood! Driving like a maniac through the tight nest of Boston city streets to the hospital, with her hysterical, crying beside him, and himself, terrified, yelling and slapping at her, trying to make her shut up. And himself back in the apartment, the studio they lived in then, when he'd had to throw away the blood-soaked rug...

Catherine lost the baby and sank into a misery that

26

lasted for years, post-partum depression, the doctor called it, made worse by the fact that she had no baby to nurture. Francis Xavier Moore, he sighed, you have a lot to answer for.

But at last she let him back in - she wanted a baby too. Thank God Alyson came along and life slipped into a normal family pattern. Catherine stayed home with the baby; he earned them a living - a good one, until the fucking recession of '08. Still, he'd done alright, got them out of Southie to this lovely home in this beautiful suburban town. Yes, he hated the commute on the Pike, but that was the cost of moving up in the world.

But was she happy? Over the years he discovered that his wife was a cold woman; only giving in to his needs when it suited her, but more often, over the years, she'd refuse him. Tired, sick, period, whatever - spoiled bitch - where did she get off calling the shots!

Frank felt anger rising again, and he pounded his meaty fist into the softly padded leather sofa arm. She shouldn't have snubbed him tonight. And then, calling the damned cops! They'd skated safely over that thin ice, damn it, but he'd break her neck if she ever did that again.

The grandfather clock in the hall struck three; loud, mournful bongs that echoed through the house. Catherine had inherited the damned thing from some rich uncle, and Frank often dreamed of throwing it down the basement stairs. He sat up, dog-tired, but they had to put this behind them, for Aly's sake. Now. In bed, in the dark. It couldn't wait. He knew himself; knew he wouldn't find the words she needed to hear in the light of day. He turned out the lights and crept up the stairs.

Catherine was awake, he could tell by her breathing. He knelt on the floor on her side of their king-size bed and laid his arm around her waist. He could feel her heart beating through the sheet.

"Catherine, honey, I don't know what came over me." whispered into her hair. "I'm so sorry–"

"Sorry? Frank, you don't know the meaning of the word." She pushed his arm away, turned toward him. Though the light was dim he could see the revulsion on her face. "This penitent routine is not going to work anymore." She rolled away. "I think you'd better sleep in the spare room."

Six

Catherine gulped the last drops of tepid coffee, dropped the mug into the sink and grabbed her briefcase in the foyer. She'd wasted valuable time on make-up, trying to cover up a darkening patch around her eye that nothing short of grease paint could possibly hide. She had better invest in a tube of stage make-up, for next time. Knowing there'd be a next time.

She checked her face once more in the hall mirror, wishing there was a way to stop Frank before he got started. But there never seemed to be a pattern; most of the time his anger had nothing to do with her. She could usually tell if it was traffic on the Pike or a bad day at work by the way he slammed things around as he walked through the door. Her coming home late didn't usually cause a row, but last night he'd been in the mood for sex, and she hadn't been there to indulge him. Last night she had sent Frank to sleep in the spare room, but that wouldn't last forever. She knew he felt ashamed, but his ego wouldn't let him stay down. The day was coming when they would have to face up to this sham of a marriage.

She shrugged, knowing full well that she would continue

to put up with his threats and occasional rages. She and Alyson were safer this way.

But what, Catherine Maude, would you do if he turned on Alyson again? She met her eyes in the mirror. *I'd kill him, Mother. So help me, God, I'd kill the bastard if he ever laid a hand on her.*

She collected her things, rushed out to the car and backed down the driveway. In the rearview mirror she saw Janice Kurtz hustle out of her front door hauling a nearly empty trash bag. Oh God. The woman must have heard or seen something during the night and now she'd be in for an inquisition.

"Yoohoo! Catherine!"

Catherine waggled her fingers through the window in a dismissive wave, but Janice had dropped the bag and was flying across the road, if flying could be used to describe a two-hundred-pound body in motion. She'd have to at least say hello. With a heavy sigh Catherine pressed the button that lowered the window.

"Hi, neighbor." Janice puffed up to the car. "Never see you. Got a minute for some fresh-brewed coffee and a homemade blueberry muffin?"

"Wish I could, Janice, but I really don't have a minute to spare." Catherine adjusted her oversize dark sunglasses. "I have an early appointment." She noticed that her lip throbbed when she moved her mouth.

"You hot ticket, coming and going at all hours." Janice's small brown eyes gleamed like raisins in her doughy face. "Heard you come home awfully late last night."

"Late meeting with a client." *And what else did you*

30

hear? Catherine dabbed a tissue at her split lip. "Hope I didn't disturb you."

"Don't worry about it," Janice's hand flapped the air. "I hardly sleep anyway now that Gary's gone. I-I mean, when he's away."

Gary was a pilot for one of the airlines, Catherine remembered, Delta, maybe, or American. He traveled a lot, but he usually spent all his free summer hours working in his gardens, and Catherine realized she hadn't seen him out there lately. She had an uneasy feeling that something was up, and that Janice might want to talk about it, but this was not the morning to get into it. "I hate to run, Janice, but—"

"I um, last night I got up to use the bathroom and I, um, saw a strange car in your driveway."

Nosey parker.

"Could it have been the police?" Janice leaned in the open window, all three of her chins quivering. "Had that little blue light on the roof."

"Kids. A prank call, apparently." Catherine made a show of checking her watch. "We got it sorted out pretty quickly. Look, I've got to get up to Hillcrest, I don't dare keep Mrs. Wetherbee waiting."

"You've got the Wetherbee listing? Well, good for you, Catherine." Janice simpered. "I wondered what Virginia would do with that old mansion when Austin passed on."

Virginia? Austin? Could Janice Kurtz possibly be on a first name basis with one of the town's wealthiest families? "I didn't know you and the Wetherbees were friends."

"Oh, we're not *that* close. They're really acquaintances." A sigh. "I know them from church."

31

A gossip *and* a namedropper. As if seeing people across the aisle at Christmas or Easter put you in their social circle. Catherine put the car in drive. "I'll be sure to give Virginia your best."

Janice's pudgy fingers fluttered to her mouth. "Oh lordy, I'm sure that poor woman has more important things on her mind than me." With both hands she pushed herself away from the car. "Can you believe it's back to school next week? Is Alyson ready?"

"She's nervous, I think." Catherine put her foot on the brake.

"Bonnie's excited, she's had her new clothes laid out for days, but Brian's playing it down, trying to act real cool."

"Seventh grade," Catherine sighed, "hard to believe they're old enough."

"Time flies when you're having fun," Janice picked up her trash bag, "they say."

Watching the woman shuffle across the road, a big sad clown in once-pink fuzzy slippers and a worn terry robe covered in huge unflattering faded yellow cabbage roses, Catherine felt a sharp stab of pity. It must be tough, raising a pair of active twelve-year-old twins, with Gary away so often.

She wondered again if something was wrong, but she'd probably never find out; Catherine had never allowed Janice to become a friend. Someone as pushy, as invasive, as Janice Kurtz would want to know her secrets, and Catherine had certain parts of her life she'd rather not share with a neighbor.

She drove slowly down the quiet street, thinking about

the Kurtz's.   Were they splitting up?   On the surface they seemed a devoted couple, but who knew what happened behind closed doors.   Just look at what went on behind her own.   Catherine couldn't imagine telling anyone about her… situation, such things were better left unsaid, but that poor woman looked as if she needed to talk to someone.   Well, it wasn't her concern, Janice Kurtz surely had many friends willing to listen to her troubles.

Gary seemed to be a devoted family man, she'd often seen him shooting hoops with Brian or riding bikes with Bonnie.   It was hard to imagine him up and leaving them but there were countless reasons families broke up, most of them having nothing to do with the children.   It took a certain kind of courage to do it; the kind she didn't have.

But she was creating a scenario when, for all Catherine knew, Gary could be on an extended trip to the Far East and she'd read far too much into Janice's few words and demeanor.

At a stoplight she flipped down the visor to check her face once more in the mirror.   Her lip had stopped bleeding, and there was just a hint of a bruise, more of a shadow on her cheek, under her eye.   She'd apparently passed the Kurtz scrutiny with no questions asked or eyebrows raised. It was safe to get on with her day.

Catherine loved her work; it had been a safety net when she'd desperately needed one.   Her first job after college had been as a receptionist at a small realty office in South Boston.   Southie, with its lively pubs so unlike the sedate drinking establishments of the Boston she knew.   She and a couple of girlfriends occasionally went for drinks after work, where she flirted shamelessly with a man with laughing blue eyes...

She stopped working when she finally got pregnant with Alyson, but she never forgot the busy little office. When Aly turned five they needed money for the down payment on their first home, and she wrote and passed the Salesman's Real Estate License exam. Salesman indeed, she mused, thinking of all the hard-working women she knew in the business. Seven successful years, most of them in Gilford with Kevin Casey. There were some late nights but putting people into homes they loved made her happy. What, she chuckled, would an analyst have to say about that?

During the last economic meltdown, when the bottom fell out of the housing market and one realty office after another closed, she joined Kevin's group and wrestled the sweet old guy into the twenty-first century. After much coaxing they had a website, they listed on Zillow, and advertised homes for sale with videos on social media like Twitter and Facebook, nearly all their paperwork transferred to a computer system. These days houses were bought and sold by clients simply scribbling their names on a computer screen! C&M had done well, survived the bank scandals, the nation-wide mortgage crisis, tough competition from the big chains. She'd recently been made a partner, and she could proudly say that Casey & Moore was the foremost independent realty company in Middlesex County.

Driving by an apple orchard Catherine lowered the windows, let the warm breeze play with her hair, breathing in the late summer scent of dry grass, the cidery smell of windfalls and apples ready for picking.

`Til Death...`

Before long it would be Autumn, her favorite season, when cooler temperatures and dry weather brought a riot of color to the landscape. Soon the maple leaves would turn brilliant scarlets and oranges, towering oaks contributing bright golden color before their leaves fell. Some trees had begun to turn already, and tall grasses waving along the roadway were golden, no longer green. End of August seemed too early; could it be climate change? In a couple of months creeks and streams would be coated with a crust of ice, these golden fields would be blanketed with cold, inhospitable snow. Catherine liked the idea of winter, softly falling flakes of snow, pines coated in white, but too often winter involved ice storms, downed power lines, and leaden gray skies. Four or five depressing months here in the Northeast, but she couldn't imagine living anywhere else.

Catherine pressed the FM button, tuned in to her favorite 'oldies' station and joined Cher's powerful alto, "If I Could Turn Back Ti-ime...! their combined voices filling the big car. Would she? *If it weren't for Alyson...*

But those were thoughts for another day. Today was a lovely summer day and her spirits lifted as the breeze carried last night's pain and humiliation out the window. Stepping on the gas, Catherine headed up to Hillcrest for her appointment with Mrs.– she laughed out loud - with Janice's 'dear friend' Virginia.

Seven

South Central Massachusetts Regional High School. The building was only a year old and the kids had already coined a name for it: SCUM. Gone were the independent school systems that had served four adjoining towns for hundreds of years, each with its small-town pride, underpaid teachers and outdated facilities.

Alyson was in Seventh Grade, Junior High, but thanks to the demo... demo-graphics in this town, grades 7 and 8 were now housed in the new high school. And what a facility! There were two pools - one exclusively for diving. Aly was a good swimmer, and she often imagined herself in their backyard pool winning gold medals for diving in the Olympics. The building also housed a theater, media center, computer rooms, indoor track, and two cafeterias. The architecture was very modern, like a pile of concrete and glass blocks a two-year-old had dumped out of a bucket and left on the ground just as they'd landed.

Nervous, chewing on her thumbnail, Alyson waited in the auditorium for Mr. Olsen, the assistant principal, to call out her name. In her new high-top sneakers, jeans slung low on her hips, the bottom hems carefully torn and a shirt big enough for her father to wear, she was dressed exactly like every other seventh-grader in the room. She looked like she fit in, but just now that was no comfort at all.

She *had* to be in the same homeroom as Bonnie, Alyson would totally die if they separated her from her best friend! Mr. Olsen was calling names alphabetically, and Kurtz, of course, came before Moore. Bonnie had already been assigned to Mrs. Bell's class. If there were only a few L's she still had a chance.

Alyson saw Bonnie all the way across the gym, talking to a thin, fidgety girl. She made friends so easily, everybody liked Bonnie Kurtz. The other girl had black curly hair, and she obviously didn't have a clue about clothes, gawd, was that really a pink twin sweater set she had on?

..."Luongo, David," Mr. Olsen called. "Massey, Peter; Montenegro, Julia." Alyson held her breath. "Moore, Alyson. Check in with Mrs. Bell over by the basketball hoop."

Alyson rushed across the gym. "Bonnie, I made it!"

"Didn't I tell you not to worry?" Bonnie hugged her. "Al, this is Gina..."

"Costello." The tiny dark girl ducked her head hello.

"Gina's dad's a cop."

"A detective."

"Oh wow."

"And they're new here."

"We moved out from Boston in June."

Alyson had relatives in the city, she'd visited one of their houses once, a tall gray building, the big rooms dark with heavy drapes shutting out the light on a steep narrow street with a tiny fenced-in park across the way and neat old-fashioned street lamps. Cousins, or second cousins, her mother had told her, and super-rich. They'd had to walk only a few blocks to visit all the wonderful shops on Newbury Street. Alyson loved the city; she planned to live in town when she was old enough. "Why did you move all the way out here?"

"Less crime, my mother says." Gina shrugged her pink shoulders.

"But your father's a policeman."

Again the shrug. "Guess there's enough work out here to keep him busy."

Alyson suddenly remembered the night she'd heard her mom scream, the night her dad scared her. And the policeman, the detective, coming to their house. She'd crept to the top of the stairs to listen–

"I really miss my friends."

"We're your friends now, Gina." Bonnie took Gina's hand and the two walked away together.

Jostled by the hordes searching out homerooms, Alyson rushed to keep up. This new girl was trying to move in on Bonnie, but Bonnie was *her* BFF and everybody knew there couldn't be *three* best friends. "So Gina," she called out, "I guess twin sets are hot in the city?"

She felt bad as soon as the words came out of her mouth, especially when a few kids turned to stare, but she felt much worse when Bonnie answered, "Gina says they're real big in Boston this year. We're going to find me a set today, right after school."

Alyson bit her lip. Bonnie was a traitor.

"Why don't you come with us, Alyson?" Gina had

stopped and turned. "I got mine downtown, but I'm sure there's a store somewhere in this place."

That was nice, but if Bonnie thought Alyson would just step aside and let this new girl horn in, she was badly mistaken. "I'd love to go with you guys, Gina." She linked her arm with Bonnie. "We have a new Mall in town. My Mom's picking me and Bonnie up after school today, I bet she'll take us over there."

Gina grabbed Bonnie's other arm. "I'll call my mom at lunch and let her know."

The sound of the bell to start classes put a stop to their conversation. Aly grabbed a seat next to Bonnie, smug, until she saw that her friend was giggling with Gina on her other side.

Alyson had heard her dad complaining about 'those uppity Eye-ties', but Alyson Moore was what were known as 'the fighting Irish', and no way was she going to lose her best friend without a fight.

Eight

The squeak of the front door opening took Laura by surprise. She'd been straining to hear the slam of Tony's car door, that irritating whistle thing he did through his teeth as he came up the walk, but she'd missed it with the thunder rolling and crashing and the rain pounding the roof like a steel drum, sounds she'd never heard in the North End.

She barely had time to pull up the covers before the bedroom door swung open. He came into the room on a flash of lightning.

"Tony? Is that you?"

Drum roll of thunder. "You were expecting maybe the angel Gabriel?" Posed like a movie star in the doorway.

Laura turned on the bedside lamp. "It's two o'clock in the morning, Tony. Where the hell have you been?"

"Where do you think, Laura?" Lightning flared, lighting up his handsome, lying face. "Policing is all done on computers these days, no more paper, and I had a shitload of work." Thunder boomed.

"Why didn't you call?" Wrong, Laura, she knew he hated what he called her interrogation. She changed her tone. "You know how scared I get in a thunderstorm."

"Yeah, I know, but we were real busy." Tony scrubbed at his face with both hands, something he did when he was very tired. "Power was off in town; some of the stoplights were out." He unbuttoned his shirt. "I'm wiped, Laura." Sat on the edge of the bed. "Lay off, okay?"

But to Laura he didn't have the gray look of a man who'd spent half the night staring at a computer screen.

Flashes of lightning lit up the room, but no more thunder, thank God. She rolled closer and rubbed his back. "Did you come straight home?" She made her voice soft, teasing.

"Laura, honey, we go through this every time I come in five minutes late! Always with the questions! Was I drinking? Was I out with some woman?"

"So give me an honest answer and I'll shut up!"

"You're making me crazy, do you know that?"

"Stop shouting! You'll wake the kids!"

Tony's voice dropped to a whisper. "How am I supposed to defend myself against things that happen only in your mind?"

He took a deep breath, and Laura knew she was in for a lecture.

"Tonight, Laura, I was at the station, at my desk, where I am every goddam night, you can check any time. We had a dozen accident reports. I texted you around eleven-thirty to let you know I'd be late, you must have already been in bed - did you leave your phone in the kitchen? I didn't phone because you always bitch when I wake you up." He threw his clothes on the floor and fumbled in his drawer for pajamas. "Let me know when you decide what you want from me, Laura. I'll try to get it right next time." He left the room, bare feet stomping the bare wood floor.

Laura listened to his footsteps fade down the hall, heard the bathroom door shut, the shower turned on. She wiped her eyes with the back of her hand. Maybe he had texted, but Claudia had probably been yakking with one of her friends on Laura's cell, always forgetting to charge up her own!

Angry, Laura punched up her pillow, wrestled with the twisted sheet; now she'd be awake all night.

Slipping into a red polyester kimono she'd picked up at Walmart, cheap but sexy-looking, Laura tiptoed past the bathroom door to the kitchen. Found the bottle of scotch where she'd hidden it behind the canister of flour in the pantry and took a quick swig. Her arm jerked when she heard the bedroom door slam, and she spilled a few drops on the new kimono. Sure, go to sleep, Tony. Bastard would be asleep in two minutes.

The thunderstorm had passed, but rain still drummed on the roof, smacked and streaked the kitchen windows. He always twisted things around, made her feel like a fool for asking, for needing to know. But where had he been, who with? *Why not here at home with me?*

The warm scotch loosened the tight knot of anger and hurt inside. After all these years she still didn't know for sure if Tony loved her. Pregnant at nineteen, she'd confessed to Tony and he had done the honorable thing - Papa would have beaten him senseless otherwise. But that age, what did we know about love? Tony, at twenty, knew everything about sex. At least, he'd told her so. And she'd wanted so badly to believe him. *Madonn',* she'd be wet in seconds when he touched her down there, she remembered his hot kisses, his mouth on her breast, fingers like butterflies working their magic all over her body - oh God, his tongue everywhere, making her crazy, until, late on the night of her nineteenth birthday, out on the back porch, she'd let him go all the way for the first time. They were stupid, caught up in the moment... but it felt so good! After that it was just a matter of time 'til something happened.

Over and over Mama had warned Laura to keep her legs crossed, keep him wondering, a man didn't respect a girl who let him have his way. *No man will buy the cow when he can get the milk for free!* And the worst possible thing, an unwed pregnancy, would bring shame on herself, on the family. But soon they were having sex often and of course it happened. She too dumb to demand protection, Tony explaining that it wouldn't be fair for him, like taking a shower in a raincoat. Mama had been so angry she had barely spoken to Laura until after Claudia was born.

You don't lock the barn after the horse is gone. Another of Mama's wise little sayings, she'd driven Laura nuts with them until she'd stopped listening. Too late the messages had hit home. But Mama didn't understand how Tony made her feel.

Now Laura wondered if Mama could have foreseen the agony she'd gone through in the long years since. How Laura watched Tony's face when they made love, wondering if he wished someone else in her place, if he had other lovers, if he regretted marrying her. He'd been forced into it, really. And all the times, like tonight, when she sat up half the night, drinking and crying, while Tony slept the sleep of the just. *Or* the sexually satisfied.

With a sigh Laura pushed the nearly empty bottle to the back of the soap cupboard and crawled into bed beside a comatose Tony. In the dim light between scurrying clouds she studied his peaceful face and felt her chest constrict with the familiar fear, the damning question in her mind already asked and answered.

After all the fights, all her tears, and all his protestations of undying love, Tony had never once in so many words actually *denied* that he'd been with another woman.

The next morning Laura woke up with a pounding headache - a migraine, she *never* got a hangover headache. This one was so bad her eyeballs hurt. Waves of sounds drifted into the bedroom; not the usual thumping rock music, thank God, but hushed voices, the chink and tinkle of cups and bowls in the kitchen, the hiss of running water in the bathroom. Tony was up; he and the kids were getting their own breakfast this morning. Good. They were old enough. She drifted back to sleep.

The next time Laura opened her eyes the house was dead quiet. Until the bedroom door opened with a shrill squeak, giving her a guilty start. She sat up too fast and sank back on the pillows, holding her head and groaning. "When are you gonna fix that damned door!"

"I'll pick up some silicone spray at the Depot." He stood by the bed holding a steaming mug. "Drink this." He gave her the coffee, went to the window, parted the drapes. "Sun's up. It's a beautiful day!"

"Shut those damned things!" She covered her eyes. "Where are the kids?"

"How the hell should I know where the kids are? It's half-past ten! They're gone wherever kids go on Saturday mornings." He held out three tablets. "For your headache."

"My head's fine."

He gave her an evil grin. "I bet."

But she took the ibuprofen, swallowed a mouthful of coffee, felt the hot liquid burn a track down her throat.

"Do you have to stand there staring at me with that shitty smug look on your face?" He knew that she hated for him to see her without makeup, hair mussed, eyes puffy and red.

But his grin only got wider.

"I'm just real tired, after waiting up for you til all hours last night." Surely he'd tell her now. "Were you really—"

The phone shrilled into the space between them.

Tony picked up the receiver, rolled his eyes, tossed it on the bed without a word and left the room.

"Good morning!" Janice Kurtz at her chirpiest. "Did you forget?"

A shaft of sunlight made its way between the shades and drilled into Laura's eyes. "Forget what?"

"We were going to bake together this morning. You were coming over to teach me how to make pizelles."

"Guess I did forget. Sorry, Jan, can we do it later--"

"Too late now." The air hummed with unspoken hurt. "The reception is at two."

A special welcoming tea for prospective members of the Gilford Chorale, she'd forgotten about that too. Laura desperately wanted to join, the group performed at concerts around the state, they had a trip planned to New York City in the Spring. Janice had promised to introduce her to the director, she thought they could use another soprano. Thank God they weren't trying out today, she'd sound like a frog for sure.

"I'm sorry, Jan, I seem to have picked up some kind of bug. But I'm feeling better now. I'll meet you there."

"Laura, you were going to drive! My car's being serviced today."

"Okay, don't panic, I'll be at your place at--"

Tony came to the bedroom door, his black leather GPD bomber jacket slung over his shoulder, reminded her of Jimmy Dean.

"Hold on a sec, Janice. Tony, where are you going?"

"Out."

"Ooh, is that your husband?" The phone receiver buzzed like a hive of bees. "Handsome. I think I saw him up here one night, a couple of weeks ago--"

"Tony?" Keys jingled in the kitchen. "Tony, wait!"

"--across the street, at my neighbors, the Moores. You know, I'm not one to gossip, but--"

"Janice, Tony never discusses his work with me." The front door squeaked open, all the hinges in this damned house needed grease. "I've really gotta run, see you later." She pressed the button to disconnect the call. "*Tony!*"

The front door slammed as she jumped out of bed.

46

Nine

He'd told Laura he had to pick up silicone spray, but he knew there was a can in the basement. The lawn needed mowing; leaves had to be raked; the kind of light yard work Tony normally enjoyed, but not today - he'd get to it Sunday with Anthony, if he could tear him away from that damned game the kid played on his damned phone, reminding himself to check if it was that creepy Fortnite they'd been talking about at the station.

Half past ten on a Saturday morning, with nothing to do and nowhere to be until three o'clock this afternoon. He jiggled the car keys in his pocket. Of course he'd have to apologize, but no way was he going back in now to fight with Laura. He jumped into the Explorer and rolled slowly down the street to the intersection. Right? Left? When that woman got a thing in her head there was no changing it. She'd been on this damn soapbox for years, and as soon as her hangover cleared, she'd be on his back again. Where in hell did she get the idea that he screwed around? When was he supposed to meet these lovers, f'r chrissake, the hours he worked! The only women he ever saw were barflies and busted hookers, and not much of that out here in this cozy suburban town.

He pounded the steering wheel; glanced at the clock on the dash. Ten forty-five. Way too early for lunch, but a cup of coffee would kill some time. He turned onto Main Street and cut across town on Summer Street, to the new Gilford Mall.

The parking lot was crowded with Saturday shoppers, but he found a space near the Stop & Shop, slipping into it seconds ahead of a pale blue minivan coming the other way. He slid out of the Explorer and turned to find the minivan behind it, with a wild-eyed woman shaking her fist and mouthing things at him through the window. Did the crazy broad expect him to back out and give her the spot? In the back seat three small children shrieked and bounced around, swatting each other with toys and making faces at him. If she didn't move on real soon he'd ticket her for not having those kids restrained, *really* piss her off.

He gave her his thin-lipped grin, the one that stopped criminals dead in their tracks, and headed toward the coffee shop, passing a gleaming Lincoln Town Car further up the row. Nice wheels. Pewter paint job; tan leather interior. *CMREAL-T* on the vanity plate. The Moore woman's car, he'd seen it that night on their driveway. Catherine Moore. Nice lady, sneaky bastard of a husband. Laura thought *she* had it rough; how would she like to be stuck with a nasty piece of shit like the Moore guy.

It had to be two, three weeks since he'd visited the happy little Moore family up there on the Ridge; he'd thought about the red-headed woman off and on ever since. The submissive droop in her shoulders, defeated glaze in her eyes. He wondered if the big asshole had been keeping his hands to himself.

She was probably in the grocery store, he could go in, buy some chips or a candy bar, maybe find her and see how she was doing. Tony spun in the other direction.

Catherine saw him as he came up beside her at the deli counter.

"Hey there, Mrs. Moore, isn't it?"

Friendly smile, acquaintances meeting once again, but she felt his brown eyes flick over her face, probing, as if checking for fresh bruises or a black eye. There were none but she touched her cheek, embarrassed, and backed away. Bumped into a grocery cart, one of a dozen surrounding her, each firmly held in place by a woman ostensibly waiting for her number to be called, all nosey harpies with nothing else to do but watch and listen. She felt as if they all knew that this man, this policeman, was singling her out for Lord only knew what crime. She tried to move her cart one way, then the other, but it was wedged in tight. Crumpling up the pink deli number, Catherine abandoned the wagon and pushed away through the crowd.

He caught up to her in Canned Fruit. "Think you forgot this."

"Oh, my cart." Embarrassed, she grasped the handle. "Thanks."

"Who would ever buy cranberry sauce in a can?"

Why was he doing this? "Working mothers, I guess." She turned the cart and walked away, eyes fixed on the shelves, sending a message. Surely he'd leave her alone

49

now.

But he followed. In Cereal he questioned the nutritional value of Lucky Charms, in Soups he wondered how so much sodium could be good for anyone. He didn't seem to be *shopping*, he just sauntered along beside her as if they were together, hands shoved in the back pockets of his jeans, black jacket spread open across his chest. The white t-shirt beneath displayed well-developed pecs.

She shook her head, annoyed with herself. "Don't you have anything to buy?"

"Haven't found it yet, but I'm looking." He smiled, moved away.

Catherine skipped the Baking Needs aisle when she saw him scanning cake mixes, but there he was in Frozen Foods, still empty-handed.

"Detective, are you following me?"

"You know how it is in a grocery store." He grinned, a gleam of white teeth. "You always see the same people, aisle after aisle." He held the freezer door open while she pored over the different brands of chopped spinach.

"Laura always buys the store brand, it's a lot cheaper, and hey, spinach is spinach, right!" He tossed a packet into her cart.

Further down the aisle Catherine reached for orange juice. "That kind's real sour." He pointed to another brand. "This one's sweeter."

Catherine laughed. "Look, if you're going to hang around harassing me," She tore off the bottom part of her shopping list, "you can help out."

She heard him before she saw him at the register,

chatting with a man in the next line, waiting by the tabloid display with a package of cream cheese, a pound of bacon and a long French baguette.

"I didn't ask for bread."

"That's for me."

"See ya 'round, Tony." The man tapped Tony on the shoulder, gave Catherine the once-over and moved up in his line.

"One of my neighbors," Tony whispered, leaning in close as he dropped the cheese and bacon into her cart. "Now that we've got people curious about us," his voice took on an intimate growl, "we should give them something to talk about."

"And what," she grinned, relenting, "did you have in mind?"

"Umm, how about a coffee?"

"Hmmm..." Could she really be going along with this?

Suppose Frank saw her, what would he think? She fixed her eyes on the crackers and broccoli moving along the belt. *No more flirting, Catherine Maude.*

"Come on, you owe me."

"I *what?*" She looked up, alarmed.

"Hey, I've done half your shopping for you." His eyes crinkled at the corners when he grinned. He tugged at his chin, and Catherine remembered a severe little goatee the night he'd come to the house.

"Didn't you have a beard?"

He stuffed his hand into his jacket pocket. "Shaved it off last week. Had that goatee for years."

"I like you better with just the mustache."

"Hey, she likes me!" He smiled. "Guess there's no accounting for taste."

Catherine felt her face flush, and, grateful for the diversion, scanned her card, signed the slip.

But he was still there, loading her groceries into the cart. "How about that coffee?" His brown eyes had gone dark, serious. "We can talk about... things."

"You mean like a follow-up?" *He's a policeman, just doing his job.* What on earth had she been expecting? Catherine felt a momentary twinge of something like disappointment; their little 'flirtation' had been amusing.

"Yeah, you could call it that."

"First I have to put this stuff in the car."

"No problem. Here, give me your keys. Yo, Billy!" He called out to a boy of fourteen or so, dressed in ripped jeans slung low around his hips and a sloppy plaid shirt that must have been a cast-off from his father.

"Hey, Mr. C."

"Take this stuff to the beige Lincoln out there, wouldya? Two rows over, four cars up." He held out the keys and two dollar bills. "No joyriding, got it? We'll be in the coffee shop."

The kid chuckled. "Sure, Detective."

"But my car, my keys..."

"Yeah, I know, your snazzy Lincoln." He took her arm. "Not to worry, Billy's a friend of my Anthony." He led Catherine past the dry cleaners to the coffee shop. "He's one of the good ones. Scary, isn't it, how they all look like bums?" He held the door open. "Why don't you grab a seat, I'll just be a sec." He left her standing alone and walked to the back of the restaurant, turned at the restroom sign.

Again, she felt that little twinge of regret, as if they were on a date, half expecting him to hang her jacket, pull out her chair. Catherine chose a booth along the wall and quickly checked her hair in the etched faux art deco mirror beside her. Gleaming eyes, glowing cheeks smiled back at her. *Get a grip, Catherine.* As she freshened her lipstick, she saw Billy come up behind her. He tossed her keys on the table with what seemed to her to be a knowing grin. Warmth crept up her neck, as if she'd been caught doing something wrong.

"Hi there, gorgeous!"

Catherine turned toward his voice with a smile ready on her lips. And saw Gorgeous coming up the aisle in front of Costello. The leggy waitress, short pink and gray uniform stretched tight over her ample breasts, tossed her bleached blond ponytail. "Hey there, Detective. What'll it be?"

"Coupla coffees and a toasted." He slid into the seat across from Catherine. "How do you take it?"

"No sugar. Cream on the side."

"Just bring the pot, Joanie."

"Something to eat?" Brown eyes on Catherine's face.

"What's a toasted?"

"Never had one of their buns? They're a big hit with the guys at the station. Sliced, buttered, grilled, dripping with cinnamon and melted sugar."

"Thanks, I've already had breakfast."

"Oh sure, hours ago, ya gotta try one of these." He held up two fingers. "Joanie, make that two."

Catherine watched the woman hustle back to the table carrying an urn of coffee, and lean close to Tony, her tummy touching his shoulder as she filled his mug. He whispered something, she giggled. She whispered back and he laughed out loud, teeth gleaming under the dark, thin Clark Gable mustache. Still flirting with him, she poured Catherine's coffee, overfilling the mug and dripping some on the table. 'Joanie' wiped up and pranced away, gray apron ties twitching back and forth over her snug pink bottom.

Tony turned his bright toothy smile on Catherine. Dazzling. "You just gotta feel sorry for a woman like that. Divorced, three kids."

And on the make. The man was clueless! He was like a lovable puppy with those big wet brown eyes, but apparently had no idea how appealing he was.

Tony stroked his bare chin. "So, how are things, Mrs. Moore?"

Time to get down to business. Catherine took a sip of the tepid weak deli coffee, instantly understanding why Starbucks had cornered the market. "Fine."

"And your husband?"

"Frank is... okay."

"But?"

God, those eyes. Dark brown and warm, not at all like Frank's icy blue eyes.

"Any more incidents?"

"Oh no."

"Is there a pattern?"

"Not really."

"Whenever the fancy takes him?"

"Oh, it's not like that. Something usually sets him off," she twisted her wedding band, "a tough day at work, maybe, or heavy traffic on the Pike —"

"Like I said, whenever the fancy takes him."

"Oh no. Often it's something I've done to... to provoke him." She rolled the paper napkin between her fingers. "Like now, if he saw me in here with you—"

"Jealous, too. The bastard is a classic case."

She watched Tony's hand make a fist, relax, make a fist, relax.

"A classic case. How reassuring."

"Mrs. Moore, you're not alone in your misery." He drained his coffee mug; slapped it down on the table. "But tell me, when did this business start?"

"Oh, I don't know, it's hard to remember back that far." A lie, the first time was as clear as yesterday in Catherine's mind.

"Try. I've got until three."

Was it his voice, the warm, sympathetic eyes? Catherine felt a crazy urge to let it all out, to share the whole nasty story with this man she quite possibly might never see again. "We'd been married about a year. I was--"

"Here we are, dear!" The buns, and more coffee. "Hot 'n' fresh!" Another series of winks and giggles before Joanie's tight little butt finally sashayed away.

Catherine watched Tony bite into the huge cinnamon bun. Butter and sugar dribbled down his chin, and Tony swiped at his face with his napkin. "You were saying...?"

She took a tiny nibble of hers, felt something warm and sticky on her cheek.

"Oops, hot melted sugar." With a quick stroke of his napkin Tony wiped it off, studied her face, then gently touched the paper to her cheek again. "Mrs. Moore, I don't want to pressure you if you really can't remember..."

Obviously giving her an out. "Detective, I--"

"Tony."

"Tony, then. For some reason I feel I can talk to you. How it all started is of course engraved on my memory. I'll never forget."

"So," stroking his chin, "you'd been married a year..."

Catherine sighed. "I was pregnant. Not an easy one." *Week after week of nausea, spotting...* "Four months, almost five. There was a problem with... the baby wasn't seated properly or something, and the doctor said no strenuous activity of any kind."

"Meaning no sex."

She felt her face flush. "How did you know?"

"Happened with one of ours, Anthony, I think. No sex, right? That's tough on the average male."

"Yes, well..." *Oh my God, I'm discussing my sex life with a total stranger.*

"You were saying...?"

Yet she felt compelled to go on. "Frank had been counting on a promotion at the firm he was with then, but he'd been passed over. He was frustrated, angry; his temper was on the boil, he was spoiling for a fight. He'd slapped me once before, guess I'd said or done something wrong."

"That's not how it goes."

She shrugged. "That night he wanted... you know." She was mumbling now. "I should have gone along, it would have been safer..."

Across the table, Tony drummed his fingers on the table.

"Other women had sex while they were pregnant and nothing bad ever happened." She picked up her coffee mug, put it down. "Stupid me, I refused. He called me names, said I was evading him. Threatened to hit me." *And did.* "Things, umm, got out of hand. He..."

She had been looking over Tony's shoulder at nothing, but now Catherine dropped her eyes, gazing at the massive bun on her plate. Took a deep breath. "Guess I can't talk about it after all."

Tony's fist slammed the Formica tabletop. "The bastard." His voice was soft, but cups and plates bounced and rattled. Drawing the attention of people in the booths around them.

But Catherine's mind had gone back in time, nearly fifteen years, feeling again the stabbing, tearing, methodical pain, and the blood, so much blood. And Frank, shouting at her all the way to the hospital that he had done nothing wrong, sex was his right as a husband, goddammit, this was all on her. Slamming on the brakes at the emergency entrance, threatening to break her neck if she ever dared breathe a word of what happened. To anyone. Ever.

"Mrs...uh, Catherine?"

She pushed the mug away, twisted her wedding band. "He said he was sorry, brought me candy. And roses, beautiful yellow ones, they smelled like raspberries." Her eyes were fixed unseeing on the barely touched pastry in front of her. "They are...they were my favorite."

"He's a prick." Tony crumpled his napkin into a tight little ball. "Pardon my French." Stuffed it into his empty mug. "Your husband is a sick man. You'd be better off without him."

"Easier said than done, Detective."

"Not if you want it badly enough."

"I'm not a religious woman, Det—Tony, but as I said, I don't believe in divorce. I stayed with Frank and was eventually rewarded with Alyson."

"But you're afraid of him."

"No." She took a sip of coffee. "I'm afraid to leave him."

"You know he will hit you again."

She looked at her watch, raised her eyes to his. "I'll deal with it then." She slid to the edge of the vinyl bench. "But now I have to get home."

"Yeah, me too." He snatched up her keys and settled the bill without flirting with the waitress, Catherine noted, then guided her with a hand on her arm out into the brilliant sunshine of an Indian summer afternoon. The sun glinting off a hundred mirrors and windshields seemed out of place, for some reason she'd expected darkness and gloom after baring her soul.

Tony clicked the remote and opened her door.

"Take care, Catherine," handing her the fob. "Good seeing you again."

She slipped into her seat. "Thanks for…"

"No worries," shrugging, "you know you can call me anytime."

Catherine watched him saunter down the row to his car. *You'd be better off without him.* As if she didn't know that. Frank might be happier too without her, but, though he rarely

58

showed it, she knew he loved his daughter.

It had taken nearly four years for her to become pregnant again after... When she cried in his office, her gynecologist asked if she was stressed, was she getting enough sleep, was her marriage a happy one. At the time Frank was building a career as an investment broker, she had a job as a receptionist at a small realty office, they were both very busy and often too tired for lovemaking. They had their share of disagreements, two people trying to settle into a partnership, but Frank was the loving husband, excessively gentle with her, desperate to show how sorry he was, how much he loved her. Over time Catherine almost forgot about the violence. When she found out she was expecting Frank was delirious with joy. He would be the best father the world had ever seen!

For nearly six months Catherine was sick, nauseous to the point of blacking out, unable to keep anything down but tea and toast-- and raw onions! They said pregnant women did not crave weird things, but what did they know! She had to quit her job, spent most of the winter cooped up in their apartment, while Frank shopped and cleaned and cooked and worried about her.

Alyson came early, at three in the morning during a wild thunderstorm, but she was a healthy, happy baby. Catherine was happy; Frank had the family he had so longed for. They would have three kids, he'd teach his sons to fish...

The severe economic recession of 2008 hit, destroying the plans of millions of families worldwide, including theirs. Frank was terminated, hired at another firm, but at a substantially lower salary. He grew bitter, disillusioned, flying off the handle with little or no provocation.

Except with his daughter, his 'darling girl'. Alyson, the shining joy of his life. Catherine saw his eyes light up when she hugged him, or climbed on his lap for a kiss, a story. But those days were gone; Aly was becoming a young woman, and Frank thought discipline showed his love, alienating her. What terrified Catherine that dreadful night a few weeks ago was seeing him turn on his daughter.

And later, after Detective Costello left, Frank swore he was sorry, it wouldn't happen again. She desperately wanted to believe it, but when he lost his temper – she remembered other times, when he'd threatened to kill her if she tried to take Alyson from him. Frank made no idle threats; he always meant exactly what he said.

Shaking herself out of her reverie, Catherine pressed the starter. It was no longer morning, the sun rode high in the sky, heating up the perishables in the trunk of her car.

A horn beeped. Detective Costello – Tony – driving slowly by in a dark green SUV, Catherine didn't know what kind, she couldn't tell one make from another. He smiled, rolled to a stop. She lowered the window.

"Everything okay in there?"

"Yes," flustered, "I was daydreaming."

"See ya." He rolled away with a quick wave. He seemed kind, sympathetic, this Tony Costello with the soft brown eyes, but compassion was probably all in a day's work. Frank would have brushed her off, quit whining, woman, you don't know what *real* trouble is. He could be so cold.

Did the detective have a wife? A family? He had mentioned a Lana, or Laura; yes, that was it. And a son, Anthony. She should have asked.

Her mother would have been shocked at her rudeness, and flirting! Foolish woman, dallying with a total stranger in the supermarket, telling him her shameful secrets. A cop, a man she barely knew. *A man with compassionate warm brown eyes*. A man she'd be too embarrassed to see ever again.

She clicked the seat belt, put the car in Drive, and drove home.

Ten

The phone was ringing as Catherine eased the big car into the garage. The landline. A sudden roar from the TV in the family room told her Frank was watching a football game. There was a phone at his elbow, but he never picked up. Had his fill of that at the office, he said. As if his secretary didn't screen his calls. But no one ever called him at home. Ben, his half-brother from his mother's second marriage, called occasionally, but Frank never spoke to him. As far as Catherine knew, he had no friends. She set the heavy bags of groceries on the kitchen counter.

"High time you get home." Frank yelling over the sound of thousands of football fans. "Bring me a soda."

Pretending she didn't hear, Catherine shoved her hands into the bags, rustling and crumpling paper and plastic packages. *Let the slob get his own drink.*

"I know damned well you heard me." Quiet as a cat, he'd come up behind her, dropped his big hands on her shoulders. She froze, waiting. Had she always felt threatened by him like this? "I politely asked for a soda."

The phone shrilled again. With her eyes on Frank, Catherine picked up. "Oh, hi Janice, can I call you back? I just got home." As if the woman didn't know; she had probably watched Catherine drive in. Barely listening, she let Janice prattle on, until--

"--a Christmas Cantata?" Catherine shook her head. "Not me, Janice, I don't even sing in the shower!"

She watched Frank shake his head as he popped the cap on a can of soda.

"And thank god for that!" hissed at her as he kicked the door shut behind him.

The choir Janice sang with was starting rehearsals for the Hallelujah Chorus. Catherine remembered her Dad playing the Messiah on his scratchy LPs on their old stereo. "Thanks for asking, but I have so little free time." Evasive. "We're dreadfully busy at work." An outright lie - in the Fall the housing market slowed down, picked up again after the holidays. But of course, it wasn't about time. Frank wouldn't approve.

He slammed the drink down on the granite counter, watched the foam overflow and drip slowly down the side of the can. Ripped open a bag of corn chips right under her nose.

"Sorry, Janice, I didn't hear that."

"We need voices! I'm betting you're a second, or an alto. I'm calling everyone I know—"

"Dip?" Frank spun around, glaring at her. "Where's the goddam dip?"

With her free hand Catherine fumbled in the bags, found the jar and handed it to him with a trembling hand.

"Sorry Janice--"

Rehearsals start in a couple of weeks."

"What is *this* crap?"   Frank had found the orange juice. "It's not the usual brand!"

Catherine reached for the juice, but he raised it high above his head.   "You know better than to fuck with the things I like."   He threw the carton across the room and Catherine, stunned, watched half a gallon of orange juice splatter the wallpaper, the stainless-steel fridge and the countertop, flow down the wall and pool on the tile floor.

After a prolonged silence she heard the phone click in her ear.   She'd forgotten all about Janice.

"Who was that?"   Frank had stopped in the kitchen doorway.

None of your damned business, Catherine thought, hanging the receiver on the wall.

"A simple question, Catherine."   Frank strode across the kitchen in three steps, beefy hand gripping her arm.   "I expect an answer."

"Janice Kurtz, across the road.   She's invited me to sing with her group."

"What makes you think you can sing?"

Catherine loved music; the Messiah was one of her favorite pieces.   It might be an opportunity to make new friends, contacts.   "It's only one night a week, Frank, until December."   Whining, and hating herself for it.

"Not a good idea."   Frank grabbed the bag of chips and stepped around a puddle of juice.   "I could be late getting home, and Alyson would be alone in the house."   He turned in the kitchen doorway.   "You spend more than enough time away from home."

"But--"

"I don't give a flying fuck!" He sauntered back to the game blaring in the other room. "Whatever it is, you're not doing it."

Catherine wadded up a bunch of paper towel and threw it on the floor to sop up some of the mess. Did he really think he could forbid her to join the chorus? Was she supposed to quake and tremble and sit at home, waiting on her lord and master? Yes, he did and yes she did and she should consider herself damned fortunate he didn't hassle her about going to work. Oh, he'd never complain about that, she was very good at her job and brought in plenty of money, in good months more than Frank. She dropped to her knees and scrubbed at the spill, pretending she was rubbing his face into the floor.

Frank at forty-six was all moody silences and violent rages, not the slightest trace left of the laughing young man she'd fallen in love with. She rose from her knees and wet a sponge to clean off the wallpaper. He flew off the handle at the slightest provocation, something as simple as her buying a different brand of orange juice. They rarely spoke, unless it was about Alyson, and it had been years since they'd had sex without violence; 'making love' wasn't in Frank's vocabulary any more.

Scrubbing hard, she remembered fighting with her parents, insisting Frank was right for her, accusing them of being snobs, of looking down on Frank because he was Irish, and Catholic. Not one of them. But he was exciting, not like the sons of their wealthy Boston Brahmin equals, the wimpy young men her parents expected her to marry. She'd been swept off her feet at twenty-four with Frank's passionate words of love and old-fashioned gifts of flowers. Roses, yellow roses, when he learned she loved them.

It had been a whirlwind courtship, only seven months before they married. Her mother, ashamed and convinced that Catherine was pregnant, opted for a small family-only wedding. No society friends were invited, no coverage of the event by the Boston papers. That had angered Frank; now she realized how badly he had craved the recognition and respect of the Boston social community. He never again spoke to her parents, hadn't attended either of their funerals. But that might mean nothing - he hadn't cared enough about his own mother to attend hers.

A year into the marriage Frank had lost whatever charm he'd held for her, growing progressively more moody, bad-tempered, controlling, beginning with the night she lost the baby, the shocking, horrible night he raped her on the worn vinyl kitchen floor of their poor little apartment in Southie...

Catherine had forced the incident from memory, but after talking to Tony Costello it had all come back, a terrible nightmare vividly relived in the light of day.

Catherine flung the wad of soaked paper towel into the trash. She was a grown woman of no small independent means who made important decisions daily. Who, with her partner Kevin Casey, ran a very successful realty business. But at the core she was spineless, a woman who let her husband bully and intimidate her... whenever the fancy took him.

The detective's old fashioned words, and how apt they were. Somehow talking to Tony this morning at the coffee shop had forced Catherine to see herself more clearly. But instead of making her shame easier to bear it had induced an eruption of self-examination, and self-loathing.

At last the kitchen was clean, except for a smidge of orange juice on the countertop. Catherine dipped her finger into the tiny puddle and licked it. Tony was absolutely right, it *was* sweeter, she would definitely buy it again.

Knowing   perfectly   well   she   wouldn't.

Eleven

On a rainy Tuesday night in October, one of Janice's friends picked them up for the first rehearsal of the Christmas Cantata. Rebellious, Catherine had phoned Janice the day after the argument with Frank. From her office. "On second thought," she gave a nervous little cough, "the market has slowed down some, so I'll probably have more time."

Catherine climbed into the back seat of the dark SUV. "Seems like everybody has one of these vehicles now."

"I never drive this ugly thing; my daughter's taking driving lessons in my car. This is my husband's Explorer." She gave a laugh. "It's green - poor guy is color blind - he thought it was dark blue!" A tiny hand, creased and brown and thin as a monkey's paw, reached back over the seat. "Hi. I'm Laura."

Catherine." She took the outstretched hand. "Catherine Moore."

"Ah, you're married to the realtor."

Janice chuckled. "Actually, Laura, Casey & Moore is Catherine's business."

"Oops, sorry, I don't know too many career women. My only claim to fame is my husband."

"The Costellos are newcomers to Gilford, Catherine.

They moved out here from Boston last June." Janice had finally settled her bulk in the front passenger seat. "Tony's a policeman here in Gilford."

Tony Costello. Of course. Laura, the wife. A son, *and* a daughter; a family. Catherine felt a little stab of - disappointment - and wondered why.

"Not to brag, ladies, but my Tony's a Detective." Laura's beaming eyes found Catherine's in the rearview mirror. "Do you know him?"

"I... I don't think--"

"Sure you do, Catherine, he--!"

"Janice." Cutting the poor woman short. "I said I don't think so."

Pretending to fumble with the seat belt, Catherine squirmed uncomfortably in the back seat. She did not want the whole world knowing her business. And if she said she knew him she'd have to make up a story about that night and she didn't remember what she'd told Janice.

"I'm Alyson Moore's mom," she forced a laugh, "and she's too young for driving lessons."

Janice opened her mouth to speak, but Catherine glared at her until she faced forward again. Then realized that Laura was staring at her in the rearview mirror. Mortified, Catherine felt her face flush, glad it was so dark in the truck.

The Chorale's rehearsals were held at S. Paul's, Gilford's only Catholic church. Lost in thought, Catherine rode the few miles down into the center of town in silence, hearing but not joining the chatter of the two in the front seat. Since their adventure that Saturday morning - a cup of coffee, for heaven's sake! - she'd had guilty fantasies of Tony's warm, dark eyes gazing into hers, his arms holding her, that little mustache tickling her lips, her nip - good heavens, the man had done nothing to set her off! Could she be in menopause? Or perimenopause, the early stages. That had to be the reason she was getting all hot and bothered.

At the church, Janice introduced her to the director and turned to chat with a friend, leaving Catherine to find a seat. Meantime, the organist and one of the sopranos, a woman with an exquisite voice, began working on a solo. Everyone stopped to listen and Catherine, stunned, turned and recognized Laura.

There were no words to describe the incredible sound that emanated from such a tiny bit of a woman. Laura's voice was joyful, rich, passionate, a haunting flute piercing the soul with sweet sadness. The final notes of the aria rose to the high domed ceiling of the church and hung there like crystals in the hushed silence. A burst of applause broke the spell and Catherine released the breath she'd been unconsciously holding. What a gift. A voice like that deserved to be heard, the woman should be on Broadway or bringing down the house at the Met! Yet it seemed Laura lived contentedly in the shadow of her husband, the infamous Detective Costello of Gilford, Massachusetts.

"Hey, a new face." Someone tugged at Catherine's sleeve. "Are you an alto?"

"I don't know - I'm definitely not a soprano if Laura is an example!"

"You could be a second." The woman slid along the pew to make room. "I'm Maureen, call me Moe."

"Catherine. Call me Catherine."

"Not Cathy." Moe laughed. "I've been warned."

Janice settled in between them. "Whaddaya think?"

"Laura? Her voice is--. It's... she's–"

"Amazing." Moe wiped tears from her eyes.

"You know what's really crazy?" Janice broke in, "Laura doesn't have the slightest idea how talented she is."

After a short run through a scale or two, it turned out that Catherine was an alto. "Altos have more fun!" Moe said with a laugh, as rehearsal commenced.

Driving back home afterwards, an obviously embarrassed Laura shook off their praises. "Really, it's not such a big deal."

"Laura thinks all Italian girls sing like that." Janice humphed her disbelief as they turned into her driveway. "Anyone for coffee and homemade brownies?"

Catherine gathered up her music. "Not for me, thanks, Janice."

"Janice's brownies are the best!"

"I'm sure they are, Laura, but I've got an early morning." Catherine opened her door. "So nice meeting you."

She looked up, again uncomfortably aware of a vague suspicion in the dark eyes that caught hers in the rearview mirror. "I'll be happy to drive next week."

Laura nodded, and Catherine shut the door, glad to get away, afraid that a cozy hour over coffee and cake with Laura would feel awkward. Catherine didn't want to gossip, but most of all, she needed to examine her strange feelings for the woman's husband.

Janice called across her thoughts. "What about Alyson?"

"Oh, um," laughing, "please send her home." She had forgotten about her daughter. "I'll wait for her out here."

Twelve

"Mo-om, I'm old enough to stay in the house by myself for a couple of hours." Aly had balked at being made to go to the Kurtz's to do homework. "Dad'll be home soon."

Exactly. At twelve, Aly probably was old enough - barely - but that wasn't the problem. Frank's threat about Catherine abandoning Aly to indulge herself had come true this first night of rehearsal, but worse, suppose Frank came home in one of his moods? She had no idea what the man was capable of doing these days and she had no intention of testing him. Yes, he said he loved his daughter, but after that terrifying night in August when he'd turned on her--

Catherine turned her face up to the sky and the stars, bright and more plentiful tonight in the moonless sky. Standing under this vast quilt of pinpoints of light it was not difficult to believe that the earth was one of the more insignificant planets in the universe. As a child that knowledge had scared her but now it made Catherine feel tiny, her problems trivial. Which started her thinking about Frank, and Tony. Why was that man invading her thoughts? No wonder Laura had looked at her with suspicion; Catherine had a guilty conscience.

A few minutes later Alyson ran out to meet her, long red hair flying free. She was dressed, as always, in a shapeless flannel shirt and pants that would have hung loose on a large man. The 'in' look of teenagers rebelling against whatever it was they rebelled against, unaware that even the most outrageous garb was a uniform if everyone wore it.

Catherine hugged her. "Hi, love. How'd it go?"

"Okay. Brian's a pain, but everybody says brothers are annoying."

"Maybe it's not so bad being an only child. Was Mr. Kurtz home?"

"Nope."

"Were you kids alone?" Catherine felt her heart beating in her chest.

"We were fine, Mom." She squared her little shoulders. "Mrs. Knight said to call if we needed her."

Doris Knight lived next door, another neighbor Catherine barely knew.

"Did the twins say where Mr. Kurtz is?"

"We don't talk about our fathers, Mom. Why?"

"Just curious, guess he's away."

"Why doesn't Dad ever go away?"

For good? Catherine shivered. *What a thought.* "Your father doesn't travel much, he has a different kind of job."

She wrapped her arm around Aly's shoulders and walked her inside. The house was quiet, peaceful. Frank had gone to bed; she hoped to sleep. "Why don't you get ready for bed, sweetie, I'll make us some hot chocolate."

Across the road Janice surveyed her kitchen. An empty

pizza box on the floor, dirty glasses on the counter, crumpled napkins on the table, she'd told the kids a hundred times—ah, so what. She'd seen worse, and tonight she was filled with beautiful music and not in the mood to nag. "Bonnie, did you and Brian get your homework done?"

"*I* did, but the girls talked the whole time."

"Brian!"

"Bonnie, hush. Did you say anything about Dad?"

"Of course not. You said not to, remember?"

"Did Alyson say anything about Mr. Moore?"

"Why should she?"

"No reason, really. I'm just asking."

"We don't talk about our fathers, Mom."

"They were too busy talking about boys!" Brian hugged himself, puckered his lips, kissed the air. "Ooooh, sooo HOT!"

Bonnie lunged at him.

"Enough, you two. Time for bed."

Long after the kids fell asleep, Janice lay on her bed, wide awake. Through the open bedroom windows a sweet hay-scented breeze billowed the curtains. It was a perfect Indian summer night, one to remember all through the long, cold New England winter, Gary would have said. She flipped the pillow over, trying to find a fresh cool spot.

Winter in this house would be dismal this year, that was certain. Staring up at the ceiling she tried to imagine Thanksgiving, Christmas... the rest of her life, without Gary. She reached over and touched his side of the bed, felt the pillows cool and undented by his balding head. She grabbed one, hugging it tight, and felt tears fill her eyes.

75

Janice still couldn't conceive of what she had done to make him leave. It *had* to be her fault; in their ten years together, Gary had never shown an interest in another woman. She knew he appreciated a well built, good looking girl, he was a normal male, but unless he fooled around on layovers in other places, he'd seemed quite content with her, love handles and all. More of you to love, he used to say, with a fond pat on her backside - a gesture she'd always hated but oh, how she missed it now!

Since Gary left, Janice had been reading up on male menopause. Apparently, lots of men went through a mental thing in their forties. Unfulfilled dreams. Time running out. Some got depressed and sat around doing nothing, jeopardizing their careers. Others did really stupid things, like whatsisname - Pam Porter's husband, running off last year with the little tramp who worked at Pizza Hut. The gossip grapevine reported that he was back in town, begging Pam to take him back. More fool her if she did!

And that Phil Henderson, with his brazen announcement that he preferred *men* after he'd been married to dear Louise for fifteen years. *Oh no!* Janice's fingers flew to her mouth. Gary had moved in with Ralph, his best friend, in a one-bedroom apartment. And Ralph was openly homosexual. Did that mean Gary...? No, impossible! Janice couldn't imagine Gary being gay, but then she'd never imagined he'd leave her either. She heaved a sigh. These days anything was possible, a person couldn't be certain of anything anymore.

She brushed tears from her cheeks, her sniffles loud in the quiet she had yearned for through all the years of Gary's loud snoring. Missing him felt heavy, like indigestion, like a weight on her chest, making it hard to breathe. How she longed for his calm presence, the sweet smell of his pipe, the crooked eyetooth that protruded when he smiled.

Gary had always been very responsible, one of the qualities she loved best about him. She'd always felt safe, protected, with Gary. Was that love? He was so different from Hank, the vagabond who loved his bike more than he'd loved her and certainly more than he loved his own two children. At least that's what she'd been forced to assume when he up and left them only a few months after the twins were born. So much for 'til death us do part.

To this day Janice was grateful that they had never married. She'd been young, immature, showing off to the girls that she - the fat one! had landed the cool guy with the free-wheeling lifestyle, that motorcycle, realizing only after she got pregnant that he was a loser. But Gary...

A bridesmaid at her brother Pete's wedding, she'd been paired with an usher called Gary Kurtz, single, and shy, and they clicked immediately. Older than Janice by six years, on their second date Gary told her how much he wanted children, but he feared that at thirty he'd missed that boat. The twins were still babies, eighteen months old, and he fell in love with them at first sight.

And loved them still, he'd said just before he left. Said he loved her too; the problem was with himself. He needed time and space to figure it out.

Another man wanting his freedom, she sure knew how to pick them. But this one was special. Janice had invested a lot of herself in Gary and she'd be damned if she'd sit idly by and lose him.

She ran her palms down her sides, felt her waist, her hips. Smaller, maybe, than when he left? Janice had started a 'nothing white' Keto diet, a fad she'd seen in one of the women's magazines. That meant no starches, potatoes, rice, bread or muffins. No ice cream, sour cream, whipping cream or (yuck) yogurt. The only sweets she allowed herself were brownies which, after all, weren't white, and blueberry muffins. Because. Janice never weighed herself, didn't own a scale, but she felt thinner, fit into her clothes better. Gary, she had decided, was worth a few cookies.

He was coming by on Saturday afternoon, taking the twins into Boston to see a travelling circus - one of the last in existence, he said, now that people realized how cruel it was to force animals to perform. Not that she didn't agree, but still... she remembered how, as a child in small-town America, she had loved the excitement, the flashing lights of the midway and thrill of the Ferris wheel ride when the circus came to town once a year.

Gary had never been one to talk about himself, but surely after two long months he'd had plenty of time to think. She had to find out if he was happy with things this way or if there was any hope of him coming back. It had to be done in person, forcing him to tell her straight to her face that he didn't want to be with her or the twins!

On Saturday she'd find an excuse to keep him talking for a minute or two. No, it had to be more than that. He never came into the house when he picked the kids up - he'd taken to sitting on the driveway in his car until they came out the door.

No, no, better to wait until he brought them home on Sunday. She could see it unfold. The kids would beg him to stay for dinner - he never refused Bonnie anything - and Janice would prepare his favorite chicken piccata. He could peel potatoes like he used to, and they'd sit together at the table like a family. Later she'd download a movie for Brian and Bonnie and they'd get a chance to talk. Perfect!

Snugging the sheet up around her shoulders, Janice fell asleep with a smile.

Thirteen

Tucked in between a secondhand bookstore and an old-fashioned cobbler's shop, the office of Casey & Moore Realty was a bright spot on a darkened street. Tony saw activity through the gleaming plate glass window every time he drove by. Which had become more frequent over the past few weeks, since their meeting at the grocery store.

The strip of shops and offices faced one side of a park, the 'Common', as the locals called the shabby square of crab grass and cigarette butts, broken glass and crumbling gazebo. Certainly didn't compare to the amazing Boston Common, he always thought. The town of Gilford was nearly three hundred years old, and the Common, once a lively summer scene of band concerts and family picnics, had deteriorated into a hangout for delinquents, vagrants, and sadly, otherwise nice people addicted to drugs in this terrible opioid epidemic. Tony's reason for being in the neighborhood.

Don Corbett, Tony's partner and a friend of Kevin Casey's, had tried to get Kevin to move his business elsewhere but the guy was stubborn in that lovable New England way and preferred to stay in the town center, where he'd always been.

But the town center had moved east, anchored by the big new shopping mall/cinema complex, as if this little burg needed six movie theaters. Another mile further east the new Super Walmart put paid to the once-thriving business district on Main Street. Now empty Victorian era shops beckoned street people to sleep in their doorways, and above, flaking gold paint on grimy windows advertised the offices of dentists and lawyers long gone.

Tony had started driving by a couple of times a week. A cop on duty, right? Detective, but still... If he saw Catherine's car he'd back into a handicapped space by the park or pull into one of the parallel slots outside her office window. With the visor down, he'd study her over a styro cup of hazelnut scented coffee from the shop with the stupid name - Earth something, no, Ground, Common Grounds. Good luck competing with Dunkin Donuts half a mile down the way.

Giving in to a compulsion, a craving, to see her. Sometimes he'd sit for an hour hoping for a glimpse of her at work. At his desk at the precinct, he'd get a sneaky little thrill logging onto the C&M website or following her on Facebook and Twitter. Officially, as he well knew, this was called stalking.

He'd noticed that Catherine usually left her office door ajar while she worked; wire framed granny glasses riding low on her nose, the tip of her tongue peeping between her lips while she did whatever real estate people did on their computers. Or she'd rock back slightly in her swivel chair, talking on the phone, twirling long gleaming strands of hair around her fingers as she listened. She drank from a black mug with the Patriots emblem on the side that sat on her desk, and she often ate lunch there - lo mein, usually, he thought, poking with chopsticks into little white Chinese take-out boxes probably from the Chinese Lantern Restaurant down the way. Oh yeah; stalking.

The passing and peering made Tony feel like a sneak, a Peeping Tom. He yearned to talk to her again, but on what pretext? The husband was either behaving himself, or she wasn't calling it in. Which she probably wouldn't do unless he went after the daughter again. He couldn't understand why she stayed with the son of a bitch, she was such a classy woman. He longed to hear that husky voice that sounded like Lauren Bacall in those old Bogey movies he'd seen on TCM.

Tonight, she had a client, a pudgy, silver haired older man. Tony loved to watch her at work, the animation in her intelligent face, the graceful gestures her hands made, the way she tilted her head to listen, as if this man was the most important person in her world. Fascinating, that's what she was. Rounded in the right places. Inviting.

Not at all like shrill, fidgety, whiny Laura - Christ, could that woman whine. And she was far too skinny. Had she always been so... unappealing? Ridiculous, he loved Laura, of course he did, but at this moment Tony couldn't think of a single thing he liked about his wife. Maybe all marriages got kind of stale over time.

Through the window he saw Catherine rise from her desk and lead the man to the outer office door. He was still talking but Catherine shook his hand with a bright smile and shut the door firmly behind him, *that's it for you, buddy!* She stood in the doorway watching the fat guy squeeze into his car which happened to be parked right next to Tony's - she *had* to see him skulking out here in the Explorer. Tony slid further down in the seat, glad that it was near dark and that he was in his black GPD jacket.

Catherine was wearing an outfit he liked; silky white shirt with long puffy sleeves and a black vest embroidered in some kind of folk pattern - what the hell did he know about fashion. High leather boots and a long rusty colored skirt. And all that wonderful hair. Tony's fingers tingled with wanting to touch her hair, her-- his fingers were not, as it happened, the only part of him that tingled as he gazed at her. Christ, she was beautiful.

The fat little guy finally got buckled in and drove off down the street. Catherine's professional client smile faded away and a wistful sadness slowly took its place, he felt he could read her like a book. She tilted her head sideways and turned away from the door, looking so vulnerable that his heart went soft and mushy in his chest.

He was out of the Explorer before he knew it. Not a clue what he was going to say or do, but he had to get inside. He pounded on the plate glass window, wanting to be with her, at the same time wishing he had stayed in his truck. She spun around fast, then smiled with relief and opened the door.

"You scared me, Detective Costello. What can I do for you?"

"Um." Tony's mind was blank. "You in here alone?"

"My client just left - why?"

"You should keep this door locked." *So lame, Tony.* "Nighttime... you work late."

"Sometimes."

He followed her into her office.

"Have you been watching me?"

"No, no, just checkin' out the neighborhood, you know...drugs and stuff, this opioid thing..." He stopped for breath. "We're puttin' in more time on the streets, around the park... a presence, you know..." Nervous, he swiped at his bare chin. "You look tired."

"I see you're still missing that beard." She chuckled, rubbed her eyes. "Was there something special, Detective? I've got a few things to—"

"Have you eaten yet?" He shoved both hands in his pockets.

A quizzical look flashed across her face. "Is this an inquisition?"

"Not at all. But it's past seven..."

"So it is--"

"How about, uh... Chinese?"

Her eyes lit up. "I love Chinese."

You are one clever bastard, Costello. "I'm on the late shift tonight and I've gotta eat too... is there somewhere...?"

"How about the Chinese Lantern?" She went around her desk. "It's not far."

"Great. I can continue my, um, inquisition there."

Her laugh tinkled like a wind chime. "Give me a sec to close up."

Fourteen

The phone rang just as Laura and the kids finished a late dinner. "Laura? I just got a text." Janice's hearty voice boomed in her ear. "We have an extra rehearsal, tomorrow morning at ten."

"Oh no." Laura studied the calendar on the wall, its big white squares nearly filled with her neat tiny print. "Saturday mornings are the worst." She sighed.

Her life seemed to revolve around the children, a whirlwind of overlapping schedules, appointments, practices, and no one to help. "It'll be nice when Claudia gets her license."

"Can't your husband help out?"

"He does what he can," quick to defend Tony, "but he often works second shift, doesn't get home until after midnight, so he sleeps in." She rolled her eyes. "Including weekends."

"Speaking of your husband, are you folks thinking of moving?"

Laura could hear growing excitement in Janice's voice.

"Moving? Where?"

"Up here, maybe, we could be neighbors."

"Oh sure, Janice, the Ridge on a cop's salary, don't get me started.   Why?"

"Thought I saw your Tony at the Chinese Lantern tonight."

"The Chinese place near the Common?"   She slid a plate into the dishwasher.   "He has to eat, you know, even when he's working."

Laura heard a sharp intake of breath.

"I know he likes the food there."   She knew no such thing, but Janice was starting to piss her off.

"He wasn't alone."   The woman was on a roll.   "He was sitting at a table by the window with Catherine Moore, she *is* a realtor, remember, Casey & Moore?   I guess I kind of speculated..."   Janice's voice trailed off.   "Just the two of them... oh my, that sounds *awful!*"   A giggle, high pitched and annoying, reached Laura's ear.

Frying pan in hand, Laura swallowed hard and waited out the long silence.

"I *could* have been mistaken, Laura."

As if.   Janice would have made damned sure it was Tony with Catherine Moore before passing on that tidbit of gossip.

"Did you talk to him?"

"No, I was picking up my order, I had a late—"

"Janice!   Were they, like, holding hands or something?"

"Good heavens, no, nothing like that."   Janice's breath wheezed in Laura's ear.   "I don't mean to imply that there was anything improper going on..."

"But?"

"I guess I was surprised they knew each other.

Socially, I mean."

Yeah, me too. "Could have been a business thing, maybe she had a break-in, or they just ran into—" *Did they know each other?* "We've been living here six months now, Janice, I'm sure Tony knows a few people." *She'd be sure to find out just how well he knew the Moore woman.* "Jan, I've gotta get this kitchen picked up. I'll see you in the morning."

Laura hung up on Janice's protests and shoved a few more dirty plates and bowls into the dishwasher, tossed a handful of flatware into the basket with a satisfying clash of stainless steel.

Tony and Catherine Moore. It did seem kind of strange, but even if it was perfectly innocent, Janice was such a gossip, she'd be talking it up all over town tomorrow.

She drained the last ounce of red wine straight from the bottle and tossed it clattering into the trash can she used as a recycling bin. Pulled it out and threw it again, harder, this time rewarded with the crash and tinkle of breaking glass. Wishing she'd thrown it at the wall. Or at Janice. Maybe smash *Janice* against a goddam wall! That woman had such a mouth.

But Laura knew very well Janice wasn't the problem here. Tony was. The Costellos were definitely not in the market for a new house, so what in hell was he doing having a romantic little dinner with a realtor? She took a few deep breaths to calm herself. Tony was always saying she jumped to stupid conclusions. Okay then, think, Laura. The Chinese Lantern was a public place, it was probably a completely innocent meeting, an accident. But how did Tony know Catherine Moore? He'd never mentioned meeting her. And only a few weeks ago she remembered that Catherine said she'd never met Tony.

Laura unscrewed a new bottle of chianti. Catherine could have been in there quite innocently having dinner and Tony could have been collecting money for charity, the cops and the firemen were always doing something for the kids. He could have sat down at her booth for a second or two and Janice just happened to see them together at that moment.

Or they met at a Chamber of Commerce breakfast - they had them every month and Tony had been to one just a week ago. Whatever, there had to be a reason and it had better be a good one because, goddammit, Tony never took *her* anywhere, so what fucking business did he have going out for dinner with some other woman? None. That's what.

Calm down, Laura, you're obsessing. She refilled her glass and swallowed another gulp of wine. Tony liked good-looking women; he had a thing for redheads. Catherine Moore wasn't a great looker, her eyes were too small, but he'd love all that auburn hair, even if it was probably dyed, and she had those lovely manicured nails that never saw a lick of real work.

Laura considered her own wrinkled hands. No wonder they looked bad. For the last forty-five minutes she'd been working nonstop and now her kitchen was well beyond clean, it gleamed. She had polished the fridge, the counters, the stove, damp mopped the floor, swigged half a bottle of wine and still had lots of energy to burn. She was anxious for Tony to get home so they could talk but it was only nine thirty. He wouldn't be home until midnight. *If* he came home on time.

She made her way down the hall, checking up on homework being done. Anthony's room vibrated with the heavy bass of some rock group or other.

Laura banged her fist on his desk. "How can you concentrate with that noise?"

"Okay, Mom," pulling an earbud out of one ear, "I'll get my headset."

"That's not the point. I'm worried about you, the bass pounding in your--"

She watched his eyes glaze, ready for the lecture. "Ah, never mind." She shut his door softly and opened the girls'.

Gina's guilty brown eyes looked up at her from the bed.

"Why aren't you at your desk? What are you doing?"

"Gawd, Mom. I'm finishing my Math."

Sure, like Laura couldn't see the flashy Smartphone on the open page of the workbook. "I've told you a million times; get your homework done before–" What's the use, she thought, kids today were never out of range.

Across the room Claudia lay curled on her bed, reading a well-worn paperback, likely some piece of trash the girls were passing around the class.

She leaned over her older daughter. "What are you reading?" Pleased that she was actually reading and not on her cell.

Claudia flipped a cushion over the book. "Geez, Mom, you scared me. Would you believe Mr. Harris makes us read this garbage for English Lit?"

No, Laura thought, *I would not*. But for a change she

didn't say.   Tonight she felt like an intruder in her own house, her children watching her with wary eyes, anxiously waiting for her to leave them to their own business.

Back in the kitchen she drained the wineglass, carried it and the bottle into the living room.   Found the remote between the couch cushions and turned on the TV - just picture. No audio. Sat down to wait.

At twenty past eleven Tony found her there, sound asleep, slack jawed and snoring, an empty glass tipped on her lap.   The TV screen flashed and blinked in silence, its eerie blue light turning Laura's tawny olive skin a sickly grayish-green.   His eyes took in the glass, the bottle lying empty on the floor.   She'd sucked down a bottle or more tonight, she'd have one hell of a head in the morning.

He pulled the afghan up over her, the wavy patterned one she'd crocheted a few years back. He remembered the skeins of bright colored yarn on the floor, Laura's dark head bent over the instruction book, the sweet curve of her cheek, her laughter and groans of frustration as she talked herself through each stitch until she had it mastered.   In the end she said she hated it and never made another.

Now he saw with a shock that those once plump cheeks were hollow, sunken.   Dark smudges circled her eyes and the laughter had died.   He touched her hand, hard and thin like a bird's claw.   This was a pale, wasted shadow of the girl he had fallen in love with so long ago.   She had changed, and it had to be all this drinking.

For years, three, four anyway, he'd been begging her to stop, to see a shrink, but Laura insisted there was nothing wrong with her. She'd go into her usual rant; sure, she had a glass or two of wine at dinner, but it was damned lonely eating without him night after night. And if she *was* turning into an alkie it was all *his* fault. If only Tony changed his job, his hours even, came home nights like everybody else's husband and stopped chasing skirts she'd be the happiest woman on earth.

Laura lived in a nightmare world, he thought, any fool could see she was not a normal, well-adjusted adult. She was like a child, a responsibility he'd been burdened with for more years than he cared to count. Tony sighed. How long had he felt this way? He had loved her once, but maybe between her drinking and her nagging he'd reached the limit, the end of that road. Else why this flicker of interest, of... attraction, to another woman.

His mind was playing games, he was dog tired, any interest he might have in Catherine Moore was purely professional, and when he thought she was safe things would get back to normal. Whatever *that* was. Tony snapped off the flickering TV and went to bed.

But not to sleep; his mind whirled with images of Laura, demanding, whining, drunk, pictures that mixed and swirled around the face of a courageous and battered Catherine Moore. Laura's dark eyes flashing with anger, Catherine's cowed and submissive. A woman with real problems. Was that the attraction? No. Tony had met all kinds of women in his career, some of them abused wives, and he'd never lain awake nights fantasizing about them.

Recalling the morning a few weeks ago in the coffee shop, he was sure Catherine had been flirting a little. And tonight, at the Chinese Lantern, they'd managed to fill nearly two hours talking, and as if by agreement the subject of the bastard husband never came up. He loved listening to her deep, sexy voice - sounded like Patsy Kline and that song he loved, Crazy... he could let her talk all night.

But Laura's voice intruded into his fantasy; frantic and shrill, smothering the low rich tones of Catherine's.

He thought of Laura's pathetic efforts to look sexy. The two, three times he'd seen Catherine she'd never been anything but well-groomed, buttoned up like a proper Boston matron, but he could imagine her naked and writhing in bed, hot and wet for him, all that wonderful red hair spread and tumbled around her and-- *down, Tony, down, boy.* A married man of forty teasing himself like a teenager. Christ, next he'd be having wet dreams.

He rolled off the bed, crept barefoot to the kitchen for a cold glass of water, soundlessly passing his wife, still asleep on the sofa. Good. Tonight he needed space. Maybe they should get a king bed. Or twins! He shut the bedroom door and crawled under the covers, tossed a few times, punched his pillow, trying to avoid the questions spinning like crazy in his head. But even as he tried to ignore it, Tony knew he had to face up to what was fast becoming a... situation. So. Catherine Moore. Harmless flirting, or more serious business. And if so, where was it taking him? Nowhere. Absolutely nowhere.

Laura was his wife, for better or worse. He was an honorable man, a good husband. Tony had never had an affair, no matter what Laura imagined in that mixed-up head of hers, and he wasn't about to start now.

He was a cop, a damned good cop. Doing his job. In the course of an investigation he had followed up with an abused woman, sadly one of many. Catherine Moore had had nothing new to report. Case closed. Job over. He had no legitimate reason to see her again and it was crystal clear that he'd better stop inventing reasons to do so before he did something he might regret.

Eighteen years ago he had vowed to love his wife 'until death', and Mauro Antonio Costello was a man of his word.

Fifteen

His booming voice followed Alyson up the stairs, through the walls, the closed bedroom door, through the palms of her hands covering her ears. Her father shouting, swearing, seemed like he was always yelling at Mom. She scooped Max up in her arms and threw herself on the bed, eyes welling up with tears. Life sucks, Max. The monkey's solitary glass eye gazed at her with sympathy. She pulled the pillow over Max's head and her own to shut it out. I hate my life, bigtime, Max.

What was she supposed to do stuck up here in her bedroom? She'd been watching a rerun of The Simpsons in the family room but Mom had sent her upstairs when the fight started. Go to your room, Alyson, do some homework. On a Sunday night, when Mom knew perfectly well Aly always did her homework with Bonnie on Friday right after school. More yelling downstairs. Did they think she couldn't hear them? A person would have to be stone deaf not to know they were fighting.

Alyson gnawed on Max's well-chewed ear. She knew he hurt Mom, slapped her, pinched her arms, and Mom just took it, she never fought back. And when it was all over, she'd say, oh Aly, your Dad has a lot on his mind, things aren't going so well at work. Always making excuses for him. Work stuff, my ass! She giggled at the forbidden word. If it really was work stuff why did he act like it was Mom's fault, yelling and throwing things around and just scaring everybody silly?

Seemed like he was always in a bad mood, unless there was a football game on TV. Even then, if the Patriots were losing, he'd holler at the TV, throw cushions around, yell at anybody who got too close. He never told a joke, or laughed, and nobody else did either when he was around. It was real sad. Mom might be telling Aly about something funny that happened during the day, or Alyson could be telling Mom one of her best new jokes, but when *he* walked through the door the fun stopped. They'd both clam up, as if they'd been doing something wrong.

Now that she was twelve - almost a grown-up, Alyson knew to be quiet, stay well out of his way. Funny how a kid learned to do stuff like that.

Children were supposed to love their fathers, but what did that mean, exactly? What was she supposed to love him for? He didn't take her to the circus and buy her stuff like Bonnie's Dad, he never played games with her or read to her, he'd never been to a single one of her soccer games, Mom did all that, because her games were right after school. *Some*body has to work to pay the bills, he'd say, keep a roof over their heads. But she knew that wasn't true, because he always missed her dance recitals and school plays, and they were at night. Parent-teacher nights? Never there.

Mom said he loved her, but he sure didn't show it.

Never talked to her, except for stupid stuff like bring me a damned napkin Alyson or I sure hope you did well in school today, Alyson, education's important, trust funds are great but money isn't everything, you know, some of us have to work for a living. Trust funds? She'd have to google that. Usually when he said that he'd give Mom this sly sideways look, what was that? Anyway, he didn't listen to anything Alyson said, she'd figured that out long ago.

Fathers were supposed to love their kids. Maybe he wasn't really her father, he was, like, a stepfather or something, and Mom didn't want Aly to know, like it was a big secret. He sure was mean, that much Alyson knew.

Max's single eye gleamed up at her. He knew. Max heard the noises coming from Mom and Dad's room at night sometimes, he'd seen and heard things he was too scared to talk about. *Like that night, back in the summer, before school started.* Max saw Mom huddled on the floor in the corner of her bedroom, whimpering like she was terrified, and Dad about to hit her with something in his hand. *And he was stark naked!* A giggle escaped when she remembered her dad's big white butt. But it wasn't funny next morning when they saw Mom trying to hide a black eye with tons of makeup. Alyson hugged the stuffed animal tighter. You saw too, didn't you?

And that other time - she hadn't even mentioned that one to Max. It happened a long time ago, back when Alyson was still a kid, eight maybe, or nine. It was summer, and she'd run in from the pool to use the bathroom. And surprised Mom with her bathing suit half off, black and blue marks on her legs and her arms, like she had bumped into something. Mom had given a little yelp and snatched up a beach towel to cover herself.

"Aren't you coming out, Mommy?"

"No, sweetie, I've changed my mind," she'd said, "I don't think I'll go swimming today after all."

But Alyson was no dummy. Well, maybe she was then but now she was older and now she knew how Mom probly got those bruises. She'd never ever forgive him for hurting Mom, even if he *was* her real father.

Poor Max was choking! She loosened her hold on his neck, threw the pillow on the floor.

Through her bedroom window she saw Brian raking leaves on the Kurtz's front lawn. Bonnie would be home too, she'd run over there; they couldn't make her stay in her room forever, like she was punished, for nothing. Alyson slid off the bed and tiptoed down the stairs. *Get out of jail free. Do not pass GO.*

"I'll be over Bon's, Mom." She shut the door carefully so it wouldn't slam. Aly had whispered but she could have yelled, they wouldn't have heard. He was still carrying on in the kitchen.

Across the road Mrs. Kurtz answered the door wearing a yellow apron with big red flowers all over it. She was fat, like the Pillsbury dough boy. Go right on up, she said, Bonnie's in her room pretending to do homework. Her chins jiggled when she laughed, and the house smelled of baking. Running up the stairs, Alyson tried to remember her Mom ever wearing an apron.

"Hey, Bon. It sure smells good in here."

"Yeah, my mom's always baking something. What's up?"

"Nothing. I just got sick of listening to my–" Alyson bit her lip.

"Your folks fighting?"

"Oooh, you got a new comforter."

"They're fighting again, aren't they." Bonnie wouldn't be sidetracked. "My mom says they do that a wicked lot."

"Oh yeah?" Defensive. "Don't yours?"

"Nah. They hardly ever argue."

"Hey Bon, how come we never see your Dad anymore?"

Bonnie's eyes rolled from Alyson to the bedroom door, back to Alyson's face. She tiptoed across the room and shut the door quietly. "He's... away."

"Where?"

"I'm not supposed to--"

"That's not fair. You know about--!"

Bonnie turned the radio volume up and sat on the bed right up close to Alyson, whispering in her ear. "He left us. And he's never coming back." Bonnie turned her head away but Alyson saw a tear trickle down her cheek.

"Mom says he has his reasons, but it's because of me and Brian, I just know it. He's not our real father, you know. Mom says we fight like cats and dogs, and I know my Dad hated that."

Alyson hugged her knees. *Not our real father.* Maybe all fathers were weird. A kid's life was awful. She played with the radio dial, found an oldies station. The rock music covered up the snuffling sounds of Bonnie lying across the bed crying into her pillow.

When Mrs. Kurtz called up the stairs, Bonnie swiped tears off her face and made Alyson swear not to say a word.

"Cross your heart. Say it!"

"Okay, Bon. Cross my heart and hope to die."

Downstairs a platter of warm chocolate chip cookies waited on the kitchen table. Bonnie's mom poured three glasses of milk and sat with them, eating cookies and asking about school and stuff but not in a nosy way. *And she never once let on she'd been dumped by her husband.* Wow.

"Aly, aren't you going to Gina Costello's Halloween party with Bonnie?"

Alyson nodded. "Yeah, but I haven't got a costume yet."

"You two should go as a pair, Tom and Jerry, maybe, or Abbot and Costell-- oops!" She laughed. Alyson liked the way Mrs. Kurtz laughed; it rolled up and bubbled out while she shook all over. "Guess that role should be Gina's."

"That reminds me, I have to call her mom." She went to the phone.

Behind her mother's back, Bonnie rolled her eyes. Alyson took another cookie and wondered if her mom would be happy like that if her father left them.

Sixteen

Catherine was on Tony's mind every minute, waking or sleeping. At work. At home. He'd drive through town, recklessly scanning every car, every shop, every woman he passed. He was beginning to understand the meaning of obsession.

More than once, thinking he'd seen her in a store, Tony put on a bright smile, practiced a casual hello, then felt his stomach sink with disappointment when he turned out to be wrong. One day, coming up behind a woman on the sidewalk wearing a black vest, he went so far as to tap her on the shoulder - scared the shit out of her - the poor soul probably thought she was getting mugged. In fact, he had yet to see Catherine anywhere besides her office, but suddenly every other woman in Gilford seemed to be a tall slender redhead, and he couldn't stop scrutinizing them.

In the three weeks and two days - but who's counting! - since their dinner at the Chinese Lantern, Tony made a point of skirting the part of Main Street where Catherine worked, but it didn't help, avoiding her made him think and worry about her more than ever.

Today he'd promised Laura he'd help supervise Gina's

Halloween party, even though he thought the mother of three kids should be able to handle a few twelve, thirteen-year-olds. Of course, this *would* be the day from hell - young father slammed into a guard rail on the Pike at rush hour and flipped the car. The little one in the car seat was fine but Dad wasn't gonna make it. A long, sad day, a shitload of paperwork.

At five-thirty he left the shop, jumped into the Explorer, texted Laura that he was on his way home, and hit the road. The shortest route was along Main Street to the Common, and Casey & Moore. He'd whip right by - Christ, he had a right to use the streets of his own town, all this slipping and sliding down side streets and back lanes was making him feel like a criminal. He sat straighter behind the wheel, a man in charge of his destiny with a belly full of fluttering butterflies.

The Main Street of Gilford, like so many in New England, was in reality the old High Road, established three hundred years earlier when horses and buggies meandered from town to town. Highway 16, at five forty-five, was a multi-colored ribbon of cars slowly heading home from work in this and other towns along the way. And damned near all of them empty but for the driver, like they'd never heard of carpools. Or air pollution. He slammed his fist on the steering wheel, rolled down the windows, tuned the radio to NPR.

He had choices. He could turn off Main Street onto Summer Street, no traffic there. Or Prospect, though longer, would take him directly into his subdivision. A sharp left on Myrtle would be a good idea, but block after block he stubbornly hugged the bumper of the little Miata in front of him like a greyhound on the track following the mechanical bunny.

Ahead at the intersection of Pleasant and Main, the traffic light turned red. Not a momentous event in itself, but for the rest of his days Tony would look back and know that this moment, this nanosecond, this random act of God, changed his life.

The stream of traffic came to a halt and Tony's Explorer, four or five cars back from the corner, stopped dead in front of Casey & Moore's plate glass window. He looked in - a casual glance - and saw Catherine standing in the doorway of her office, apparently talking to someone out of Tony's range of vision. A shaft of sunlight gave her silky blouse a golden glow where it touched, to his eyes it looked like a painting by one of those ancient Dutch guys. A pair of gold-rimmed granny glasses on a beaded cord nestled in the vee of her shirt and her hair was pinned up on top of her head, a few escaped strands lay against her cheek, her neck.

Or maybe God and the red light had nothing to do with it. The woman Catherine had been talking to walked out the door, her secretary or a client, what did it matter. The setting sun lit up Catherine's face and Tony realized that seeing her through the window wasn't going to be enough; now he had to hear her voice, touch her hand, stroke that gleaming copper hair, instead of sitting out here like a damned lovestruck fool. The light changed, cars started to move, but the woman who'd been in Catherine's office was in her car, waiting for a break in the traffic. An omen, surely. He let her back out and slipped into her spot and quickly let himself into the office before he could change his mind.

"Who's there?" She turned from her desk, peering at him over her granny glasses. "May I help you?"

"It's me, Mrs. Moore. Tony Costello." His voice sounded rusty, and he cleared his throat. "You should keep this outer door locked when you're in here alone." Realizing as he said the words that he'd used that excuse the last time.

"Tony! It's been ages." She sounded pleased. "My secretary just left, but you're right about the door, it'll be dark soon and I should have locked it behind her." Realizing as she said the words that she remembered last time too. She tilted her head, obviously wondering why he was really here.

"I, ah...I was on my way home, got stuck in traffic, rush hour gets longer every day, it's like a parking lot out there. *Geez, Tony, quit your babbling.* But he couldn't stop. "Saw you in here and thought I'd stop in, say hi, chinwag a few minutes, let the traffic die down a bit."

She walked around behind her desk, but stayed on her feet, like she was waiting for him to leave.

"But you're busy," turning to the door, "I don't want to keep you from--"

"It's okay, I'm about done." She locked a file drawer. "I often stay late to avoid the traffic."

An invitation to stay? Tony couldn't tell. "I've gotta get moving soon anyway, I'm the official bouncer at my daughter's Halloween party tonight."

"My Alyson's going to that party..." She laughed, and Tony heard the bells. "She's one of Macbeth's three witches, along with your Gina and Bonnie Kurtz." She leaned her hip against the desk. "Three beautiful young girls transformed with green paint and fake warts into ugly old crones."

"What color are your eyes?"

"What color…?" She smiled. "Green. Your wife said you were color blind."

"Only blue and green." Tony tried to laugh. "I can see red as well as everyone else. Like your hair."

With her eyes shining and the way her mouth tilted up like that it was all he could do not to rush over and kiss her. Fortunately, his legs refused to move.

"Auburn, my daughter's hair is bright carroty red," she chuckled, "and she hates it."

"Alyson, right? Will you be picking her up later?"

"No, I've got the night off. Janice Kurtz drove them to your house and the girls are sleeping over."

"So you're not rushing home?"

She shook her head no.

"Got any plans for dinner?" Laura would be pissed but the party was hours away yet. He smoothed down his mustache with a nervous hand while the clock in the lobby ticked ten loud seconds.

Her smile had faded, she was suddenly looking real serious, and he'd give anything to know what she was thinking.

"I was planning to grab a bite on the way home." He'd thought no such thing but if it bought him an hour with her it was worth the lie. "Italian… or maybe Chinese?"

"Frank—"

His heart stopped.

"—won't be home for dinner."

Tony's heart started beating again.

"We can walk to the Lantern." She nodded her head, slowly, thoughtfully, like this was the most important decision she'd made all day. "Chinese it is." She smiled. "Again."

Catherine said she had a quick phone call to make and he sat in the waiting room, or lobby, whatever, listening to the damned clock tick away the minutes and telling himself to run - don't walk - tear right out that door and never look back. He was getting in way over his head and he didn't even know into what! He was deliberately walking down a very dangerous path here and—

"All set."

--and that was that. Outside he stopped beside the Explorer.

"I thought we were going to walk."

He glanced up. "Be dark soon." The sun in all its glory had just set behind the oak trees in the Common. But she just nodded her head and moved, robotlike, to the Explorer.

He held the door open and watched as she struggled with the high step in her tight skirt, wanting to help but not daring to touch her; afraid he'd get his arms around her and never let go. He slammed the door shut behind her and jumped in on the driver's side.

Maybe it was PMS. Catherine felt shaky, quivery inside, a sloshing in her stomach of motion sickness, though they had only driven a couple of blocks and she never got seasick. She didn't look at Tony, but stared straight ahead through the windshield, concentrating on the road as if she were the one driving. Something shiny on the dashboard caught her eye. A gold ball; an earring. She'd seen it before, Laura wore earrings like this all the time; that earring belonged to Laura. *Like this vehicle, Catherine, and the man driving it.* The gold ball, gleaming in the light like an unblinking yellow eye, watched her.

She felt as if she were doing something wrong, but goodness, they were only getting a bite to eat. Frank had a meeting in town, wouldn't be home until late, even *he* wouldn't have a problem with what she was doing. *What she was doing.* The words sounded ominous, even though she wasn't *doing* anything.

Her stomach churned, she felt nauseous, when they got to the restaurant she wouldn't be able to keep a bite of food down. She would simply ask Tony to let her out. At the next corner, or the next light. Now. As she wondered why she didn't open her mouth, the moon showed itself on the horizon, an impossibly huge orange balloon suspended like a stage prop behind a small stand of birches.

Tony drove slowly down Main Street, right on past the Chinese Lantern. He had intended to stop, there were empty parking spaces near the door, but, as if directed by remote control, the damned SUV kept on rolling down Main Street, aimed straight at the big orange ball of a moon hanging in the trees at the edge of town. So. Not the Chinese Lantern. Okay by him, there were other places in town to eat.

"Guess I missed it back there. Italian okay with you?"

From the corner of his eye he saw her nod her head.

With the window down the breeze tugged at the knot of hair twisted up on Catherine's head, whipping long strands around her face. Tony clutched the wheel with both sweaty hands to keep from brushing her hair out of her eyes.

He noticed that the traffic had died down on Main Street. He noticed, too, that since they got into the car she hadn't spoken a single word.

Shivering a little, Catherine undid the knot in her hair and tucked it behind her ears, but left the window open partway. It was hard to breathe, she felt asthmatic, as if there was a tight band around her chest. The cool fresh air, redolent of dry leaves - and pine needles, seemed to help. She stared out the windshield and listened to her heart pounding, wondering if Tony heard it too and wondering why he was so quiet and if he was wondering the same thing about her and hoping he wouldn't try to make small talk because she didn't know what was going on but words couldn't describe what was happening if anything and she knew that a single word would spoil it all. Whatever *it* was.

Meantime the car rolled smoothly on down the road as though in a dream. Dry leaves scraped and swirled around in the wind and the moon rose inexorably, smaller now but still deep yellow, just above the trees.

Catherine didn't dare look at Tony but the little hairs on her arm stood on end, her whole body sensed him beside her, as if electrodes were attached to her skin, if he touched her she would burst, or cry. She didn't have a clue where Tony was taking her and she soon realized that she didn't care, she'd given up responsibility for her actions when she stepped into his car. Back in town, when they passed the Chinese restaurant and she didn't open her mouth to object or question, she understood that her fate was out of her hands.

Six-thirty on the dashboard clock. Turn around, Tony, go home. But all he wanted was to drive to the edge of the world with this wonderful woman beside him. He looked at Catherine's hand, resting calmly on the seat between them, long fingers tapering to pale polished nails, diamond wedding band winking in the streetlights as they left town. She seemed composed, like this was an everyday thing they were doing. Or was she as stunned as he was? And what exactly were they doing? He was glad she was so quiet, he couldn't think of anything to say that wouldn't sound stupid, and anything he did say would break the mood. The silence was safe.

The road was smooth and he shifted into fifth gear, pushing the stick way over to the right. The back of his hand brushed Catherine's leg, felt the warmth of her skin through the skirt that was riding up her thigh. *Jesus Christ,* his whole arm tingled, it was like getting an electric shock. One hand clutched the wheel, the other tugged at his beardless chin. Nine years since he had a smoke and he suddenly craved a cigarette.

Mile after wordless mile he followed the road out of Gilford, into Southwood and out the other side, driving around Tyler Lake, to the Old Log Cabin restaurant. Beyond that he knew the unpaved road was nearly impassable and he swerved into the gravel parking lot. It was empty, but he drove the truck to the farthest corner, over by the trees where it was dark and as far as possible from the building, like a man who knew all about sneaking around.

As the car bumped across the ridges and potholes in the parking lot the gold earring rocked and rolled back and forth on its post, an implacable eye gazing first at her, then at Tony, then back again. Catherine was afraid to touch it, as if it might burn her hand, but Tony must see it there rolling around, Laura's earing spying on them, why didn't he take it away?

The instant the car stopped moving Catherine jumped out but instead of heading across the parking lot to the restaurant she made for the thick fringe of pines that edged the small lake.

Tony grabbed his jacket from the back seat and followed the long slender shadow slipping through the trees, easy to see by the light of the amazing harvest moon over the lake. Look at her moving gracefully, so carefree, so natural, while he was a jumble of nerves, tripping and stumbling over roots and shrubs, no idea what to do next except that he desperately needed to take a whiz.

"Ooh!" He couldn't see her now but he heard her voice out of the silver shadows. "The water's cold." She laughed, a short high-pitched giggle.

How could she laugh when the whole damned world was spinning upside down? But then he caught up to her and he saw her face, ghostly pale, eyes big and round and-- afraid.

"Catherine, what is it?"

"Nothing. Everything. This isn't…"

"You're shivering."

"Aren't you?"

Funny how they both knew without saying that something was going down here. He draped his leather jacket around her shoulders, let his hands linger on her arms. He felt her stiffen, pull away.

"Tony, I—I'm not sure what's happening to me. I feel afraid, but excited too. I think I'm falling down the rabbit hole, letting myself get into something I can't control."

"Yeah, I know…"

Catherine's eyes stared into his. "I have to know if it's the same for you."

"If you're asking have I ever done this before, the answer is no. I've only ever been with one woman in my whole life."

She stood quite still, inches away in the pine-scented dark, so close he could smell her shampoo, her sweat, see the fear in the dark pools of her eyes. So near he could kiss her mouth if he wanted to. His chest ached, he could hardly breathe, with wanting to.

"Why me, Tony?"

Her voice trembled, and Tony wanted to wrap her in his arms, keep her safe. What was it about this woman that had him tied up in knots, standing out here in the middle of nowhere wanting to make love to her and to hell with the consequences?

"Damned if I know." The moon peeped over the hills on the far side of the pond. "Geez, would ya look at that moon."

She tilted her head back to see, exposing her long white neck, and Tony felt a surge of emotion so strong it left him breathless. His arms closed around her, startling them both. He bent to kiss the curve of her neck. Felt her go rigid.

"No." He saw terror in her eyes. "I... no."

"I'm sorry, Cath — "

She pushed him away and ran out of the woods, slipping, skidding on roots and rocks until she heard the crunch of her shoes on gravel; ran past the car and stopped to lean against a post to catch her breath, feeling afraid and weak and hollow from wanting Tony to kiss her, touch her, rip her clothes off and make love to her in the bed of dry pine needles under the trees.

He caught up to her under the single dim light that illuminated the center of the parking lot, took her hand. "Catherine, I'm sorry!"

She snatched it away. "I...I can't, Tony. I can't do this."

She saw his Adam's apple leap in his throat as he swallowed. "It's okay." His fingers tenderly brushed tears from her cheeks. "Really, it's okay. I don't think I can either."

She laughed, bursting the tension like a bubble. "Know what?"

"No." He was still so serious.

"I'm hungry."

He chuckled. "Then we'll get you something to eat."

The restaurant was dark, just a couple of burglar lights lit, *CLOSED FOR THE SEASON*, big sign out front and everything. She hadn't noticed before.

"I'm starving."

"There's always Chinese."

She gave him a thin, watery grin. "I think I'd better get home."

"Me too, I was supposed to be home ages ago."

He helped her into the Explorer, feeling like he'd been robbed, cheated. But of what? A kiss in the moonlight? A grope in the dark? A cheap fuck they'd both regret before it was over? There couldn't be anything else. They were two married people, stuck in their own lives. He climbed in his side and slammed the door. Lacy moonlight flickered through the bare branches, touched her face, glinted off something shiny on the dash.

Tony's truck plunged in and out of potholes, rocking one way and the other across the parking lot. The gold eye wobbled and winked at Catherine from the dashboard. It had been so long since she'd felt like this, breathless with wanting a man to kiss her, to feel his hands move slowly in all her secret places, arousing her, undressing her, entering her... knowing it was wrong yet wanting the feeling to last forever.

Laura's stupid earring seemed to be grinning at her. Catherine reached out to grab it but the truck lurched and the gold stud rolled across the dashboard and out of her grasp.

Tony caught the bright little ball as it skittered over to his side. "Laura's." He picked up the tiny gold earring and twirled it between his fingers. "She thought it was lost."

Like me, he thought, his hungry eyes fixed on Catherine's mouth.

"It's been staring at me, Tony, like a golden eye."

The fucking Eye of God, Tony thought, *watching us*. Or worse, Laura's eye, he felt as if Laura was here with them in the car. He dropped the earring into his shirt pocket, then took it out, rolled down the window and tossed the shiny little ball into the trees. He hit the brake, slammed the car into park, turned to her. "And now I'm lost."

Catherine felt Tony's fingers touch her cheek, trace her lips.

"Gone." She heard tears in his voice. "Laura isn't watching us now."

She took his right hand in hers, kissed the palm, each one of his fingertips. Unbuttoned her blouse and drew his hand across the swell of her breast, placing his fingers over the nipple, stiff and hard. His touch was like fire. "Oh my God, Tony," and, whispered, "Please, please make love to me..."

With a groan Tony turned off the engine.

Seventeen

Laura did not remember a time when she was not afraid of clowns. She hated the circus for that reason, and when the kids were small she let Tony take them by himself. She didn't like masks either. Not the monsters or the Draculas, they had real facial expressions, no matter how scary. Much more terrifying were the shiny white clown faces, with their wide empty grins and stupid red noses, hiding everything but a pair of glassy eyes.

Tonight though, the Miss Piggy masks, smooth and pink and wearing identical simpering smirks, were the worst. Four of them arrived together, young men - definitely *not* seventh-grade boys - dressed in droopy blue jeans slung low around their hips like they were about to slip right off and baseball hats turned backwards.

She'd gone all-out for this party of Gina's. Spent the day baking pumpkin cookies, carving five different Jack-O'Lanterns, cutting out cobwebs from old pantyhose. Inflated dozens of black and orange balloons with Gina's new friends Alyson and Bonnie, trying to make them comfortable so they'd come around more often. They seemed to be real nice girls, from up on the Ridge, good families, and she hoped they'd be good influences on her rebellious younger daughter.

Since turning twelve in July Gina had grown sullen, withdrawn, pulling away from the family circle while at the same time demanding attention by doing things she obviously knew they wouldn't like, just to see how far she could push. Like the spiked dog collar and black lipstick she had on tonight, where in hell did she find stuff like that? Her friends had come dressed as witches from Shakespeare and Gina was supposed to be the third. They were pretty upset, especially Bonnie, who had come up with the idea and now said she felt dumb.

Gina had been allowed to invite fifteen kids but in the dim glow of the Jack-O-Lanterns Laura had counted twenty, now twenty-four with the Miss Piggys coming through the door. A buzzing, shouting swarm of teenagers jammed the living room, squatted against the walls down the hallway, perched on furniture. The whole house rattled and vibrated with a cacophony of young girls' high-pitched giggles and the pounding basses and garbled lyrics of music Laura couldn't and didn't want to understand.

Bedlam, but still under control. Too soon for congratulations, she thought, as another car turned into the driveway, discharging three more of these creepy pink Miss Piggys - they must have cleared out the Dollar Store shelves! Some of them old enough to drive - who were these kids? Had Gina invited the baseball team? When confronted, her daughter didn't seem to know, or care.

"You know how it is, Ma, kids hear about a party going down and they just show up." Gina's eyes glowed, her first party had been crashed, she was going to be the talk of the school Monday morning. "And you're here, so what's the big deal?"

Seeing three boys go into the bathroom together, Laura pushed her way down the hall and smelled cigarette smoke. She banged on the door and told them they'd have to put them out or leave. Looking sheepish, they slinked out, promising not to do it again and she relented, proud of herself for handling the situation.

Her mouth was bone dry with nerves. She'd hidden a bottle of liquor in the hamper in her bedroom, just a few steps down the hall, she could use a swig now, but she'd hold off until Tony got home. Which should have been an hour ago. She checked her cell; no message since four-thirty. She sent him another text.

"Keep it down, kids." Her voice, powerful enough to shatter glass, couldn't penetrate the wall of noise.

In the orange gloom of the Jack O' Lantern light she watched Gina dancing with one of the Miss Piggys, if that sexy swaying could be called dancing. He was built like a man, not a boy, with her tiny daughter pressed right up against him, his big hand stroking her little girl's butt. Laura's temper flared, but she didn't want to cause a scene and embarrass Gina in front of her friends. Stay cool, Laura, what could happen, really? The room was crowded and as long as they didn't try to escape to the basement or a bedroom Gina would be safe. Laura remembered herself at that age, doing everything in her power to get the boys to notice her.

Claudia was supposed to be helping but she must be

dancing; Laura couldn't pick her out in the crowd of dark-clad figures.

When she saw the flare of a lighter across the room Laura shoved through the crowd and planted herself in front of the boy with the cigarette. "I thought I told you–" Not a cigarette, a joint! Four, five Miss Piggys silently closed in, one of them towering over her. She trembled, but there would be absolutely no drugs in her house. "Don't you know Gina's father is a cop?"

The tallest one laughed. "Who's Gina?"

Laura felt stupid talking to a mask, but her voice held firm. "Please leave."

Dark eyes gleamed with scorn behind the rosy mask while the kid deliberately and slowly put the joint in his pocket. He snapped his fingers, like a Mob boss, and two of the Miss Piggys followed him out the door.

A small victory, Laura thought, watching them drive away, but her hands shook just thinking about what might have happened if he'd balked. Now she was dying for a drink, her nerves were shot and where the hell was Tony?

She squeezed past a dozen kids into the kitchen and dialed the main precinct number, changed her mind and hung up before it rang a second time. Surely she could handle a kids' party by herself. She crammed a handful of candy corn into her mouth and went back into what she now considered a battlefield.

A flash of glass, or tin, being passed from one hand to another. They didn't even bother to hide it, these kids swigged straight from the flask. She knew they were laughing at her behind those smug, smiling plastic faces.

Liquor and pot were a far cry from cigarettes, who knew what might happen next, and this time Laura hurried to the bedroom, punched in Tony's direct line at the station. Long gone, Don said when he picked up, Tony left early to help chaperone Gina's party, must be hung up in traffic. Thanks, Don, clicking off before she screamed into the phone that it was now well past seven and Tony had a fifteen-minute drive home. Where in hell was he? She couldn't hold on much longer alone.

Laura heard the front door slam. Tony at last.

Digging the bottle out of the hamper, she took a sip, a swig, for courage, but a crash sent her scurrying back into the now throbbing silence of the living room. Miss Piggy and Mickey Mouse were rolling on the floor, fighting. The door of the stereo cabinet hung open, shattered glass sparkled like raindrops in the carpet.

"Stop!" She grabbed Mickey Mouse by the back of his shirt. "Stop this now!"

"Let go, Ma!"

"Who--?" She pulled off the mask and her heart did a flip. "Anthony? I thought you were at a school dance tonight."

"I was, but I heard that a bunch of seniors were gonna crash Gina's party and I came home to tell you. Damn good thing, too." He poked the pig in the chest. "I caught this motherf --!"

"Anthony!"

"--ucker with his slimy paws all over my kid sister!"

A blur in black, like a cat with a spiked collar flew at him. "You shut your fuckin' mouth--"

118

"Gina!" Laura reached out to stop her, the pig swiped at Anthony's face with a piece of broken glass, missed and slashed Laura's arm.   Pain, swift and sharp, followed by nausea when she saw all the blood.   Laura sagged to the floor.

Anthony dropped to his knees. "Jesus Christ, Ma."

Laura saw him through a fisheye lens, slowly going black around the edges.   *Madonn',* she was going to black out. Anthony's frightened face up close, distorted and bug-eyed. Gina wailing, her voice small and tinny, as if it came from far away.   Laura saw Anthony run out of the room, race back with a handful of wadded tissues and collide with Tony, finally coming through the door. Suddenly the room seemed empty, as if all the kids had melted into the walls.   She breathed easier.

"Laura! Jesus! What the hell's going on here?"

"Tony, about time..."

She watched him take in the broken glass, the blood on the rug.   Their audience, still and silent, stood around the room like figures in a wax museum.

"What are you all staring at?"   He flipped on the overhead light. "Party's over, kids. Time to go home."

Tripping over each other they rushed the door, the air deafening with the sound of tramping feet, all in a hurry except for a pair of witches cowering in a corner.

"Don't you two have any place to go?"

Gina burst into tears.   "Dad! Alyson and Bonnie are sleeping over."

"Sorry, girls." Tony's eyes flicked over Laura. "Anthony, get your mother into the bathroom. Can somebody tell me what in hell happened here?"

"Anthony was fighting with--"

"Ma!" He turned to his father. "It was an accident, Dad."

Laura saw the look of gratitude Gina shot her brother. "Anthony, you know damned well you were fighting--"

"Where was your mother?" Like she wasn't even there.

"*She* was in the bedroom."

"At least *I* was in the house." Laura tried to catch his eye. "Where were *you?*"

But her husband stayed by the door, wiping his shoes over and over on the mat. "Geez, Laura, you should be able to supervise a few kids."

"Damn you, Tony, there were twenty-five, thirty kids in here!" Laura's lips were stiff, she was trying hard not to cry. "You're saying this was my fault?" The bastard wouldn't even raise his head to look at her. "Look at me when I'm talking to you, dammit!"

He crossed the room, knelt beside her. "How much have you had to drink?"

"Nothing, Tony..."

"Laura, I can smell it on your breath!"

"A drop. I thought I heard you--"

"Yeah whatever." He turned away, disgusted. "Good night, kids. We'll clean up in the morning."

Somewhere in the dark strange house Alyson heard a clock chime once. She still hadn't shut her eyes, and on the air mattress beside her Bonnie was whispering what sounded like prayers. In her bed on the far side of the room, Gina sniffled, Aly could tell she was crying. *Too bad about Gina's party.* Just when it got going good Anthony started that fight and then Mrs. Costello threw a fit and ruined everything *right* at the minute Dave asked her to dance. Wow, Gina's mother was one scary lady. Poor Gina. It would be all over school on Monday.

She nudged her friend. "Psst, Bonnie!"

"What?"

Alyson put her lips near Bonnie's ear. "D'you think Mrs. Costello was drunk?"

"My mother says she drinks like a fish." Bonnie's whisper held the ring of authority.

Alyson didn't know anyone who drank like a fish. "She gets like that from drinking?"

"What are you two whispering about?"

"Oh, nothing, Gina."

"It's okay, my folks fight a lot."

"My mom says it's because your mother drinks." Bonnie's voice was smug. "My parents never fight."

"That's because they're split up."

Across the room Gina sucked in her breath.

"Al, you weren't supposed to tell."

"Well, it's true."

"Your folks fight too, Alyson Moore. You said so!"

"Yeah, they do."

"Like my mom and dad?"

"Worse, even, Gina. My father hits--" Alyson bit her lip, she hadn't meant to go that far.

"Oh my God." Gina's voice was shocked.

Somebody pounded on the bedroom door. "Hey, keep it

down in there."

Alyson buried her head deeper into her sleeping bag. A door slammed and through the thin walls she heard Mrs. Costello's voice, whining, just like her mother did sometimes. Mr. Costello's voice sounded ticked off, like he was half asleep. At first she couldn't make out any words, but Mrs. Costello's voice kept getting louder, higher.

"I d'serve some respeck, Tony."

"Oh yeah, respect. Why don't you just shut up, Laura, and let me sleep!"

Gina sniffled louder. Bonnie clutched at Alyson's arm.

"I'm s-scared, Aly."

"It's okay, Bon." She rolled over and took Bonnie's hand. "Don't be." Feeling brave, this was nothing compared to some of the rows at home. Movement at her back told her Gina had slipped from her bed to the floor. "C'm'on in, it's cozy in here." She lifted the corner of the sleeping bag and felt her friend snuggle close. Aly pulled the covers up over their heads, closing out the sounds still coming at them from beyond the wall. In a weird way she felt comforted; it wasn't just her folks, it seemed like everybody's family was... fucked   up!

Eighteen

Tony had been looking for an opportunity to corner Frank Moore, talk to the man, find out what made him tick.

His opportunity came early in November. Gina was going to see a movie on Saturday afternoon with Bonnie and Alyson, Aly's dad was driving them to the Cinema Complex. Immediately a plan began to form in Tony's mind.

"Look, we live down here in town, I'll drop you off at the show." He realized he didn't spend enough time with his youngest when he saw her face light up.

"Sure, Dad.

"What time's the movie?"

"2.15."

At 1.45 on Saturday afternoon he bundled her into the Explorer.

"Dad, it's a ten minute drive!"

"You never know about the traffic, and I know you don't want to be late."

Waiting for the others, he and Gina chatted a bit, a rare event and more or less an inquisition on his part. He asked about school, her friends; did she like this town, but her relief obvious when she spotted a silver Lexus pull up in front of the theatre.   Tony was out of the car before his daughter, leaned into the driver's window.

"Frank? Tony Costello.   Nice to see you again."   Oho, by the look on the guy's face, the feeling was NOT mutual. "Laura's real busy cleaning house and she doesn't want me in the way.   Let's go grab a beer."   Not a question.

"I don't drink beer."

"How 'bout a Coke?"   But now he remembered the morning in the Coffee Shop where he'd met Catherine and learned of Frank's violent behavior.   "Coffee.   Follow me."

"How long you been married, Frank?"

"Why do you want to know?"

"I've been married seventeen long years, how about you?"

Frank took a minute sip of coffee.   "Sixteen."

"Yeah, long enough.   Do you sometimes get tired of the monotony?"

"I never thought of it that way."

"Ah, come on, Frank.   The commute; the chores around the house; the wife."   He swallowed, glad the coffee was lukewarm, he was getting into deep water here.   "The same day, over and over, like the movie, Ground Hog Day.   Don't you sometimes wish for a change?"

Frank slammed his mug down on the table.   "Listen, copper, I don't know what you're aiming at here, but I am not playing your game.   My life is none of your damned business!"

"Oh, but it is, Frank.   I see battered women every day, and your wife is a prime specimen.   I can't help but wonder why." He turned, waved two fingers in the air.

"Drink up, Frank," when the waitress, not Joanie, filled their mugs.

He mopped up the spill when Frank pushed his away.

"What has my wife told you about me?"

"I haven't spoken about you with your wife since the night I answered the 911 call." He took a huge gulp of coffee, avoiding any thought of what he and Catherine *had* spoken about in the intervening time. "I'am sure you remember that night, Frank?"

"A one-off."

"I don't think so. You've done it before, and you and I both know you'll do it again." His fingers drummed on the table. "I've always wondered, Frank, what kind of man beats on his wife?"

"Shut the fuck up before I—" A hoarse whisper. Frank slapped his palms down hard on the table, kicked his chair away and leaned over, towering above Tony. "Stay out of my life and my wife's life, you little pissant."

"That's Detective pissant to you, Frank." He watched the big man stride out of the coffee shop, heard the door slam shut behind him. "And I'll be watching you like a hawk, you bastard."

Nineteen

Catherine's well-ordered world had turned upside down. In a few short months Tony had moved into her dreams and taken over her waking hours. Images of his eyes, his mouth, his cute habit of tugging at a beard he no longer wore flitted across her mind, interfered with work - Kevin had commented a few times on foolish mistakes she'd made.

And miracle of miracles, Frank was easier to take. Where once the knife-edge of his cruelty cut deep now it barely glanced her skin. He'd sensed her distraction, become rougher and more demanding, but somehow she felt less vulnerable, protected by the knowledge that she had Tony to rely on, to shield her.

Weirdest of all in this strange world were Tuesday nights driving to rehearsal with Laura. Repelled, mesmerized, Catherine would listen to Laura complain about Tony, repeating over and over like a broken record that she was positive he was fooling around, he wasn't paying her any attention; if she had proof she'd kill the bastard. One part of Catherine wanted to block her ears, to drive alone or stop going to rehearsals, anything to escape the constant whine but instead she'd sit, ears tuned to Laura's rant in horrified fascination, pinned to the very seat where she and Laura's husband had almost--.

She'd started telling lies. When Laura said she'd been seen with Tony at the Chinese Lantern a tale sprang whole out of her mouth, how he'd been canvassing for the Police Children's Fund - was there such a thing? - and simply joined her for a cup of coffee. All the while noticing a sly grin on Janice's face, not too difficult to guess who had reported seeing them together.

Fortunately, Janice hadn't seen her drive out of town with Tony on Halloween, the night they'd come so close to making love. She wouldn't have stopped him, in fact, Catherine had begged for it, but Tony said he couldn't, he wasn't prepared. Her lips curved in a secret smile, remembering Tony's warm hands, his lips on her mouth, her neck, her nipples, his gentle hands pressing and probing her most secret places, bringing her to life, until she came, oh God, for the first time in years, writhing in agonized joy. She sighed, feeling an urgent throbbing between her legs.

"You okay back there?" Laura's eyes met hers in the rearview mirror. "You're real fidgety. Need more heat?"

The damp chill of November permeated the SUV and Catherine's reply floated on a frosty cloud. "No, no, I'm fine."

They had not gone 'all the way' yet; smiling as she remembered the phrase from her college dating days. He wanted somewhere private for their first time and she was as excited as a schoolgirl with anticipation. Tony was a romantic, as different from Frank's cool sophistication as beer to Dom Perignon. Catherine admired his straightforward honesty and childlike candor. She was quite certain that anything illicit was as foreign to him as it was to her; realizing at the same time that contemplating having sex with him was about as dishonest and illicit as could be. But she also knew that, unless things in her life changed drastically, he would soon take her to bed. What things? *Welcome to my crazy world.*

"Catherine, you're so quiet back there. How's it going with Mrs. Wetherbee's house?"

"Mrs....? Oh, um. Pretty good, Janice. I've had a few showings, but that house is a tough sell."

"You're talking about the stone mansion, up on Hillcrest, right?" Laura's dark eyes shone in the green glow of the dashboard. "What I'd give to live there."

"Well over a million bucks; closer to two when all is said and done. All the wiring needs to be replaced, the kitchen is a total gut-job, and the bathrooms are a throwback to the 1950s, pink toilets and all! It was beautiful once, but it's been woefully neglected. I'm having trouble finding a buyer with both the money and the interest to restore the place."

"I'd do it, in a heartbeat."

"Sure you would, Laura, on a cop's lousy salary."

Catherine rolled her eyes, Janice had *such* a way with words. But the house was a white elephant; older folks were downsizing these days and young people with money wanted to live closer to downtown, with access to all the city had to offer.

"So Catherine, what do *you* think?"

What had she missed? *Too bizarre.*

"Sorry, Laura, I didn't—"

"As I was sayin' before Janice here interrupted, Tony's a

man who's always needed lots of sex and if Tony's not having sex with me, who is he getting it with?"

In the dark, Catherine shrugged. How would I know. She kept silent.

"I wouldn't care if Gary had an affair."

"Janice, what on earth are you saying?" Laura's head swiveled to her passenger. "I don't believe you! You'd never forgive Gary if he--!"

"Oh yes I would, if it meant keeping him." Janice nodded her tightly permed head slowly. "Absolutely. Yes."

Laura's eyes caught Catherine's in the rearview mirror, her raised eyebrow asking if Janice had gone nuts. "Talk's cheap, Jan. Your Gary's a puppet, dancing to your tune. Now my Tony--!"

"Ah, but the puppet has cut his strings." Janice's whisper cut through Laura's strident whine like a knife.

"He what?"

"Gary left me and the kids, back in August." She sniffled. "Needs to find himself or some such stupid thing!"

"You never said!"

"I thought he'd be back in a week, but it's been months and it sure doesn't look like he's ever coming back."

"Where is he?"

"In Boston. Living with his friend Ralph."

"The one you don't like? The gay one?"

Janice nodded.

Laura slapped the steering wheel. "Do you think Gary is...?"

"I don't think so," Janice's sigh was heavy with tears, "but anything's possible. A few months ago I'd have laughed at the idea of Gary leaving me."

"Did he say why?"

"Nope. He said he didn't know why, couldn't give me a reason. Just had to be alone for a while. I think he got tired of me. I'm a whale, as anyone can plainly see."

"Oh now, Janice—"

"Don't feed me platitudes, Laura. I'm obese, ugly, and a very boring person."

"Janice, you are far from ugly."

"Well thanks, Catherine." Laughing, Janice turned to the back seat. "That just leaves fat and boring."

"You are *not* boring!" Laura skidded around a corner. "Oops, sorry, ladies." She slowed down. "I'll admit that you are kind of hefty, Janice, but that's easily remedied."

"Easy for you to say, Laura. You're thin as a toothpick."

"But I have to work to keep my weight down."

I doubt it, Catherine thought, you're anorexic, Laura. But Janice needed reassurance. "Have you thought of joining one of those diet groups?"

"I didn't want to say but yes, I joined Weight Watchers® last--"

"If I caught my Tony messing around I'd kill him." Laura's mind was one-track. Her tiny palm struck the rim of the steering wheel. "*And* the bimbo he was fucking."

"Oh, Laura, maybe you're imagining—" Catherine clutched her arms to stop them trembling.

"And what suddenly makes you an authority on my husband?" Vicious eyes glared in the rearview mirror. "What did he tell you the night he took you out for dinner?"

"Your husband did not *take* me out for dinner, Laura.

He told me a bit about the, umm, the Fund, and the kids they were raising money for."

But when Laura was on a roll there was no stopping her.

"Have you seen him since?"

Like a dog with a bone. "He came by the office to pick up our donation." More lies.

Janice's voice, wistful and sad, cut across her thoughts. "I just want Gary back."

Laura had parked on Janice's driveway, engine idling.

"I had Bonnie invite him for Thanksgiving dinner. He loves my cooking, turkey's his favorite, I thought, how could he refuse?"

"And did he?"

"Yes, he did." Sniffling, soon the tears would start.

"Well ladies, gotta run." Catherine's cheerful goodbye sounded fake to her but the other two were too intent on Janice's troubles to hear.

She crossed the road and let herself into the house. Her husband lay sprawled on the couch in the den. "'Bout time," he grunted, absorbed in the nightly news. *Missed you too, Frank*. She turned to the stairs. Seeing a light in Alyson's room, Catherine looked in and saw her daughter lying face-down on her bed.

"It's late, Al, how come you're still awake?" Catherine heard her sniffle. "What's wrong, love?"

"Dad." Sniff. "Being his mean old self."

Catherine's heart missed a beat. "He didn't... what did he...?" She couldn't say the words.

"He didn't hit me, if that's what you mean. But he

threatened to."

"Why? What did you do?"

"Nothing. I was talking to Gina on the phone."

Gina. Her lover's daughter; Alyson's new BFF. Catherine was back in the Twilight Zone. "Did you finish your homework?"

"Of course, what do you take me for, an idiot? Dad asked me the same thing but he yelled at me anyway, I was so embarrassed." Alyson swiped at her dripping nose with the back of her hand. "Gina heard everything."

Catherine handed her a tissue.

"I wish he would just go away, like Bonnie's Dad."

"You know about Mr. Kurtz."

"Of course, Mom, I've known for ages. We're not babies, you know."

"No, I guess you're not." Catherine sat on the end of the bed, stroking Max's long furry leg. "Al, your father has a lot on his mind, but —"

"Does he drink?"

"What makes you ask that?"

"Gina says her mother does and it makes her do crazy stuff."

Catherine gazed at her daughter, so young to be aware of facts like these. When had children begun discussing runaway fathers and alcoholic mothers? "No, sweetheart, your Dad doesn't drink. You know he loves you. He's under a lot of pressure and stress at work. It's best if we don't get him riled up at home." The grandfather clock in the downstairs hall struck half past ten. "Anyway, you know you're not supposed to yak to your friends on weeknights."

Softened with a kiss and a hug. "Now under the covers with you."

Yawning, Aly pulled Max in with her and Catherine left them snuggled together, a cozy tangle of arms and legs. She'd have no trouble getting to sleep.

Not so her mother. Catherine undressed and slipped into bed, pulling the duvet up over her ears. With any luck Frank would fall asleep in front of the TV and she'd be in dreamland before he came up the stairs. But she guessed wrong. Frank burst into the room a few minutes later.

"What have you been telling your friend the cop about us?"

"I don't know what you mean, Frank."

"He cornered me on Saturday, when I dropped Aly off at the theatre. Asked me all kinds of questions. Do I love you. Why do I hit you." He leaned closer, snarling, "I'll ask you one more time. What does he know about us?"

Huddled under the duvet, Catherine watched him tear off his shirt, unbuckle his belt, drop his trousers.

"Know what his parting shot was?" He peeled off his socks. "What kind of man beats on his wife!" His boxers joined the clothing strewn on the floor. "Roll over, bitch, I'll show you what kind of man I am!"

Afterwards, she realized he'd have taken her awake or sleeping. He entered her from behind, like a dog, without invitation, his clear intent to degrade her. Crushing her face into the pillow, whispering curses, pounding into her and finally grunting his release, he rolled off her back and immediately fell asleep, oblivious to - or completely ignoring -

her humiliation and pain.

When she heard him snoring Catherine crept to the bathroom and ran the shower. She needed to forget, to get clean, to wash him off. Sitting on the tile bench under the warm spray she closed her eyes, let her mind drift. And couldn't remember a single instance, not a day or a night after the whirlwind months of their courtship, when she'd been truly happy with Frank. This was not a marriage; it was a life sentence - if she had any spine she'd take Alyson and leave, before something really bad happened. She stepped out of the shower, wrapped herself in the cozy warmth of a bath sheet. He had threatened to kill her, surely something said in anger.

In the steamed mirror her face, pale and ghostly in the soft glow of the nightlight, reminded Catherine of her mother. *You were right, Mother, he is a cruel and evil man.*

The very reason, Catherine Maude, that I made the Will I did.

Mother's Will. On her death nearly three years ago, the Will stipulated that the estate pass to Catherine and her sister Elaine, then to their children. At the reading Catherine hadn't been paying attention, other than to learn that the estate was tied up in land deeds and Trusts; she couldn't remember if the estate included their spouses. Catherine pressed the thick towel to her bruised and aching body. If excluded from sharing in or profiting from any part of the Barstowe estate, and if she continued on the road to divorce, Frank would be incredibly angry, but he wouldn't have a leg to stand on, and Alyson would be financially safe.

She slipped back into bed, curling up on her side as far

away from her snoring husband as possible. Back in August, after only a couple of nights in the guest room, he had returned to the 'marriage bed', carrying on about his 'rightful place' and "it looks bad to Alyson" and lots of other nonsense. Too bad they didn't have twin beds.

As she drifted off to sleep the name of the family solicitors crossed her mind. Burgess, Hawthorne… she'd call Thorny first thing in the morning.

Twenty

One frosty Friday morning Catherine fought the wind on State Street searching for a coffee shop. With all the construction in this part of town she had been forced to park in a garage near the Aquarium and walk to the lawyer's office; a pleasant trip in decent weather but nasty today, she couldn't remember a worse November.

Around Boston Harbor the howling wind stank of salt and fish, swirling up sand and bits of paper and cigarette butts into wild tornadoes that stung her face and whipped up her skirt. Chilled through, wishing for her old sheared beaver coat - this faux fur jacket was not doing the trick - she caught the heel of her boot in a crack in the broken sidewalk, still undone after the "Big Dig' construction. The project had cost the city countless millions more than estimated and had dragged on for years; damn all crooked politicians to hell! Fortunately, the boot was intact, but she had twisted her ankle. In pain, she looked around for a place to sit. Spotting the ubiquitous green sign above a doorway down the block she hobbled into Starbuck's, grateful for the warm coffee scented air that enveloped her as she pushed the door open. At midmorning the shop was nearly empty, and Catherine claimed the tiny bistro table for two in the bay window, sensing more than feeling the warmth of the weak winter sun filtering in.

Still in her coat and gloves, she gazed idly at the blur of pedestrian traffic rushing past in the narrow old lane. One couple, a man in a trench coat and an Asian woman, caught her attention. They stood quite still, holding hands and gazing at each other, an island of calm in the constantly swirling tide of people. She was tall, her slenderness enhanced by the long black cashmere coat she wore. Catherine's quick eye took in and admired the multi-colored Pashmina shawl wound around the woman's neck, then froze on the man who now held her in a close embrace. Could it be? Gary Kurtz, or someone who looked very much like Gary Kurtz, was kissing this woman in broad daylight on the sidewalk not twenty feet from Catherine's vantage point. She couldn't take her eyes off the pair. Determined to make sure it was Gary, she continued to stare at them from the safety of her perch.

Lovers? They looked comfortable together, their affection for each other obvious both in their eyes and the intimate way his hands rested on her shoulders.

Gary, if it was Gary, looked quite handsome with his thinning blond hair brushed back, emphasizing a high forehead and clear blue eyes. There was self-confidence in the squared shoulders, the coat hanging unbuttoned across the broad swell of his chest. This simply couldn't be the harried, absentminded man who was Catherine's neighbor. The Gary she knew *had* no chest.

As he hugged his— the woman, his eyes slid to the

137

windows, past Catherine, then swung back and locked on hers. He had recognized her. He waved, pointed one finger in a little gesture that said don't go away, I'll be right there. With another hug the woman turned away, and Gary came through the door and bent to kiss her cheek. Quite the Lothario, Catherine thought, smiling and nodding and completely tongue-tied.

"Here, let me help you with that."

Her coat was half off her shoulders. "Oh, um, thanks." She slipped her arms out of the sleeves and rested her elbows on the table. "Well, fancy meeting you here." Lame, but something.

"Not so odd, really, considering I work out around the corner."

"Oh, I didn't realize." She took a deep breath and plunged right in, she'd handle this meeting better if she got the burning question out of the way first. "And your friend?"

"Of course," he smiled, a wicked grin, "you saw me kissing Soon Li." He leaned back in the dainty ice cream parlor chair, crossed his legs and laughed out loud. "Maybe it's not the way it seems."

"And how is it?"

"Soon Li and I go back a long way." He shrugged out of his coat, folded it carefully over a chair at the next table. "Have you got a few minutes?"

"Well, I have an appointment on State Street in–" she checked her watch, "--in forty-five minutes."

"Then you have time for a cup of coffee."

"A latte for me, thanks." He went to the counter to place their order, and Catherine watched him flirt with the

138

multiple pierced young girl behind the counter. This Gary was definitely not the man she knew.

"So." He set the two cups and a few napkins on the table, topped the foam on his coffee with a flurry of chocolate flakes. "How are things with you?"

Catherine shook cinnamon into her cup. "Great."

"Frank?"

"Good." He picked up the cinnamon shaker, put it down, fiddled with a packet of sugar. "And Janice?"

"Fine, I think." She took a tentative sip of her latte. "Mmm, hot."

Gary blew on the steaming mug, fingers drumming a tattoo on the table. "Soon Li and I are old friends, grew up together in Revere." *Revee -ah.*

"Gary, it's really none of my business."

"She made me join a health club. Said I needed to improve my image."

Catherine glanced at his chest, the suggestion of strength in his shoulders. "I'd say it's paying off."

He grinned. "Thanks, I'm happy with my new buff look." But there was no smile in his blue eyes.

"She's lost some weight."

"Janice?"

"Weren't we talking about Janice?"

He studied her over the rim of his cup.

She nodded, ready to listen.

"Janice and I were married ten years last July. Second time for her." He swirled the coffee in his cup. "Well, not really; they never tied the knot."

Catherine gulped hot coffee, trying not to betray the

surprise she felt. "His name was Hank. He skipped town with his motorcycle and a backpack soon after the twins were born. Guess he couldn't face the responsibility of marriage, or kids." He gave an ironic little shrug of the shoulders. "I, on the other hand, represent the soul of responsibility." He tore open a sugar pack. "It's been a pretty good marriage, I guess. A lot like my folks'."

"I don't mean to pry, Gary, but, like your folks?"

"Well, that's the thing. My mother was a strong-willed woman, ruled the roost, much like my Janice." Gary's fingers toyed with another sugar packet. "My father was a very gentle man, never raised his voice, loved his gardens. Guess I take after him. Died at fifty-four, henpecked to death, I always thought."

Catherine watched him dump more sugar into his cup.

"One morning last August I looked in the mirror at the face I was shaving and saw my father looking back... same thinning hair, double chin, dark circles, faded blue eyes. It wasn't so much the physical resemblance that bothered me, can't do much about genetics, but my eyes frightened me. Blank and lifeless, like my old man's. I looked as if I'd been sentenced to a life term without parole. Scared the shit out of me."

He sipped his coffee, made a face. "I hate coffee with sugar." He pushed aside his cup. "Janice and I had already had a bit of go round that morning and, well..." He raised his eyes. "My wife, gets hold of an idea and won't let go."

"What did you argue about? If you don't mind telling--"

"I'm glad you're letting me talk." He waved her imagined rudeness away. "It was stupid. Janice suggested I try the stuff that stops you losing hair, said I was starting to look like an old man." His fingers started drumming again. "She was teasing, I know, but that morning I just couldn't take it."

He dropped his head. "I suddenly felt like I was marking time, waiting to die. I fly around the world for a living, but I don't even get to see the places I visit. And at home, caught up in the minutiae of life; mowing lawns, shoveling snow, barely enough time to spend with my wife and kids... like the old song, "Is that all there is?"

"Gary, you are not old enough to feel this way," she reached across the table, put her hand on his. "She loves you, you know."

"Yeah, I know that. I love her too, damn it. And I miss my kids like hell." He laughed, a snort of regret. "I really miss my family but I don't want to go back to the same old grind."

"But you'd go back?"

"In a heartbeat, if Jan can forgive me."

"She misses you very much."

"But how can I explain..." He shook his head slowly. "I'm not good with words. Not like Janice."

Catherine averted her eyes. "She does get her point across."

"You've gotta admire her for that. She's very outspoken but you always know where you are with Janice. Me, on the other hand, I've spent a lifetime afraid to speak my mind."

"Gary, if you expect things to change, you have to get your feelings out in the open. Talk to her, tell her what's bothering you. She loves you; she'll listen. You can't spend your life with your head stuck in the sand like an ostrich.

141

Heh." She touched the napkin to her lips. "Sorry, I didn.'t . He mean to lecture."

"You're not, Catherine, you're absolutely right. Communication makes a relationship strong. I guess that's what makes your marriage work so well."

Ye*ah, right.* "It's the creed we live by in my house, Gary."

"But how to start--?" He slumped, defeated.

...Thanksgiving dinner... Catherine heard Janice's wistful voice. "Thanksgiving is a couple of weeks away, Gary." She felt like a conspirator, but she knew Janice would be pleased. "Get yourself invited home for dinner." She shrugged into her coat. "Now I have business to attend to."

"Realty business?"

"Um no." She adjusted her scarf. "Family business."

Outside on the windy sidewalk Gary hugged her, kissed her, thanked her again for her help. "That ostrich image has me thinking, Catherine. I will try to let Janice know how I feel."

Walking to Thorny's office building, Catherine mulled over their conversation and realized that she gave a really good imitation of an ostrich herself.

Burgess, Hawthorne, Sedgewick & Greene, Solicitors, had been administrators of the Barstowe Family Trusts since the eighteen forties, originally in the person of Chief Trust Officer Lawrence Q. Hawthorne, and since nineteen sixty by Lawrence IV, one-time fiancé and lifelong friend of Catherine's mother Maude Halliday. Catherine often wondered why their relationship ended, how Maude and Arthur

Barstowe came together, but her mother never shared that information. Perhaps an arranged marriage; these old Boston families were so intertwined.

This session proceeded precisely like every other one Catherine could remember. 'Thorny' spent two minutes fussily removing her coat and settling her in a straight-backed chair at one end of a mahogany table more suitable for forty. He seated himself beside her and summoned his secretary, one of a long succession of attractive and nubile young women, to bring on the tea and Pepperidge Farm biscuits. Then he reminisced for six minutes, no more, no less, about the golden days.

"And how is your little one, my dear?" Dabbing at miniscule crumbs in his dainty white goatee with the damask napkin.

"Alyson is twelve now, Lawrence." Catherine couldn't bring herself to call him by his nickname in person. "Not so little anymore."

"A young woman." He chuckled into his hand. "How well I recall my Laureen at that age." He sighed, and Catherine remembered that he and his wife 'Muffy' had also had a son, Lawrence V, who died of a brain aneurism at the age of fourteen.

"And your husband, my dear?"

"Fine." She remembered to smile. "Perfect."

"And now, to business, Cat?"

All her mother's friends called her Cat. Catherine hated it, but it beat Thorny. Or Muffy.

She had told his secretary that she wished to discuss the Barstowe Estate. Now, the old lawyer opened a folder, and in a murmur as soft as the droning of a bee, he began to recite the same information she'd heard for years. Catherine gazed out the window at the town of Hull glistening in the cold sunlight across the harbor and forgot to listen.

"Catherine?" His whispery voice brought her back to the business at hand. "I think you were, ah, thirty-eight last birthday?"

He knew perfectly well how old she was.

"Your grandfather's trust provided first for your mother, then passed to you on the date of your thirty-fifth birthday, I believe." He scanned the last few pages of the document, as if he weren't absolutely certain of every word printed there. "Yes, I am correct. The conditions of the Barstowe trust stipulate that... blah, blah--"

She nodded, impatient. "Yes, yes, Lawrence, but *Mother's* Will? How was it drawn up?"

"Maude's will? Why, I don't recall. Not as sharp as I once was, you know." Again he buzzed the blonde, and while Catherine assured him he was still sharp as a tack the young woman returned with the Last Will and Testament of Maude (Halliday) Barstowe. "Now what was it you wished to know, Cat dear?"

"Who inherits." She might have to explain eventually but for now—

"Give me a moment, my dear." He flipped slowly through a few pages. "Ah, here it is..." As I believe you know, Maude left her entire estate, barring a few charitable gifts, to be divided equally between you and your sister Elaine. Your issue, if any--"

"--Yes, yes, our issue." She took a deep breath.

"Spouses?"

He pursed his lips. "If I may--?"

She felt herself blush. "Of course."

"The codicil, dated shortly before Maude's death, specifically excludes one Frances Xavier Moore." He glanced up over the rims of his glasses. "Your spouse, I believe."

She nodded. "Lawrence, I –"

He raised one hand in the air. "No need to explain, my dear." The slightest flicker of an eyebrow, as befitted a Trust Officer as discreet as Lawrence Quincy Hawthorne, Esq., said he understood all.

And yet, she needed to clarify. "I want to protect Alyson from my- financially, I mean." She rushed on. "If one were to sue for divorce" - she could hardly get the word out -

"My dear, be calm." He rested a veined old hand on her thigh. "Being excluded from gain from the Barstowe Estate, your, ah, your spouse would have no legal recourse to contest the Will."

"Hypothetically."

"Of course, dear Cat. Enough said."

And apparently it was.

She nodded, mute. His wise old eyes understood, and she wondered how often he had encountered a situation like this over the years. His sympathy was conveyed in the slight pressure of his hand on her shoulder as he helped her into her coat. "I'll have a draft of divorce drawn up whenever you say the word."

Catherine drove out of Boston mulling over a decision seemingly made on impulse but really years in the making. She realized that taking the leap had nothing, and yet everything, to do with Tony. Falling in love with him had opened her mind to freedom from the trap of her marriage. Was she in love with him? No matter, with or without him, she was going to move on to the next step. Which would take time, and far more courage than Catherine thought she had.

But she had the ball rolling, at last, and that in itself empowered her. She flicked on the radio. With the Eagles singing 'Take It To The Limit' she sped up the ramp to the Mass. Pike. Maybe she wasn't such an ostrich after all.

Twenty-one

She flicked on the overhead light, the glare blinding him as he entered the bedroom. "Where the hell have you been?"

"Did I wake you up?" It was past one; most nights by this time Laura would have drunk herself into a sleep so deep that a tank roaring around in the next room wouldn't have disturbed her. Truth be known, Tony preferred getting home after Laura had fallen asleep. Five minutes late and she'd be on his back, an hour late and he'd have a fight on his hands. Most nights he'd pull up on the driveway and glance at their bedroom window, hoping for darkness, dreading the arguments and ridiculous accusations Laura would throw at him.

Accusations that, sad to say, were no longer ridiculous. Tonight, although she didn't know it, Laura had good reason to be angry. Tony had left the station early, pleading a cold and ignoring the raised eyebrows that accompanied him to the door, and had spent the evening with Catherine. While Laura recited her dreary litany of complaints, Tony's mind revisited the dark, run-down bar in Auburn, one of the few places where both he and Catherine could pretend their real lives didn't exist. And where, though Tony knew very well that what they were doing was wrong, he didn't feel like the shit his loving wife believed him to be. Amazing how the right woman could make you feel so good about yourself.

"I want to know where you've been!"

"Work, honey," he whispered. "I had--"

"Don't give me the bullshit, Tony." Laura's voice rose. "I called the station hours ago. Don hasn't seen you since six o'clock!"

"Geez, Laura, the kids. Keep it down." Trying to buy some time, Tony shut the door softly behind him.

"Don asked if your cold was worse." She folded her arms across her bony little chest. "Cold, my ass. Tell me what you're up to, Tony. I have a right to know!"

Then at least one of us would know, he thought. He dropped his clothes on the floor, shoved the whole bundle into the hamper in the corner. He wondered if he should have a shower, but that would not be his normal routine, he always showered in the daytime before work. Unless he and Laura intended to have sex. He'd love to put on a pair of pajamas or boxers, but that would give Laura more to gripe about, since he never wore anything to bed.

Ah Tony, you've become a schemer, a liar. He sat on the bed, careful to stay on the very edge. "What's got into you, Laura?" The bedroom was cold, but he was clammy with sweat. "I'm here now. Go to sleep."

"You think I can sleep with you gallivanting around all night? Talk to me, you son of a bitch!"

She'd been drinking, that was obvious. "Laura, for chrissake, keep it down!" Searching his mind for something

148

to explain the missing hours.

"I really wasn't feeling well. I'm sure I'm working on a cold." To lend credence to the claim, he gave a little cough. "But I saw some of the guys at Butchie's, you know, the bar on Main, where all the cops hang out." Not a lie; he'd seen them there as he drove by. "We got to kibbitzing... you know how it is." He dimmed the light almost to nothing, much easier to tell lies in the dark. Shivering, he slid under the covers. "Damned cold in here."

She turned the light back up to bright. "You couldn't call?"

He looked away. It was impossible to lie straight to her worried little face. Scrunched his pillow, made a great show of getting comfortable, tugged at his bare chin. "Um, my phone... dead." He faked a yawn, turned his back to her. "Now lay off, Laura. Maybe *you* can stay up all night, but I need some sleep."

Her punch caught him squarely between the shoulder blades. "And which one of the *'guys'* wears Obsession, you lying bastard!"

So it was called Obsession, the perfume Catherine wore. She didn't like driving half an hour out of town for a drink, she said it made her feel sneaky. But the dim lights at Moroni's, the high-backed booths, the fact that it was off the beaten path provided privacy for people like him and Catherine, two highly recognizable stars in their own galaxy. Tony remembered her breast rising and falling, the little mole just visible in the vee of her blue crocheted sweater, the links of gold chain around her neck gleaming in the candlelight. Her shy smile. And her scent. Obsession.

Next time he'd be smarter, make a plan. Because there definitely would be a next time. Ever since Halloween night at Tyler Lake he'd seen it coming, been drawn in deeper and deeper against his will, even though he knew that getting involved with Catherine was begging for trouble.

Laura snapped on the bedside lamp. "You're going to tell me who you were with if it takes all night."

Tony rolled over slowly, squinting his eyes in the bright light. Next to him Laura sat hunched up against the headboard, hugging her knees, wrinkled cotton nightgown rucked up around thin sticks of legs and arms. She was no bigger than a child, but dark rings circled tired eyes, and her thin lined face was creased and blurry from crying. She looked old.

"I'm waiting, Tony."

'Tell one lie, Tonio,' his mother used to say, 'you have to hide it with ten more.'

He dredged up a story he'd heard a week ago. "There was this hooker, honey, in the bar, coming on to me, hangin' all over me, bet I'm covered in the stuff." Laura was hardly breathing. "You don't know how those gals are. See a coupla guys, a chance to pick up a few quick bucks." He couldn't meet her eyes, but Tony saw tears slipping down Laura's hollow cheeks. He threw off the blankets. "I'll go jump in the shower."

She grabbed his arm. "You wouldn't... you know, do anything..."

"Nah, the woman's a pross." And then, driving it home, "Laura, you know I'd never sleep with a hooker." But he'd give his right arm to sleep with Catherine, to make love with her. He wanted that so much it hurt.

Laura wriggled down beside him, her head close to his, her mouth on his ear. "You're not lying?"

Tony sighed, turned away from the stale smell of alcohol on her breath. "No, Laura, I'm not lying."

"I love you so much, Tony. I couldn't live without you."

Now he should put his arms around her, tell her how much he loved her, he knew she needed to hear that, but the words stuck in his mind. Tony couldn't say what he didn't mean, and he had finally realized that he didn't love Laura anymore. Overnight, it seemed, his side of their marriage had degenerated to nothing more than responsibility, duty, and now, lies and evasions.

Laura nestled close, after all these years fitting snug into the familiar hollows of his body. Her fingers played in the thick hair on his chest, brushed his nipples.

Tony was shocked to feel himself respond. He lay still and hoped she wouldn't notice. He *couldn't* make love to her, couldn't be that dishonest.

"Promise you'll never leave me, Tony." Laura's lips closed around the nipple she had been fingering, and he felt heat spread through his groin. Her hand moved slowly down to his erection. She laughed, a lusty chuckle.

"The ideas you get, Laura." He gave the top of her head a dismissive peck and turned over. "Now let's get some sleep here."

Laura turned off the lamp and rolled up against his back. "Oh, I don't think you're ready for sleep just yet, big man." She giggled, licked his ear. "I'll be your hooker, honey." With darting tongue, nipping teeth and teasing, toying hands she brought him quickly past all thought, his traitorous body ready and oh so willing, his mind in turmoil.

Laura settled herself on top, riding him slowly, trailing her tiny breasts back and forth across his lips. Tony sucked hungrily, desperately, making moaning sounds through teeth clamped shut, afraid to call out the name blazing in his mind, his imagination. Catherine, with the long lithe body, the generous curves and full womanly breasts... he flipped over, and with Laura beneath and himself on top in the dominator's role, thrusting like a bucking, mindless horse, he went over the edge into oblivion.

Laura gave a triumphant, knowing laugh. "A hooker couldn't make you feel this way, could she, Tony?"

With a grunt, Tony rolled away to his side of the bed, embarrassed and suffused with guilt. Laura fit herself in behind him, spoon fashion, her bent knees tucked in behind his, thin arm clutched tight around his ribs. Long after he thought she'd fallen asleep, Laura spoke. "If you ever leave me, Tony, I'll kill myself. I swear it."

He had nothing to say to that, and Tony waited, not moving a muscle, until Laura's even breathing told him she had finally gone to sleep. He eased out of her grip, wiped his sweaty face with the edge of the sheet and padded to the kitchen, wishing he knew where Laura kept her stash.

He turned on the tap, mind swirling like the water filling the glass. He'd always considered himself an upright, honest man, a man with a great respect for truth and justice. A cop, for crissake. Could such a man also be a liar and a cheat? The kind of man who made passionate love to his wife minutes after kissing another woman good night? It was obvious he had the soul of an adulterer, no matter that he had not yet committed the sin, that was just a matter of time and the right woman. But how could Catherine be the right woman when she was someone else's wife! And Catherine, so trusting, so pure, he'd be dragging her down that road with him. Ah, what a mess.

Tony backed into a chair, sick with shame, with remorse. And worse yet, confusion. Okay, he had to admit that he was a liar, and a cheat. But which woman was he deceiving?

Twenty-two

Catherine had taken a shower, dressed, packed a lunch for Alyson and sent her off to school with a hug.   Normal. Finished the last of her coffee, put the mug into the dishwasher, turned off the overhead kitchen light, went into the garage to the car... still normal.

She had an appointment.   Had to get going.   Yet Catherine sat unmoving in the car, waiting for - what? Inspiration?   The Word of God?   A solution; a plan.

She pressed the remote and the heavy double garage door lumbered open.   Backed the big car down the drive. Drove down the hill and into town - was almost at the office when she remembered she was to meet the folks up in Hillcrest at the Wetherbee house in... twelve minutes.

An illegal u-turn, ignoring the horns and raised middle fingers of disgruntled commuters, her mind a maelstrom of disjointed thoughts.   More horns.   She was doing 45 in a 35mph zone; had to get her mind focused on driving. But how?   Her world was in complete chaos after— another horn blared and she pulled into the Walmart parking lot to think without distraction.

Since Halloween, and that incredible night at the lake,

she and Tony had met a few times. In public, except for once or twice in the back seat of her car, when they'd behaved like teenagers. But, openly, for the most part. The Chinese place after work, lunch or a sandwich in the privacy of her office, the dimly-lit bar in Auburn for a drink, hardly what one might call an affair - oh, be honest, Catherine - an affair. But the... the tryst in Boston last week was a whole other kettle of fish.

The fourteenth of November had started out on a high note. She and Tony had a date, shrouded in secrecy and lies, but admittedly, thrilling. Frank thought she was attending a Real Estate Award evening - sorry, no spouses - as if he had the slightest interest in her business, but at her suggestion he agreed that she'd be better off staying in town instead of driving back to Gilford on a cold wintry night after a few drinks.

Kevin thought she was in Albany helping her sister Elaine after an emergency appendectomy - thank technology for cell phones, you could be anywhere in the world and no one would be any the wiser. Catherine had no idea what Tony had told his wife or his precinct, but she didn't want to know; it would have been lies.

The weather was decent. Massachusetts was enjoying a break in the steady cold drizzle that had been around for days.

They drove into Boston in Tony's Explorer - not the Lincoln, that would have been too obvious, as if olive green SUVs were thick on the ground in the city. She would have preferred his other car, the nondescript dark blue Toyota, but apparently it was in for service.

Tony drove too fast; it made her uncomfortable.

"This is the Mass Pike, Cath, what the f–"   Edgy, stressed. But he slowed down.

The rest of the drive was tense, but she thought they were over it when they parked at the hotel in Cambridge– now, less than a week later, she couldn't remember which one.   They checked into their room - actually, Tony checked in; she followed him up a few minutes later with the creepy feeling that all eyes were on her as she crossed the lobby to the elevators.

She remembers dropping her bag just inside the door and staring at the enormous King-size bed, backing away from it.   "Tony, I–"

"Let's go for a walk."   He takes her hand to dodge the traffic on Memorial Drive, drops it as soon as they reach the path along the Charles.   Dry leaves scuttle in the brisk wind and the river is choppy and black.   Three in the afternoon and the sky is dark with the heavy gray overcast of November, skies that will look like this until March. Sometimes she hates the weather in New England.

Tony zips up his jacket.   "No rowers today."

"Umhmm."   No small talk either.

They find a bench and sit for an hour, huddled in cocoons of fleece, side by side but not together, each lost in silent, brooding thought.   This would be a big step, far more serious than necking and stroking in the back seat of one of their cars, or a quick stolen embrace in the dark of her office.

Not an auspicious beginning, but back at the hotel, they try to move on.   A quick change of clothes, a bottle of red over a candlelit dinner in the hotel restaurant - she can't recall what she ordered for dinner but remembers leaving most of it.   No conversation.   She throws furtive glances at every person walking through the door.

Eventually, "see you upstairs," he whispers, pushing his chair back from the table. She nods, stops at the bar.   After a shot - two - she feels relaxed enough to stroll across the lobby to the elevator, hating the way her heels tap on the marble, advertising her presence to the room.

Should they turn on the TV?   Hotel porn? he grins.

Not funny, she snaps, turning to the bathroom.

Avoiding the mirrors, standing under shower water hotter than hell, her mind shouts run!   Wrapped in a huge towel, perched on the edge of the wing chair, waiting for him to get done in the bathroom, her mind shouts run!   Some sports thing is on mute - soccer, she thinks, or rugby.   When she can't hear the shower anymore, she drops the towel on the floor and slips into the bed.   He leaves the bathroom, snaps off the TV and gets into bed.

Where they lie, uncomfortable and totally un-aroused. Ah, she thinks, this is not going well.   Covers pulled up, lights out, waiting... his hand brushes her breast and she turns, mentally wanting to melt into him but physically cold and stiff.   With embarrassed giggles and grins, they turn from each other, hinting at a better time later.   Tony dozes, and Catherine goes to the window and pulls the drape aside, gazing out at the river, the brilliant glow of Boston by night. Is she in love with him?   Are they meant for each other?   Is this something special or just a new experience at a time when she desperately needs one. All the while feeling cheap and tawdry; she knows this behavior is not for her.

She slips back into bed and settles in among the pillows, trying to relax, chuckling when she notices that the ceiling is embedded with shiny specks that sparkle in the soft light leaking through the partly opened drapes. At least it's not a mirror! Her giggles shake the bed and waken Tony. They laugh and turn to each other and at last they make love; sweet, slow, tender, wonderful.

As if they don't have a care in the world.

As if they have the rest of their lives together.

As if they know that this is the end.

They spent the rest of the night talking about the future, their families, the D-word, was this really love or merely a titillating break in marriages gone sour.

As morning dawned, after hours of negotiation, decisions were made. Sneaking around did not sit well with either of them. There could be no future together unless they both initiated major changes in their lives, steps they tearfully agreed neither one was quite ready to take. But until they were ready to take those steps, they would stop seeing each other.

The drive back to Gilford was quiet, each wrapped in silence. This time Catherine was grateful for the speed.

Twenty-three

"Mom, you won't believe what happened at rehearsal today." Alyson's beautiful deep blue eyes gleamed through a curtain of thick, wavy red hair, the elastic 'Scrunchie' meant to hold it back twisted around her wrist like a bracelet.

Smiling, Catherine put her fork down. "Please don't talk until you've swallowed your food, sweetie."

"But Mo-om!"

Every day she heard fascinating new details about a young man, a bronze god, apparently, named Daniel Garcia, the reason Alyson had joined the stage crew. "I'm all ears, Aly."

"Remember I told you Mrs. Kurtz took over as stage director when Ms. Lopez left?"

"Janice Kurtz?" Not the boy.

"Mom, I told you but you never listen–"

"Yes. Yes I do, Al, I remember now." But she didn't, hadn't even been aware that Ms. Lopez had gone. Where had her mind been lately?

Alyson shoved her hair back with both hands, "she is *so* bad, Mom, even *you* could do better!"

"Thanks so much, Aly."

"Oh, you know what I mean. I like Bonnie's mom, but she just doesn't have a clue. She clomps around the stage in long skirts and high heels."

Catherine sighed. "And what's wrong with that?"

"Daniel says" - Catherine noticed Alyson's voice soften - "Dan says Mrs. Kurtz doesn't even know what a scrim is and she's the stage director! All the kids make fun of her!"

"I don't think--"

"But here's the thing, Mom. Mrs. Kurtz backed into a set of risers, flipped over and fell right on her butt! Big flowery skirt all the way up to there, those spiky shoes waving in the air. It was hyster--"

"My God! When did this happen?"

"Today."

"Was she hurt?"

"Maybe." Alyson's smile wavered. "Mr. Stewart drove her to the hospital."

"Good heavens!" Catherine pushed her plate away and went to the phone. Bonnie said her mother was home, in bed, the doctor said she had dislocated something. Maybe. Her hip, or her shoulder.

"Can't you be a little more specific, Bonnie?"

"Well, they gave her stuff to make her sleep, but my--"

"Is there anything I can do for you, Bonnie? I have to go out to meet a client now, but I can swing by Stop & Shop on the way back."

"Oh, you don't have to worry about us, Mrs. Moore. I called my Dad." Pleased, as if she had masterminded the whole accident.   "He'll be home real soon." Catherine imagined Gary swooping in like Sir Galahad. She hoped

Janice wasn't badly hurt, but with her laid up in bed they would have the opportunity to talk things over. Sometimes things turned out for the best.

Catherine's new clients, Minnie and Walter Brown, turned out to be a twig of a woman with a horrible smoker's cough and a rotund little husband. Walt said they needed something in a ranch because 'Min' couldn't take the stairs no more. Minnie, seemingly disinterested, sat with an unlit vape clutched in her hand and sucked in long rattling breaths that reminded Catherine of Darth Vader. In under half an hour they found three houses to visit in the morning, and Catherine saw them out, hoping the woman would make it through the night.

She should have gone home, there was nothing else to do this evening, but she stayed on, as she had for the past week. To catch up on paperwork. To wash out the sparkling clean coffee pot. To stare through the wall of windows facing the dismal town common. Monday was normally a quiet night in this part of Gilford, but Tony had been known to drive by.

At seven-ten she pulled on her raincoat, turned off the lights, and watched a dark SUV roll to a stop outside the rain-spattered windows. Catherine's heart started beating double time. Tony got out but stood by his truck, shoulders hunched, hands shoved deep in the pockets of his leather bomber jacket. When he moved it was sudden, jerky, as if he'd been pushed from behind. He stopped in the reception area, looking through her office door with a strange, lopsided smile. Catherine felt her stomach knot.

"Hi." He strode into her office, a man on a mission, dropping into one of the client chairs that faced her desk. Catherine's hands turned to ice. She searched Tony's face for a clue, but he avoided her eyes, stared at the carpet, hands locked together, white-knuckled.

"Guess I'll just jump right on in. We--I... I can't go on like this, Catherine." He raised his big, dark eyes, soft with hurt. "I know we agreed to stop seeing each other until we figured our way out of this." He hung his head. "I said what I knew you wanted to hear, but this uncertainty is killing me." His eyes closed. "I love you."

Waiting for the 'but' that had to be coming, Catherine moved slowly around her desk, perched on the edge of the other client chair. She wanted to touch him, but she kept her hands tucked in her lap. Silence beat like a pulse in her ears.

He smoothed his bare chin with strong stubby fingers, over and over, in that nervous way he had. "Yesterday I was all set to talk to Laura about a divorce."

A big, hollow space inside Catherine was filling up with lead. Please stop, she begged silently, don't say another word.

"Laura needs–" Now he looked at her. "The other night, she threatened to..." His eyes hardened. "Ah, what's the use, I'm not going to use her as an excuse. We're both married, Catherine. To the wrong people, as it turns out, but fooling around won't fix things. I can't leave Laura, certainly not now, and you're not the kind of woman to… to have an affair."

With her eyelids clenched tight, Catherine felt him stand

up beside her, his warm palm rest lightly on her head. *How do you know what kind of woman I am, Tony?* She'd do anything to keep him, she'd have an affair in a heartbeat if that was the only way to have him. She dug sharp nails into her palms and kept her eyes closed, fighting the urge to wrap her arms around his legs, to beg him not to leave.

"Well, I've done what I came to do." His voice was hushed, tired. "I'll get out of your life now."

Catherine waited for him to take her in his arms, to kiss her, flash his sexy smile. But no. He was backing away.

At the door he stopped. "I'm so sorry, Cath..."

She heard him cross the tile reception area, heard the outside door close. The roar of his engine filled her with rage. It was all over, this love affair, before it had really begun. Catherine jumped out of her chair, kicked the office door shut, pounded the wall with balled fists until they hurt, dropped into the chair still warm from Tony's body, rocked back and forth and let the tears flow.

Why couldn't they go on like this? How could Tony decide what was fair to her? She was just learning the lightheaded joy of seeing his face, feeling the rush of heat deep inside from his touch. For so many years she had not felt much of anything. She had been playing a role. In a few short months Tony had broken through the pretense, shattered the glass cocoon she'd hidden in, taught her to feel. Without him she had to face the stark reality of her empty life, made hopeless with his leaving. Oh no, Tony, you're dead wrong about me. This would have been enough.

Grateful for routine, for day following familiar day, for the welcome intrusion that was Alyson, for a part to play. Catherine felt as though she was living behind a curtain, her heart heavy, the world a uniform gray. How melodramatic, she would have said once.

She visited with Janice, a hobbling walrus on crutches making the most of her poor wrenched back while chubby fingers sorted through a box of candy for her favorite soft center, an indulgence during convalescence, she said, smiling, a gift from Gary. So wonderful to have Gary back home, they were a family again. After commenting that Janice seemed to be shedding pounds, Catherine let the details of Janice's convalescence wash over deaf ears while her mind drifted to Tony.

Work was a blessing. November was always a quiet month, but she kept herself occupied with closings, helping families like the Browns settle into their new homes before the holidays. Every time the phone rang Catherine held her breath, said an unconscious prayer, fearful and anxious and pathetically hopeful that she might hear "Hi there... it's me," in his gruff, tender voice. But he didn't call.

Each time the office door opened her heart leaped with hope, imagining that she'd look up from her desk and see him slouched against the wall, dark eyes sparkling with mischief, that lazy, sexy smile spreading slowly across his face. And he didn't come.

She felt hollow. Leaden. Maybe she *was* getting sick. Barely able to eat, lying awake at night, living out every sad or trashy romance novel ever written. But now she understood the plot.

She saw Alyson's concern, her pinched little face, fended off her anxious questions. It's probably the flu, love. Don't worry. I'll be better soon.

And Frank? He lived in the same house, slept in the same bed, came and went as usual, but his nasty remarks, his bitterness and anger didn't penetrate. He was coming home later. Traffic, he said, icy roads; they rarely ate dinner together anymore. Wouldn't it be ironic, she thought, if he was fooling around. She let him use her body, mind and thoughts far away, but for the most part he left her alone, as if he sensed her distance.

She stayed late at the office, there was always something to do; calls to make, figures to check, files to straighten, ensuring the stapler and tape dispenser lined up perfectly with her laptop and the phone, shapes to doodle on a pad. But night followed day followed lonely night with no visit, no phone call, only once a hang-up, and another heart stopping moment of pregnant silence before the caller cradled the receiver with a whispered "Sorry, wrong number." She pretended it was Tony.

He'd said he loved her. How could he stay away?

Twenty-four

"Alyson!"

"Yeah, Mom?"

"Come down here and help me with the groceries!"

Barefoot, Alyson thumped down the stairs, took two loaded bags from Catherine's overburdened arms, and led the way to the kitchen.

"Wow, that turkey is huge, Mom!   Are we having company for Thanksgiving?"

Catherine dumped three heavy bags on the kitchen table. "Dad home?"

Alyson mooched through the bags, making a mess. "Not yet."

Of course he wasn't here, the house was too quiet. Somehow Frank's mere physical presence filled a room. "Al, please, help me put the food away--"

"Gawd, Mom, Brussels sprouts!"

"I got broccoli for you."

"You got tons of vegetables," Alyson screwed up her face, "Who's coming?"

Tons of vegetables.   Out of the blue Catherine remembered the dining room of her grandparents' massive Victorian home in Lincoln, the long mahogany table, the lace cloth, the silver and crystal gleaming in the candlelight, the air redolent of roast turkey, pumpkin pie, Butcher's wax on the glossy hardwood floors. And tons of vegetables. The Barstowes were not a boisterous family but she remembered the cozy warmth of blazing fires, the refined laughter of aunts and uncles, the giggling and good-natured teasing among the cousins.

Alyson barely knew the relatives on her mother's side.

Frank liked to say that he preferred the peace of his own home for the holidays, but Catherine knew the real reasons. Her wealthy family intimidated him, made him feel dirty, and Mother had made no secret of her dislike of Frank.

And Frank's side? Only Ben, half-brother, from his mother's 'other' life. Catherine knew that in Frank's mind her second marriage repudiated his father, and his childhood, bad as it had been. Until her death, he considered his mother a widow. Catherine met Ben, a bachelor, once, years ago, at her mother-in-law's funeral, where she'd gone without Frank, over his furious objections--

"Mo-omm..."

"Sorry hon."

"Is Aunt Elaine coming?"

I wish. "Not this year, sweetie, maybe--"

"But you've gone and bought enough damn food to feed ten starving people!"

Catherine swiveled to the doorway, where Frank, handsome and remote in tweed coat and cold blue eyes, scowled. Suddenly it seemed gloomy in the kitchen. He could do that - simply walk into a room and change the atmosphere.

"The stores will be closed, Frank, and I always shop for the week."

"Long as you're not wasting my hard-earned money."

Catherine's jaw dropped. He said the dumbest things. Livid, she stashed the 'tons of veggies' in the fridge. *His* money! *His* house! But always *her* fault.

"Can't you at least be civil?"

"Not when I'm tired and hungry." He held out his coat to Alyson.

Aly's face was a stubborn mask. "I'm not your maid, Dad."

"Don't get smart with me, Missy. Hang this up before I tan your little butt."

Alyson stomped down the hall.

"She used to be a good kid."

"She's a teenager."

"Not yet she's not!" He turned to leave the room.

"Frank? Have you noticed that we don't talk to each other anymore?" She rested her hip against the counter. "I can deal with it, but God only knows when you last had a nice word to say to Alyson."

"Yeah, whatever." He pulled out a kitchen chair. "Where's dinner?"

"In the oven, keeping warm." There would be no heart to heart tonight. "Aly and I have already eaten."

The front door slammed. "Where's she going?"

"To Bonnie's - they have a project." She grabbed her music bag. "And I've got rehearsal."

"But—"

"Sorry, I'm running late." Wow, both of his women

getting lippy - what was the world coming to!

In the garage, Catherine hit the remote to raise the garage door. She settled into the Lincoln and tapped the starter, amazed as always as the engine roared to life. But backing down the drive her thoughts turned to her husband and the widening gap between Frank and his daughter.

Frank left his dirty plate in the sink. In the den he picked up the remote, but it was past seven. He'd missed the news, and there was nothing to watch on a Tuesday night. He flicked the switch that started the fire and collapsed on the leather couch. Cozy, he thought. Quiet, with Catherine and Aly out of the house. Nice and–no, Frank, be honest, lonely.

When had he and Catherine started down this road of evasion and stony silence? He couldn't recall the last time they'd enjoyed a good laugh. And Alyson, the sassy little imp - his darling girl! - went out of her way to stay out of his way.

Is this the life you wanted, Frank? Ah, sure, he'd seen the Barstowe wealth and decided to hitch a ride, but he loved Catherine, and she-- a smile tugged at his lips when he remembered the light in her beautiful eyes when she looked at him in that shy way she used to have. Gone, and you have no one to blame but yourself, you miserable son of a bitch.

Was it stress, the job? Nah, he'd resigned himself to just putting in the hours until retirement, turned out he wasn't the brilliant executive he'd dreamed himself to be; he was a loser like his father, and like his father he blamed everyone

it better. Maybe
there was something left of this marriage to salvage.

170

Twenty-five

But as she drove down into town, Catherine chose not to go to the church. With Janice laid up, she had declined Laura's offer to drive all the way up to the Ridge to pick her up. But in truth, she couldn't bear facing Laura alone, with her endless complaining and whining about Tony. And she didn't feel like singing; she felt depressed. She turned the other way on Main and drove to her office.

It took great concentration to keep her mind off Tony, to resist glancing at the doorway where he wasn't, but it would have taken a far more heroic effort to simply shut her office door. A distracting wind came up, tossing sand and dry leaves up and down the street, scraping against the plate glass window, making her look up frequently, but she finally became engrossed in the work on her laptop. After an hour or so, hearing an insistent tapping at the window, she looked up from the rows of figures, removed her reading glasses to rub her tired eyes, then rubbed them again.

Tony, slouched against the window, waiting to be noticed. Catherine floated across the dim reception area, unlocked the door. "How long have you been standing out here in the cold?" Without the overhead lights on it was too dark to see him, to take in every detail of his face, his brown eyes, the thick black lashes. Clutching his arm as if he might disappear, she pulled him into the bright warmth of her private office.

"Not too long... I was in the neighborhood."

She smiled. "You're a terrible liar."

"I love watching you work, these sexy granny glasses..." His eyes glowed, his hands touched her face, her hair, as if making sure she was real. "I couldn't help myself. All hours of every day and night you've been on my mind. I ... God help me, Catherine, I can't stay away from you."

Happiness flooded the empty cavern inside, dissolved the leaden weight she'd been carrying for days.

His hands cupped her face, he looked into her eyes for an eternity until, at last, his mouth found hers; his kiss a soft, sweet pressure, a drifting feather, a glowing flame. A promise.

When he slipped his hands up inside her sweater Catherine caught her breath; she'd been aching for his touch. He crushed her to his chest and she melted into his arms. Just before she gave in to the sensations engulfing her Catherine kicked the office door shut with her foot.

"And His name shall be call-ed WON-derful..." Laura's voice resounding in the car made her blood race. *Madonn',* she loved to sing, and the Messiah had such terrific soprano parts. Rehearsal had gone well tonight, thank God, with just about three weeks until the first performance. The tenor section could use some help from a Pavarotti or two but in a backwater like this, unlike the North End, men who liked to

sing or sang well were in short supply and you took what you got.

She drove home along Main Street, wondering if the town had yet lit the decorations around the gazebo on the Common, but it was in darkness. Unlike the Mall, which had been decorated for Christmas since Labor Day! They had already extended shopping hours in anticipation of post-Thanksgiving Black Friday sales and the Christmas rush, but the little independent shops in the town center were closed - no surprise in Laura's mind that business had gone elsewhere. In the middle of a dark block, Casey & Moore's lit windows shone out in the night like a beacon. Laura slowed down and peeked in, saw Catherine standing by her desk and realized that the poor woman had missed rehearsal to work tonight. Laura chuckled; the job hadn't yet been invented that would keep her from singing.

Figuring her friend might welcome a break, Laura whipped into the driveway at the coffee shop on the Common seconds before nine, chirping brightly to the sullen, pimpled teen who slammed the drive-thru window open. If Catherine was too busy to chat she'd just say hi and leave the coffee. She seemed nice, this Catherine Moore, quiet, polite, a bit higher up the food chain but not snotty about it. Old Boston money, you could tell. She'd never met the husband, Janice didn't like him, but Laura had grown fond of Catherine's daughter; Alyson was a good influence on Gina.

Leaving the car parked at Common Grounds - stupid name - Laura crossed the street balancing two burning hot paper cups of coffee while the biting cold wind whistled up under her too-thin quilted jacket. Winter was definitely here, and Laura resolved to ask Santa for a full-length, down-filled coat, like the one she'd seen on sale at Macy's. As she raised her hand to rap on the plate glass window of Casey & Moore she saw movement in Catherine's office.

Damn. Looked like she had a client, a man, in a black leather jacket just like... Laura felt the air leave her lungs. Like Tony's. He had his back to the door but it clearly *was* Tony; Laura certainly knew the shape of her own husband's body, his dark curly hair, the red and blue Gilford Police crest on the shoulder. She watched him move toward Catherine, put his arms around her, saw her tuck her red head on his shoulder, like she was crying. Something bad must have happened to Alyson, maybe, or Catherine's husband.

But wait! There was something wrong with this picture - Catherine's arm was around Tony's neck, the beautifully manicured fingers playing with the dark curls that hung down to his collar. Spellbound, Laura watched Tony touch Catherine's face, she could feel the tenderness in his fingers all the way out here, right down to the pit of her stomach. Now he pulled her close, crushing her in his arms and oh my God now they were kissing... like, like lovers. It was like watching a movie. Only it wasn't. Oh God, no. This was real.

Catherine's office door slowly swung shut and Laura sagged against the wall, sweating. Maybe she'd had some kind of hallucination, maybe it never happened, but no, the sick feeling in her stomach was proof enough. She stood for an eternity with her face pressed against the cold glass, wanting to run, to get far away from here, but her legs were limp like boiled spaghetti, they refused to move.

Hot coffee streaming over her hands jerked her back to reality. Laura let the cups fall, watched the coffee splatter her jeans in slow motion and collect in a puddle on the sidewalk. Finally, she tore herself away and climbed into Tony's SUV parked behind her. She had reversed into the street when she remembered that she hadn't driven the damned thing here, her Toyota was parked across the road. Well fuck him, let the cheating son of a bitch work it out for himself.

Laura peeled off down the empty street in a screech of grit   and   rubber.

Twenty-six

Scotch exploded down her throat, spreading warmth and relief to rigid muscles, relieving the queasiness in her stomach. She knew it wasn't the smartest thing to be drinking tonight, she needed to be sharp when Tony got home, but ice had formed around her heart, spread to her fingertips, her toes. She just needed to relax a bit. To face him. Laura tossed off another shot. And another.

When she woke up a vicious headache throbbed, and her neck was stiff. She was in the living room in the dark and the house was deathly quiet. She had fallen asleep on the couch under the ugly ripple stitch afghan she'd worked on for months all those years ago. She didn't remember covering herself with it, Tony must've... Ah, Tony.

Tucked into a tight little ball of hurt, Laura sat rocking back and forth, trying to ease the gnawing, twisting pain, heavy as lead in her chest. She had imagined the scene a hundred times, seen herself towering in righteous anger over Tony, humiliated and writhing in shame at her feet. She had not anticipated this nausea in the pit of her stomach. While that bastard, oblivious, slept in comfort down the hall.

In the dim glow of the nightlight his handsome face was soft and peaceful, and for a second Laura told herself she had imagined the whole thing. Until she saw them again in her memory, two bodies molded into one fiery column in the dark behind her eyelids. Fondness turned to revulsion, and she strode into the bedroom and flicked on the overhead light. "Wake up, greaseball."

Tony squinched his eyes, scrubbed at his face. "Laura?"

"I saw you tonight!"

"What are you talking about?"

But she could see the light dawning in his lying eyes. "I saw you with that two-faced bitch!" Laura's chin started quivering. "I knew it! I knew you were fucking somebody!" Her voice trailed off in a whisper.

Tony lay there, staring at her like she was crazy.

"Don't look at me like that!" She threw a pillow at him. "Say something!"

He tossed the pillow aside and sat up, his eyes cold and hard. "You're drunk, Laura."

"I wasn't drunk last night at ten past nine." She heard the defensive whine in her voice. "When I drove by Casey & Moore. I saw you kissing that bitch in her office... Don't you dare try to deny it!"

But Tony wasn't denying anything, he just lay on the rumpled bed, staring at her like she'd grown two heads. "I know what I saw, Tony." Why did she have to convince him? And what was this flat, cold look in his eyes? It made her feel worthless, like nothing, less than nothing. But his silence confirmed everything.

"Don't do this to me, Tony. Please don't." She grabbed

for the lamp, to throw it, to hurt him, but tears blurred her vision and her fingers hit the shade and knocked it over. The light swung in a blinding arc, fizzled and died. "You're killing me, Tony." In the darkness she crept back out to the bottle she'd left by the couch.

The kids got themselves ready for school in the morning. Laura heard them tiptoeing around, feeling guilty but incapable of lifting her head off the cushions.

Around noon, judging from the shape of the bright patch of sunshine on the rug, she felt Tony bump the couch. "I'm leaving."

He smelled so good; showered and shaved. Laura kept her eyes shut tight, burrowed deeper under the afghan.

"I'll try to get home early." She heard the jangle of his keys. "We can talk then." Footsteps padded across the carpet. "If you're sober." The door slammed.

Laura sat up and watched him drive away, hating him, hating that reasonable tone of voice that always put her in the wrong, made her out to be the hysterical, jealous wife, the alcoholic, with delusions. Tony hadn't even bothered to make up an excuse. And why should he? They'd been here before, her ranting and raving like a damn fool... but this time was different. *This* time she had proof.

And where had that got her? Nowhere. Already she was second-guessing herself, maybe she'd imagined the whole thing. She had to get away, by herself, to think this through. Not for good, just long enough to scare the shit out of Tony. A day, two at most. And she had to leave before the kids got home, before she got caught up in the grind of drive me here, take me there, what's for dinner, Ma.

It didn't take long. She dragged a suitcase up from the basement, tossed in underwear, jeans, socks, didn't matter what. She stripped a dozen dresses from their hangers, stuffed two into the bag, left the rest heaped in a pile on the floor. It looked theatrical. Laura Costello, runaway wife. In the still dead air of the closet her burst of laughter sounded a bit hysterical. She wiped tears from her eyes, suddenly remembered her make-up, Tony would never believe she'd gone without it. She slid the whole tray of cosmetics into the overstuffed bag, grabbed her wallet and keys and raced to the car, heart pounding and legs trembling from the weight of the case and her frantic need to get out before Tony called - *as if!* - or she chickened out and changed her mind.

Her shaky fingers fumbled with the clump of keys but finally Laura gunned the engine and roared in reverse up the driveway. Sleet had fallen overnight, leaving a thin glaze of ice on the pavement. The car veered to the right and the passenger side wheels squished through the white-dusted flowerbed planted alongside. Tony's prized roses, the only living proof of his not-so-green thumb, carefully wrapped against the winter, nurtured and loved as much as his children. She shifted into drive and drove over them, laughing hysterically as branches snapped under the wheels, then backed up through them again, shocked when she saw the broken mess she'd made. In a surge of guilt, she wiped tears from her cheeks, slammed the lever into drive and screeched off down the street.

But where could she go? Boston, Mama? Not in a million years, after the kids came her mother thought the sun came out of Tony's ass. Laura would find no comfort there. Janice? There she'd be in for fresh from the oven chocolate chip cookies and a lecture, not to mention that she might run into that bitch Moore, a woman she'd cheerfully strangle about now.

After a wasted hour driving around suburban neighborhoods, she spotted the I-495 entrance and whipped up the nearest ramp. It led south.

The pale wintry sun was low in the sky when Laura pulled off the highway in Provincetown. The tip of Cape Cod. The cold gray Atlantic ocean crashed and sprayed angry spume twenty feet away. After a quick stop for gas she'd driven like a crazy person and ended up here on this narrow strip of sand between a forlorn salt marsh and the dismal winter sea. The end of the line. Well, it matched her mood, and Tony wouldn't have the faintest idea where she was. Teach the son of a bitch a lesson!

The town was lifeless, deserted. Empty fudge shops, shuttered restaurants, T-shirt shops boarded up for the winter. Myrtle Beach crossed her mind, with its wide white sandy beaches, happy crowds and sunshine and inviting warm blue ocean. Not for the first time she wondered why they lived here in this godforsaken place.

She pulled into the parking lot of 'Seagull's Roost', a string of tiny weather-beaten cabins, each with a green roof and its own teensy porch, all vacant. She wanted to hide the car between the cabins, and it took a while to convince the old bat at the desk that she really preferred a middle unit, she didn't care about the splendid view from the more desirable and still available end units - as if the place was going to fill up any time soon.

It was only three-thirty in the afternoon, but Laura could hardly keep her eyes open. Dusty, mildewed Cabin #5 with its bare wood floor crunchy with sand might have been a suite at the Ritz for all she noticed. She dropped her bag inside the door, pulled down the cracked and brittle yellowed shades and crawled fully dressed under the damp, ugly orange and brown comforter.

It was bright when Laura woke up, the clock beside the bed said six-forty a.m. - she'd slept all night, but the morning light came from the wrong side of the room, and it took a few thudding heartbeats to get herself oriented. Then it all came rushing back, along with a desperate craving for a big mug of hot, strong coffee. She threw on her jacket and picked her way along the row of units to the office, settling for a tepid imitation from a vending machine. The desk clerk - same woman, same stained sweatshirt, said far's she knew P'town was closed up 'tighter'n a drum' for Thanksgiving, most folks are home with their families; her mean little eyes dying to find out what Laura was doing here alone this time of year.

Laura picked up a tiny bag of Sun Chips and two Snickers bars and shuffled back to #5 to celebrate the upcoming holiday. She couldn't form a coherent thought, her mind churned with questions, but she wasn't worried; the answer would come. Bundled in the smelly comforter she'd yanked off the bed, Laura sat in the open doorway of the unit and stared at the steel gray ocean, mesmerized by the never-ending bands of ruffled whitecaps whipped up by the cold, raw wind, rushing to break against the dark granite boulders that lined the bay. So not Myrtle Beach with its white sand beaches and warm breeze.

Later in the morning she drove around town until she found an open liquor store and bought a couple bottles of Jack Daniels. By two in the afternoon she had killed one. The cabin was a mess, clothes tossed on the floor, the dresser littered with dirty glasses, empty chip bags, crumpled candy wrappers.

Three times she chased the maid away from her door, surprised that there actually was such a person in this place so long after the season, realizing it was probably the old bag in the stained sweatshirt.

She lay on the bed and slept off and on, dreaming of swaying palm trees, long walks with Tony in the moonlight on the beach, making love to the sexy sound of waves gently slapping sand– but wait! Forget sex - he never even held her hand! He was already messing around with Catherine Moore way back in the Spring!

The stupid TV set didn't work, and she missed Ellen. She imagined herself on one of the talk shows, talking to America.

"My husband cheated on me, with my, my best friend!"

"They all do, hon, you have to live with it."

"Oh no I don't!"

But really, what choice did she have? She knew in her heart that she'd drive back to Gilford in the morning, ready to forgive. Laura couldn't imagine living without Tony; she'd been in love with him since she was fourteen years old and had spent more than half her life with him.

But how could she go back, pretending everything was fine. Divorce was out of the question, she'd have to stick it out until the kids grew up, while he ran around with his–his whore! In a tiny place like Gilford, everyone would know her shame. This was the stuff of weepy soaps and TV movies, where contemptible lying bastards cheated with their devoted wives' best friends and got away with it.

She unscrewed the other bottle of scotch with a crazy kind of fear in her gut. What to do? One thing sure, she wasn't going to spend the rest of her life in this hole waiting for Tony to find her.

The kids must be worried about her, and she missed them so much it hurt. Laura picked up the phone ten, twelve times to call, to let them know she was okay, that she'd be home in a couple of days, Sunday latest, that she loved them, she was just giving their father a bit of a wake-up call. But she couldn't do it, knew she'd break down in tears.

She would call them in the morning, but right now she had to eat, couldn't remember the last time she'd had a meal. But first, a swig, then another, and eventually she sank into a dreamless sleep with the half-empty bottle on her lap.

Twenty-seven

Thanksgiving dinner was over in forty minutes. A meal that had taken Catherine many hours to prepare, that should have been a joyful family celebration, had been eaten in brooding silence interrupted only by the unsavory sounds of chewing and swallowing. Alyson, after gulping down a glass of milk, had begged to be excused and escaped across the road to Bonnie's. Frank had pushed his chair away from the table without so much as a thank you or a kiss my ass and gone into the den to watch more football. Catherine had the dining room to herself. *And a happy Thanksgiving to you, Mrs. Moore.*

Sitting at the table looking over unappetizing trays and dishes of congealed gravy and withered vegetables, Catherine wondered about taking some of the food to a shelter. Frank was adamant about leftovers, always said he'd eaten enough table scraps as a child to last a lifetime. In his mind, financially secure people didn't eat yesterday's food.

Draining her cup of cold tea, she noticed that a few leaves had accumulated in the bottom. One of Mother's friends used to read fortunes in tea leaves. She'd turn the empty cup upside down in the saucer, spin it three times and flip it over. Catherine tried it now. Leaves clung to the bottom and the sides of the cup in a shapeless clump. If there was a message, like some tall, dark stranger coming to her rescue, Catherine couldn't read it. She added more lukewarm tea from the pot at her elbow.

The day had started out really well. Frank had taken Alyson to the football game at the High School and stayed with her to watch Gilford defeat Southwood 27-10. They'd had hot dogs for lunch - he knew Catherine wouldn't approve, but it would be their little secret, his and his daughter's, grinning happily as he told Catherine. He'd come back full of the game, pleased that the home team, the underdog, had beaten its powerhouse archrival for only the eighth time in fifty years.

"Everybody was talking about the Costello boy, Anthony?"

She nodded, unable to speak.

"Kid's not big but fast as hell; scored two touchdowns."

Built like his father. "Wh--where's Aly?"

"We sat with the Kurtz's. They drove her home."

She'd obviously hurt his feelings, ditching him to go home with her friends, but how long did he think he could reject his daughter and not alienate her affection?

"But you had a good time together today, right?" She moved closer to him. "It's a start, Frank."

"You sayin' I should be grateful?"

"No, but I don't think one hot dog is going to make up for all the--" She'd expected anger, but the sadness in his eyes stopped her cold. "Frank?" In a rush of sympathy, Catherine touched his hand. "Maybe we can--?"

He jerked his hand away. "Spare me the lecture,

Catherine."

Candles flickered through the lace curtains in the Kurtz dining room across the way, Catherine could make out figures moving around the table. Alyson said the Kurtz's had started working on a puzzle, the Sistine Chapel ceiling, "the hardest puzzle in the whole world, Mom", and she'd been invited back to help with it after dinner.

Gary was home, possibly for good. It seemed Janice wasn't improving very quickly, she was in constant pain, but her accident might turn into a good thing, giving herself and Gary the opportunity to work out their problems.

Everyone had problems, Catherine thought, as she carried dirty plates into the kitchen, loaded them into the dishwasher. Family dynamics, dysfunctional families, their family. It couldn't be healthy for a child to grow up in this kind of environment, maybe staying with Frank was doing Aly more harm than good. As soon as she heard from Thorny she'd leave him, God knew she was tired and sick of this marriage; this life. But Frank could get so violent, suppose he followed through on his threat to hurt–to kill her. Catherine knew she was too afraid of Frank to leave him.

Scraping greasy pans with a vengeance they didn't deserve, she fantasized about starting a new life, hopefully with Tony, knowing full well she'd never get up the courage to ask Frank for a divorce, risk his wrath. So, what was she going to do?

Kitchen chores done, Catherine curled up on the window seat in the living room to read but the book lay unopened on her lap as she gazed into space. She got up and roamed around the house. Put away a pair of Alyson's shoes, hung a jacket in the front closet. Stared out of windows.

"Jesus, Catherine, settle down, willya? This pacing of yours is driving me nuts!" Frank stormed past her on his way back to the game with another can of soda.

"Oh, I'm so sorry, I'll try to stay out of your way."

He threw a dirty look over his shoulder as he left the room. She 'paced' to the front door. Only four o'clock but it was nearly dark, and snowing. Scattered flurries had been forecast, but half an inch had accumulated on the lawns, draping the neighborhood in white, a preview of the long bleak New England winter to come. A minivan sprayed a wide tail of slush in its wake before it stopped at the house next door. Three children jumped out and raced up the walk. Their grandparents, Doris Knight and her husband Al, ex-footballer, and as far as Catherine knew, the neighborhood's only black family, waited in the open doorway. Up and down the street, unfamiliar cars were parked in front of brightly lit homes; chandeliers glowed over festive dining tables crowded with happy families gathered to give thanks.

Catherine's thoughts drifted to Tony, as they so often did these days, no doubt celebrating the holiday with his big family in the North End. Italians, he said, knew how to enjoy themselves, tons of food and wine and music, big boisterous parties that lasted well into the night. Catherine's silent, empty house mocked her.

This year, as always, Elaine and Tom had invited them to Albany, a place Frank absolutely refused to visit. Lucky for Elaine and Tom. She'd told her sister they were spending the holiday with Kevin and Jean Casey, told Kevin they were going up to her sister's in Albany, the same lies she told every year, always hoping they'd never meet to compare notes.

What was Tony doing now, right this minute, at - she checked her watch - four twenty-two. Probably living it up in the bosom of his family.

Down the hall, in the den, the football game roared on the TV. Frank had built a cozy fire, and Catherine stood in the open doorway watching the dancing flames, wondering, not for the first time, how they had come to this. She had seen hurt, and love for his daughter in his eyes earlier; maybe that was a place to start, to get past the cold emptiness that had become their life together.

The front door slammed, distracting her. "Mom!" Alyson kicked off her wet boots in the front hall. "Mom! Guess where Bonnie's going for Christmas!"

"Get that kid to quiet down, would'ya!"

"Disney World?" Ignoring Frank, Catherine stayed where she was, in the hallway at the den door, waiting for Aly to come to her.

"Aw, Mom, you knew!"

"Well, Mrs. Kurtz did kind of hint--!"

"Shut the fuck up out there!" Frank suddenly loomed in the doorway, red faced and angry. "Take it somewhere else!"

"Your daughter has some news to share, Frank." Catherine felt her jaw tighten. "Go on, sweetie."

Alyson's eyes shifted from one to the other. "S'okay, not important." She turned and scurried up the stairs.

"*Very* nice, Frank." Catherine spat the words out.

"Would you be happier if Aly and I lived in the basement, the garage? How about if we left altogether?" Trying that idea on for size.

"You wouldn't dare." Frank smacked the wall with his fist, rattling a few of the plaques and trophies she had won over the years. "What makes you so fucking perfect, Catherine?" He picked one up, the million-dollar sales award she'd earned in 2017, hefting it. "Why am I always in the wrong!" He threw it at her, and Catherine ducked as the brass figure hit the wall where her head had been.

"Frank, are you crazy?"

"Crazy?" He followed her across the wide hallway, Catherine backing away and Frank stalking, hand raised to strike, pale gleaming eyes fixed on hers, obviously enjoying her fear. His slap caught her across the cheek, slammed her head against the wall. Catherine saw stars, and, when her eyes focused, saw Janice Kurtz moving toward her, looking for all the world like a deer caught in the glare of headlights.

"Aly wanted her iPod and I, um, I came with her to… to wish you a happy Thanksgiving."

Of course, there was nothing to say, all Catherine could think was *Janice Kurtz, of all people*. By tomorrow *everyone* in town would know. Without a word of apology, Frank had retreated back into the den. She closed the door, muting the swearing and crashes of trophies and plaques hitting the walls inside with frightening regularity.

"This doesn't seem to be a good time for a visit, Janice." With her eyes on the floor and a firm hand on Janice's back Catherine walked the woman back toward the door. Janice balked, but instead of the juicy gossip gleam Catherine had expected she saw compassion in the other woman's eyes.

"Come over to my place." She took Catherine's hand. "I'll make us a pot of tea."

"I–I have to see to Alyson."

"Then I'll wait here for both of you."

Too surprised to protest, Catherine left her in the foyer and followed Alyson up to her room. Her daughter lay in what could only be called a fetal position, curled around her beloved Max. Catherine often imagined her taking him with her to college.

She bent to kiss her daughter. "I'm going over to the Kurtz's for a cup of tea, sweetheart. Would you like to come?" Alyson snuggled deeper into her pillow. "Stay up here, then, have a nap. I won't be long." Closing the bedroom door softly behind her.

Downstairs, she donned boots and a jacket from the hall tree and helped Janice across the slushy street.

"Home at last!" Gary tenderly settled Janice in a rocker by the kitchen window and made their tea, chatting about meeting Frank at the terrific football game this morning, Janice's fantastic pumpkin pie. He cut Catherine a huge wedge and pushed a fork into her hand, overly solicitous. Catherine didn't see a signal, no exchange of winks or significantly raised eyebrows between the Kurtzes, but after he served them Gary quietly left the kitchen to go back to the puzzle in the dining room with the twins.

Catherine nibbled a crumb of pie. "This is good, Janice." She sipped the orange flavored spiced Chai. "I guess you're wondering..."

"Not a word, Cath." Janice patted her hand. "I don't want you to say things you'll regret after you and Frank make up."

Comforting thought. "I'm afraid there is no making up."

Janice smiled. "Every couple has problems, Catherine, every marriage has secrets. Look at what happened to us. Most of the time things work out for the best."

With Gary home God's in his heaven, all's right with *Janice's* world, Catherine thought. But there was no smug satisfaction on the woman's face, she radiated peace and… friendship. As if, after witnessing Frank's performance, a door had opened and they could be friends. Did she realize how badly Catherine needed a friend?

As she sat, relaxed, in Janice's kitchen, warm and cozy with its wooden beams and a fire crackling in the hearth, Catherine sighed. "Janice, I wish that were true..."

"Maybe it's a male thing, kind of a midlife crisis, like what happened to Gary. Sometimes people are not satisfied with the blessings the good Lord gave them and have to see if the grass is greener somewhere else."

"Frank is not having a midlife crisis, Janice." She twisted her wedding band.

"You mean he's always…?"

Catherine nodded, exhausted and unwilling to explain.

But Janice needed to make sense out of what she'd seen. "Does Frank drink?"

"Never. Frank grew up in Southie with an alcoholic father who routinely lost his monthly wages at the dog track, beat his wife and son weekly. He was hit by a bus outside the local tavern when Frank was thirteen."

She watched horror and pity chase each other across Janice's round face.

"Frank is filled with all the rage he needs."

"He...oh my God." Janice's eyes were huge in her pasty face, Catherine could see the wheels turning. "He hits you."

"I guess I'm lucky, it's not a weekly event. But Frank has to be in control, he needs someone to dominate. Unfortunately, that seems to be me." And what, she wondered, does that say about me?

"How did you meet?"

"In a bar." She chuckled at the irony. "I was twenty, slumming in Southie with a few of my friends, four innocents from the white bread world of Beacon Hill. I was smitten by Frank's good looks, his amazing blue eyes, his independence. He was so different from the pale, polite, well-bred boys I knew and much older, a mature man of twenty-six. He courted me with flowers and promises...I didn't realize it then, but I think he saw me as his ticket out of poverty. My mother saw through him; didn't care for him at all, but I refused to listen to her, or my dad, when they warned me that he was too smooth, didn't treat me with respect."

Janice's eyes dropped to her mug. "Respect in a relationship is so important. I'm learning that after all this time."

Apparently Gary had said his piece. "I'm glad Gary's back."

"We're so happy, Catherine." She giggled, sounding girlish. "He thinks I look terrific now that I've lost a few pounds."

Keep eating like that and it won't stay off long, Catherine

thought, watching Janice attack another slice of pie.

"Since you're laid up, what's happening with the school play?"

"In college Gary had experience with stage work - the man is so talented - and he's taken over as director of the Christmas show." Janice bent awkwardly and rubbed her ankle. "I can't go on, of course, with this."

"Isn't it healing?"

"My ankle is coming along fine but I still have a lot of pain in my back. The doctors want to run some tests next week." Fear crossed Janice's face. "Routine stuff, they said. Nothing to worry about."

Catherine carried their cups and plates to the dishwasher. "Guess I'd better get back home. If I can help at all —"

"Thanks, but Gary's here." A sly grin. "He told me you two met in Boston, you know. It couldn't have worked out better if I had planned this accident." Janice hobbled to the door. "Catherine, if you ever need... anything, anything at all, you can count on me. On Gary and me. We're your friends."

"Thanks, Janice, but I don't--"

"Promise?"

Eyes blurred with unshed tears, Catherine nodded.

At her own door, she squared her shoulders to face Frank, but she met only Alyson, huddled at the bottom of the stairs.

"Are you okay?" Catherine's eyes raked her over. "Where's your Dad?" If Frank had laid a finger on Alyson, she'd walk out that door right now.

"I'm fine." Alyson's tiny voice told a different story. Eyes like saucers stared out of her tearstained face. "I'm scared, Mom."

Catherine kissed the top of her head. "Yes, sweetie, but it's over now."

"But it'll happen again. I've heard him, in the night..."

Catherine stiffened. Alyson wasn't a baby anymore, it was too much to hope that she'd sleep through Frank's rages as she had then. This poor angel lived in terror of her own father; how much damage was that doing to her? How could they go on living this way? I *have* to do something, I've been selfish. This isn't just about me anymore.

She walked barefoot to the den. Stretched out on the couch, asleep, Frank looked like a homeless vagrant, gray stubble on his cheeks, snuffling and snoring like a wild boar. Some of her trophies lay on the floor. Disgusted, relieved, and ashamed, Catherine wouldn't wake him or do anything to disturb him now. She and Alyson were better off with him sleeping and God knew there would be other opportunities to tidy up.

As she watched, Frank abruptly changed position, settled deeper into the soft leather cushions. Lying on his side, face relaxed, mouth closed, she glimpsed the handsome young man who had lured her from her staid, comfortable family - from everything safe and familiar - with his adventurous plans. All bluster and talk, as it turned out, the chip on his shoulder too large to set aside. She kept her eyes on his sleeping face, remembering those soft full lips curved in a sweet smile... But the charm had worn away, like cheap silver plate on brass. She could pity him while he slept, but for too long she had lived with an angry man who punished her with his sullen moods, his violent outbursts, who found ways to hurt her, humiliate her, to make her pay for... what? His insecurities?

From the doorway Catherine glanced back at the man she had once loved to distraction. The earth did not move. She and Alyson would be happier and safer without him. Shutting the door silently, she prayed for the courage to act.

Twenty-eight

At four fifteen on Friday, the day after Thanksgiving and her third day in this godforsaken place, Laura heard a fist pounding on the door of her cabin.

"Laura?" Not the crone in the office; a male voice she immediately recognized.

Her heart stood still. "Who is it?"

"Jeeze, Laura, who do you think?"

She jumped off the bed, scattering dirty clothes, styro cups and newspapers to the floor. Instinct sped her to the door, but the bottle of Jack Daniels on the dresser stopped her. Dark eyes, big as saucers, red-rimmed, stared back at her from the mirror. Reflected behind her were the torn shades, stained rugs, dingy furnishings. This was all his fault, damn it, and here she was ready to rush into his arms like an idiot. If the last few days were to have any meaning she'd have to be strong. Laura leaned her forehead against the door. "What are you doing here?"

"We've all been worried sick." She heard him try the doorknob. "Are we going to talk through the damned door?"

"Leave me alone."

"Laura. We need to talk."

"I have nothing to say to you, you cheating sonova... wait a sec, how did you find me?" Tony was a cop, they probably had some fancy system that tracked people down. She opened the door but left it on the chain, gratified by the look of worry and concern on Tony's face. "How did you know I was here?"

He sighed. "Plastic, Laura. You used the card for gas in Buzzard's Bay, the liquor store in Truro, this place. It's all on VISA."

"Shit. I should've taken out some cash."

"It might have taken longer, but I'd have found you." One brown eye peered through the narrow gap in the door. "C'm'on, hon, open up."

Laura longed to let him in, to lose herself in the warmth and safety of Tony's arms but the sane voice in her head held her back. She always crawled to him, looking for comfort, but it had been a long time since she'd found it there. With her fingers wrapped tight around the neck of the bottle she held behind the door, Laura went on staring at him through the crack in the door.

"Laura, it was a long drive. Can we at least talk?"

"Don't expect any apologies from me."

"I have to take a piss. Will you please let me in?"

She snickered, nearly gave in. But in this mess, with the unmade bed and the empty bottles, she'd feel ashamed, on the defensive. "No. Go to the office. I'll be out in a sec."

This time of year it was damned cold, and would be dark by five. "There's a bar not too far away, saw it when I drove in." He stopped beside the Explorer. "Hop in."

"I'd rather not." She moved away. "Let's walk."

It was windy, her jacket wasn't nearly warm enough, her teeth chattered, but she felt safer out here; she wouldn't be able to trust herself in his car. She hugged herself tight and wondered what Tony was going to say. Would he beg forgiveness, plead with her to come back? Not very likely, knowing Tony. He'd probably tell her to pull herself together and follow him home. But dammit, he owed her an explanation, an apology, something-- or she wasn't going anywhere. Behind her, Tony muttered Italian curses as he lost his footing but at least he was dressed for the weather.

On the boardwalk Laura turned, watching him stroll toward her with his hands stuck in the back pockets of his jeans, bomber jacket unzipped halfway, a tee shirt proclaiming him the 'World's Greatest Dad" - a gift from the kids last Father's Day - pulled taut across his muscular chest. Still gorgeous. After twenty years she was still crazy for him, the bastard. She felt a hot throbbing start between her legs, *oh yeah, I'd go home with him in a heartbeat.*

He stopped in front of her, close but not touching, a sad little smile deep in his eyes. Now, now he'd say something; the right thing. Over Tony's shoulder she could see black clouds low in the darkening sky, the flash of lightning out over the bay. Imagine! A thunderstorm, at this time of year. Laura hated thunder and lightning, they'd better get this over with soon. But he stood there, awfully quiet for someone who wanted to talk. She leaned against the railing, tucked her icy hands in her armpits. "Tony, I'm freezing. I thought you came here to talk."

He looked blank, as if her voice surprised him. He could thank his lucky stars this damned rail was nailed down! While he rubbed his bare chin and looked stupid the rain started, fat icy globs that splatted when they hit. Laura's thin shell of a jacket was immediately wet and cold. Spotting the bar a hundred yards away, she ran for shelter. Tony caught up and pushed the door open, releasing a burst of warm smoky air, laughter, the tinkle of glass.

The walls were hung with nets and lobster traps, tacky but dry. The whole room was a bar, big wooden thing that ran the length of the room along one wall, all the stools taken. The rest of the narrow space was crammed with miniature tables and tiny wrought iron chairs jammed tight.

Surprisingly, there were other people down the Cape. The place was mobbed, but Tony got them a table right away, calmly walking through the crowd with that arrogant cop strut of his and claiming it, though Laura could see there were other people waiting. That always ticked her off, that way he had of getting what he wanted. And spoiled as he was, he took it as his due. He snapped his fingers at a passing waiter.

It was so noisy; they'd never be able to talk in here. Laura picked up a bunch of paper napkins and patted angrily at her wet hair.

Tony tipped his hand up to his mouth as if it held a glass.

She shook her head.

His eyebrows shot up in surprise.

"Coffee's fine." She had to repeat it. "Coffee."

"My wife here will have coffee." Tony shrugged. "No

cream." Knowing she took it black, all the years of voiceless communication across crowded rooms, over the heads of children. "Regulah for me."

"How are the kids?"

"What?"

"The kids?" She had to shout.

Tony leaned closer, she felt his warm breath in her ear, but Laura noticed from some faraway place that it didn't give her a thrill.

"They miss you."

"They'll survive." Feeling her heart break at how much she missed her children.

"That doesn't sound like you."

"People change, Tony." She looked deep into the steaming cup the waiter had banged down on the table in front of her. "As you know."

"They love you, Laura."

"And how about you, Tony?" Again with the chin rubbing - she knew he missed that stupid goatee - while he thought about it. God, he wasn't *that* dense, he had to know she needed to hear him say that he loved her, that he was sorry - he *had* to be sorry!

He said nothing.

The table was so small it barely held two mugs of coffee. Jammed in against the wall, thighs touching, Laura could hear Tony breathing, smell his after shave. "God damn it, Tony, did you drive all the way down here for coffee?" She slammed her tiny fist on the table, rattling the cups. "Talk."

And still he said nothing, just stared down at his hands,

but his leg started jiggling, another nervous habit. Laura felt a rush of sympathy. The poor guy didn't know what to say, how to apologize. She touched his hand, ready to--

His head came up, he looked her straight in the eye.

Laura never knew what she'd have been prepared to do, because in his eyes there was no guilt. Instead she saw a cool distance, the soul of patience dealing with an overwrought woman. His cop face. She realized with a shock that Tony had not come here to apologize.

What, then? Did he think she'd just fall right into his arms? All these years she'd worried that maybe Tony didn't love her, that he fooled around, that she'd die without him. But faced with this-- defiance, Laura went cold with fear. She tried to push it down but it rose in her like bile. Tony really *didn't* care for her. And suddenly she didn't want to hear what he had to say.

The table tipped when she stood up, an abrupt move that sent their coffee mugs skittering to the floor. Leaving Tony to worry about the mess - fuck him, Laura fought her way through the crowd of happy talk and laughing faces. The door slammed behind her, shutting off the music and the buzz of conversation with a bang.

Tony followed her outside, caught her arm and spun her around. He looked weird, sinister even, in the flashing blue and red neon lights of the beer signs. Laura felt trapped in a nightmare. Thick, damp fog and fine silver strands of rain mixed with sleet had turned the green and white striped awning into a private place, like a prison cell. Nearby she heard the muted thud of the ocean hitting the shore, the hiss of rain on pavement.

She pulled her arm out of his grasp. Tony backed a few steps - a hundred miles - away from her. "So what now, Laura?"

"You're asking me?" Her legs felt like wobbly rubber, too weak to hold her up. Laura backed up to the wall. "You started all this, remember?"

She liked that hard edge to her voice. Laura pressed her back into the shingles and tried to look like she didn't care. Watched little beads of mist form on her sleeves. Wished she didn't feel like throwing up, that she didn't need a drink so badly. But she was determined not to give in, back down, submit, accept, or go back home with this cold stranger. No matter how much her pussy ached or her legs trembled.

A gust of wind drove icy needles of rain through her thin, wet jacket and she shivered. The dampness always made Tony's wavy hair curl, and wet ringlets dripped inside his collar, down his face. He looked uncomfortable, and bewildered, as if he'd caught *her* fooling around with his best friend instead of the other way around. *Dickhead.* It was probably too much to hope he was hurting. Laura could give lessons on hurting, how the pain grew and filled you up and ate at your insides until you wanted to puke and only a good slug of scotch took it away. Tony couldn't possibly imagine what he had put her through. Go ahead and hurt, damn you, it's good for the soul.

"Laura, look..." Tony had stopped his pacing and stood facing her, legs spread in a tough cop pose. "Where do we go from here?"

His face was so close to hers Laura could see a web of

fine lines at the corners of his eyes, feel his warm breath on her face, almost feel his soft full lips touching hers. She turned her head away.

"You tell me, Tony."

"Laura, be reasonable, here. We have to--"

"Reasonable? You mean like forgive and forget?"

Angry tears sprang to her eyes and she tossed them away. Behind her the big oak door squeaked open and shut two, three times. More maybe. People leaving the bar, laughing, pausing under the awning before running out into the cold driving rain.

"Laura, hush..." He caught her shoulders.

"Don't shush me, Tony, and keep your hands off me!"

"People are watching, Laura." The patience of Job through clenched teeth. "I just meant..."

"I know exactly what you meant, Tony." She twisted away from him. "You meant come home with me, stupid, we'll go on like nothing happened, while I keep right on fucking your friend right under your stupid nose!"

Around them people huddled under the awning, pretending not to listen. Laura could imagine their ears stretched to hear but she couldn't care less. "Do you really think you can keep shitting on my head and I'll keep wiping it off?"

"Laura, I never--"

"Never what, Tony? I saw you kissing that cow with my own two eyes!" His eyes filled with tears but she stared him down, heart pounding with fear and an exhilarating sense of power. "And now you're going to stand here and lie to my face?"

His face crumpled, at last she'd hurt him, offended his honor. "Laura, please."

"For the last time let go of me, Tony." Again she pried his fingers off her arm.

"Laura...!"

"Go fuck yourself, Tony."

One of the women under the awning clapped her hands as Laura stalked off into the icy November sleet.

Twenty-nine

Today's meeting had gone well, business seemed to be picking up after a lousy November. Catherine closed her eyes and let herself relax into the cushy leather comfort of Kevin's Cadillac. Over a pricey lunch at a cozy, New England restaurant in Worcester, they'd signed an exclusive agreement with a tech firm planning to transfer a dozen or more families into the area.

"I'm hearing some pretty heavy sighs over there, Cath, considering."

"I've got a few things on my mind."

"Anything you want to share?"

"Not really, Kev, but thanks."

He patted her gloved hand. "You know you can count on me."

She nodded. Kevin Casey was business partner, comforter and father confessor rolled into one. Sixty-ish, a jovial, kindhearted man known for long involved less-than-funny jokes, whose twinkling blue eyes hardened like diamonds whenever she mentioned Frank's name. Which wasn't often; Kevin guessed about her troubles with her husband early on in their partnership when Catherine, with less than artful makeup, had tried to cover up a bruised cheek. He had sworn years earlier that he'd chop Frank's balls off the next time he laid eyes on the bastard.

"Catherine, we've been friends for too long. You know I'd never pry but you've been in the dumps for months now, and if there's anything I can do..."

"I'm working on it."

"Leave him."

"I would, in a minute, but I'm afraid of what he might do. You know, with Alyson and all..."

"Catherine, if you need a lawyer, or a place to sleep-"

"Just be my friend, Kevin."

He patted her hand. "You know you can count on me, love."

She felt like a creep, with Kevin pouring out his affection and concern. She was not worrying about Frank or her marriage; but thinking about Tony. The whole town, it seemed, was buzzing with the news that Laura Costello had run away, leaving home and family for parts unknown. Catherine heard it from Alyson, who'd heard it from Gina, Tony's daughter, and from Janice Kurtz, whose eyes gleamed with the excitement of it all.

"I wonder if her husband, the detective, is fooling around? Remember, Cath, what Laura said that night in the car about-"

"About Tony cheating on her?" *How could I forget?* "Yes, Janice, I remember."

As Kevin pulled into his private parking space, his headlights picked out a man in dark leather slouched in the doorway. "Hey, isn't that Detective Costello?"

Tony? Catherine's breath caught in her throat.

206

"Hey Detective," Kevin called from the car. "What's up?"

Tony turned tragic eyes on her. "I wanted a word with Cath–Mrs. Moore."

"Everything okay?"

She watched them shake hands, Kevin's sharp blue eyes studying Tony.

"Yeah, just needed a word..."

Kevin turned to her, his eyes holding hers for a long moment. "Anything at all, Cath, I'll be in my office."

He'd probably think the detective's visit had to do with Frank.

"Tony, what's going on?" Catherine threw her jacket on a chair in the reception area, led him into her office. "I hear your wife--"

"I found her in a cheesy motel down the Cape."

Catherine didn't know what to say. "Where?"

"In P'town, day after Thanksgiving." He raised his hand to his face, changed his mind, shoved his hands in his pockets. "It didn't go well."

"What happened?"

"She said she'd seen us together, you and me, can't imagine where, kissing or something. I didn't know what to say, I practiced all kinds of speeches in the car on the way down but when I got there the words stuck in my throat. I'm sure Laura expected me to beg her to come back, and she certainly deserved an apology. But I didn't want to lie, and I'm sick of pretending. I don't think I *am* sorry."

Catherine gave him a long look. "About us or about getting caught?"

"Good question." He slumped his shoulders. "I'm not

sure."

"How was your...Laura?"

"I can't quite put my finger on it. She seemed defiant, independent. Definitely not sober, Christ, I don't remember the last time Laura's breath didn't smell of booze."

"She didn't come back with you."

"We didn't part on very good terms. I called the motel this morning, woman there said Laura checked out, but I don't think she's coming home. Probably hiding out someplace else on the Cape." He sighed. "She needs to get her head straight."

All about the wife. Catherine studied his face, the dark circles under his eyes. "And how about you, Tony?" She took a deep breath. "How about us?"

"I don't know." He looked away. "Maybe we both need some time."

Time for what, she wondered. To work it out? Get back on track? Get a divorce? She sneezed. Snatched a tissue from the box handy on her desk. Grateful for something to hide behind. What did Tony expect from her?

"Bless you."

"Starting a cold." She waved a hand toward the window, where gusts of wind swirled snowflakes into a mini tornado. "This weather." As if it mattered a damn.

"I don't know what to tell the kids about Christmas." He hung his head.

"That's weeks away, Tony, I'm sure Laur—your wife will be back by then." Back to her cozy home, her loving family, and Tony. Catherine felt weird, disassociated, as if none of this mattered. She didn't care anymore; she'd had enough of this merry-go-round. She popped a twelve-hour cold capsule out of the foil pack, the second one this morning, and swallowed it with a sip of tepid coffee from the carafe. "Has she called the kids?"

"Apparently not." He glanced at his phone. "Too busy getting herself together, I guess." He slumped forward in the chair, head cradled in both hands. "What the hell am I going to do, Catherine?"

What indeed.

Did Tony still love Laura? Would he beg her to come back? Would he declare his undying love for Catherine? Which woman did he really love? Tune in tomorrow for the next episode of--

My God, this medication was making her crazy. Catherine snapped back to reality. "Do you still love her, Tony?"

"I thought I didn't," rubbing at his chin, "but I'm confused. I feel responsible for Laura, the same way I do about my kids. I'm worried about her all alone out there, pretending she's one of the grownups." He raised tired eyes. "She's like a child, Laura is. Never made an important decision by herself, never earned a penny on her own, and for a lot of years she's never been two days in a row without a drink. I'm afraid for her, Catherine. Is *that* love? You tell me."

"Oh no, you're on your own there, my friend." Whatever Catherine had expected from him, it wasn't this waffling. Either he loved the woman or not, all other decisions were based on that. Meantime, her own future hung in the balance. If she let it.

Catherine glanced at her watch. "I've got an

appointment, gotta run" - a lie - "but why don't you give me a call after Laura gets home, when you two have had a chance to talk."

"Does this mean you don't- " His eyes pleading, big brown puppy dog eyes.

"Better that way, don't you think?" She forced a sympathetic smile and shooed him to the door, dismissing him and his problems. "Who knows, you lovebirds might just work it out." Picking up her coat as the door swung shut behind him, she let the tears fall.

She drove straight home. Was she hurt? Angry? Dazed seemed to sum it up nicely. Dog tired and weary of men and their inflated egos, their childish ways, their need to be dominant, their hunger to be mothered. Sick of it all. Or maybe it was just the cold, her head was clogged something awful. She took another cold capsule, went upstairs to her room and lay on her bed staring at the ceiling, sinking into the out-of-body-ness the medication produced.

The white ceiling was plastered in cloudlike swirls and her eyes drifted from one to another, thinking of the glass ceiling the newsmagazines said held women down. She'd crashed that barrier long ago, was a very successful businesswoman, a decision maker, a mover and shaker, certainly in the small puddle that was Gilford, Massachusetts, and a woman with wealth beyond measure in trust funds. Yet she chose to remain shackled to a man who abused her and yearned for another who didn't know his ass from his elbow.

She rolled over onto her side. Why? Was it true that a

woman was incomplete without a man? An old-fashioned notion, surely. But how else explain why she and Frank had traveled so far along this road? He'd been abusing her mentally and physically for years. After the first time he hit her, why had she ever allowed a second? Where was her self-esteem, that central core that said, 'this far and no further'!

Slowly, a feeling of strength swelled in her; Tony's waffling, maybe, or the drugs, but Catherine felt empowered. It was there, her self-esteem, buried deep inside her. She had no need of men, she was a successful woman who could stand on her own two feet. Frank would be home in an hour, Aly was at Bonnie's, this was the night she would tell Frank she wanted a divorce, break the chains of bondage and rise like a phoenix out of the ruins...

Drifting among the clouds swirling over her head, Catherine fell asleep dreaming of a new future.

Thirty

The Myrtle Beach Laura remembered was a warm, sunny place where a woman couldn't possibly be lonesome, where strangers' faces didn't break with the effort to share a smile. On the long drive south she'd kept herself awake with memories of white sandy beaches and noisy, crowded boardwalks, but in the bleak gray rain of late afternoon in early December, the place looked abandoned, like fairgrounds after the carnival has moved on. She had to find a place to stay but all she saw were towering condo buildings lining the street and blocking any view of the ocean. What the hell was she going to do now?

All the parking areas obviously belonged to the condos but she turned into one isolated spot and made her way to the boardwalk. A strong onshore wind was blowing the palm trees every which way, and fat salty raindrops smashed against her face, burning her eyes. Laura backed away from the railing, wrapped her wet jacket tighter, wishing she had another sweater, missing her big fleece coat and hat. A little way down the beach a string of colored lights swung crazily in the wind, and she let herself get pushed along the boardwalk to a one-room shanty attached to a screened-in porch that apparently went by the name of Beanie's. She shook herself like a wet dog and opened the door on a dimly lit bar. It was foggy with smoke, but dry and warm.

"Dewars, double," Laura mumbled to the bartender, "rocks." She climbed onto an unsteady wooden stool at the end of a well-worn gray Formica counter.

"Sorry, hon, this ain't a bar."

Laura glanced around. There were ten people in the place and every one of them was drinking. "Are you saying I can't get a drink in here?"

"I'm sayin' this is a restaurant, hon."

The nametag on her soiled white shirt said Sam. She looked tough, muscular, with brassy blond hair pulled into a loose ponytail and big boobs stuffed into a blouse that didn't quite meet where it should. At *least* five ten. Not a bartender. More like a bouncer.

"But I don't want to eat." Tired, gritty eyed, Laura wanted a drink and a bed.

The Amazon's smile showed a gap between her front teeth. "You c'n order chips, or grits, long as it's food. It's Sunday, this here's South Carolina, and rules is rules."

"Well then, bring me one of those." Laura pointed to a plate in front of the man a couple of stools down the bar.

"Hush puppies."

She'd forgotten what they were called. "Whatever. Don't forget—"

"Dewars, rocks. I got it, hon."

"It's Laura. Stop with the hon. Call me Laura."

"Sure, hon." Again the smile. "Laura."

Watching the woman pour her drink, Laura tried to come

up with a plan. First thing, she needed a place to sleep. Where were all the motels she remembered?

"Here we go, hon."

Laura looked down at the plate. Three little brown logs, like firewood. Or dog-doo. With a dish of ketchup alongside. "Where's my--"

"Right here!" Sam smacked the glass down and rested her elbows on the counter. "Looks like you could use some sleep."

Laura downed half her drink, felt the warmth spread through her chest.

"Where y'all from?"

Laura dipped a hushpuppy into the ketchup and bit off the tip, chewing slowly. A cop's wife, she knew when to keep her mouth shut. "Up north." With her Boston accent it sounded like 'nawth'. The hushpuppy was greasy and barely warm but she stuffed the rest of it into her mouth.

"Well now, I knew that, hon."

"I wish you'd call me Laura."

"Touchy, ain't we." Sam popped one of Laura's hushpuppies into her mouth.

Laura caught the laughter in the woman's eyes and forced a smile. She was just being friendly, one of those Southern things. "Sorry. Been on the road for two days straight and I'm tired."

"Whatcha here for?"

Laura swirled another log in the ketchup. Drained her glass. "That's a very good question." She shrugged her shoulders. "Hit me again."

Where did she learn to say that? And what *was* she

doing here? It was one thing to leave home for a couple of days, show Tony she could take care of herself. But to drive hundreds of miles to South Carolina - now she was a runaway wife, a mother who had deserted her family.

"You okay, Laura?"

"I was just thinking about my kids." Laura sipped the fresh drink. "My Gina has a gap between her teeth, just like yours. She'll be getting braces soon."

"Well I say what's okay for Lauren Hutton is fine with me."

"Lauren who?"

"Old movie star, never mind. Got any pictures?"

Laura shook her head. "Nothing recent." She hadn't got around to putting their latest school pictures into her wallet, but she could see them all. Claudia's thick dark hair. Gina's impish grin. Anthony's expressive brown eyes, so like his father's. Were they eating well? Did they have clean clothes? Who was taking them to practice and dance lessons and rehearsals?

"I'm a *good* mother." Her eyes locked on Sam's. "You know?"

Sam nodded. "Yeah, me too, hon. It was the old man I couldn't stomach."

There was no one else sitting at the counter now, and Laura watched the woman pour two glasses of amber liquid. "Here's to all the sons of bitches!"

Laura clicked her glass against Sam's.

"I'm off in half an hour. What say you 'n me hang out for a while?"

Tired, strung tight as a wire. Laura would never get to

sleep tonight. "Well, I--"

"I don't bite, hon."

"Okay, but only if you stop calling me hon." Laura laughed out loud. Suddenly she felt like living dangerously. This woman had never heard of Tony or Catherine or Gilford, Massachusetts. She could forget about the whole damned mess for a while.

Laura sat beside Sam out behind Beanie's on wide wooden steps that led to the beach. Before locking up Sam had scooped a bottle of Jack Daniels off the shelf, and Laura tipped the bottle to her mouth, feeling the liquid dribble warm down her throat. The rain had stopped and the moon came and went through holes in the thick cloud cover.

"I thought she was my friend." Seemed she'd told Sam the whole sorry story.

"Nobody's your friend when it comes to love, or sex."

"But Catherine has a husband of her own, what does she want with mine?"

"Maybe the question is what your Tony wants with her."

But Laura didn't want to go there tonight. "That's not the point here."

"No? Laura, it takes two to –"

"She was my friend, okay? And she took advantage." Laura got up and moved a few steps away in the soft white sand. "I was here last spring. Where are the lights? The people?"

"Gone south for the winter." Sam chuckled and fumbled in the pocket of her jacket, coming up with a crumpled looking cigarette. She lit it carefully, hand cupped around the flame of the match until it caught. "Drag?"

"Don't smoke, thanks."

"This ain't just smokin', hon." Passing her the joint.

Trying to imitate Sam, Laura took a tiny mouthful of smoke and blew it out.

"No, ya gotta get it back there. Like this." Sam took a long drag, inhaling with her mouth open to show Laura, let the smoke trickle slowly out of her nostrils. "Now you."

Coughing, choking, Laura managed to get a couple of good hits to the back of her throat. She started feeling lightheaded, loose, yet thick and syrupy, all at the same time. "Wow."

"It's pretty good shit."

"Where do you get this stuff?"

"Beanie grows it in the kitchen garden."

Laura laughed, thought about being a police detective's wife. In another life. She giggled, took another drag.

Sam - don't-*ever*-call-me-Samantha - shuffled off the steps to the beach. To Laura's muddled eyes the big woman was graceful as a leaf floating on a gentle breeze.

"So, you've run away." Sam's voice was muffled, and Laura drifted down the steps herself, settling like a cloud beside Sam. She wrapped her arms around her drawn up knees, making herself as small as possible, no more than a dark speck on the white sand. If she tucked herself tight enough she might disappear. "I didn't mean to. I just-- started driving. And ended up here."

"So, stay a while."

"Where?"

"With me. Got a cute little one bedroom place, futon in

the front room. A mite crowded, but it'll do 'til you make up your mind."

She'd almost done it, almost disappeared, but now Laura felt herself getting bigger, like Alice, floating up and growing like a genie out of a bottle until she was one of the clouds in the sky. She hung in the air overhead, overflowing with sympathy for this pathetic little bundle down below that was Laura Maria Costello. Tears filled her eyes. "I don't think so. My kids need me home."

"I thought you said they were teenagers. They'll survive."

"Gina's still… ah, you don't know much about kids." She'd have to phone first thing in the morning. Or no, after school was better, when Tony would be at work.

Sam sat up. "Look, hon. Laura. You want the son of a bitch to worry about you for a while. Be incomm…" Sam laughed. "Mouth's real loose. What I mean is, you gotta play hardball with this guy."

"Now that would be different." Laura thought about Tony's soft brown eyes. "I've always been a fool for Tony." Hardball? Sure. After she'd gone and run away, leaving Tony and Catherine together. Not the best bargaining position.

"Ever notice, Sam, how nothing ever turns out the way you expect? There you are thinking you've got a good life and a faithful husband and a happy marriage and suddenly it all blows up in your fuckin' face!"

"In my experience those things aren't sudden at all, hon. Let's face it, men are dickheads, every one. Sweet talk you into cookin' and cleanin' up after them, raisin' their little brats, watch you get old and tired with it all and meanwhile the bastards are fuckin' anything that moves."

"Put that way, we're the fools."

Sam's head had dropped to her knees. "Mine took a fancy to the babysitter. All of fourteen years old. My sister's kid."

Laura's mind filled with the disgusting image of a man's pale shiny butt stuck in the air, pants down around his knees, big guy so flabby you couldn't see the little girl under him. There was nothing to say. She patted Sam's shoulder.

"Jolene blames me," Sam sniffled, "says I should've kept my husband out of her little girl's panties." Sam's broad shoulders shook. "There's a kid."

"Oh my God. When did this happen?"

"Few years back." Sam wiped her eyes on the sleeve of her smock. "Had to get out, left them up in Raleigh. Damned rednecks! Little gal and the kid're with him but my sister says the shit's still screwing around."

Laura watched the clouds scudding across the sky, thin as gauze drifting by the moon. Was Tony worrying about her? Or screwing Catherine Moore, both of them glad she'd run off and left them together.

The clouds broke apart and moonlight hit the water like a long silver ribbon narrowing down to nothing in the distance. If you walked out on it you might touch the moon. Laura kicked off her shoes and walked slowly toward the thin, still, mirror-like sheen of water reflecting the moon.

"Watch me, Sam," she called out as she stepped onto the magic carpet. "I'm walkin' on water."

Thirty-one

Catherine had come down with a nasty cold and spent several miserable days in bed, tanking up on cough medicine and popping cold capsules like candy.

When she was conscious she thought about Tony, she hadn't heard from him in the week since he came to her office. True, she'd been sick, but her phone went everywhere with her. She sneezed, grabbed a tissue from the half empty box beside her bed. If he wasn't making up with L–his wife, he surely would have tried to get in touch by now. Maybe they had decided to give it another try, good for them. But, Tony or no Tony, she was finally going to have it out with Frank. She was going to ask for a divorce. Tonight, she thought, she'd put it off long enough, and drifted off to sleep.

It was dark when she heard Frank's car on the driveway, listened to a skim-coat of ice crackling under the wheels. Wind-driven snow had drifted up against the garage doors; he'd have to shovel to get the car inside.

Crossing to the window, she tugged the drapes aside and watched him pull his briefcase out of the back seat and shuffle slowly up the snow-covered flagstone path. God, when was the last time he'd taken a vacation? It had been years since they'd gone to the Barstowe cottage on the Cape-- she felt a rush of sympathy, then shook her head to stop the tears forming in her eyes. From up here he looked old and tired, slump-shouldered with the weight of his demons; not a trace left of the charming, brash, confident man she'd married. That man was long gone. But this was no time for pity.

Wrapped in her warm fleece robe she stumbled down to the foyer and made it to the bottom of the staircase when Frank barreled through the door on a gust of icy wind.

"Had to leave the car outside, guess I'll have to shovel the driveway." He dropped his wet coat on the floor. "Damned weather! Traffic on the Pike was one hell of a mess tonight - people don't know how to drive in this--" Kicking off his boots, he turned to look at her. "What the hell are you, the Statue of fuckin' Liberty?"

"Frank, can we talk?"

"Okay with you if I come into my home first?" In his socks, he crossed the floor, let his briefcase fall on the tile floor at her feet, and leaned in close. "You look like hell."

She felt like it too, maybe this wasn't a good time, but, "Frank, I–"

"Don't start with any shit, Catherine." He turned away.

She stood a little taller, determined not to lose the momentum that had brought her this far. She was tense, nervous, terrified of the outcome. But she'd steeled herself for this moment. It was now or never. "We need to talk."

"And I need to eat." He turned back to pick up his coat. "Will this take long?"

"Frank, I-- we can't keep going like this."

He turned to stare at her.

"I want a divorce." Pleased with her firm, strong voice.

His shocked silence hit her like a physical thing, but it didn't last long. "You stupid bitch, you hit me with this as I walk through the door after the shitty day I had?"

Catherine flinched. Tired, hungry, of course Frank would be spoiling for a fight. In two long strides he closed the gap between them, standing so close to her that the paisley pattern on his tie blurred. Catherine's stomach knotted.

"You sure know how to pick your time, Catherine."

"I'm not looking for a fight, Frank."

"Oh no?" He shoved her against the railing with the flat of his hand, she could feel the pineapple finial dig into her back. "Well, you've fucking got one now!" His voice rose to a high-pitched whine, mimicking hers. "Oh, Frank, I'm so unhappy." His face reddened, thick veins stood out in his neck. "Maybe I'm not happy either, ever think of that?" He dropped his voice to a menacing whisper. "You're my wife, smartass, 'til death and all that bullshit." His hand closed around her neck. "Don't you forget it."

In the breathless silence the grandfather clock bonged the half hour.

"So what's the deal, got a new man in your life, Cath?" He loosened the knot on his tie. "Ole Kev finally making his move?"

"Of course not, Frank. I'm just sick of living like this."

His head swiveled to the living room, the formal dining room, the gleaming kitchen down the hall, so different from the crowded space he'd grown up in. "Like what?"

"Do you think we have a good life, Frank?"

One-handed, he pulled his tie off, his other big paw kept her pinned to the railing, where the spike-edged wooden pineapple cut into Catherine's back.

She winced with the pain.

Frank's lip curled in a smug grimace. "Scared, aren't you?"

"No, but you're hurting me." She pushed weakly at his chest. "Take your hands off me so we can talk like intelligent adults." Cool, calm, courageous, a little bit out-of-body thanks to the drugs she'd taken.

His twisted mouth made his handsome face ugly. "Said the spoiled Beacon Hill bitch." The slap came out of nowhere; it stung, she tasted blood.

Once the slapping started only God knew where it would end. This beating thing was methodical, and there was no way to tell from the blank expression on Frank's face if he derived satisfaction from it or not. But Catherine had learned over time that crying and pleading fueled his anger. Silently she prayed for strength.

Turning inward, to shut out the fierce gleam of violence in his eyes, trying to distance herself from the blows and whispered obscenities. Curling into herself, hiding, for protection, for sanity. As always.

She covered her face when he punched her in the ribs. Gasping for breath, sobbing now but not begging, not yet. She tried to kick him, but Frank had pinned her body with his leg. Catherine felt her knees giving out, soon she'd be a crumpled bloody heap at his feet.

"Frank, please stop." Pleading, hating the sound of her

223

whine, but hoping for once that he might listen, that the beating might stop before he really hurt her. It had never worked before, anything she said angered him more. But hadn't she promised herself that she'd never again let Frank beat her into submission? She had to do something now, right this second, or it would go on and on and -- "Stop! Now!"

Catherine didn't know she had shouted the words until she saw the shock on Frank's face. Adrenalin surged. Her fingers curled around the handles of his briefcase at her feet. She brought it up between his legs. He roared in pain and backed away. She tore down the long hallway to the kitchen, almost tripping on her robe. She heard him slip and fall in his socks on the polished tile floor, where he let loose a string of curses. Force of habit made her stop, see if he was okay, but she quickly took off again, hellbent for the back door.

She didn't make it. Frank caught her just as her fingers touched the doorknob. He grabbed her arm, twisting it behind her back, silencing her shriek of pain quickly with his fist to the side of her head. Squealing like a trapped animal, bent over backwards on the edge of the counter, Catherine felt his thick fingers close around her neck, choking her, this time he was really going to kill her! With a strength she didn't know she had, Catherine twisted around, stretched out one arm and grasped one of the razor-sharp knives clinging to the magnetic rack on the wall beside the stove as blackness closed in.

Frank lay on his back on the kitchen floor near the door,

a pool of red spreading slowly under his shoulder, around his head, a rigid mask of terror on his face, in his horror-struck eyes. Through the wooly haze in her head Catherine heard a distant metallic clatter as the big knife dropped from her hand and hit the tile floor.

Her teeth were chattering, she could hear them in the sudden humming silence. Stepping cautiously around the – around Frank, she opened the door to the half-bath and sank to her knees beside the toilet. After she threw up Catherine rinsed out her mouth, wet a cloth with warm tap water and wiped her face, carefully patted it dry, checked her hair in the mirror over the vanity, and closed the door softly behind her.

But Frank still lay motionless on the floor. No nightmare, this, as she'd hoped in the bathroom. She dropped to her knees beside him, close but not touching, and stared at his face, waiting for his eyes to blink.

After what seemed like hours the Westminster chimes in the grandfather clock cheerfully played its tune, bonged the hour. "Five, six, seven. Come on, Frank, time to get up.

Years earlier, still in love and awestruck with his presence in her bed, she'd watch Frank sleep, watch the rhythmic rise and fall of his chest. She remembered her fear when he seemed to stop breathing and she'd hold her own breath until she saw the almost imperceptible swell of his chest. She felt that fear now. "Breathe, you sonofabitch!"

She heard dripping, droplets of blood slapping the tiles, but Catherine kept her eyes on Frank's shirt, away from the growing red pool on the floor around his neck, his fixed, horrified, staring eyes. Waiting for his chest to rise and fall.

Now he would take a breath, or now--

The squeak of the front door opening penetrated the cotton wool feeling in her head. Boots slapped the tiles in the hall. "Mom, I–" A strangled scream, running feet and the boom of the door as it slammed shut, the single bong of the grandfather clock striking the quarter hour.

But still Frank didn't breathe.

Shivering, Catherine crossed the room on wobbly legs to the land-line phone on the kitchen wall.

"De-detective Costello."

"Your name, ma'am?"

"Cath–um, Moore. Mrs. H-he'll know."

And after a long silent moment. "Costello."

"T-t-tony? Catherine. F-" Hard to form the words with her stiff lips. "Fr-Frank's dead. I think I killed him."

Thirty-two

Tony damn near flew out of the car, slipped on the icy crust covering the driveway and went down flat on his ass. He'd grabbed his jacket on the run but left his boots behind in favor of speed. He picked himself up and raced across the snow-covered lawn just as a cruiser, sirens blaring and lights whirling - followed closely by a fire truck - screeched to a halt on and around the Moore driveway. He scanned the houses nearby, couldn't see anyone but sensed them behind sheer curtains, all wondering what could possibly bring police cars to their sedate upper middle-class suburban neighborhood.

"Thank God you're here." A large woman stood in the doorway, brown eyes big as dinner plates in her pudgy face. Arms around a shivering little girl. Annie Moore? No, Aly, he remembered from the red hair. "Terrible! This poor little thing saw everything!"

To Alyson, "I've got to go inside but you can tell me about it in a bit, okay, sweetie?"

The girl nodded, zombielike.

And to the woman, "get her outside, please. The EMT's will take care of her."

From deep inside the house Tony heard a low keening, the sound of a wounded animal.

She didn't move. "You've gotta go, Mrs., ah…"

"Kurtz; Janice Kurtz. You must be--"

"--Costello, Ma'am. Detective."

"Laura's husband."

"Yes, Ma'am." Wasting time; he had to get to Catherine!

"They fought a lot, the Moores, and I just know something dreadful has happened this time." Eyes bright, double chins trembling. Tony knew the type, they were usually the ones babbling on TV with the thrill of it all.

"You been inside? Touched anything?"

"God, no…! The reason I'm here at all is that Aly ran screaming across the road--"

More sirens. An ambulance; men with stretchers. "Mrs. Kurtz." With one arm he guided her unsteadily back to the door. "I need my cane."

"Guys! Got a little one here." Two burly men wrapped the shivering body in a tan blanket and led her to the ambulance.

"Mrs…ah, you live there, number 110? Look, when the EMTs are done, take Alyson to your place." He shoved the cane at her. "I'll need a statement from you later." Magic words.

"Of course." Regret in her voice, but he heard her mumbling about hot chocolate as she limped away.

Tony took a deep breath and finally walked slowly toward the kitchen. The room was in darkness and he felt along the wall for a switch. He set the dimmer on low, providing just enough light to illuminate the scene.

Frank Moore lay inert on the floor, a pool of blood under his shoulders. Beside him a woman knelt, the front of her shirt bloody, telephone receiver buzzing in her hand. Catherine.

Tony moved closer to the tableau, stooped, took the receiver from her cold hand and replaced it on the wall, his policeman's eye taking in the knife on the floor, eight, ten inch bloodstained blade, the blood-spattered cabinets and stove, the thread of blood still trickling from a wound in the side of the victim's neck. He bent quickly to study the body, fingers feeling automatically for a pulse in the man's neck.

Beside him, Catherine rocked slowly back and forth. "I killed him, oh my God, I killed him..." A mantra, repeated over and over in a low monotone.

"Holy--!" Two uniforms crowded into the doorway.

"Jesus!" One of the patrolmen. "She says she ki–"

"Shut up, assholes!" Don, Tony's partner, shoved them aside and moved into the kitchen. His eyes darted around the room, took in the woman - the perp? kneeling beside a man - the vic, stretched out on the floor.

"He's dead, Tony, I killed him."

"Tony? She knows you?" With a raised eyebrow and a look that shouted 'we'll talk later', Don began to scribble rapidly in his notebook. "Ma'am…"

"Moore," Tony whispered, "Catherine Moore."

Don turned to the woman on her knees. "Mrs. Moore, we have to ask you a few questions."

She raised her head and Tony groaned. Catherine's face and arms were scraped and bleeding, one eye nearly shut, her robe torn and bloody. The son of a bitch had

229

been beating on her and she knifed him in self-defense. He didn't realize he had taken her in his arms until Don's fist came down on his shoulder, hard, and in the doorway the uniforms shuffled, exchanging glances.

"Get those two out of here, Don, please." His voice shook.

"Hey, Jerry, get on the radio to the chief, give him the picture. We need the crime scene boys over here right away."

"Staties, too." Tony called, pleased that his voice was under control. "Looks like a homicide."

They scurried down the hall, and Tony pounded one fist into the other, wishing he'd stuck the bastard himself. Restless, angry, he couldn't just stand around waiting. "I gotta get her out of here."

"Tony, we can't move her!"

"Don't be ridiculous, Don. The poor woman's husband is dead on the kitchen floor," he leaned in closer and whispered, "don't give me the hairy eyeball."

He picked her up from the floor where she sat crumpled like a rag doll and carried her to a kitchen chair. "It'll be okay," he murmured into her hair, "I love you." Patted her shoulder. "I'll get you some water." And to the two numbnuts staring, frozen, in the foyer, "find a blanket, take the lady to the couch in the living room."

"Nothing looks dead like dead, huh, Tony?" His partner still squatted by the body, dropped his voice. "The fuck's going on between you and the woman?"

"Nothin'." But Don kept staring at him, waiting. "I said nothing, f'r crissake."

"Sure, Tony." Don got to his feet; disbelief written clear across his face. "Whatever." He turned on his heel and left the room.

Tony stared at the dead body on the floor, it would feel so good to spit on the bastard! With a backward look at Frank's distorted face he followed his partner down the hall to the front room.

Catherine sat on the edge of a padded gray chair, feet primly crossed at the ankles, hands clasped in her lap. She looked like a queen, holding court. The blues stood around looking tough. Don hung back, ready to take his cue from Tony.

"Is there anyone else in the house, Catherine?"

"Aly? My daughter...?"

"*Mrs.* Moore." Emphasis on the 'Mrs.' Tony let Don take over, realizing he'd called her by her first name. "Mrs. Moore, where's your daughter now?"

"She's fine, Don, neighbor's got her." Tony remembered his promise to Janice. "One of you bozos go across the road to one-ten, get a statement from the lady of the house."

There was a commotion at the door and Tony saw Phil Mulvey, the Medical Examiner and his team of experts, ready to begin their forensic work. He closed the frosted glass French doors and all was quiet.

"Oh my God," Catherine turned pleading eyes to Tony. "Aly came in, I heard the door slam while– after- maybe she saw something. Oh God!"

"We need to talk to the kid sometime." Don made a note on his coiled pad, shoved it into his pocket. "Let's get Mrs. Moore downtown, Tony, maybe she'll have something to tell us there." And to the uniform, "Make sure they've got somebody from Psych ready to talk to her when we get there."

"We need you to come with us now, Mrs. Moore." Don grabbed a damp tweed coat from the hall tree and draped it over her shoulders. "Will your daughter be okay with the neighbor?"

Catherine showed no sign of seeing or hearing, her eyes gazed blankly just past Tony's shoulder, walking zombie-like as Don led her by the hand to the door. Following close behind, Tony snatched up her boots, realizing that she was wearing the bastard's coat.

Thirty-three

The room was claustrophobic, airless, a closet, stinking of sweat and guilt - she couldn't imagine this space in the heat and humidity of summer. It was painted a nasty shade of beige, with bars over a small frosted window set high on the wall. No clock, no phone, a table and two gray plastic chairs. Someone told her she had the right to remain silent, if she said anything it could and would be used against her in a court of law. She had the right to a lawyer – she started wondering about the attorneys she and Kevin knew -- and missed the rest. She tuned in when the door slammed shut behind the woman, leaving her alone with her guilty thoughts, she supposed, so that when the detectives came in she would break down and confess all. Which she did, there was nothing to hide, and in a scrawl she barely recognized as her own Catherine scribbled three pages of the yellow legal pad with all the details as she remembered them.

"Am I under arrest?"

"No ma'am, but we have to hold you overnight as a person of interest in the death of your husband, Francis Moore." Sergeant Perkins, according to the badge on his chest. The other one had identified himself as Detective

Corbett, Tony's partner.

Of course I'm a person of interest, I killed him! She turned to Corbett. "Where's Ton- Detective Costello?"

The two men exchanged glances, raised bushy eyebrows, said nothing.

Within an hour she'd been fingerprinted, photographed, booked and led to a small room in the basement of the police station. Shivering, though it was unbearably warm, Catherine was taken to a holding cell, she supposed, with bars on three sides and no window. Overhead a bulb protected by a screen provided light; a video camera watched from high up in a corner, and against the dirty green wall, a tired gray blanket folded on a thin mat on a bench bolted to the wall.

Tony was pissed, he should have been in on the interrogation, he belonged in that room, how could he protect Catherine out here? He'd been kept out - Don must have given the chief a heads up - soon there'd be questions, questions he dare not answer.

He rocked back and forth in the chair at his desk and brooded in silence, sensing in the air around him that everybody knew, the uniforms had obviously been talking, people tiptoed around him like he was the bereaved.

It was past eleven when Corbett stopped beside his desk in the squad room. "She's fine," a rough whisper, "tucked away safe for the night."

Tony rolled his chair back. "I'm going in there."

"Not smart, Tony." Corbett jabbed at his chest.

"Smart gets you diddly." He spun his chair around.

His partner raised a significant eyebrow. "Tony, tell me what's up–"

"--Later, Don, I'll fill you in later."

"Don't forget, Tony, the walls have eyes."

"Yeah, I'll remember." He took off at a run.

Downstairs in the cell he sat beside Catherine on the hard, narrow cot. She didn't even turn her head.

"Catherine?"

No answer.

"Catherine, you've got to come out of this trance. Your husband's dead and you're a person of interest and you're gonna need a lawyer."

Now she raised eyes round with fear and he took her hand, fuck the camera. Her hand lay in his palm, limp and cold like a dead fish.

"Kevin." Her voice was rough, like bare branches scratching a window.

"Your partner?"

She nodded.

"I'll call him right away." Searched his mind for something good to report. "Alyson's gonna be okay; she's sleeping over at her friend Bonnie's tonight."

"I want Elaine."

"Who's Elaine?"

"My sister. Elaine Browning. In Albany."

She had a sister; he knew so little about this woman. She recited a phone number but he didn't hear, he'd get it later off the tape. Something huge had been on his mind ever since this happened. He leaned toward her. "Catherine, did Frank know about us?" Remembering to whisper.

Her eyes fixed on his, her mouth a thin line.

"Were you fighting about--?"

"You arrogant bastard." Eyes gleaming with anger, Catherine came alive. "There *is* no '*us*', Tony, remember?" She turned her face to the wall. "You've got a wife. Somewhere." She huddled in the corner of the bunk, as far from him as possible. "Go find her."

Tony rubbed at his chin, glanced up at the camera in the corner of the cell. It was all going to be on record, but he couldn't leave her like this. "Catherine, I lov--" His throat closed, choked with tears. "I'll see this through with you."

"I don't need your kind of help, Detective. Go away."

For the second time in a week a woman had flipped him off; he might find that amusing someday.

In the Men's he threw cold water at his face, grimaced into the tin mirror bolted to the wall, and climbed the stairs slowly, trying for composure.

Don Corbett cornered him at the top of the stairwell. "I erased the video, you stupid bastard. Now you'd better talk to   me."

Thirty-four

Laura missed the kids something awful, she had a constant pain in her chest from worrying about them. Her cell had run out of power days ago, they were probably texting like crazy. She itched to phone home, time a call for when Tony would be at work but had no idea what she would say. She was their mother, she loved them, but she had run away. How could she explain what she was doing down here? Time and again she'd pick up the receiver in Sam's kitchen, then hang it up again. Later, she'd call later, when the right words came.

Sam tried to make her see that she had to make contact, to explain her side.

"They're kids, Laura. They'll stop crying for you soon enough, hon, when they're stuck doing their own laundry and feeding themselves. You've gotta get to them before they resent what you've done and won't let you say your piece."

The first time she got the answering machine, listened to her own voice saying sorry we missed you, your call is important to us, please leave your... She hung up.

The next time Anthony picked up, answering with a breezy "Yah?" Thrilled to hear his young man's voice but she couldn't talk to him, she really needed Claudia, the only one of her children who might understand. Once again Laura hung up, hoping he hadn't made note of the number. Come to that, how come Tony hadn't checked caller ID? He could have called her by now.

Finally, Sam talked her into some sense. "You've been sittin' around here eatin' your heart out over those kids. Call them, for heaven's sake, talk to whichever one answers the phone, tell 'em you miss 'em, set your mind at ease." She plucked a jacket off the hook by the back door. "I'm going for a walk." Pointedly leaving Laura alone with the telephone.

"Who's this?" Gina's voice, timid. Hopeful?

In the background Anthony's voice yelling. "Gee, get off the phone."

"Shut up, Ant."

"I said get off the fuckin' phone, I'm waiting for Rob to – "

"Gina? It's Mom! Stop the fighting!"

"Lay off, Anthony!" Whispers through a partially covered receiver. "It's Mom, you stupid turd!" Sounds of scuffling and a door slamming; Gina had taken the phone into the bathroom.

"Mom, where are you?"

"I'm, ah..." Of course, they'd want to know where she was, she'd been stupid to call without having some kind of answer ready. Laura chose to ignore the question. "How are you, *bambina*?"

Laura heard pounding and banging, Anthony's muffled

voice through the door. "Gina, let me talk to her!"

"Sweetie, I just wanted to know how you guys are."

"Well, I guess we're all fine." Gina's little girl voice full of tears.

"Gina, please, don't cry. I'll be home soon."

"Well, you better." Gina sniffled. "Bad things are happening around here. Mrs. Kurtz, Bonnie's Mom?"

"What about her?"

"Bonnie says she's got cancer, she's probably dying. Mom, you gotta come home."

Gina gave a loud shriek, Laura heard the door bang against the wall, then Anthony's voice. "You don't own the phone, you little shit. Give it here.

"Ma? Dad said you'd likely call when you heard."

Hello, Mom. Miss you Mom. "Gina already told me about Mrs. Kurtz."

"Nah, I don't know about that...but Ma, did ya hear about the Moores?"

"Catherine Moore?" Laura's mind raced. The bitch must have left her husband, she'd moved in with Tony, she'd...!

"Not her, Ma, him. Mr. Moore. Well, her too, sorta."

"Jesus, Anthony, get to the point. What the hell happened?"

"He's dead."

Laura tried to take it in. "An accident on the Pike?" She knew he worked in Boston.

"Nope, not in a car, right there in their house!"

"Like a heart attack?"

"No, Mom. Like murder."

"What!" Please God, don't let Tony be involved.

239

"It was all over the news, don't you have a TV?"

"I haven't been watching— When did it happen?"

"Um, couple, three days ago. Mrs. Moore's in jail, and everybody says she did it. Ma, where are you?"

"Didn't you see my texts?"

"I can't find my phone."

"I'm, uh, away for a bit." She heard footsteps, Sam back from her walk on the beach with a thumbs up. "I, I needed a rest."

"Dad says you'll be home soon."

Wishful thinking. "Is Dad there?"

"No, we haven't seen him in ages."

"He left you alone in the house?" *I'll kill the bastard!*

"Ma, I'm hangin' up, Rob's calling—" And he was gone.

Clutching the buzzing phone in Sam's tiny galley kitchen, Laura's mind whirled.

"Guess that didn't go well." Her friend took the receiver from Laura and hung it up on the wall.

"Sam, I don't know where to start." Laura backed into a chair. "All hell's broken loose up there."

"Because of you?"

"Nothing to do with me at all. One of my friends has cancer, and Tony's, um, *lover!* has apparently gone and killed her husband."

"Well, if that don't beat all." Sam's whisper sounded like a prayer.

Stunned, Laura watched the other woman calmly stir the rice simmering on the stove, set the table with two plates, two forks, two knives. "Janice is a big woman, kinda like you, robust, you know? She looked in the peak of health,

240

well except that she fell, hurt her back, sprained her ankle."

"What form of cancer?"

"Gina didn't say."

"Maybe you should give your friend a call, let her know you care. At a time like this that woman is going to need her friends." Sam turned back to the stove. "Dinner in half an hour." Laura picked up the phone.

"Gary? " She took a deep breath, prepared for the inevitable questions. "Laura Costello here."

"Hi there. Howzit going?"

He didn't seem surprised to hear from her, maybe he didn't know, everything he had on his plate. "Fine, great. Look, Gary, I was just talking to my Gina and she said Janice..."

"...has cancer." He sounded robotic. "Diagnosed a week or so ago."

"Can they do--?"

"Ovarian."

The worst.

"Doctor says by the time the tumors are big enough to see it's too late."

"Is there anything I can do?"

"Pray." His voice broke. "My Jan'll need all the help she can get."

"Gary, take down this number. I'm down in, ah, South Carolina, visiting a friend, but I'll be home soon. If you need me for anything, just call. Tell Janice I'm pulling for her. Give her my love..."

Laura waited until he'd repeated Sam's number, then hung up fast so he wouldn't hear her burst into tears.

Thirty-five

Catherine didn't sleep that night, the longest of her life. Every time she closed her eyes she saw Frank staring up at her, dead on the kitchen floor. The knife in her hand, and the blood, one drop at a time pinging on the tile floor.

The silence was terrifying. Oh, there were sounds; clanging steel doors, boots tromping up and down the corridor past the row of steel cages. There were three other cells, only one occupied by a very old man, a street person, she thought, who snuffled and snored on his narrow bench throughout the night.

But no voices, she hadn't heard a single word spoken after Tony left her. Until this morning. She knew it was morning by the increased activity around the guards' desk and not by any hint of sunrise. "Arraignment at 9. Get up." It was 5.30 a.m. She'd been on the move ever since.

A hefty, pear-shaped female officer led her by the arm to a massive white tiled room. Along one wall half a dozen shower heads hung from the ceiling in plain view of each other. On a narrow steel shelf were a sliver of yellow soap, a cheap plastic comb, a folded towel thin as toilet paper, and an unwrapped toothbrush, possibly left there by the last woman in here. She wouldn't touch it, rubbing her teeth with a corner of the sad grayish towel instead. She turned on the shower and stood under it facing the wall, grateful to be in here alone, trying not to think of the person undoubtedly watching on a hidden camera.

Every sound echoed off the tiles, making the weak stream of water sound like a raging waterfall. She towel-dried her long hair and tugged the comb through it, her thoughts turning to Alyson, surely terrified and feeling abandoned by the mother who loved her.

She dressed in her own clothes. Someone, Janice, she hoped and not some ham-handed cop, had brought her a fresh sweater, slacks and clean underwear along with boots and her warm down filled coat.

A tray had been left for her in the cell. Cold toast, a tiny packet of cream cheese - no knife - and terrible coffee. Breakfast.

Next had come the humiliating walk, the perp walk? With yet another pear-shaped - was the big butt a requirement for the job? - female officer's gloved hand clamped onto her arm, a large male in front and another behind. Catherine was taken outside, shivering, to a police car. No handcuffs - a small mercy - especially when Catherine spotted a young man with a camera; she'd be front-page news in the *Gilford Daily* this afternoon. They drove to the courthouse. No lights. No siren. No talking. Seven a.m.

At the courthouse, Catherine was taken to a stuffy little room without windows, paneled in dark wood, an empty bookcase on one wall and two chairs. The officer pointed at one. She sat. The woman stood by the door, legs spread, arms loose at her sides, near the holster. Did they expect her to make a run for it? It was funny; except it was not. The door closed with a loud thud and a click. She was locked in this tiny room with the stone-faced woman.

"What is arraignment?" She had screwed up the courage to ask, now that it was imminent.

"You'll find out soon enough." With a hint of a smile, the officer glanced at the heavy gold watch on her wrist.

After an exhausting wait of an hour or more a section of the paneling opened inward and Catherine was pushed into a tiny vestibule facing two massive oak doors. With what might have been a sympathetic smile, the female cop handed her over to a male. The doors opened, and she was looking into a courtroom. Oak paneled walls, soft gray chairs, and a cloudy December sky through huge windows. A raised seat, for the judge, or the Lord High Executioner - she covered the nervous laugh with a cough.

At the back of the room Kevin paced, and beside him, a young man, tall, slender, hugging a thin laptop to his chest. Most likely a paralegal, from Larry Sheldon's office, dressed in jeans and plaid flannel shirt and, oh my god, a tie. He couldn't be more than twenty years of age.

Kevin rushed toward her. "Catherine, thank God! I tried to get you out of here last night but–" The deputy stopped him with a hand in the air.

"Hey! Get the hell–"

"It's okay, Kevin, I'm okay."

A male voice bellowed "All rise!" and a firm grip on her arm led her to the front of the room. "This court is now in session."

"Good morning," from the Judge. No one responded.

"Madam Clerk, please call the first case."

A woman stood up. "Your Honor, though the defendant has no priors, this is capital murder case, and the Court recommends that she be incarcerated without bond until trial."

"Who is she?" Catherine whispered to the young man who had rushed to her side.

He had thick dark hair that fell over his eyes when he bent his head. He turned to answer, and she saw intelligent, attentive brown eyes magnified by plain gold rimmed glasses. "The ADA."

"And the defendant's position?" From the judge.

"Good morning, Judge." The young man stood up. "David Sheldon for the defendant." He cleared his throat. "This arraignment came to my attention very early this morning, sir, and I apologize for my casual dress."

"Right. How does your client plead?"

Arraignment seemed to mean entering a plea before a judge. What language did that come from, Catherine wondered, her mind a million miles away.

"Not guilty, your Honor."

Thanks to her confession, she was no longer a 'Person of Interest" but a criminal, charged with Murder Two.

"Your Honor, the defendant has no priors, and is not a threat to society. She is a well-respected local business woman, the mother of a young child. She has the right to assist in the preparation of her defense, and it is necessary for her to be free on bail to assist her attorneys."

Catherine followed the proceedings strangely detached, as if she were watching *Law and Order* on TV. A million dollar bond was posted, using her house and the brokerage as collateral. The judge and the clerk, a wizened little elf of a woman, set the trial date for March the twenty-first, a Monday. What could be finer than to go on trial for murder on the first day of Spring? Catherine stifled a nervous giggle.

She signed a pile of papers and followed the young man out of the courtroom into the brilliant sunshine of a cold December morning, and Kevin's hug. "Free as a bird, isn't that right, Counselor?"

"Yes, with a few minor constraints."

Kevin gave her a resounding kiss. "This, my dear, is David Sheldon. Esquire." He took the boy's hand. "Your attorney."

This child was going to defend her.

"I know he looks young," said Kevin, apparently seeing her look of disbelief, "but the boy's getting himself quite a reputation."

"Has the… this boy finished high school?" Rude, she was being terribly rude.

"Yes, dear," a chuckle, "graduated Harvard Law and passed the Massachusetts bar first try!" He patted the young man's shoulder. "Larry's son."

Larry Sheldon, the lawyer they retained for legal advice and representation in their real estate dealings, and a close personal friend of Kevin's. "Where is Larry?"

"He practices civil law, but his pride and joy is a criminal lawyer. Kid looks twenty-one, but he's thirty-seven and a partner in a small firm in Roxbury. Defends people who can't defend themselves." Kevin rubbed his hands together, content that her fate was in the hands of this child.

"But why did you know to call Larry?"

"I got a phone call late last night, midnight I think, telling me what happened." He looked uncomfortable.

"Who called--?"

Kevin looked off into the distance, as if trying to remember. "Umm, one of the detectives. Costello, I think."

Thank you, Tony, God bless you, Tony.

"Now, son, what's next!"

"Now I talk - privately - to Mrs. Moore. We only have thirty days to present…

Blah, blah… she knew it was important, but he was talking in a language she didn't understand.

…before March twenty-first." He turned away from Kevin. "Mrs. Moore, can we go somewhere and talk?"

"Let's go ho —no, I don't think I…"

"No problem, you're staying with us." Kevin's head bobbed into view around the thin young lawyer. "Jean would love to have you, we've got that guest suite downstairs. It'll be perfect, Catherine, until you get your head together. I'll just call Jeannie…" He turned away to mumble into his cell phone.

"Mrs. Moore," Sheldon leaned in close, "you'll be permitted to travel in town from your home - or wherever you are registered to live for the next three months - to your office; the grocery store; your daughter's school."

Catherine breathed a sigh of relief.

"Do not talk to anyone but me. Anything you tell me is confidential, I cannot repeat it, but whatever you say to anyone else can be used in court against you." He rested both hands on her shoulders. "Am I making myself clear?"

"Yes, yes, of course."

"You will be subject to electronic monitoring. You'll wear an ankle bracelet–" He saw her look of shock. "You're imagining the Denver Boot, but they are quite thin now, almost invisible."

After she had the damned thing clamped around her ankle - thin and invisible, my ass - David led her to Kevin's Cadillac. "Now we talk."

"No. First a long, hot bath - I feel filthy. And coffee, I can't describe the gunk they served me at the station this morning."

"Sometimes Frank would come home in a rage, go straight to bed and sleep until morning ..." Catherine faltered, stopped. *There would never be another morning for Frank.*

He had given her a couple of days to get herself together. Despite his warning, she had called her sister, Frank's brother Ben, and tried to talk to Alyson, a one-sided conversation;, her daughter refused to say a word. Today, sitting across from Sheldon's intent young face, Catherine tried to describe her life.

"And other times, Mrs. Moore?"

"You had to know Frank. He was an angry man, felt he'd been shortchanged in life. Put himself through night school and got a decent job in an investment firm. Frank is... was a very bright man, but he had a temper. He felt shafted at work, got angry when promotions he thought should be his went to other people. But he didn't have the, I don't know, the courage, the self-confidence, to leave.

Instead he'd come home and take out his frustrations on me." She took a sip of water from the bottle he'd thoughtfully put in front of her.

"He didn't like me working ... Frank had this old-fashioned notion that a man looked bad if his wife had a job! Hated my success but envied me at the same time, dealt with it by intimidating me, humiliating me... but I'm rambling, and you're a very patient young man."

"My job. Can you tell me how Frank humiliated you?"

"He'd put me down, in public, or talk around me as if I wasn't there."

"And in private...?"

"Physically." She mumbled. "Sexually."

"Tell me what happened the other evening."

She took a deep breath. "Apparently he'd had a lousy day and the roads were bad. He said there'd been accidents and traffic on the Pike was a nightmare. But I had a horrible cold, and I'd been psyching myself up all day to talk to him. In an incredible example of bad timing I met him at the door and told him I wanted a divorce. In a flash he lost his temper, started shouting, punching me."

While she talked, he typed furiously on his laptop, the tip of his tongue tracing his upper lip. "For no reason."

"I guess asking for a divorce might be seen as reason enough."

"But the other times?" The attorney's dark eyes pierced hers.

"Frank would invent things to feed his anger, like his crazy idea that I, uh..." She stared down at the carpet, wringing her tightly clasped hands.

"And were you?"

"Um. No."

"Mrs. Moore, if I'm going to help you, I have to know it all. Were you having an extramarital affair?"

"No. I...not really."

"Not really...?"   He pounded a fist on his desk. "Mrs. Moore, in all the years you were married, were you ever involved with another man?"

She hung her head.

"Mrs...Catherine," gentler now, "the prosecution will dig up as much dirt as they can."

"There was, ah, once—"

"When?"

"For a very short time." She raised her eyes to meet his. "It's over now."

"But your husband knew about it."

"God, no - he wouldn't have let that slip past him." *He would have killed me.* "Throughout our marriage Frank's fantasies gave him an excuse to intimidate me, Mr. Sheldon."

"Please, call me David. What do you mean by that?"

"It was a game he played." She folded her arms and curled in on herself. "He'd accuse me of having sex with other men, threaten to kill me, slap me around a little, and when he was good and mad, he... he'd..."

His voice was soft. "Rape you?"

She nodded.

"Did that happen last Tuesday night?"

"No. I was stupid. Said I wanted a divorce, and of course he went... ballistic!"

"Catherine, this is not on you. You didn't ask for a

beating, and you fought back with whatever came to hand."

"Frank is- was, a big man." She clutched her arms across her chest, trembling.

"Tell me what happened the other night."

"Oh God, um…" trying to remember the sequence of events and not the terror. "Frank had me pinned to the newel post at the bottom of the stairs. He punched me and I started to fall. Picked up his briefcase." The words were coming faster now. "I hit him with it, and I kicked him. Hard. When he clutched himself, I shoved him and ran to the kitchen… he was after me like a shot, cursing, swearing, damn it, he never stopped cursing…!"

Sheldon waited, patient.

"…He caught me near the back door..." She could hardly breathe, reliving the terror.

"I know this is hard, Mrs. Moore, but I need the whole picture. He cornered you near the door..."

"By the stove, yes... had his hands around my neck, choking me."

"The bruises around your neck." David made a note on his pad. "And then?"

"The knife rack, on the wall, a magnetic bar - Frank put it up last summer." She felt in her pocket for a tissue. "All my knives. I grabbed one and, I, uh ..." She sniffled.

"Was the blade, say, seven or eight inches long?"

"Eight..." She could see the knife in her trembling hand. "French chef's knife. Very sharp. F-Frank liked to keep them sh-sha..." Tears streamed down her cheeks.

The lawyer handed her a tissue. "I'm sorry, Mrs. Moore, but we have to go on. You say Frank trapped you in the kitchen and tried to strangle you." He consulted his notes. "In your panic, while your husband was trying to kill you, you grabbed a weapon, a carving knife, and stabbed him twice, once in the in the shoulder, once in the neck, striking and puncturing the jugular vein. Is that right?"

Shuddering at the harsh words. "Yes."

"In court the prosecutor will suggest that you lured your husband into the kitchen so you could conveniently bump him off."

"Oh, my God…"

"Because you were fooling around with another man."

"No!" Again she broke down; he tossed the box of tissues into her lap. "Tell me about this other man."

Dropping her head, Catherine twisted the diamond on her wedding band around her finger. "The…my friend was sympathetic, cared about me. He came to my office to talk…" All the while memories flashed through her mind. The night at the lake, meetings in her office, drinks in one out-of-town bar or another, the hotel in Cambridge…

"A Prosecutor will say you wanted your husband out of the way. Could she dig up anything - photos, credit card receipts, witnesses - regarding this aff--?"

"I told you, there was no affair!"

He snorted his disbelief. Stared into her eyes. Waited.

"It was short and… it's over."

He rocked back in his chair, crossed his long, skinny legs. "Better hope you didn't leave a trail." Scanned the laptop screen. "How often did your husband beat you up?"

"Frequently."

"Catherine, I'm your attorney; your only friend. How

often did your husband physically abuse you? Once a month? Every week? Twice a year?"

"What difference does it make how often? He did it, he hurt me. Once should be more than enough."

"Yes Ma'am, but you tell me it was frequent, and yet you stayed with him."

"I was afraid of him, of what he might do to me if I left him. And I was worried about Alyson."

"Did he ever attack her?"

"He went for her once, but I called–"

"911? There'll be a record..." His fingers flew over the keys. "Who answered the call?"

"Ton-- Detective Costello..."

Her voice had softened, and David was ready. "Ah, at last, the other man."

She sighed. "It's over... "

"It's relevant. Detective Costello. Gilford P.D.?"

She nodded.

"He was the first officer on the scene. After you... did you call 911 or call him directly?"

"I asked for Detective Costello."

"Well, won't the Prosecutor have fun with that!"

Catherine gazed out the window, noted that it was snowing again.

"Did you and Costello go out in town together? Restaurants, clubs, anywhere people might see you together?"

"Never- yes, once."

"And that was...?"

"Last August. Just after a really bad, um, incident with

Frank, a week or so after Tony came to the house the first time. We met in the grocery store, by accident, you know how you run into someone, and we got to talking and went next door for coffee. But there was nothing-!"

"Yeah, sure..." He leaned back in his swivel chair. "Did anyone see you there, someone who might testify?"

"Oh, Lord, I don't know - the waitress in the coffee shop, I guess. She seemed to know Tony pretty well ... but what would she say?"

"The prosecutor can make it sound like you two looked pretty cozy together - doesn't take much to plant doubts in the minds of a jury... was that the only time you were out in public?"

"A couple of times we grabbed a bite to eat at the Chinese place on Union Street. But that was before... After... it started, we were careful."   In retrospect, even to her, "it" sounded cheap, and dirty.

At last he let her go. She had to get to the house, needed clothes and toiletries. Driving slowly up to the spacious white colonial - home for the past four years, she wondered what it would sell for. Alyson had chosen to stay with Bonnie, but this time of day the girls were at school. Just as well; Catherine didn't think she could face her daughter today. She trudged up the unplowed driveway in shoes, reminded herself to find winter boots. Gathering courage, she ducked under the yellow tape, tapped in Frank's birthdate with trembling fingers and stood inside, dazed. Studiously avoiding the hallway leading to the kitchen, she took a deep breath and turned up the stairs to her bedroom, the bathroom, threw a few things into a duffle bag and let it drop over the railing to the foyer below. Slowly following it down, she crumpled on the bottom step and stared vacantly at nothing.

Sheldon found her there half an hour later. "I told you to wait for me," he said, "Do you have boots?" Grabbing her bag in one hand, he led her to her car with the other. "Think you can drive?"

"Yeah, I'm fine."

"I see that. I'll follow you to Kevin's."

Once she was settled in an armchair in the Casey's living room, he got right to the point. "We have a good case for self-defense. You were a battered wife for many years, afraid to leave your vicious husband, he threatened to kill you. And your little girl. During one of his violent beatings you ki-!"

Catherine flinched.

"Self-defense..." He leaned back in the chair, traced his upper lip with the tip of his tongue. "Any of your neighbors see or hear anything?"

"Only one. Janice Kurtz - from across the street - came in while Frank was shouting and throwing things at me."

David wrote down Janice's name and address, as well as the names of the neighbors on either side.

"I have to talk to your daughter."

"She's only twelve. Can't we spare—?"

"You said she came into the house; saw what happened. The prosecution will try to make her testify. I'll see what I can do." With a grave smile and a firm handshake, he turned to leave.

"Oh, one more thing. You'll have to go for an evaluation."

"You mean an insanity kind of thing?"

"Nope. For self-defense to stand up in court it has to be determined that you were a victim of abuse and not a conniving, evil murderer." Grinning, he took her stone-cold hand in his. "Meantime get your life in order. Take care of your daughter." He looked around Kevin's living room. "You'll want the best facility, I'm sure. I'll make arrangements to get you into McLean."

She had eight days to get ready.

Gary Kurtz offered to take care of things at the house.

Kevin wondered if it was too soon to start the process of putting the place on the market.

Frank's half-brother, Ben, arranged the cremation, the obituary. "Suddenly, at home...survived by his wife Catherine and loving daughter Alyson..." *Bless you, Ben.*

Her dear friends, trying to help, but Catherine's biggest heartbreak was Alyson. She was still at the Kurtz's, having flat-out refused to come near Catherine. Janice reported that Alyson stayed in the bedroom she shared with Bonnie, wouldn't talk to anyone, including the police or Catherine's lawyer. "She keeps asking for Max," Janice said, "Who is Max?"

"Her stuffed monkey; she never sleeps without him."

"I'll send Bonnie over to get him."

There was only one more week of school before the Christmas holidays, but Alyson refused to go. Bonnie said she hadn't been to school since the... since. She didn't want to face the other kids. Worse, she wanted no contact with her mother.

It was Janice's uninformed (and unsolicited) opinion that the girl was torn between love for her mother and horror of what she'd done, and mixed emotions for her father, whose approval she'd probably spent all of her twelve years trying to obtain. "I think she needs to see a therapist, and soon." But Alyson refused that too.

Elaine offered to drive down and take her up to Albany for the Christmas holidays. Aly had barely nodded her head, but she let Elaine pack a little bag for her. "Not to worry, Cat, I'll pick up whatever else she needs."

On the twentieth of December, a short service was held at the mortuary for Frank. Catherine attended; Alyson came with Gary Kurtz but did not cry or acknowledge her mother. Immediately following Frank's burial, Elaine took Alyson to Albany.

Later the same day Catherine checked into McLean's.

Thirty-six

"That was Tony."

Fifteen minutes earlier Sam had passed the phone over to Laura and discreetly left the kitchen. "So he said." She poured two glasses of chilled tomato juice and led the way to the front room.

Laura leaned against the wall, one eye on the game show Sam was obviously pretending to watch. "He said he got your number from Gina, who copied it from Janice Kurtz's bulletin board."

"Unhunh."

For some reason Laura felt she had to justify talking to her husband. "Well, he'd gone to the trouble of calling, I couldn't just hang up on him." She folded herself into one of Sam's director's chairs. "He *begged* me to come home, Sam."

"And you said?"

"I'm not ready." Laura studied Sam out of the corner of her eye, anxious for her reaction. "I thought that was pretty good, I'm not ready. I need more time, I said."

"Good girl!" Sam slapped the table with her palm. "And what did good ole Tony say to that?"

"He wants to come down here. To see me. To talk."

"And you said...?"

"I said yes. What else?"

"No. You could have said no. If you really didn't want to see him."

"But I don't know if that's what I really want." Laura tossed her head. "That's why I need time."

Running away had only made things worse, it was all so frustrating. "I've been here three weeks, Sam, and the only thing I'm sure of is that I miss my kids like crazy. But Tony? I've spent most of my life with him." Laura squeezed her eyes shut. "I just don't know."

Sam stood up, wrapped her arms around Laura, and whispered, "changing your life takes time."

Laura rested her head on her friend's chest. "If I go back it'll look like I'm okay with what he did and I'm not." She sniffed. "But I miss him, you know?"

"Yes, hon, I do." Sam's strong fingers began kneading Laura's shoulders, her neck, gently tracing her ears - it all felt suddenly too intimate and Laura tried to pull away.

"Sit." Sam believed a person could be healed body and soul simply by touch. Laura remembered the night Sam brought her here from the beach, nearly had to carry her after the pot experiment, made her lie down on the bed. Laura had felt a flutter of fear, was this a sexual thing, what if Sam's oiled, scented fingers went places they shouldn't? But they didn't, and from the first stroke of those strong hands her tension and anger drained away like melting ice cream. Laura sighed, relaxing under the big woman's soothing hands.

"You've given that man how many years? Fifteen?"

"Seventeen. Nearly eighteen."

"So, he owes you a few weeks. When's he coming?"

"Soon as he can." Laura slapped her forehead. "I've got to find him a place to stay." She tried to wriggle out of Sam's grasp.

Sam's powerful hands held her in the chair. "Let the man worry about himself. It's off-season, he'll have his choice of empty motels up and down the strip - *if* he forgets to book a room. In my experience, men usually manage to see to their own comforts. What you need to focus on is what you want to do with the rest of your life."

Restless, Laura wandered back to the kitchen, dropped into a kitchen chair. Sam brought their glasses and sat across the table in the other half yellow/half blue vinyl and chrome chair, 'not antique, hon, just real old'. Laura's fingers traced the row of brass tacks around the seat. "I've been afraid to think about that."

"I'm bettin' you won't go back."

Laura raised her eyes. "Why do you say that?"

"If you intended to go back home with Tony your li'l heart would be just a-thumping away, bumpity bump, in that tiny bird sized chest of yours." Sam's eyes held Laura's over the rim of her glass. "My sense is that it's not."

"You're right. I don't seem to care much about what Tony did. The only feeling I have is a sick one at the pit of my stomach whenever I think of my children." Laura dropped her head on her arms. "Oh Sam, what am I going to do?"

Sam's voice changed, hardened. "Now you listen up,

woman. Let that man bamboozle you into going home with him and you've gone through all this for nothing. You've gotta *want* to go back to him, it should be burnin' a hole in your heart and your soul. If you don't feel one hunderd and one percent ready don't you take a single step. You've made the break, Laura, the tough stuff is behind you. Now it's time to worry about yourself." She stood and pushed Laura's glass closer. "Drink up, hon."

"Oh yeah, plain old tomato juice is *exactly* what I need."

"You've been doing real good. Don't you go fallin' back on me now."

With her lips pursed, hands on ample hips, Sam reminded Laura of her mother. Laughing, she drank the juice in one long gulp. "Sam, you're an angel." She kissed the big woman on the cheek and felt herself blush. She pushed her arms into one of Sam's shapeless gray sweatshirts drooping from a hook by the door. "Think I'll take a walk."

Sam's little cottage was not on the ocean, those expensive views were for the tourists, who stayed for a week or two in the 20-30 story condos obliterating the beautiful beaches of Myrtle Beach from the peons. But, unlike most of Massachusetts' oceanfront, the beach beyond the towers and the dunes was public land, and Laura covered the few blocks to the wide strip of white sand in five minutes. After weeks of hard daily walking with and without her watchdog Sam, Laura felt strong, like she could easily walk five miles without coughing and wheezing now that she'd quit drinking.

She sat on the beach with her back to the seawall,

zipped up the gray sweatshirt against the chill breeze. Breathed in the salt-laden air; *Madonn'*, she loved this place. Less than a week to Christmas and she was sitting on a beach in a sweatshirt. Tony had said it was snowing again in Massachusetts, might be a white Christmas after all. Like that was supposed to lure her home.

She watched the sky turn rose and mauve; counted the interval between waves. Each one took seven, eight seconds to roll in, spread and darken the sand, tugging at pebbles and shells on the beach as it went back where it came from and crashed into the next one.

She drew up her knees, tugged Sam's huge shirt down over her bare legs and asked herself something she'd been avoiding all week. What was going on with her and Sam? The question filled her mind, driving out any thought of Tony and the kids. Was she attracted to the big woman in a sexual way? Had she felt a little tug of desire back there? Would she have liked Sam to touch her--? Could she be a—? Nah; grateful, thankful, nothing more. But still...

She watched a tiny crab pick its dainty way toward her over shells and ropes of seaweed until a sudden wave lifted and carried him off to sea. Poor thing, all that work. Did crabs know how to swim? She watched him tumble round and round, tossed this way and that by the water, then he seemed to give up the fight and get dragged under, only to come up on the beach not ten feet away from her. Hurray! He stood for a moment, waving his claws in the air as if to celebrate his lucky escape, then rushed off again, like Alice's rabbit. A survivor, that little guy.

And me? Can I make it on my own? All her life

Laura'd had someone to depend on, first her father, then Tony. It was scary to imagine being without him, but the past few years, with all their fighting, Tony and his other women - she knew he'd had others no matter what he said - drinking away her days and nights, was no life at all. They were all losing that way, especially the kids.

Down here she felt independent. Kind of. Laura shuddered. If it hadn't been for Sam she probably would have drowned herself that first night. But here she was taking vitamins, drinking tomato juice and tea and eating like a pig, Sam was on a crusade to put meat on her bones. Sundays she went with Sam to her church, a Southern Baptist kind of place where everyone swayed and sang at the tops of their lungs - she was turning into a fuckin' holy roller. 'S'cuse me, Sam, a plain old holy roller.

She might even have a job. Beanie was looking for a way to attract more people to his restaurant, and Sam had suggested Laura put her voice to use, she claimed to be sick of hearing her humming and singing around the house day and night. Sam had an alto voice, not a good one, but they'd been having fun harmonizing *Amazing Grace* and old standards from the forties; *Whispering Hope, Harbor Lights*, stuff her father used to sing.

Laura's relationship with her father had been one of love/hate. She remembered sneaking into the *Mezzanotte,* the local hangout her uncle Santino owned on Hanover Street, while the guys in Papa's band rehearsed on a Friday or Saturday afternoon. Sometimes they let her sing with them, she couldn't have been more than fourteen, fifteen. She could still remember the cold of the chrome mic in her hand, the sweet smell of beer and sawdust, like hay in the sunshine. The little black cheroot clutched in Santino's wet lips, her father's mustard yellow suspenders.

"Let the girl sing with us, Aldo. That sweet voice will charm the money right out of their pockets."

"And something else right out of their pants," with a snap of his suspenders, "I'll be in my grave, Santin', before my *bambina* sings in a bar!"

Laura brushed sand off the backs of her legs, remembering family friends who'd offered to take her to New York, stay with her. "She's opera material, Aldo, give her a chance."

"My little girl stays here where I can keep an eye on her."

Thanks, Papa. He'd been in the ground seven, eight years, maybe her time had come. To sing in a bar. To stand on her own.

Were all men like him? So protective of their daughters, so cruel to their wives. All the years of her parents' marriage, papa leaving the house after dinner, saying he was going to the Italian Club, Santin's, or the bowling alley, when the whole neighborhood knew Aldo Mercurio was visiting a woman.

Tony's father had been the same, maybe every man in the North End had a mistress. Did her mother know? Of course, everyone knew. Did those wives accept it as normal? Was Tony merely following in his father's footsteps?

Tony had sworn for years there hadn't been any other women, not in Boston or in Gilford, but Catherine Moore was living proof. And after catching him in the act only a fool would believe a single word that came out of that liar's mouth. Laura could never go back to trusting Tony. And wasn't that the bottom line in a marriage, trust with a capital T? Well, she'd lost it.

And she had to admit that their marriage had been in trouble long before Catherine came on the scene. If Tony had been in love with her, no other woman would have been able to turn his head. And if she had truly loved him, trust would not have become an issue.

Maybe Tony had fallen for Catherine, maybe she hadn't deliberately set out to trap him. If she met Catherine on the street today Laura probably wouldn't push her in front of a bus, but no way was she going to forgive her or Tony; those two deserved each other. And if Catherine really did kill her husband for Tony, well, good luck to them.

The only attraction back in Gilford were the kids. They were almost adults with lives of their own, didn't have a thimbleful of respect for her, their mother. She knew they saw her as a drunk, and sure enough if she went back she'd turn into that woman again. Lots of people had long distance relationships with their children, and they all survived, selfish as that sounded. What did she have to gain by going back? Absolutely nothing.

But this place, and her dear friend Sam, were good therapy. If she stayed here and got a job - any job - she could contribute her share. Looking deep inside herself, Laura saw that in the past few weeks she'd regained some of her self-respect.

Overhead stars began to twinkle, faint but visible; she should think about getting back to the cottage. Wiping sand off her legs, she noticed that her feet had been digging trenches in the damp sand. Not one, but two separate tracks. It seemed significant in some stupid way and she began to cry.

"I see by the tears that you've made up your mind." Sam's voice behind her, whisper soft against the rumble of the surf.

Laura nodded, swiped at her eyes with the back of her hand, stood and turned to face the other woman. "I'd like to stay here for a while. I'll get a job, find a place—"

"You know I'd like you to stay with me." Sam's heavy hand on her shoulder was reassuring. "Friends. Unless or until you say otherwise—"

Friends? Maybe more... Realizing she was stepping off a ledge into the unknown, Laura moved into the circle of Sam's arms. "I think I'd like that."

Sam held her close for a long moment, then whispered, "When are you going to let the dear man know?"

"As soon as possible."

Thirty-seven

Goddam piece of--! The zipper on this old suitcase always stuck. Tony willed himself to work it gently so the damned thing wouldn't split on him, it was the only one left since Laura had taken off with the new one.

In the girls' bedroom Claudia and Gina were screaming obscenities at each other - he didn't want to get into it. No doubt about it, life was much easier with their mother around. He rapped his knuckles on their door on his way to the kitchen. "Cool it ladies!"

Tony still wasn't thrilled about dragging the kids down to South Carolina, but they were his ace in the hole. One thing for sure, Laura was nuts about her children. One look at their faces and she'd come home, damn it, she had to, they had to get their shit back together.

He'd never been much of a drinker, but he liked the occasional beer. He drank straight out of the can, enjoying the cold bitter liquid trickle down his throat, then he aimed the empty can at the overflowing trash bag in the corner. It missed, rolled across the kitchen floor. Be good to have Laura back, live in a tidy house again. Plus, he was damned sick and tired of trucking kids all over town, buying groceries, fighting with the girls to keep up the house, smelling cigarette smoke - or worse - on Anthony's breath and unable to catch him. These kids needed a full-time keeper and Tony wasn't it, he had too much on his plate and more important things on his mind.

He couldn't sit still. Grabbed another beer - maybe Laura wasn't the only alkie around here. Rested his forehead against the cold slider window. Watched the snowflakes fall and thought about Catherine. He hadn't seen her at all, his big-mouth partner had felt honor bound to tell the boss about Tony's involvement in the Moore thing, even though he, Tony, didn't know the first damned thing about why she did the bastard in. Took a lot of guts for a woman to stab her husband to death, she must have been under incredible provocation. Tony did not know Frank very well, but he knew the man was a prick, understood the abuse she had taken. Well, maybe he'd get called as a character witness, screw that guy's reputation right into the ground.

He was pacing again; back and forth across the living room. Thanks to his hypocrite partner, who probably had his own little chickie on the side, everybody in the precinct now knew about him and Catherine. Tony had seen the smirks, the raised eyebrows, the dirty little minds wondering if he'd had something to do with the perp offing her husband. But right now he had to finish packing. It would be good to get away from here for a few days, give the rumor mill time to grind to a halt.

Claudia and Gina were still going at it in their bedroom. Tony flung open their door. "Girls, girls! *Basta!* Enough!"

"Daddy, Claudia's hogging the whole bag for her stupid

289

make-up!"

"Gina has five pairs of jeans in there, Dad. But it's okay, I'll shove my stuff into a grocery bag for all I care!"

"Girls, fighting isn't going to help anything."

"Don't see why we have to be dragged all the way down there anyway." Gina had her back turned but she grumbled loud enough for Tony's ears.

"Gina, we're a family."

"Oh sure, when it's convenient." She turned to face him, eyes shiny with tears.

Convenient? What the hell was that supposed to mean. Tony knew he should try to get to the bottom of Gina's discontent, but tonight just wasn't the right time. "Look... Gina, we're not getting into that now. We're all going, so just pack up your stuff and stop this damned fighting!"

Tony opened Anthony's bedroom door. "How you doing, son?"

The boy sat cross-legged on the floor with his back to the door, nodding and bobbing his head to the squealing noises spilling out of the red earbuds stuck in his ears.

"ANTHONY!"

Pulling one of the plugs out of his ear, his son slowly turned a long-suffering, aggrieved face toward him. "Geez, Dad, ya don't have ta yell."

"You're gonna go deaf with that damned racket blasting in your ears!"

Demonstrating his irritation, Anthony slowly removed the other plug from his ear and held them both in his lap, his expression blank. From across the room Tony heard the tinny sound of rock music squeaking in his hand.

"Whattaya want with me?"

"Are you all packed?"

"Sure, Dad.   Anthony waved a ragged pair of jeans in the air.   His tiny backpack, too small for Claudia's make-up, overflowed with disks and a portable CD player, a plaid shirt and one pair of socks.   Tony didn't see any underwear.   He watched his son stuff the jeans in on top and zip the bag shut.

Tony rolled his eyes to heaven.   "Don't forget a toothbrush and a change of underwear, for crissake!"

"Right, dad.   Shut the door on your way out."

Tony did as he was told, walked past the argument still raging in the girls' room to the living room.   He had to step over hockey equipment and about fifteen pairs of shoes and boots by the front door; Laura would have a fit if she saw the mess.   Tony didn't know how she did it, yelling at the kids got him nothing but sulking and slammed doors.

Outside, the drizzle that had been falling all day had turned to wet heavy snow, the first real snowfall of the season.   The weather guys didn't expect much accumulation, but the woman at the airline advised him to check with Logan in the morning.

He'd booked a two-leg flight - direct was too expensive. He hadn't told the kids, but they had a two-hour flight to Raleigh, a couple of hours to kill there, and another two and a half hours to Myrtle Beach, they wouldn't be landing until four!

"And remember, sir, be at the airport two hours before flight time."

Seven; he had to get the kids to Logan by seven, they

had to be ready to leave the house by five-thirty, six. Goddam terrorists. Might as well stay up the rest of the night for all the sleep he was going to get.

He dropped heavily on the couch, grunting like an old man, and shoved Laura's afghan out of his way. Now she was hiding out in South Carolina. Catherine was stuck in a psych hospital over the Christmas holidays for a ten-day 'victim of abuse' eval. At least she could afford McLean's and escape the humiliation that was Bridgewater.

It had to be obvious that she'd killed that asshole in self-defense, Christ, Tony had seen right off the bastard was trouble. If Catherine had simply left the jerk none of this would have happened. What bugged him the most was that if he'd had his shit together they might have had a chance. But he hadn't, and now Catherine didn't want anything to do with him. He felt responsible, somehow, for the whole damned mess.

If it went to trial, which of course it would, he'd be called to testify, him and Don, probably, the first responders at the scene. The prosecution would be digging around for dirt, suppose they found out about him and Catherine? If they hit him with the right questions, how was he going to answer without perjuring himself?

Tony, he sighed, look at you, pining over another woman the very night you're going to try to get your wife back.

Had Laura heard about it? Probably not, a piddly little incident of domestic violence didn't go national unless an O.J. Simpson was involved.

Down the hall the girls were still at it, their shrill voices rising over Anthony's music and all of it blasting through the house. They were all so angry, everybody in this damned house was angry! Here he was taking them to the ocean, sunshine and beaches, a Christmas vacation most kids would jump at, and these little snots didn't want to go. All he'd heard for days was whining about the parties, the dances they were going to miss. And worse yet, they didn't seem to care about Laura at all.

"Your mother needs you," he had explained, a few days ago. "We all have to go."

"Sure, Dad. Mom really cares about us, guess that's why she took off."

"Gina, can't you think of anybody besides yourself?"

Were they hurting, or just selfish? "This is a bad time for your mother, guys."

"Why don't you go by yourself?" Gina's tiny fist slammed into his bicep. "It's all your fault anyway."

Claudia with tears in her eyes, Gina lay sobbing on her bed. Nobody was happy, and he supposed that was his fault too. And here, he almost laughed out loud, here was the irony. At the crack of dawn, after worrying all night about another woman, he'd be hustling a trio of miserable brats onto a plane to coax their mother, his wife, a woman he didn't love any more, to come back home. Christ, life was the pits.

Thirty-eight

She stood at the barred window, seeing nothing in the gathering darkness but the rain. Christmas Eve in Boston had turned into a miserable night. The fresh snow that had fallen only a few days before had been washed away by the steady gray drizzle. The weather report said it would rain and sleet right through Christmas Day. As if it made the slightest difference to her, she was stuck here for another week for evaluation. Not to decide if she was sane enough to stand trial, but to determine whether or not she really was a victim of abuse. As if a woman who had put up with years and years of mistreatment wouldn't finally try to defend herself. Such belated resistance had to be attributed to something far more sinister, like premeditated murder, anything other than simple self-preservation. David - surely the youngest lawyer on the planet - had explained that for a plea of self-defense to stand up in court, her response to Frank's violence, the rising up and finally hitting back, even in the midst of a brutal beating, had to be classified as 'abuse-victim syndrome'. As the kids said, WTF?

These days everything had a name, a slot, a category, and apparently the 'syndrome', this disease, had been growing and festering inside her all this time, finally erupting in behavior so uncharacteristic that it had to be studied and evaluated. Unimaginable that a woman might strike out at her abuser in a frantic effort to save her life.

But the outcome of all this didn't matter, they could call it whatever they wished. She could never have planned to kill Frank, in her wildest dreams had never imagined herself doing any such thing, but now it was done and she was rid of him and finally at peace.

Or she would be, if not for Alyson.

As the pallid afternoon light dimmed to the insubstantial gray of a winter twilight Catherine stared past the raindrops and thought of Christmas, and her daughter, a little girl who would probably be damaged for life. She ached to hold her, but Aly was up in Albany with Elaine and her cousins for the holidays. She'd have a good Christmas there, Elaine had been blessed with a loving husband and two delightful daughters only a couple of years older than Alyson.

Just this morning Elaine had called with good news.

"She was sullen at first, Cat, refused to eat anything, wouldn't leave her bedroom. Yesterday was a better day. The girls took her sledding at the golf course and she had a good time. She's thin as a rail, still not eating much, but she had a cup of hot chocolate and helped decorate the tree last night. You'd have laughed - on the lot it looked like a Charlie Brown disaster but with Mother's old glass ornaments and the things the girls have made over the years it blossomed. It's beautiful. And tomorrow for Christmas dinner-_"

"Please, Elaine, spare me the details." Knowing her

dinner would be rubbery turkey and tasteless wet bread for dressing.

"Sorry, Cat, it's hard to remember. Listen, when I bring Aly back next week, I'd like to stay with you a while. Lord knows you can use the support and Aly needs a guiding hand. She has to get back to school when vacation's over."

"She'll die, Elaine. Her friends— it was in the paper!"

"Better to tackle it before the story becomes distorted and exaggerated."

Her sister, the psych nurse.

"After years of listening to you and Frank fighting, she can face anything."

"Oh Elaine, what have I done?"

"The best you could, my dear."

"She blames me, I know." Alyson hadn't kissed Catherine goodbye; she had climbed into Tom and Elaine's car right after the service for Frank and slammed the door on her mother. She'd hardly spoken a word since... since it happened. "Do you think she needs therapy?"

"Do I? You bet! She has to start facing facts, Catherine."

"Yeah, the fact that her mother killed her father."

"With good reason. You will have to see someone too when this is all over."

Catherine grunted.

"On the good side, she's bonding with Jennifer."

Elaine's sixteen-year-old.

"Aly's sleeping in Jen's room, and this morning she told her she'd had a nightmare. She dreamed that Frank had chased her with a knife and grabbed her— I hope to God that never happened!"

"She never said anything to me—"

"She wouldn't, she'd be too scared of the consequences."

"I think she saw Frank after I—after what happened." Catherine had relived that moment a hundred times, the squeak of the door, the little yelp of shock in the doorway, herself glued to the kitchen floor, utterly incapable of turning even to see who it was, waiting in terror for Frank to take a breath.

"The nightmare proves it."

"Catherine, assume for the moment that it was merely a dream, that she is starting to address the fighting and the fear that has been your life for most of hers. She seems relieved that it's all over, though I don't think she has associated that with the reality that her father is dead, by her mother's hand."

Spoken not as her sister, but as the psychiatric nurse she was. Catherine heard footsteps on Elaine's end.

"I'm talking to your Mom. Can you wish her— no, no, sweetie, that's okay."

Catherine fumbled for a tissue, picturing her baby pushing the phone away.

"I know you're crying, Cat, but listen, this morning Aly said she misses the things you do together at Christmas. She wants to be with you. And I agree. You two belong together, in your own house."

"Oh God, I couldn't set foot --!"

"Cat, you have to go home, start the healing."

"I'll be fine," nearly choking on the words, "but…"

"There are a hundred reasons for her to have bad

dreams, Catherine. I think Alyson should revisit the scene, get her mind around what happened there. One of our friends is a psychologist. He strongly recommends that people, especially children, face their demons."

"If only I had done that years ago, Elaine—" If only... Frank would be alive and Aly wouldn't be having nightmares and Catherine wouldn't be sitting here wondering if she was criminally insane.

"Yes, sweetheart, but the past can't be undone."

"Elaine, wish her a merry Christmas, tell her I love her."

"Aly's coming around, you'll see. I love you."

With total darkness the window had become a mirror, reflecting the bare room and a thin woman in the foreground, hugging her elbows and rocking slowly back and forth, a visual image of the despair that ate at Catherine's heart.

Was that woman a murderer? Had she madly joyously insanely grabbed a knife and killed her husband because marriage to him had become a burden? Should she have submitted to yet another savage beating and let things go on as they were? These questions nagged at her day and night, aggravated by the constant probing of doctors and therapists, twisting and muddling and crunching Catherine's words and thoughts until she thought she must be crazy. And terrified - if *she* didn't believe in her heart of hearts that she had been defending herself, who would?

At that moment thousands of tiny multi-colored lights flared into life on the trunks and the bare branches of the towering oaks that lined the drive. Hundreds more twinkled on shrubs and bushes, twisted around the stone gateposts, topped the ten-foot high wrought iron fence surrounding the compound.

Merry Christmas, Cat.

Every year she took Aly to the Episcopal Church parking lot in town to find the perfect tree. Humming along to the Christmas Carols coming out of an old boom box; breathing in the cold, pine-scented air, laughing to hear her daughter's sweet little voice from behind the tallest, bushiest tree on the lot. "Mommy, mommy, this one's the best!" Sipping hot chocolate while the two of them hung decorations - Catherine couldn't remember Frank ever joining them - Aly's latest creation always front and center, no matter how big or un-beautiful it was. And after shooing Aly off to bed, she'd enjoy a few peaceful moments in the luminous glow that filled the room, from the gleaming star at the tip of the tree to the little stable nestled at its foot, reminiscing...

… recalling the butler setting up the perfectly shaped trees decorated fashionably in twinkling white lights and tinsel - lead tinsel - handed down from past generations, hung by a maid, then wrapped and saved from one year to the next. Ornaments she and Elaine created; admired by Mother; never adorning any tree in her memory. When both girls reached their teen years, the family attended the midnight service on Christmas Eve, mingling with friends in a 'see and be seen' holiday atmosphere. Until they were old enough to share in the giving of gifts, Christmas morning was devoted to Catherine and Elaine formally unwrapping sensible items like sweaters and gloves.

She chuckles now, in this cold, gray place, remembering

her excitement on finding the hair dryer she'd been begging for; toned down by Mother admonishing her to 'keep her rebellious curls in place'.

The miniature nativity scene had been a gift, a peace offering, from her parents the year Alyson was born. Its message seemed to say that although they did not approve of Catherine's choice of husband, they would love her child. And they had, in their cool, detached way. She pictured the tiny bisque figures grouped inside, shepherds and lambs and gaudily colored Magi surrounding the holy family, the baby asleep in a manger, his doting parents looking on, a few moments of peace in their soon to be turbulent lives.

The birth of the Christ child had no religious significance for her, yet she set it under the Christmas tree every year. The little scene gave off an aura of... peace, and hope. She remembered Frank telling her to get rid of the thing, but she'd kept it, mainly because you couldn't throw the baby Jesus into the trash. And glad she did, because Alyson loved the story and so it remained a part of their Christmas celebration, but as an ornament, a myth, like Santa.

Catherine had long since lost belief in any kind of God but imagined what a comfort it must be to have some kind of faith to hold on to; if a mystical powerful force could make everything right, she might not feel so empty. For a while she had turned to Tony, searching for an anchor in the storm-tossed sea of her life. She had begun to believe in the possibility of a new beginning for herself and Alyson, a life free of Frank. She'd been a fool! Tony had given her dreams, but that dream was over. Now Frank was gone but she was stuck here, lonely and alone in this nightmare.

But alone she didn't have the strength, alone she was inadequate, and helpless... Suicide had crossed her mind many times in the past few weeks, but she didn't have the luxury of giving up, of letting go. *If it weren't for Alyson...*

Somewhere a gong sounded; time for dinner.

She'd dredge up some courage and stick it out, for Alyson. After the trial - assuming of course, that she'd get off, she'd sell that damned house and get out of town. They'd start a new life somewhere - London, maybe, or Tibet!

Outside, thick, wet snow had begun to fall, the flakes coating the barred window like lace. Perhaps it would be a white Christmas after all; it seemed like a good omen. With a final glance at the shadowy woman in the barred window, Catherine squared her shoulders and went down to the dining room.

Thirty-nine

Janice shivered with cold, she had so little fat on her noticeably thin–thinner, body. Wrapped in a thick fleece throw, she sat by the bay window in her living room in the new comfy rocker/recliner Gary had surprised her with a week ago. An early Christmas gift, he'd called it. She heaved a huge sigh. Outside heavy flakes of snow fell thick and silent, building up rapidly on the evergreens, spreading like a white blanket over the lawn and Gary's tenderly wrapped shrubs and covered flowerbeds.

Brian and Bonnie had carefully decorated a live blue spruce that now stood in bright shining glory beside the fireplace, aglow with a merrily crackling fire. Gary had decided to buy a live tree and replant it outside in the Spring as a kind of memorial to all the happy Christmases they had enjoyed in this house. He had loaded the CD player with some of her favorite holiday music - Mannheim Steamroller; Celine Dion; Perry Como. Janice smiled at the beaming Santa by the fireplace. She felt as if she were in a Christmas card, one of those romantic scenes covered with the tiny bits of sparkly stuff she'd loved as a child. How quickly the years passed-- with a sudden jolt she realized that this would probably be her last Christmas on earth.

These bursts of reality hit her periodically and had of late struck more frequently, like the night early in December when she had settled down at the dining room table to write Christmas cards. It was a task she had always enjoyed, scribbling notes that started out as a line or two and expanded to fill one whole side of the card inside, often spreading to the back - Gary said Janice had invented the Christmas letter.

But she couldn't do it. Surrounded by cheerful greeting cards waiting to wish friends and family peace and joy, Janice had felt a huge sorrow well up and overflow into tears that coursed down her face. What kind of note would she write? *Dear friends, this will be my last Christmas greeting...* She had gathered up the address lists and boxes of cards and shoved them into a drawer in the den.

A sudden burst of laughter from the kitchen brought her back to the present. Sounds of scissors snipping, the rustle of paper being cut, or torn, the excited voices of her children and their father calling out to each other for the tape, a pen, gift tags. But instead of the warm spread of happiness she'd anticipated, a feeling of melancholy fell over her like a... a shroud - my word, Janice, how maudlin.

But it really wasn't fair, forty-two was far too young to even think about dying, she should have another forty wonderful years ahead! She and Gary had just begun to understand each other, the kids were growing up into lovable people, she'd never been to the South of France. No matter... she was faced with the possibility, or rather the *prob*ability, that she'd be dead within the year.

Armed with a stack of brightly wrapped packages and hoarse giggles, the twins tiptoed into the room to deposit a few more gifts under the tree.

"Hey guys…"

"Oops, sorry Mom, Dad said you were asleep."

"I'm awake." She perked herself up. "Come over here and look at this snow!"

Brian scooted out of the room, tripping over himself in his rush to leave. He hadn't come near her in the weeks since she and Gary had shared the awful news with the twins, wouldn't let Janice touch or hug him. But Bonnie was a different story. She skipped across the room and snuggled beside Janice under the fleece.

"Hey, we both fit in here!"

Janice had noticed the same thing. "Must be the new chair." Couldn't possibly have anything to do with the thirty or more pounds she'd lost.

"No Mom, you are so thin!"

She sat with Bonnie nestled in the crook of her arm for a few minutes, savoring the scent of her hair, her firm young body. I could sit like this for hours, she thought.

"Mommy?"

The baby name, not the Mom she'd become in recent years.

"Mmhm?"

"What do you think it's it like to be dead?"

Janice chuckled. "How would I know? I'm not--!" Dead yet, she had been about to say. Small comfort at this juncture. She'd been worrying at the same question for ages, and obviously death, her death, was on her daughter's mind as well.

"I don't know, love. I imagine you go to a quiet place where your house never gets messy and you don't feel any pain."

"Can you see your children, do you think?"

"Most certainly." She hugged Bonnie close. "I plan to watch you grow into a brilliant and beautiful young woman with a first-class education who accomplishes great things in your life."

"Like what?" Bonnie's little body fidgeted with anticipation.

"Oh, I don't know, maybe you'll be a doctor, or become President of the United States or–"

"–or I could be a great Mom, like you."

Tears welled, damn this medication that kept her emotions so close to the surface.

"Or you could be a great Mom, with terrific kids like mine."

"Dinner's ready, Bon. Sweetheart, do you fancy anything?" Gary's welcome voice, gentle with concern.

She looked at him over Bonnie's head, the man she'd been lucky enough to marry, the man who loved her. "A bowl of soup, dear, would suit me just fine."

Yes, she'd been blessed - how many people lived to their eighties and could say the same?

"Help me out of this chair, Gary. It's Christmas. I'd like to eat at the table with you tonight."

Forty

Tony stood in the center of the darkened motel room, too wound up for sleep. What time was it, past midnight? Big day tomorrow and here he was, wide awake. Around ten he'd left the kids watching TV and taken a long walk through town along the concrete boardwalk that ran behind the row of high-rise condos, block after block of towers. Progress, he snorted, ugly and crowded. But, between two buildings, he followed a crooked, narrow pathway that led to the magnificent Atlantic Ocean, hillocks of grass covered dunes and the white sand beach. He walked slowly, watching frothy white foam dancing to the shore on waves that broke and crashed on the sand. Half a mile or so down the beach he spotted a shack, gaudy with strings of multi-colored lights swaying in the chill breeze off the water. A bar. Beanie's. He stopped, considering, but he kept on walking; beer wasn't going to help. He made his way back to the motel, his mind still in turmoil, wondering what in hell was he going to say to Laura in the morning.

The kids had finally fallen asleep in the room behind him, Claudia and Gina in one bed, Anthony sprawled across the other, the one he was supposed to share with his father. Guess it's the couch for me, Tony thought, noting with a quick flash of pride how muscular his son had become. Getting a blanket from the closet he squirmed into the most comfortable position possible on the couch and stared up at the pebbled white ceiling.

Christmas Eve. He listened to the waves slapping the beach outside the slider he'd left open. Definitely not like Christmas up north, with snow that sparkled and crunched underfoot, and the glittering tree, and the kids asleep in their beds, and him and Laura... well, that meant turning the clock way back and that probably was never going to happen.

This was shaping up to be one shitty Christmas! First thing this morning he'd run into Laura's keeper, a huge woman, big as a bear, wearing red shorts with white polka dots that must have been made out of a table cloth and the most unsympathetic face he'd ever run across.

"What do you mean she won't see me? I'm her husband, dammit."

"A privilege it seems you've abused."

So, she was a well-spoken bear. "Y'know, I don't know what Laura's told you about me, Pam, but she's got a fertile imagination."

"Watching you make out with her friend in a shop window seemed pretty real to her, Tony. And it's Sam."

Tony felt his stomach clench. "Laura was pregnant when I married her, did she tell you that?"

"What's that got to do with the price of bananas?"

"She's always had this complex, that I don't really love her, that I married her out of pity."

"So you did her a big favor and that gives you the right to mess around?"

"Of course not.   Claudia was my kid and I was nuts about Laura, we'd have got married anyway.   And I never had other women, that was all in her fucked-up mind."

"Sir, this is a Christian home."

Yeah, whatever... Tony saw a guy come out of the tiny cottage next door. Watched him hook his foot on the railing, pull a pack of cigarettes out of his shirt pocket, squinting at Tony through the smoke, planning to enjoy every word. "Look, do we have to have this conversation standing out here on the porch?"

"We could sit in your car instead."

Tony turned away from the door and sat on the top step.   "Sam, how can I make you understand?"   He left space for her to sit next to him.   "Laura never gave me room to breathe, checking up on every move I made.   Did she tell you I gave up a sweet promotion to Detective Sergeant in Boston to move out to the boonies?   I did that for her.   All these years I've put up with her whingeing and whining, her irrational jealousy, her drinking but Christ, I go and make one mistake and she's up and gone."

The big woman sank slowly on the step next to him. "So, are you tellin' me it was no more than a quick grope in the dark, a one-time thing?"

Tony opened his mouth to answer but words wouldn't come.   "I... I can't say that, no.   But until then I'd been as good a husband as I knew how."

"Maybe it wasn't good enough, hon.   You know, I was prepared to dislike you.   Poor Laura came here wounded and hurting, all because of you."

"Or all because of what she made up in her tortured

308

mind."

"Oh no, catching you together confirmed what she already thought she knew. What Laura saw that night threatened her safety."

"Aw, that's crazy--!"

"But now," Sam went on as if he hadn't opened his mouth, "now I pity you both. Yoked together all this time and never really knowin' love."

"What the f--!"

Sam held her hand up for silence. "She's been out walkin' the beach every night wonderin' where love has gone and you're here lookin' for the missing parts but you know what I think? You never had it, either one." She sniffed, fumbled in her jeans for a tissue. "You married her out of duty and she married in fear."

Tony shrugged, this woman was some kind of loony-toon. "But we have to talk. I have to make Laura see that her place is with me and the kids."

"Are you certain that's what you want, Tony? Or are you just trying to make things smooth at home, so you'll be free to make your own choice?" Sam clucked her tongue. "Laura's entitled to the same deal, don't you think?"

"Excuse me, Ma'am, did somebody die and make you God?" Tony's world was falling apart and this fat smug-faced Southern broad had all the answers. "I just want to talk to my wife, dammit."

"Come back tomorrow, I'll try to talk her into seeing you. But don't expect me to intervene. Every woman has to make her own decisions."

And now it was two in the morning and he couldn't

sleep, why the hell had he given up smoking? Heaving himself off the stiff, mildew-smelling couch, Tony went out to the balcony. The moon shone a silver path on the water, reminding him of that first, wonderful night at the lake, with Catherine-- Christ, he was *so* screwed up!

He'd come down here to do the right thing, hoping to atone for his sin, but would making up with Laura get him what he wanted? No, not if what he really wanted was Catherine.

Which Laura's friend Pam or Sam seemed to know, as if she'd seen into his soul and read all the confusion there. But even if he couldn't love Laura any more, he still wanted the best for her and the kids. And that meant having her at home with them.

And then, if he really was in love with Catherine Moore, then dammit, *then* he would fight for her. If he could sort out his own confusion, then coming down here might turn out to be a good thing after all.

He slid the glass door shut quietly so as not to wake the kids - as if, they slept like hibernating bears, and took a tiny bottle of vodka from the fridge concealed in the armoire - fuck the expense! He swilled it neat, and shuddered as it went down, hoping it would help him sleep; thinking of Laura and her supply of hidden bottles. How long had that been going on? Was that how she dealt with their failing marriage? He stretched out on the sofa under the thin cotton blanket and shut his eyes, waiting for oblivion, and tomorrow, when he'd get everything sorted out with Laura.

"Who's ready for dinner?" Sam set another platter on

the table. Tony sat with his children at the table in Sam's tiny kitchen. A Southern Christmas dinner sure was something else, dishes of stuff on the table he'd never heard of. The kids turned up their noses at the okra and collard greens but dug right into the crispy fried chicken.

"This is way better than turkey, Sam."

His children had fallen in love with her. She had caught their attention with some story or other, that woman sure had a way with people. He and Laura sat facing each other at one end of the table, a world away from the fun at the other end. Across from him Laura kept her eyes on her plate and chewed mechanically.

"Different from the big Italian holiday spread we're used to, huh?" Making small talk.

"Yes, it is Tony. But, you know, that's okay. We get locked into one way of life and haven't a clue how other people live. I didn't ask for this to happen but now that I've been forced into it, I'm willing to give it a chance." Laura speared a forkful of chicken.

Great! He'd been talking about collard greens and she was giving him her new philosophy of life. Tony tried to catch Laura's eye, trying hard to see what was in there, but she kept her head bent over food she couldn't possibly be enjoying.

And that's how the whole meal went, Sam and the kids yukking it up, Laura off in space somewhere and him trying to read her mind. And yet, with her never saying word one, by the time Sam sliced up the sweet potato pie Tony knew for certain that Laura wasn't coming home.

He phoned her from the motel, just before they left for the airport, damn near begging, but she was offhand and vague. "Laura, I don't like this game you're playing."

"If this was a game, Tony, I'd be having fun. I'm just not sure what I want to do. First time around we jumped right in, we had no choice, but this time I want to give it a lot of thought."

"Whaddaya mean, *this* time? What's to think about? Huh? We're married, Laura, we have a family together, your place is home with us."

"Go home, Tony. I'll let you know."

And she did, at the end of January.

"I want a divorce."

"That's how you greet someone comes a thousand miles to see you?" He sat down, hard, on some kind of beanbag chair in the corner of Sam's miniature living room. "I didn't come all this way to hear this."

"You came here for an answer, Tony, just like I did."

He didn't like that the big woman was in the room, standing beside Laura looking all smug and possessive. Instead he looked out the window at a cloudy, rainy sky, the same steel gray color as the ocean. Drab and dull, no better than home. Myrtle Beach wasn't far enough south to get the gorgeous sunny hot weather that made Florida so popular with the snowbirds.

"We're Catholic, we can't get divorced."

"Right. And we get this from a bunch of pedophiles?"

"Laura—"

She leaned against the big woman's chest. "We married

for the wrong reasons, Tony; the Church recognizes that. But if we can't get divorced, we can get a legal separation. I certainly don't ever plan to marry again." Her laugh sounded like a witch's cackle to Tony's ears. "And you can live in sin with that bitch."

He cringed when Sam laid her hammy paw on Laura's shoulder, like it was all settled. "Laura, you're stressed, and still upset. Don't make a decision about this now."

"Stress? That's a laugh. My entire life with you has been stress. Now it's over, Tony, and I know what I'm doing. I'm not crazy, you know. I was depressed, yes, and I drank a lot." She reached up to cover the other woman's hand resting on her shoulder. "I did some crazy things, but me and Sam think I've recovered."

"You and–" Watching the two women gaze into each other's eyes; he realized they'd forgotten him; he could've been a hundred miles away. *Aw, geez, they've got a thing going!*

"I know my own mind, Tony."

Tony scrubbed at his face with both hands, hoping to erase the image that had leaped into his mind of his wife with that-- that Neanderthal.

"Laura, I know you're upset over this thing with the Moore woman. She came on to me," casually throwing Catherine under the bus, "and I caved. You have every right to be pissed about that, but it's behind me now. It's over. I won't see her any more, Laura. I swear it!"

"Of course not, Tony. She's going to prison for killing her husband - over you."

"Now that's stupid. That bastard abused her for years,

she was defending herself."

"That's what *she* says. Anyway, this is not about you or Catherine Moore. If I hadn't caught you with her it would have been someone else - I know you never truly loved me, Tony. But I was so crazy in love with you I pretended not to see, not to know."

"Laura, there was nothing to know." *Christ, she was obstinate.* "Believe me!"

"I don't, Tony. I can't. How can you stand there looking me straight in the eye after what I saw? Not to mention all the times I didn't see."

She was going to cry, always a good sign, and he reached out to—

"Don't you touch me!" She folded her arms. "Drinking made the pretending easier. Nothing's real when you're blind drunk, and reality is much less harsh, like a faded memory, when you're not. But Sam has been a great help. Now I'm cold, stone sober, Tony. Haven't had a drop to drink since the night I got here."

She stood and put her hands on her hips, which to Tony didn't look so skinny any more, and thrust her chin forward.

"You look just like your mother."

"Ah, but I'm not as forgiving as she was. Now listen up, Tony. Get this through your thick Italian skull. I am not going back to live with you, you can have all the fancy women you can handle. I'm getting a divorce." She turned her back to him. "And now you need to go."

Fancy women? Tony's jaw dropped, realizing that all along he figured she'd get over this little tantrum and come to her senses. "But Laura, what will you do? Where will you go? And how about the kids?" Now he was whining.

"I've got plans, ideas... it's time I had a life of my own, don't you think? In the spring I'm going to New York, see if I can get work. I'll need some help from you until I'm on my feet, but it shouldn't take long, and it might ease your conscience. Meantime, you keep the kids with you, like the good ol' dad you are. I've talked to Claudia, she says she understands, and anyway, she'll soon be starting a life of her own, heading to UMass Amherst in September. And we'll help her get ready for school - we are not going to punish our kids for this. We've been texting, they know I'll see them when I can, and they're already excited about visiting me in New York." She stood up. "Now goodbye, Tony."

He watched her open the porch door, a homemade looking half screened thing with flaking multi-colored layers of paint, while he sat with his mouth hanging open.

"And don't bother to come back here again," she said, holding the door ajar. "I won't change my mind."

He backed through the door, watched it swing slowly, firmly, shut. Through the grimy window he watched Sam put her arms around his wife's waist - saw Laura crying on her shoulder, gettin' all cozy in her embrace, like a pair of lezzies! Tony stared at that door for a long time before he turned   away.

Forty-one

In mid-January, when Catherine's incarceration at McLean's was finally over, Elaine picked her up and drove her back to Gilford, to the house at 107 Silver Birch Road. Light snow fell as Elaine's Jeep rattled up the long driveway to the big white Colonial, softening the rigid lines of the house, frosting the junipers that lined the walk. "Looks pretty in the snow, doesn't it, Cat?"

Catherine had lived here for four years, but it had been Frank's dream, and she felt no attachment to the place. It could have been any house on any street, anywhere, but she was determined to pick up the pieces of their lives with Alyson.

As she tapped 0823 into the keypad at the door the shock of reality hit, hard and painful. Those four numbers represented Frank's birthday!

"Elaine, I just wanted a divorce! And now I'm caught in a nightmare that will never go away..." She staggered across the foyer and crumpled on the bottom stair.

"It's okay, sweetheart, I'm here with you..." Holding Catherine in her arms as her sister's face twisted. "Cry it out, love, it's good to feel..."

Elaine sat with her until she was done. "You will get through this, Catherine." She hung their damp coats in the hall closet. "Sounds like a platitude now, but time does soften pain." She stood and dragged Catherine to her feet. "You have to heal, sister dear, for Alyson's sake."

"You sound like a psychologist."

"Funny you should say that," said the psych nurse with a laugh, "now let's get some heat going in here. Go sit in the den; I'll scare up the kettle and make some tea."

Soon a cozy gas fire warmed the room, and between sips of hot tea, Elaine turned to Catherine. "Something I've been meaning to tell you. Your, ah, friend Tony has called me a few times. A compassionate man, your Detective Costello."

"Not mine, Elaine."

"Oh, no?"

Catherine could feel Elaine's antennae quivering, but she had no intention of sharing anything about her short-lived affair with Tony.

After the initial shock of walking through the foyer to the kitchen for the first time and reliving the images that were now engraved in her mind, settling back into the house wasn't so difficult. The tile floor in the kitchen had been cleaned; the yellow tape was gone, everything was in order and familiar. As day followed night followed day, Catherine began to put the horror behind her, she'd had years of experience at that. There were no warm memories to flood her heart, like *that was his favorite chair* or *we made beautiful love in that bed,* she convinced herself she was beginning to heal. She had absolutely no doubt that she'd acted in self-defense, and she trusted in her young attorney to take care of the rest.

February was a nasty month of sleet and rain and icy roads, but Catherine rarely went outside. She'd become a celebrity of sorts; a nine-days-wonder. She soon learned to keep shades and drapes shut against slow-moving cars. She stopped answering her door to people she didn't recognize - neighbors, allegedly, cookies and casseroles in hand, offering condolences, but obviously hoping for a glimpse or a word from the now notorious murderer. She let all phone calls go to message, ignoring numerous requests for 'the backstory' from the newspapers and tabloids. Anything she needed could be bought online; bags of de-icer from Amazon, groceries from Stop & Shop. A worried Kevin begged her to come back to work, but she said she'd wait, until March, until... after. Her life would start up again... after.

Aly was her chief concern. She'd gone back to school near the end of January, after Martin Luther King Day, but her teachers said she was inattentive, there in body only. At home the girl hardly ate a bite, she was pale, tired, lethargic. To Catherine's knowledge, Alyson hadn't shed a single tear over her father's death, and Max had been relegated to the toy chest in the corner of her bedroom, where he sagged, sad and lonely. She had shut up tight as a clam, rarely spoke, except to refuse therapy. Catherine began praying to a god she didn't believe in for a way through to her daughter.

On a Sunday in early March, after a gentle shower had

sprinkled gleaming droplets of rain on greening lawns and shrubs, when the stalks of forsythia came alive with bright yellow blossoms, Catherine resisted Spring no longer and took a mug of coffee outside.   The buds on the PJM rhododendrons along the foundation wall were opening and soon they would bloom, a riot of huge red and white blossoms.   Frank had been so proud of the display.   The pink dogwood on the front lawn was covered with bulbs ready to burst, and the heady scent of lilacs carried to her on the breeze.   She walked slowly toward the flowering crab at the side of the house, to the park bench Frank had placed there, for her…   there were not many happy memories, but this was certainly one.   Tears threatened as she remembered that Mother's Day when he dragged it out of the garage–she was about to sit when the faint sound of Janice's distinctive *hallooo*, a weaker version of her normally booming voice, called out.

"Hi! I'm over here, on the sunny side of the house."

Catherine plodded across the road - no matter what they said, the ankle bracelet was a drag - working up an excuse as she went, she really should have come over before this to visit, but her words were swallowed up in shock - Janice had lost at least thirty pounds since Thanksgiving.   Her neighbor sat in a wheelchair in the sunshine wearing a huge smile and her loose flesh like a baggy old sweater.

"Janice, you've lost so much weight!"   Regretting the words instantly.

"Yeah, nearly forty pounds! I know I look dreadful; guess I wasn't meant to be thin.

"You don't look–"

Janice waved the words away. "I knew you were back."

"-- I've been meaning to come over–"

"Don't, Catherine." Janice touched her arm. "You're going through hell just now and I don't have time to waste on guilt or excuses. Let's just enjoy the moment, okay?"

Relieved, Catherine nodded.

"Grab that lawn chair and sit a spell, as they used to say. But first, turn my chair into the sun, would you? I'm going to my maker with a tan if it's the last thing I do, which it just may be."

Catherine laughed. "Good heavens, Janice. You're so… so –"

"Flip? You could say that, I guess. I sit in this wheelchair all day and think of the great laughs a dying comedian could get."

"How are you feeling?"

"Pretty good, considering. I've got drugs for the pain and I've got the twins and Gary, don't know what I'd do without him."

"But when… how…?"

"My dear, it must be such a shock for you."

Catherine took Janice's hand, amazed that the woman was concerned with her feelings.

"I was diagnosed with ovarian cancer back in December, around the time of your, ah, troubles. There's no pain, no telltale signs, you don't know you have it until it's too late. They tell me it started long ago, possibly a year." She grinned. "I'm in good company, though. Gilda Radner from SNL had it."

Catherine had a flashback to Rosanne Rosannadanna;

one of Radner's characters.

"Remember around Halloween, when I started losing weight? I was so proud, my diet was working..." She laughed. "But that's enough about me, Catherine, how are you holding up?"

Alert and curious as always, but she seemed sympathetic, interested, not nosey. Sensing the other woman's compassion, Catherine opened up to Janice as she had to no-one else, her years of terror with Frank, her fears and worries about Alyson. Janice listened, sympathetically, and Catherine surprised herself by telling her about Tony.

"Please don't let Laura know, it never really amounted to anything and it's long over."

"You know she's in South Carolina?"

"Last I heard she'd gone to the Cape."

"Oh, that was months ago, you really have been out of the loop. The Cape was a short flight from home to think things over. This is a full-fledged escape. Last time she phoned she said she might never come back here."

"But the kids? T–her husband?"

"Yeah, the kids. She's nuts about them, too protective, I always thought. But they'll get along. That little Gina's a tough one and she's going to be fine. And as for Tony, guess he'll have to figure things out for himself." She gave Catherine a sly little grin. "It seems poor Laura's suspicions about him were right all along."

On March fourteenth the uncontested Costello divorce was made final.

The following Monday Catherine Maude Barstowe Moore went on trial for murder.

Forty-two

The courtroom was bright, very different from the cold marble and stuffy mahogany paneling Catherine had imagined. Morning sunlight streamed through long windows set high up along one wall, painting stripes of light on soft gray carpeting and pale oak walls. Comforting, kind of like being in church, Catherine thought, an effect heightened by the judge's massive raised bench at one end of the room and the Great Seal of Massachusetts centered on the wall behind it. Rows of oak benches upholstered in a medium gray shade that matched her suit... *if not for my red hair I'd be invisible!* She chuckled, then quickly covered her mouth, wondering at her sanity.

David turned from the whispered conversation he'd been having with one of the paralegals. "You okay?"

"Sure." *It was self-defense, Catherine, you'll be fine.* The words, like a mantra, flashed through her mind. "Fine."

He gave her a tight little smile, meant to be encouraging, but his young face was pale above the red bow tie. A lucky color, Catherine always wore something red when she had a big deal to close; a red scarf, earrings, or panties. Today, however, she was dressed in a gray suit and white blouse, like a nun, she thought, hiding an unwelcome grin with a trembling hand. And she didn't see a single red spot at the prosecution's table, ha! they were bound to lose. Laughter bubbled up and spilled out, nervous giggles she smothered in a fake coughing spell. Good grief, she was losing her mind!

The air in the big room had the closed-up smell of the weekend and the air conditioning's sluggish Monday start, but Catherine shivered. Nerves, she supposed. Her mother would have said something about a goose walking over her grave, too near the truth to be amusing.

Twelve gray padded armchairs in two rows filled the jury box, empty but poised for anything. Besides Catherine, her counsel, and two prosecuting attorneys at the other table, there were a handful of spectators, most of them strangers. She was surprised to see Gary Kurtz, in the third row, sending her a thumbs up. Beside him sat her brother-in-law Ben, the dot.com millionaire, as a jealous Frank used to call him. He looked anxious, and she wondered if he and Gary had met. She raised her hand to wave but was suddenly struck by the realization that they were here for her trial. For murder. She hugged her elbows; Catherine in Wonderland, unable to adjust to the absurdity of it all.

Alyson and Elaine sat in the front row directly behind her, and her sister smiled awkwardly when she turned to peer at them. Aly had refused to let Catherine speak to her or hug her before they left the house - thank goodness Elaine had come to stay for a while. Aly looked anxious and fidgety yet grown up, her childhood a far-off memory. She had lost a great deal of her hair - stress, according to the doctor, and surely that pale drawn little face would someday smile again! As Catherine watched, a blue uniformed woman took Aly's arm and escorted her out of the courtroom.

She clutched David's arm. Where are they taking my daughter?"

"She will be called as a witness. She can't be here."

Catherine felt a sudden yearning for Tony, to feel the encouragement she knew she'd see in his fierce dark eyes. "Where is Detective Costello?" Too loud, but who knew now or cared didn't matter to her any more.

"As the first Detective on the scene of a homicide, Costello will have to testify." David patted her hand. "Are you okay?"

Catherine nodded, unable to speak. *Homicide.* This was not a TV show. She was in this courtroom today on trial for a crime she had committed. Forget self-defense; she had murdered her husband, and she would have to pay. Her hands began to tremble. Her whole body went dead with chill, she was shaking, she was going to throw up, to black out. David forced her to sip some water. "Ready?" He squeezed her hand as the jury filed in, the show was about to start.

Catherine scanned their faces for some emotion - pity, revulsion, anything. As if they'd been warned to ignore the defendant, not one of the seven women and five men glanced at her as they passed, each face rigid and unsmiling in the performance of its awesome duty. She'd never been called for jury duty and now Catherine wished she had, she wouldn't feel so ignorant.

"All rise," said the bailiff, his voice booming out over the whispers and rustlings in the huge room.

The judge, a woman, swept majestically into the room in billowing black robes.   Tall, thin, hatchet-faced, with graying hair and black-rimmed glasses.   *Our Father,* Catherine prayed, *who art in heaven.* The nightmare had begun.

In their opening statement the prosecution promised the jury that they would prove beyond a reasonable doubt that Catherine Moore had callously murdered her husband for reasons to be disclosed during the trial, blah, blah, all the while hinting at a secret love affair.

David vowed to prove that Catherine was a victim of her husband's brutality and had killed him 'in self-defense while enduring another attack by the man who beat her, raped and emotionally abused her throughout their marriage.'

The long days passed in a muddle of legal rhetoric, background stuff they never showed on TV.   Voices swirled around her, establishing this and clarifying that.   Police photographs, taken the night Catherine was arrested, were admitted into evidence.   The split and swollen lips, the bruises beginning to darken on her neck, her blackened eyes, sad testimony to the battering she had taken.   All David had to do was prove that Frank had inflicted them.

On day three Catherine was jolted from her daze when she heard Alyson's name called out, saw her daughter escorted into the courtroom by the bailiff, followed closely, thank God, by Elaine.   Aly came up the aisle wringing her hands, searching out Catherine's eyes the instant she sat in the witness box.   Catherine nodded encouragement.

A young guy, one of the lawyers for the prosecution

came out on the attack, with blond brush cut hair and a tiger's smile.

"In your statement to the police, Alyson, you said you once heard someone screaming and smashing things in the den."

"Yes." Near tears. "My Dad."

"Did your mother call the police?"

"I-I - no, I don't know." She hugged her elbows, obviously distraught.

"No police officer came to the house that day?"

"I didn't see or hear anyone, I was hiding upstairs in my room..."

"No police, Miss Moore, your mother didn't think your father's behavior was that bad."

"Objection! The prosecutor is badgering—"

"Sustained."

The prosecutor, with a grin. "Is it possible you dreamed the whole incident?"

"Objection!" David, rising.

"Overruled," from Hatchet-face. "Answer the question."

"No! Stuff like that happened all the time," Alyson insisted, visibly upset.

"Did you ever actually see your father hurt your mother?"

She shot a terrified glance at Catherine.

"I-I could hear them fighting, at night, when they thought I was asleep."

"Didn't you tell me she saw him hurt you?" David's whisper rang in Catherine's ear.

"Not that time."

"Thank you, Miss Moore. No more questions."

David was on his feet. "Miss Moore, Alyson, you have previously stated that your father, Francis Moore, mistreated the defendant on more than one occasion."

"Who?"

Aly's face was screwed up tight, she was very near tears. Catherine looked away.

"I'm sorry, dear, your mother. You saw bruises on her arms."

"Yes."

Now tell the court what you saw," David consulted his blank notepad... "on that horrific night last August."

"I was asleep," with a glance at Catherine, "but I when I heard him yelling, and a crash, stuff breaking, like glass, and I ran to my mo...my parents' bedroom."

"And what did you see there?"

"My mother all huddled up on the floor in the corner. My, um... my father was... he had nothing on!" Tears filled her eyes. "H- he was holding something in his hand over her head, like a flashlight, and it looked like he was going to hit her with it."

"But did you see your father hit your mother that night?"

A little shake of the red head. "No." Whispered.

"Did you ever actually see him hit your mother?"

"He was always yelling, and he threw things at Mom."

"What things?"

She shook her head, long auburn locks swaying like a curtain around her face.

"Alyson, honey, you need to answer the question."

"Stuff. Plates and awards. Just stuff." Her eyes pleaded with Catherine.

Listening to her daughter, her baby, Catherine felt tears spill over. Does she have to go through this?

"Did you hear often your parents fighting?"

"I'd hear noises at night, from their room, my father grunting and my mother saying Frank, please, for the love of God, stop, you're hurting me, and the squishy sound of slaps and her crying and it went on and on and on and I'd have to hide my head under the pillow!" Tears streamed down her cheeks, but her voice had grown stronger as she spoke, and now she nearly shouted. "He was a horrible man and I'm glad he's dead!" She took the tissue David gave her and dropped her head, her pathetic little face hidden at last by the thick veil of curls.

Catherine watched her daughter's thin shoulders heave; they were far too slight for their burden. After all she'd seen and heard, how would Alyson learn to trust again?

David led Aly across the carpeted floor, her sniffles the only sound in the hushed room. Elaine slid out of her seat and took Aly outside. Catherine wiped hot tears with the back of her hand.

The parade of witnesses continued for days, five, six, seven, Catherine lost count. Medical and forensic people, a psychiatrist's evaluation of Catherine's mental state - as if anyone could imagine how she felt. Frank's despised boss, who testified about Frank's appalling and rude behavior with his co-workers, particularly the women, his bouts of unprovoked and excessive anger, all of which had prevented his advancement in the firm.

Catherine had little or no interest in their testimony.

David sat hunched forward, eyes and attention fastened on each and every witness, he was determined to prove she had killed Frank while defending herself. She watched the proceedings from a distance, as if the outcome of this trial had no relevance for her.

Kevin Casey was called by the prosecution. "Mr. Casey, you consider yourself a personal friend of the defendant?"

A little smile for Catherine. "Yes, I do."

"Did Mrs. Moore ever talk to you about the alleged abuse on the part of the deceased?"

"Many times I saw bruises, a black eye--"

"But did the defendant say how she got those injuries?"

Kevin's head shook no. "She didn't like to talk about it, most of the time she made something up."

"Thank you, Mr. Casey."

"There was one time..."

"I said thank you, sir." And to the court, "no further questions."

David sprang up. "Mr. Casey? Mrs. Moore told you what happened once?"

Kevin nodded. "It was last year; last Spring, maybe? Catherine's poor face was bandaged. When I pressed her, she said Frank had thrown a jar at her."

Catherine uncrossed her arms and rubbed the tiny scar on her cheek, remembering that morning. Frank was having trouble with the coffee maker, and she offered to help after the second pod hit the trash bin amid a flurry of curses. "I am *perfectly* capable of making myself a cup of coffee!" He picked up the jar of marmalade as smoke rose from the toaster, and, "You let the damned toast burn!" He flung the jar at her head and left the room.

Doris Knight, their next-door neighbor, told the Court that she'd heard the Moores fight many times, and though Catherine had tried to cover them up, she had once seen dark bruises on her arms.

"Did you ask Mrs. Moore how she got those bruises, Mrs. Knight?"

"Oh, no, I couldn't embarrass her..."

"She didn't say how she got those bruises." The prosecutor turned away. "Thank you."

"Mrs. Knight." David's turn. "Did you hear fighting prior to seeing those bruises?"

"No."

David's shoulders slumped.

"But I saw Mr. Moore back his car out fast just before I saw her. He looked angry, and he raced down the street, there might have been children—"

"When did this happen?"

"Breakfast time."

"You seem very certain—"

"I was drinking coffee."

"Yes, Ma'am. Can you tell us when this occurred?"

"Well, I was outside admiring my daffodils."

"So, early May, perhaps the fifth?"

"Objection, your Honor. Leading the —"

"Overruled. Mr. Sheldon, please make your point."

"On the morning of May fifth last, your Honor, Mr. Moore was given a ticket by police for passing a school bus at sixty miles per hour." Theatrical pause. "Children were boarding at the time." He looked at the papers he held. "In her notes Officer Belcher tells us that Mr. Moore was belligerent, refused the roadside drunk driving test, tore up the speeding ticket she presented to him, dared her to take him to court. The officer called for backup and escorted Mr. Moore to the precinct for a breathalyzer test. His blood alcohol level was negative, but Mr. Moore continued shouting abuse, hitting out at two officers. He was detained for several hours in a holding cell until he cooled down." David turned an ominous face to the jury. "The behavior, ladies and gentlemen, I think we all agree, of a deeply disturbed and angry man."

Shocked, Catherine realized Frank had never mentioned the incident.

Catherine's mind drifted, she couldn't follow all the legal jargon, but she came to when Janice Kurtz - in a wheelchair - was brought into the courtroom. Weak and pale, she testified that she had seen and heard for herself Frank's violent behavior to his wife.

"I saw that man throw brass trophies and a silver bowl at Catherine. He was screaming that he'd like to kill her, shouting a verbal stream of abuse the likes of which I've never heard in my life."

"Thank –"

"And then he tried to choke her - I saw it with my own two eyes!"

"Afterward I said to my husband, Gary, I said, that man is deranged."

"Yes ma'am."

"He should be locked up!"

"Yes, ma'am. Thank you."

Sending an encouraging grin to Catherine as they wheeled her out.

At the end of the week David was almost euphoric. "We're looking really good, Catherine. Your daughter's testimony was very powerful, your friends painted a flattering picture of you as a woman doing her best under severe circumstances. Juries are sensitive to that kind of thing. Added to your husband's arrest, his behavior at work and the recorded incident of domestic abuse, I think we are going to win this case."

Catherine permitted herself a tiny glimmer of hope.

Then   Tony   took   the   stand.

Forty-three

He was dressed in a dark blue suit and so nervous his hands trembled visibly as he smoothed his hair, tugged at his chin. Catherine's spirits rose when she saw him, her heart beat a little faster, but he avoided eye contact. His statement, which he was permitted to read, was brief and limited to what he had seen when he arrived at the Moore household the day of the murder, delivered in an unemotional monotone.

"Detective Costello." Paula Hawkins, another prosecuting attorney, approached the stand like a hungry barracuda. "You said that Mrs. Moore phoned you at the station immediately after she killed her husband--"

"Objection, your honor! Implies the Detective had prior knowledge."

"Sustained."

Hawkins changed her tactic. "When Mrs. Moore phoned the station did she or did she not ask for you?"

"Yes," head bowed, "I was the officer on duty."

"But she asked for you by name, Detective Costello. Why is that?"

"Uh, maybe she remembered my name! I was assigned

to her case when she reported her husband's abuse in August of last year."

"And since then, Detective Costello, have you had any contact with Mrs. Moore?"

"I followed up on the case, yes."

"By phone, Detective?"

"Yes."

"And personal contact."

"Yes ma'am."

"Is this normal procedure?"

Tony's eyes dropped to his hands, clenched in his lap. "Sometimes."

"Detective? Didn't you have a personal interest in Mrs. Moore?"

"Objection, your—"

"Your Honor, speaks to the bias of the witness."

"Answer the question, Detective Costello."

"I was concerned about Mrs. Moore's welfare."

"You cared for her."

"I care about all abused women."

"But your interest in Mrs. Moore was, shall we say, more... intimate?"

"Objection! The prosecutor is leading--"

"The question is relevant if there was an illicit association between the defendant and Detective Costello, Your Honor."

"Overruled, Mr. Sheldon."

"Detective Costello, did you have a personal relationship with the defendant prior to the night she brutally murdered her husband?"

"Your Honor--!" Once more David was out of his chair. The Judge waved him down.

"I knew her. Mrs. Moore and my w-wife were friends."

"You refer to Laura Costello?"

"Y-yes."

Catherine clutched at David's arm. "Why is any of this important?"

"You asked for him by name," he whispered, "so they've been digging around, looking for dirt."

"But I wasn't involved with Tony when--"

"Sounds like they've got something, maybe a witness, who says you were."

"When did your wife leave you, Detective?"

"November of last year."

"Because you were having an affair with Mrs. Moore?"

"No, sir," Tony's shoulders slumped, "my wife was, ah, unbalanced."

"But she knew about this extramarital love affair, did she not?"

"Your Honor! This witness is legally incapable of stating what was or is in another person's—"

The prosecutor held up her hand, okay, okay. "But your wife left you, Detective?"

"Yes."

"And you did have an affair with the defendant."

Once again Tony's head bowed. Catherine eyes were fixed on his face.

"Answer the question, Detective."

"Nothing you could call an affair. My wife, as you have probably discovered, is a sick woman. An alcoholic, anorexic, she suffers from depression and who knows what else! She always imagined I was fooling around, getting it on the side" - a glance at the jury - "since I wasn't begging for it at home." Now a sly grin crept across Tony's face. "Mrs. Moore, here - you know how it is, counselor, a woman with troubles up the yinyang - lookin' for a little TLC, right?"

"You had sexual relations with the defendant."

Tony's eyes glittered. "Yeah, but it was nothing."

A physical change had come over Tony during his lengthy speech, and now he sat back, relaxed, legs crossed, jacket unbuttoned, all impudence, welcoming further questions.

Silence crackled throughout the room. Catherine's mind registered shock, then hurt, as she reacted to Tony's words. What was he implying?

"That's all, Detective," disgust clear in her dismissal. "No more questions."

Between them, the female prosecutor and Tony had established that Tony was a pig who took advantage of a woman in crisis; Catherine a whore who just might pop her inconvenient husband off when it suited her. She dropped her head in shame.

"Do you intend to cross-examine, Mr. Sheldon?" the judge asked for the second time.

David took a deep breath, squared his shoulders, and addressed Tony from his seat. A sheen of sweat glistened on Tony's forehead, but an insolent grin curled his lips.

"Detective Costello, you knew Mrs. Moore prior to last December, when this incident occurred?"

Tony cleared his throat, uncrossed his legs, leaned forward a bit, intent on David's every word. "Yes, as I have stated, Mrs. Moore and my wife were friends. Our children attend the same school, our daughters are in some classes together. We met occasionally."

"Were you acquainted with Frank Moore, the deceased?"

"Met him for the first time the night Mrs. Moore reported the abuse."

"Is that when you became interested in Mrs. Moore?"

"No. She was a battered wife. I hoped to prevent Mrs. Moore from suffering further brutality at the hands of a cruel, insensitive man."

"And when did you become attracted to the defendant?"

Tony took a deep breath. "Mrs. Moore is a very attractive woman, anyone can see that. But like I just said, counselor," - that filthy leer again - "the *relationship* the prosecution is so eager to explore didn't amount to more than a quick roll in the hay."

David consulted his notes. "So, you saw the defendant again prior to the night her husband was killed."

"Well yeah. She was unhappy, so was I..."

"And you had sex?"

"You could say it was inevitable."

Not once had he glanced her way.

"Were you in love with Mrs. Moore?"

Catherine couldn't tear her eyes away from him.

"Nah. It was nothin', really, we both knew it was just a fling. The last time we were together, I told her I wanted to reconcile with my wife." His hand tugged at his chin, and for the first time Catherine noticed his little mustache was gone. "And she was going to work things out with her husband."

"Thank you, Det—"

"And I believe Mrs. Moore killed her husband in self-defense."

A whoosh of indrawn breath filled the courtroom.

"That's enough, Detective. Thank you."

Catherine didn't see Tony leave the courtroom; her head was buried in her arms. And she dare not look at the jury, terrified of the verdict she'd see in their eyes.

Tony's testimony had to be damning, her life was over. Despondent, she heard David speaking but his words barely registered in Catherine's brain, until—

"You mean I have to testify?"

"Absolutely. We have to convince the jury that you're not a whore or a nutcase, but an intelligent woman. And whether you were involved with another man is immaterial to this trial. That night you were defending yourself from yet another incidence of your husband's cruelty, and in protecting yourself, he was unfortunately killed."

His defense was based on the physical and mental cruelty and abuse she had endured for years from a vicious, sadistic husband who terrorized her. She called 911, not for herself, but when he attempted to hurt her child. That she had endured it for so long was astonishing, she had made a herculean effort to keep home and marriage intact. Catherine Moore had been under "extreme provocation" at the time she killed her husband. There was no ulterior motive.

The prosecution attempted to show that Catherine had "knowingly caused the death of her husband" for some far less exalted reason, perhaps the secret lover? But Tony had clearly squelched that as a motive, in the process tarnishing both his and Catherine's reputations, but they had uncovered no other dirt on Catherine Moore.

Her young lawyer insisted that she take the stand in her own defense. "The jury needs to see how terrified you were of the man, Catherine." He looked deep into her eyes. "He gave you no choice but to save yourself from a violent death."

Trancelike, Catherine solemnly swore to tell the truth, and sat in the box, answering David's preliminary questions clearly and carefully.

"And so, Catherine, your husband attempted to kill you."

"Objection, your Honor. Hearsay."

"Mr. Sheldon?"

He turned gentle eyes on Catherine. "Mrs. Moore, in your own words, please tell the court what led up to that horrific night in December last."

In a whisper, Catherine took them through the years of fear and abuse that had been her marriage. The humiliation, the resentment, the threats. Meantime, at the back of her mind like a half-remembered tune, the words of the wedding vows played over and over. *"...to love and to cherish, until death us do part.*

"Catherine," Sheldon glanced at the jury box, "your husband was a violent man who abused you, physically, mentally, sexually."

"Yes." Catherine crumpled a sodden tissue in her fist.

Suddenly a commotion rose from the prosecutor's table. "Your Honor?" Paula Hawkins rose and strode toward Catherine, buttoning her gray jacket as she closed in.

"Mrs. Moore, why didn't you leave him?" Sneering, she

turned to the jury box under the bank of huge windows, the glare of sunlight casting the faces of the people sitting there in shadow. "I'm sure these ladies and gentlemen would like to know why you thought stabbing your husband to death was preferable to, say, divorce!"

She closed her eyes, reliving the entire fight.

"I asked for a divorce. He tried to kill me."

After nine hours of deliberation, agonizing even though David said that was no time at all, the jury found that Catherine had killed her abusive husband in self-defense.

She was acquitted. Completely exonerated.

"Mrs. Moore, you are free to leave." The judge's words echoed in her ears. Entirely free to live as she pleased for the rest of her life. But she felt like an island in the middle of a deep, dark ocean. Where to go? What to do?

Tony's testimony had changed everything. With his callous words he had twisted her love and trust into a tawdry liaison between a disillusioned housewife and a bored cop. And as if to underscore that, he didn't phone or text. Fine with her. Catherine had no interest in anything he had to say.

In a small community like Gilford Catherine had been a recognizable figure before all this; now her sin was engraved on her forehead and forevermore in this town she would be the woman who killed her husband for a lover who then turned against her.

Life was hardly worth living.

If it weren't for Alyson she'd kill herself, but she had to keep going for her daughter; hadn't she promised to give the child a life without fear?

Janice   Kurtz   showed   her   how.

Forty-four

Thanks to television, the newspapers and social media like Facebook and Twitter, Catherine's notoriety in Gilford was such that a trip to the grocery store or the bank had become an agony of stares and whispers. She feigned indifference, telling herself that she didn't like small-town Gilford or, with very few exceptions, the small-minded people who lived in it. The big white Colonial, identical to every other one on the suburban street, was Frank's house, a monument to his success. That he'd never invited a single business acquaintance or any member of his family - Frank had had no friends - only served to underline the enigma that was her husband.

As it does, March became April became May, and by the middle of the month Catherine admitted that she disliked the house, its rooms boxlike, devoid of color. She was fed up with Frank's dull grays and beiges, as if it had been decorated out of an office supply catalogue. Frank had sneeringly refuted any of her decorating ideas, probably gaining some grim satisfaction by overruling Catherine's taste and upbringing.

Recalling the homes of her childhood, she grew nostalgic

for the venerable old Victorians of Brookline and Chestnut Hill, towered and mullioned and gingerbreaded to the nines, with their winding staircases and twelve-foot ceilings, stained glass transoms and window seats and fireplaces.

Catherine remembered the listing for the Wetherbee place, the house Laura had once called a Victorian mansion. Not Victorian - Catherine knew her architecture, but Queen Anne, a more delicate style. Bearing the somewhat pretentious name of Hilltop Manor, the large, well-proportioned two-story house stood on a rise surrounded by four plus acres of lawn and gracefully curved gardens and flowerbeds. A dozen peach and apple trees, a pond complete with gazebo, a sweeping flagstone terrace, and a balcony off the master bedroom offered a hazy view of the Boston night skyline some fifty miles off in the distance. All this beauty enclosed by an ivy-covered stone wall that promised peace and solitude.

She'd been inside a couple of times, a year ago or more, shortly after Mr. Wetherbee passed and his widow 'bestowed' on Casey & Moore the honor of the listing. Kevin said it was still for sale.

"The old gal really wants to downsize, but it's priced too high for today's market, and it's been on the market for a year. Catherine, I believe you're the only one of us who can convince her to get the price down."

She wouldn't take the bait, but the more she thought of living there the better she liked the idea. The old house badly needed repairs and substantial upgrades; there were modern amenities Catherine wouldn't live without, but she had the wherewithal and what good was money if you didn't spend it? She loved old houses, she'd always fancied herself a decorator, and she desperately needed a distraction. It would be a pleasure to restore this one.

"Kevin, make sure she understands that if she lowers the price and sells it as is, she gets out from under costly repairs and upgrades. And if she agrees, I will buy it."

On the first of July the 'Manor' in Hillcrest belonged to Catherine.

The house on Silver Birch sold within a month to a young couple from Rhode Island who professed to love its neutral colors - go figure! They weren't the least put off by the requisite disclosure that the 'previous owner died in the house'. The school system in Gilford was very well regarded, and they wanted to move in before Labor Day so their eleven-year-old princeling would be in place for the new school year.

Catherine told Elaine that though Alyson refused to discuss ideas for decorating her new bedroom, her friend Bonnie had disclosed that Aly was pleased that they would still be attending the same high school. "Small steps, Cath," her sister said, adding, "you might start looking into therapy."

"I'll think about it." But she dismissed the idea of putting Alyson through the horror of that day, the loss of her father, the trial. "She's young, Elaine, "give her time."

Over the summer, serving as her own general contractor, Catherine hired and worked with contractors and tradespeople, discovering that she enjoyed this phase immensely.

She became a hospice volunteer, mainly for Janice' sake, but she had other clients as well, terminally ill people

345

who were grateful for a few hours of care and consolation. It was healing work, as if ministering to others made up somehow for causing Frank's untimely death.

"You don't have to come by so often, Catherine."

"I don't mind, Janice." She tucked the throw around her friend's now bony frame. "I enjoy our time together."

"And that surprises you." Janice still laughed heartily like the large woman she had once been. "Don't give me that look, it doesn't bother me. We're both different people now. I'm glad we've had the chance to become friends."

"And so am I." Catherine felt her eyes fill with tears. "Look here, pictures of my new kitchen!"

Janice reached out for Catherine's iPad but her weakened arm couldn't support the weight. Catherine held it on her lap, zooming in on the wide-board hickory floor, the massive refrigerator/freezer and commercial gas range - "all the rage these days, Jan. I might start cooking."

"I'd love to see it." Janice's voice was wistful.

"You will, it'll be finished in a few weeks."

"That long."

"Now that's the first time I've heard you sound defeated, Jan. It's not like you."

"No, I'm just being realistic, Catherine. The meds aren't doing the job anymore. Yesterday the doctor put me on a heroin derivative pump for the pain."

They had talked about this, Catherine and Janice and Gary. When her pain became unbearable Janice would take whatever drugs enabled her to stay home as long as possible with her family, hoping to spare Bonnie and Brian the frightening and impersonal visits to a hospital in their mother's last days.

To this end Gary had turned the kitchen into her headquarters, with Janice's bed set up in the sunny walkout bay window overlooking the back lawn. "The hearth room," she called it, "the heart of our home." From her bed she had an unobstructed view of the gardens, watching Gary putter to his heart's content. And though Janice could barely hold down solid food, each weekend Gary and the twins cooked up some culinary masterpiece to delight her olfactory senses.

Now she turned her face to the window where Gary attacked the weeds threatening to invade his beloved herb beds. "It's not fair."

"Life isn't fair, Janice, you know that."

"Oh, I've accepted my lot, Catherine. But I worry about them, especially Gary. Bonnie and Brian are young, they'll eventually accept my going as part of their lives and move on. But Gary… he thinks I don't know that he cries." Her tired gray eyes sparkled with unshed tears. "Ah, Catherine, it's heartbreaking that we won't grow old together, that I won't see our children's children…"

Catherine wiped away the tears that rolled slowly down Janice's withered cheeks. "Jan, I'll watch over him for you. I promise." She had developed a great affection for Gary over the past few months. He'd changed his job with the airline, working ground duty three days a week to be with his wife as much as possible. His compassion, sense of humor, and obvious love for their children had shown her how a good husband and father behaved.

"Oh sure, take him on now that he's learned to cook

and clean and do laundry!"

"I never said I'd marry him!" Laughing, Catherine hugged her friend, sending the iPad to the floor. "You're amazing, Janice," picking up the device.

"No, just trying to get through each day." She tapped the screen. "Your new kitchen will be lovely."

Catherine stood up. "And you, my dear, are going to see it." Through the window she saw Gary's straw hat bobbing among the tall gladiolas stalks. "Today."

Gary carried Janice out to their customized van while Catherine clipped the wheelchair into the restraints. Gary started the engine, and a commercial blasted their ears. "Sorry." He reached for the knob to change stations.

Janice's weakened voice called out. "Wait, Gary, I know that voice."

"...there's one in every town...!" A snatch of music, a woman singing, then a voiceover giving details on where to find the *Pop's Pizza* nearest you.

"You know, Janice, I heard this the other day and I thought the same thing." Catherine settled beside her as the jingle came on to end the commercial. "--to west, Pop's is the best!"

"I've heard her in another ad, for one of the airlines." Gary called out, reversing down the driveway.

Catherine buckled her seatbelt. "She sounds familiar, Gary. I must say, this woman has a very melodic voice, seems wasted on radio commercials."

In a few minutes they turned onto a narrow country road lined on both sides with rock walls low enough to allow a view of rolling meadows heavy with the golden light of late summer. "And here we are!" She pushed Janice's chair across the lawn, noticing that the woman was light as a feather. "Let's go around back, to the orchard. Bosc pears, and my favorite, Cortland apples."

"Catherine, this spot would be perfect for a small vegetable garden." Gary was enthusiastic as he pointed to a level, sunny spot by the house. "Dig it up now, plant in the spring. I see herbs here along the path to the kitchen."

"I'm a city girl, Gary, I wouldn't know a parsley from a dill!" Catherine laughed as she unlocked the kitchen door.

"Gary will help, won't you dear?" With a sigh, Janice turned to gaze at the windows high on the wall.

"You know I will." But her husband had seen the wistful little smile, and he picked his wife up in his arms. "You're going to see every room in this house, my love, upstairs and down."

"Couldn't do this a few months ago, could you, Hercules?"

"Janice, you know I'd be the happiest man on earth if I still couldn't."

Catherine turned away as Janice brushed his cheek with her parched lips.

Wordless for once, Janice gazed in wonder at the six-burner gas stovetop, the wall ovens and huge double door fridge and freezer. "You've got yourself a dream kitchen, Catherine, professional yet warm and homey. I love the alder wood cabinets and the quartz countertops. Remember how Laura used to rave about this place? I bet she'd turn green with envy."

Catherine took a deep breath, tried to sound calm. "Have you seen her lately?" *Or Tony?*

"No, she says she's pretty busy. She called a while ago; said she'll visit when she gets a chance."

Bet she tells you how much she loves you and misses you, Catherine thought, uncharitable but so what. "How can she call herself a friend?"

"A lot of people don't know how to deal with death, Catherine, or dying. I guess Laura is one of them."

Catherine left them chatting in the dining room and went out through the french doors to the flagstone patio. The sweeping view was restful, patches of forest and meadows, rolling hills in the distance. She and Aly were moving in on the sixth of October, when the maples would be wearing their brilliant autumn hues. And once settled there would be parties; she could hear the tinkle of ice cubes, vivid conversation, the laughter of a dozen people. She'd order a cozy firepit, for dining *'al fresco'* with friends as the sun set. *Who are you kidding, Cat.*

Sitting on the low stone wall, she faced the enormous house. It would be beautiful at night when, from the master bedroom windows, she would see the twinkling lights of Boston in the distance. She'd have a window seat installed. But six bedrooms, three with ensuites? A conservatory, a library… good grief, she and Alyson would be banging around this echoing place alone. Melancholy fell over her like a cloud passing in front of the bright sun. She'd made a huge mistake, buying this mausoleum could be nothing else. Why had she thought living in a different house could change her life?

She had imagined friends coming to visit, to stay over, but which friends? She had no one but Kevin and his wife Jean. Gary and Janice, of course, perhaps the best friends she'd had in years, but soon, too soon, Janice would be gone and she'd likely lose touch with Gary. Relatives, then, family? But Tom and Elaine rarely left their beloved farm near Albany and Catherine was completely out of touch with her Barstowe relatives.

Face it, she chided herself, in her fantasies she had imagined living here with Tony, Alyson and his three kids. She had envisioned Alyson's wedding here in the stately Barstowe tradition, and Gina's, a rollicking feast celebrated the way they did it in the North End with the big Italian family he'd raved about. Catherine had dreamed all that when she'd expected Tony to come to her. So much for dreams.

Tony had said he loved her, but in the long months since the trial he had disappeared from her life. Fine! She certainly didn't want him after the cruel way he had humiliated her in court. She didn't miss him at all...almost, but even more than the loss of her husband, Tony had left her with a vast emptiness that she didn't know how to fill.

She had an empty house, while he enjoyed a cozy bungalow, and Laura, smug and secure there with her Tony after his undoubted eloquent apologies. Those two hypocrites deserved each other!

"Sorry to intrude on your thoughts, Catherine," Gary poked his head out the door. "I'm taking Janice back to the van; it'll soon be time for her meds."

Catherine dragged herself back to reality, to the sun

slowly disappearing behind the oaks lining the back of her property, noticing the sudden chill in the air. "I'm so sorry, Gary, why didn't you come for me sooner?"

"Jan was fine, and you looked deep in thought out here."

"Dreams, Gary, lost in dreams."

"I hope they all come true for you, Cath."

"Yeah…"

Don't be discouraged, my dear." He closed the distance between them, locked eyes with her. "You are a courageous woman, Catherine Moore. After all you've been through, I see happiness in your future."

"Easy for you to say…"

"A dear friend once told me not to live my life with my head in the sand–"

"–like an ostrich!" They both laughed.

"I don't know if that is the right allegory here, but--"

"I get it, and thank you, Gary."

"You know you can count on me, and Jan–"

"Hey, you two, I'm still here!"

Catherine helped Gary settle Janice into her chair, tucking the fleece close around her emaciated hips.

"Let me look at the garden one more time, please." Janice looked weak, her voice thin and tired. "This might be my last visit out here."

"Oh Janice, you'll be out here often." All of them knowing that wasn't going to happen.

"You know how they say you should live every day as if it's your last?"

Catherine nodded.

"I'm about there, my dear. And I'm ready."

Tears sprang to Catherine's eyes. Janice had taught her so much in the past few months about healing, about looking ahead and letting go of the past. She should be moving on with her new life, but still... "I think the Costellos are very selfish people." She chose to ignore her friend's look of surprise.

Janice phoned her the next day. "Catherine, remember the commercial we heard yesterday on the car radio? The pizza jingle...?"

"I remember."

"It's Laura. Laura Costello!"

"You're not serious."

"I knew I recognized that voice. Listen carefully next time it's on."

Between pizzas and airline commercials she seemed to be on the air frequently, and it wasn't long before Catherine heard it again. This time she paid closer attention to the voice. Rich contralto, a little sexy, bright overtone - Laura's unique sound. She grabbed the remote and clicked the radio off.

Forty-five

When Alyson came home from school that day Catherine set out a plate of cookies. "Al, have you heard the commercials for Pop's Pizza?"

"Yum, oatmeal raisin. Did you bake them?" Alyson began munching.

"No, love, picked them up at Whole Foods this morning. Did you know Amazon owns them now?" Her daughter munched on, oblivious. "But about that commercial…"

"Yeah, I guess I've heard it. So?"

Catherine began humming the tune.

"I said I've heard it, Mom."

"I think Gina's mother does it."

"Mrs. Cos-*tello*?" Cookie crumbs sprayed out with the words.

"Gina must be proud--"

"I don't have a clue how Gina feels, Mom." Alyson popped another cookie into her mouth and slid off the stool. "She doesn't talk to me."

Another huge change in her daughter's life. "Is it about–"

"Oh, Mom, don't start." Her clogs stamped across the

kitchen floor.

"I'm not *starting* anything, Al, I was just wondering—"

"Kids don't talk about their parents." She stopped at the doorway. "And anyway, I don't have to - everybody in the world already knows everything about *my* mother."

Everybody knows about your mother... The words Gina had spit at her the first week back at school; their last conversation.

"Gina, Aly's our friend and you're being mean."

"She's no friend of mine," sneering at Alyson. "Bonnie fighting your battles now?"

Alyson and Bonnie had grown close as sisters over the summer, hanging out together while Bonnie's dad helped her and her mom move into their new house, but Aly had not seen Gina since June. Still in the same school, but on different bus routes and class schedules. They were not friends, but Bonnie kept trying to get them together.

Alyson scanned the enormous cafeteria, hoping nobody had heard Gina's nasty remark. She had prayed all summer that this year would be different, that everyone would have forgotten what happened way back in December.

Even Mom believed it was all over. "Al, I'm sure your friends have other things to talk about."

But not Gina. Like a dog with a bone, she wouldn't let it go.

"Don't you dare talk about my mother, Gina Costello. Your mother's so screwed up she ran away from home."

"Oh yeah?" She raised her voice. "Well, your mother's a ho."

Suddenly the hum of conversation around them went dead, and Alyson noticed a few of the kids leaning in closer. But she couldn't let that remark go without an answer.

"Yeah, thanks to your pig of a father."

"You leave him out of this, bitch."

Bonnie covered her ears with both hands. "Please stop it, you two. At least your mothers aren't dying."

Ashamed, Alyson hung her head, but Gina plowed on.

"She was making fun of my mother."

"No, I just said that singing commercials for Pop's Pizza doesn't seem like such a big deal."

"Not as big a deal as your mother, the–"

"Shut up, just shut up!"

"C'mon, Gina, give her a break."

"Bonnie, butt out. Why do we have to listen to miss goody-two-shoes here preach at us when her mother is a whore and a… you know what."

"Gina, we promised…"

The bell rang. Alyson stood and picked up her tray, grateful that lunch period was over.

But Gina wasn't finished. "Bonnie," in a voice that could be heard across the cafeteria, "don't forget Friday! Jason - my boyfriend - is having a party, and everybody's going.

"Not everybody, Gina."

"Everybody who's anybody!" With a glance to make sure Alyson heard. "Aly's pissed off because she didn't get invited."

"I'm not going, Gina."

"I told you about it weeks ago, before school started."

"Well, I'm not going. I have better things to do."

"Ha! You're just sayin'--"

"No, Gina. Everybody knows that Jason's folks are away, and you can bet they'll be drinking and doing drugs there."

"So what."

Alyson turned around. "If your father ever found out--"

"Alyson Moore, if he does find out I'll know it's you that squealed and I'll make your miserable life even more miserable, hear me?" Waving her fist in Alyson's face.

Bonnie grabbed her arm. "You know Al would never tell, Gina, but I don't like that gang either."

"They just happen to be the most popular kids in the whole school. *And* they like me." Gina was fuming, a short fuse about to blow. "And here's another thing. My mother did *not* run away from home. She went to New York to start her career. Maybe she just sings commercials right now but she's going to be on Broadway one of these days. She's got a real neat apartment and she knows lots of famous people and I went to New York three times over the summer to visit her." Gina banged her fist on the table and stood up, tugging her miniskirt down over her behind. "Now I'm goin' outside for a smoke with all my friends so both of you, fuck off."

"Did you hear that?!"

I did, Al." Bonnie stacked Gina's tray with hers. "I guess she's found better friends than us to hang out with this year."

Alyson shook her head. "That ring in her nose creeps me out."

"It's a fake, you can tell it doesn't go right through."

"Even so... she's different since her Mom went away." Alyson studied her fingertips, noticed that the artificial nail on her thumb was peeling off one side. "Lots has happened in the past year, Bonnie. We're all different now."

"I wish my mother wasn't sick."

"Yeah, me too. And I wish..." What? That her mother hadn't done what she did? Nine months gone and the kids were still talking about it. *That's Alyson Moore, her mother murdered her father, you know.* Notorious. She'd looked the word up in the dictionary. The Moores were notorious.

"Al, do you miss your Dad?"

Not really, she'd decided that pretty quickly. He used to scare her and abuse - another new word - her mom. They were better off without him. But Bonnie's Mom, now that was a different story, she was sure Bonnie was really thinking about losing her mother.

"Yeah, I do, some. But I bet you'll miss your mother more."

The second bell rang for class. Alyson pried the fake nail off her thumb and dropped it into the trash on the tray.

Cookie in hand, Alyson had run up the stairs and slammed her bedroom door so hard the walls shook. "Max, Mom has ruined my life!" She threw herself on her bed, the stuffed animal clutched tight in her arms. "I'm never going to leave this ugly house again."

Listening outside the door, Catherine's heart broke. Aly was far too young to bear a burden like this.

Forty-six

The Costellos had only lived in Gilford for about eighteen months, but news about Laura's commercial gigs spread through the small town like wildfire. Many people had heard her sing at Mass, weddings, funerals, community concerts - her voice stood out, rich and clear, like bells ringing, hard to mistake. There were umpteen messages on Tony's machine every day and he was questioned wherever he went. Though six months had passed since the divorce he hadn't told a soul about it and it was hard to know what to say.

"Yup, that's Laura, all right.

"No, we don't see much of her these days, she spends a lot of time in New York, real busy with commercials and studio work.

"Laura took voice lessons before we got married but, with the kids and all...

"Oh yeah, me'n the kids are real excited about it.

"Thanks. We'd love to come over sometime, but with Laura's crazy schedule..."

One of those invitations came from Gary Kurtz, both of them shopping for groceries one Saturday morning. "Hi, aren't you Tony Costello?"

Tony pushed his cart on down the aisle--

The guy followed. "Recognized you from the newspapers, when...ah..."

"Okay, bud, whaddaya want?"

"Sorry, I don't mean to... I'm Gary Kurtz."

Tony kept both hands on the cart and ignored the outstretched hand.

"We've never met but my Janice and your wife are friends."

"Nice." He smiled, turned, ready to move on.

"Laura might also have told you that Janice is, ah, isn't well. She's heard Laura's voice on the radio and she'd love to congratulate her, and Lord knows my poor wife could use some good news. Does Laura have any free time?"

"Um, she spends most of her time in New York just now..." Tony couldn't bring himself to tell this man about the divorce. "She calls and gets here when she can, you know, to see the kids, whatever."

Truth was Laura rarely phoned, if she called at all; she and the kids texted back and forth these days. And she'd only been home once in the year since she left, to drive Claudia to Amherst and her dorm at UMass. Tony didn't like to think about that miserable day, but he saw no need to advertise that to a stranger.

"Janice really would love to see Laura before she...ah, while she's still able to enjoy company. Maybe the next time she's home, huh? Ask her to call."

"Yeah, sure."

The obit was in the paper a month later. Tony had

Gina text Laura to tell her that her friend Janice had passed away.

Forty-seven

Alyson had never seen the inside of a church. Mom said they were Protestant, whatever that was, but they never attended services. The closest she'd ever come to a church was the Christmas Tree lot at the Episcopal Church in town. Dad was supposed to be a Catholic, but he never went to church. When he died, they held a little service in the chapel at the Mortuary, somebody sang a couple of songs and a few people said what a great guy he was - guess they didn't know him very well. Anyway, she'd never been in St. Paul's Catholic Church.

Bonnie and Brian's mom's funeral was an eye opener. There was a big table that Bonnie said was an altar, where a priest stood and mumbled stuff. Behind him was a huge stained-glass window full of people that Alyson imagined was a bunch of saints, one of them apparently knocked off his horse by a beam of golden light - she'd have to ask Bonnie about that after the, uh, the mass.

She felt weird, sitting up here in the front row with Bonnie, her brother and her Dad. "Bon, why is it called a mass?"

"Shut up, Al," Bonnie hissed, "we're in Church."

Mr. Kurtz frowned. "Alyson, please try not to fidget."

He put a finger on his lips. "Say a prayer, ask your questions later."

"Sorry." But Aly didn't know any prayers, and if she didn't gaze around at all the statues, the stained glass windows, the chandeliers, the pictures on the walls of some guy dragging a cross, she'd have to look at the polished wooden box with the brass handles in the middle of the aisle that held Mrs. Kurtz. Were there holes in the sides, she wondered, so Bonnie's Mom could breathe in there? Alyson felt herself choking and turned to find her mother.

Several rows back, Catherine waggled her fingers at Al, smiled her support. It took courage to sit up front with Gary and the twins, and Catherine was proud of her daughter. She'd suggested keeping Aly back here with her, but Bonnie had begged.

"Now's when we need our friends, my Dad says so."

Catherine wasn't about to argue with that logic, but her heart skipped a beat when she spotted Gina Costello, with an ugly black ring in her pert little nose, sitting alone a few seats further up the aisle. For over a year the three girls had been inseparable; but since the scandal that involved her father, Gina didn't 'hang out' or sleep over at their house with Bonnie, nor, apparently, did she stay at Bonnie's when Alyson was there.

After the trial, hoping to protect her, Catherine had confessed the entire sordid story to her daughter, from her miserable marriage, her affair with Tony and the horror of the night Frank died. Hoping to make her understand that no shame attached to her; it was all on herself.

But the incident at school confirmed that her poor

daughter would have a tough row to hoe. Gina had obviously severed her friendship with Alyson because of Catherine's connection to her father. She sighed, hoping the girls would work it out on their own. If they did, she'd probably never find out now; Alyson didn't communicate with her at any level but the most superficial.

Her eyes roved about the church, took in the rather gaudy plaques between the stained-glass windows. Stations of the cross, Frank once told her, depicting Jesus' walk to his death on Calvary, and the huge cross above the altar with a pierced and bleeding Christ hanging on it - even with all the gold trim and painted statues, it was depressing, so unlike the unadorned Protestant churches she knew. Her eyes swiveled back to the front row where Alyson sat with Bonnie and Brian, their bent heads barely visible over the back of the pew. Such tiny shoulders to bear this sadness, Catherine thought. And Gary, poor, poor man, how lost and alone he must feel. The Kurtzes had been a happy, loving couple, they should have enjoyed many more years together - life was damned unfair! If only she and Frank-- sitting alone midway down the center aisle of the huge church, Catherine suddenly felt lonely.

The organ droned into a hymn Catherine had never heard and a gentle blend of voices rose to the high ceiling, descending on the congregation as if from heaven. For obvious reasons she was not part of the choir, but the loft was filled with people come to honor their friend's passing. Catherine couldn't imagine singing at a time like this, but the music gave her the opportunity to think about Janice.

Tears threatened as she realized how much she would

miss her friend, her wit and wisdom. She'd gone so quickly, a few short months from beginning to end. Ovarian cancer was merciless. Too late by the time it was diagnosed. She sent up a prayer that research would someday find a cure.

Across the aisle a slight figure swathed in a purple Pashmina shawl genuflected and slipped into the pew next to Gina. When she unwound her scarf and removed her dark glasses Catherine recognized Laura Costello. Alone. Catherine turned her head for a glimpse of Tony but didn't see him among the group of people standing at the back. She commanded herself not to think about Tony, but worried that he might come up and sit with his wife. She saw Gina gaze up at her mother with an expression of pure joy, saw Laura put her arm around her daughter and kiss the top of her curly head. At that moment the organ swelled into an entrance hymn and the service began.

After a rather lengthy sermon, in which the priest did his best to convince one and all that he had known 'Janet Katz' intimately, Communion was distributed. From her pew Catherine watched Laura and Gina approach the altar, take the bread and wine, then slip out the side door.

Finally, the choir director invited the congregation to join in singing *Precious Lord*, the recessional hymn, while six blank-faced pallbearers wheeled Janice slowly down the aisle, and a sobbing Alyson stumbled behind the coffin with Bonnie. Catherine took her daughter in her arms and put the Costellos out of her mind.

At Gary's house after the burial, Catherine passed platters of sandwiches and cake, made sure glasses and cups were filled, cleared dirty plates, always with an eye on the front door.   Laura did not come to pay her respects. Nor did Tony.

Catherine found out about Tony and Laura's divorce at The Sunnyside Café early the next morning.   And she heard it from Laura.

A petite woman, wearing a well-cut tan suit and enormous sunglasses, shoved the door open to leave and collided with Catherine coming in, swearing when hot coffee splattered her hand.   "Aw shit, look what you—"

"Sorry, I… Laura?"

The woman raised her head.

"Catherine--"

"*Madonn',* like I didn't know."   She turned back to the door.

"Laura, please, can we talk?"

"Why the hell not?   Coffee with a murderer and a chance to catch up on my husband's philandering all in one fell swoop!"

Catherine collapsed into an empty booth, feeling like she'd been punched in the stomach.   Eyes ablaze, Laura scooted in across the table and opened her mouth to speak.

But Catherine spoke first.   "I'm sorry about... about everything, Laura."

Laura slammed her paper cup down on the faux-marble tabletop.   "I just bet you are.   But in the end, you got what you wanted."   She pried the lid of the paper to-go cup.   "He's all yours now."

"Tony? I haven't seen him since--"

"You and me both."

To hide her shock, Catherine took a sip of black coffee from the mug the waitress slid across the table. Always tepid, but today, scalding hot, and burning as she swallowed.

Laura crossed her legs and sat back against the cushion with a self-satisfied grin. "You seem surprised."

Everything about Laura advertised success, from the neat blunt cut hair tinted a flattering soft brown, chunky heeled brushed suede booties and Coach handbag, tasteful diamond studs that twinkled in her ears.

"Don't tell me you didn't know I'd divorced the cheating bastard?"

"No. No, I didn't."

"I thought he'd run straight to your arms." She checked her cup. "Bah, they forgot the chocolate shavings." Shoved it aside. "This backwater sure ain't New York." Leaned across the table. "Here's the scoop, Catherine. One, he is a cheating bastard, as you well know, and two, I divorced him back in March." Manicured red nails tapped the tabletop. "I can't believe you're not together, that you didn't know he was free."

Catherine shook her head. "I told you, I haven't seen Tony in... since the trial."

"Ah yes, let me recap." Dark eyes glared into Catherine's. "That's when you killed your husband to get your grubby hands on mine."

"It wasn't like that." Both hands cupped the coffee mug. "I know you must hate me, Laura, but--"

"You mean you, personally? Not really. If it wasn't you it would have been one of his other floozies - surely you didn't think you were the one and only?"

Catherine sipped more coffee for something to do.

"It's sad," Laura's eyes were full of pity, "to go through all that and end up with nobody."

"Laura, it was an accid –"

"Oh, spare me, please, I really don't care one way or the other why you did what you did. But I guess now you know. Tony is a selfish man; he pleases only himself." She began to laugh, a low rumble deep in in her chest that rose in pitch and volume until the rich sound filled the coffee shop. People stopped talking to watch as Laura stood to leave.

"You were a fool, Catherine, murdering your husband for a man who could care less about you." Her laugh and her words floated behind her as she walked to the door.

Face burning, Catherine buried her face in a napkin.

"Refill?" The waitress' face bore a look of intense curiosity.

"Half a cup." She had to calm herself before she took the walk of shame out of here. "And bring the check."

Janice must have known, she and Laura had been close friends, but she never mentioned a divorce. And if Tony were free, why hadn't he tried to get in touch? A phone call, a letter, a text, a not so accidental meeting on the street, or, like before, in her office, the grocery store? Apparently, what they'd had, whatever it was, really meant nothing to him. She felt her face heat up, remembering with shame his damning words on the stand. Maybe Laura was right; he had so many women he had no need of her. Well, she was over him too. She didn't need him, or any man. So what if he'd been free all this time, she'd been on her own for longer.   She was a wealthy, independent woman, with a lovely daughter and an exquisitely renovated house. Her life was complete.

The waitress was talking rapidly to a man at the counter, by her gestures and head nodding obviously recounting the embarrassing scene.   Rather than wait for the check, Catherine dropped a ten-dollar bill on the table and made her way along the amazingly long aisle, head high and eyes fixed on the door ahead, pretending to ignore the rude stares.

Forty-eight

Over the summer Alyson had gone from uncommunicative and sullen to totally compliant, zombie-like behavior Catherine didn't trust in a thirteen-year-old. Now, a few months into a new school year, her teachers said she was quiet and attentive, but according to her guidance counselor, who knew the circumstances, Aly displayed only a superficial interest in her surroundings. She thought Alyson's compliance was a façade, a wall she hid behind to make her more acceptable to the people close to her.

There was no question that Alyson had developed an eating disorder. The dinner table was a battleground, and when she did swallow a morsel of the food that Catherine bullied her into eating, she gagged and left the table to bring it up. When asked, Bonnie said, "At school she takes a bite and throws the rest in the trash."

Alyson grew wan, listless; spoke only when spoken to, had no interest in television and worse, always an avid reader, she hadn't cracked a book in months. Catherine's heart broke as she watched Aly's bright, inquisitive personality disappear.

Lying awake at night, with terrifying images of that bleak

December night racing across her mind, Catherine wondered how anyone ever again could expect normal behavior. She had killed a man-- her husband. Alyson had seen her holding a bloody knife over that man-- her father. Catherine could see that Alyson needed therapy, but she had to find a way through her daughter's stubbornness.

The breaking point came one afternoon shortly before Halloween. Alyson raced into the house after school, ran up the stairs and slammed her bedroom door. Catherine quickly followed. With her hand on the doorknob, she heard a tiny, tear filled voice.

"Max, my life sucks." Heartbreaking sobs, and then, "-- wish *I* could die."

Rushing into the room, she found Alyson huddled on the floor, a miserable bundle, with Max clutched in her stick-thin arms. Catherine fell to the floor beside her and tried to hold her, but Aly fought her off. So much of her young life had been filled with horror. She took the sad little face into both hands and kissed the top of her head. "I love you so much, little one." Pushing Aly's hair back from her forehead, she noticed that it had lost its shine. "What is it, sweetheart?"

"Nothing. I was having a private conversation with Max."

"I know, love, but please tell me too."

Finally, "Remember Daniel?" Catherine didn't, but she nodded. Alyson was not fooled. "Dan, Mom, my boyfriend!"

Boyfriend? She longed for the days when Aly would have shared that. Catherine had been busy, but too busy to know about a boyfriend? Too late for regrets, but an adolescent lovers' spat couldn't be too difficult to handle.

"So tell me about ah, Dan."

"Well, I like him, and I thought he liked me."

"But?"

"There's going to be a party on Halloween - not at Gina's! - and I was sure Dan was going to ask me to go with him." She peeked up at Catherine with one eye. "I would have asked you if it would be okay."

Catherine squeezed her a little tighter.

"But today he said he was going to take another girl, Marie." Her chin began to tremble. "When I asked him why, he said he couldn't date a, a… a girl whose mother was a m-mur-murderer!" And she burst into heart wrenching tears.

"I'm so sorry, sweetheart, I've let you carry the burden of my actions on your little shoulders way too long." She gazed into her daughter's deep blue eyes, filled with tears and underlined with dark circles. "I'm going to make an appointment for you with a doctor as soon as possible."

"Oh no. I'm fine, Mom."

Catherine felt panic but kept her voice calm. "I know you think so, love, but you - we - are broken, and it's time for us to see someone who can make us better."

It took a long moment, but her sweet baby's arms reached up and clung to her neck. "I hope so, Mommy."

Catherine's heart overflowed with love. "Why don't you take a little nap before dinner."

Without a word, Alyson rolled over and scooted under the covers.

"Things will look better when you wake up, I promise." Kissing her damp cheek, Catherine tucked Max in beside her, closed the bedroom door and sped down the stairs.

"Elaine?" Breathless, tearfully sharing Alyson's story. "I can't believe I didn't see something like this coming. What should I do?"

Her sister knew immediately. "My roommate in med school, Sonia Ranthala, is a child psychologist in the Boston area. We are still in touch." She called Catherine back within the hour. "Dr. Sonia will see her Monday morning."

After one session the psychologist diagnosed Alyson with serious clinical depression, prescribed Zoloft®. "She's deep into the woods, Mrs. Moore. After what your daughter's gone through this comes as no surprise, but I believe she wants to talk about it." She patted Catherine on the shoulder. "I'm confident that we will soon see a spark of interest in the world around her."

"And Mrs. Moore," handing Catherine a business card, "I recommend that you make an appointment for yourself."

Forty-nine

Catherine and Alyson spent a quiet Thanksgiving in their beautiful home. Alone. She had invited Elaine and her family down but one of the girls was competing in a swim meet in Albany. "They think Amy might be Olympic material, Catherine. We're all so excited!"

So are we, Catherine said, keep us posted, all the while wondering how it felt to be truly excited about something-- anything, anymore.

The Caseys were on a Caribbean cruise, wouldn't be back until after Christmas.

Ben, Frank's half-brother, when he called to wish them Happy Chanukah, said he had made plans to spend the holidays in Florida.

"I'm going to meet Beth's folks, Catherine, but if you need me--"

Since the trial she and Ben spoke about once a month, and he had recently mentioned meeting a woman. Ben, at thirty-four, and wealthy, would be quite a catch. "They'll love you!" Lord knew they needed some good news in the family. "You and Beth can tell us all about it when you come back."

Gary had taken the twins to visit Janice's family in Iowa.

374

Catherine couldn't bring herself to invite anyone else who might turn her down.

It was a day to forget, a meal like so many others they'd shared lately, with Catherine making small talk and Alyson chewing her miniscule portions in remote silence. But she smiled behind her napkin as Aly left the table. "Thanks for dinner, Mom. It was good." Progress! The welcome words rang in Catherine's mind for the rest of the day.

Christmas came quickly, Alyson's favorite holiday. Catherine bought and set up a fresh-cut tree in the living room bay window, placed it exactly where she'd imagined it would go and decorated it with the new LED lights, reveling in the brilliant hues of purple and orange, nothing traditional here. Alyson, showing a spark of interest, helped with a few ornaments, but left her to finish. Catherine found solace in decorating the house, shopping for gifts, planning Christmas dinner.

"Bonnie and Brian are coming, with their dad." Catherine loved the twins, they were good company for Alyson, and Gary? Gary. After Janice passed away, he needed comfort, but of late she thought it might develop into something more.

"How about Beef Wellington, sweetheart? Your favorite."

"Yeah, Mom. Whatever."

She tried to create a festive mood, but the specter of the previous December was fresh in her mind. She concentrated on pleasing Alyson, with Christmas CD's - John Denver & The Muppets; Aly's favorite since childhood, brought a few moments of light to her daughter's wan little face.

Bonnie said she knew what Alyson would like for Christmas, and the pewter colored puffy quilted jacket and tall faux-suede UGG boots brought a smile and a hug on Christmas morning. Another bright spot was the card Alyson had made for her, now tucked into the holly garland on the mantel.

A few evenings they sat quietly, basking in the warmth of the fire and the lights on the tree. Alyson asked about the creche, in its rightful place under the tree, and Catherine told her the Nativity story. Small steps, but flashes of light in the dark tunnel, and she was grateful.

She trimmed mantels and doorways with ribbons and greens gathered from the bushes on their property and the forest beyond, keeping busy and resolutely cheerful, but long before the pine and juniper boughs lost their scent Aly had retreated into herself.

Otherwise, she filled the days with long, introspective walks, evenings reading by the fire or watching thick snowflakes blanket the pines and bare oak branches in white.

A festive time, Christmas.

New Year's came and went and suddenly it was the end of January, and Catherine had to acknowledge that she was bored. There was very little left to do inside the house and nothing could be done outdoors. It was a time she had disliked ever since childhood; the dingy winter gray sky, the dirty snowbanks, darkness falling at four in the afternoon. She called Kevin the day after Alyson returned to school.

For months he had been asking to come back, the market was hot, and he needed her experience. Also, Catherine was a bright light in the office, everyone missed her cheerful attitude. "Ah, Kevin, flattery will get you everywhere!" She had laughed, but always refused, but now she saw that it would be good, both for herself and for the company of which she was a partner.

"I will not deal with clients!"

"But you're so good at it."

"You know how people talk." Firm, but as the year progressed, she became more comfortable in town. Being publicly embarrassed by Laura Costello in the Sunnyside Café had been the absolute low point of her life and there was nowhere to go but up. Now she faced the world with proud head held high and a calm, unruffled demeanor. Little did she know the world saw a woman with eyes of steel and tightly pursed lips that never softened into a smile.

She rarely thought of Frank, but she was lonely, and she missed Tony, with his earthy humor, his candor, his silly mustache, their stolen moments of bliss.

She began scanning supermarket aisles, parking lots, faces in crowds. Her heart leaped whenever she saw a rare green Explorer on the road, leaving her shaken for hours. She'd drive slowly past the Gilford police station, a glitzy new building at the corner of Main and Prospect Street, straining to see movement through the tinted glass windows, as if Tony might be gazing out at the street at that moment and their eyes might meet...

She knew she was behaving like an idiot, yearning for a

man whose cruel words, so casually uttered in court, were burned into her memory. Why had he said such hurtful things? Had all his kisses and tender loving really been meaningless? Had she, as his nasty wife had thrown at her, been one of many? Catherine longed for an answer, but in the long, long year since her trial he hadn't tried to get in touch. Not by phone, not even a text or an email. Now that he was free– face it, Catherine, he had found someone else to seduce, and lie to. She was filled with shame, yet, in her heart of hearts she continued to hope that in a small place like Gilford it was inevitable that she'd run into him sooner or later.

Her days were full, but nights were long and empty, and in the dark hours before dawn, she would lie awake on a pillow wet with tears. Try as she might to forget him, Catherine longed for Tony like a schoolgirl with a crush, dreaming of him sailing up her driveway to declare his undying love. And a few times, at dusk, she had imagined him sitting in his green Explorer at the foot of the drive, pining for her. All the stuff of tacky romance novels.

Sometimes a desolate yawning emptiness overtook her, a craving for intimacy, for a lover, for the kind of relationship she'd been denied with Frank but one she'd hoped for with Tony. Some mornings she'd wake up with the memory of his kiss on her lips, the deep murmur of his voice in her hair, the delicious heart-pounding sensation when he touched her, moved inside her. Then her hands would rove over her body, pressing, caressing, arousing, until she turned, writhing and moaning, into her pillow.

Tony, aching with love for Catherine, waited and prayed for the right opportunity to explain why he had trivialized their love. He resisted calling or texting, they had to meet in person, to give her the space to walk away, pride intact. Even though he was responsible for bringing it all to an end, he refused to believe he would never again see her beautiful ocean-colored eyes glow with love for him, or hold her in his arms, But he had done it - damn near perjured himself f'r Chrissake - he'd done it to protect her. Surely she understood that.

He prowled the streets of town hoping for a glimpse of her. After she moved to Hillcrest he often drove up there, parking by the stone walls surrounding the beautifully restored old mansion, by his presence keeping her safe. Leaving only when the last light went out. Knowing that she was asleep, he was content. He haunted the Chinese restaurant and drove by Casey & Moore daily, feeling like a complete fool when he dredged up the courage to stop at her office. Kevin Casey said she had not returned to work, all the while looking at him the way a person might regard a cockroach in the bathroom.

Sweet Jesus how he missed her, the smell of her hair, her silky skin, their long talks, her sighs and moans the few times they made love. Night after night he saw again the shock in those trusting eyes, her gentle heart his to break. He wanted to spend the rest of his life with her, but first he needed to explain, to beg forgiveness, only then could they move on.

But he was afraid. Why would she agree to see him, listen to him? She'd probably hang up on him if he tried to phone. He'd compose a text and immediately delete it, too impersonal. When the right moment came along, he'd be ready, but meantime months slipped by. She needed time to heal, and he could wait, certain that in a small place like Gilford it was inevitable that they'd meet up sooner or later.

Fifty

There is no greater love than that of a mother for her child, Catherine grumbled, peering through a windshield smeared and streaked with dirty snow and ice, the mess piling up on her windshield faster than her wipers could move it. In April! It certainly made you wonder about climate change.

She had planned to be at the high school well before seven but slogging through the slushy back roads from Hillcrest to Gilford had nearly doubled her estimated driving time. Scanning the crowded parking lot, she'd had to drive around back to the ice-covered soccer field behind the school, finally finding a spot between a massive snowbank and a big yellow Hummer - at least she'd have no trouble finding her car later. She arrived at the auditorium, wet, bedraggled, and fifteen minutes late for the show. The students who should have been taking tickets had deserted their posts to go inside and watch the performance. She crept down the walkway in the pitch dark, grateful to find a seat on the aisle in the third row from the back of the crowded auditorium.

Onstage the show was underway, a skit about women

shopping for underwear. The women were being played by boys, large young men who had to be football halfbacks in real life, and the crowd loved it.

Alyson was part of the production crew. She had come such a long way in the past few months. Some days she was her old sweet self, flashing a big smile at breakfast, and singing - slightly offkey! with her favorite music. She had filled out, grown a tiny bosom, started her periods, and the bulimia was just a bad memory, if the plates scraped clean at dinner were any example. Dr. Sonia said she was beginning to share her feelings, and the therapist felt confident that Aly would soon be mentally ready to confront what she'd seen the day Frank died and hopefully get it behind her.

While the audience laughed and applauded Catherine shed her wet woolen coat and the magnificent striped scarf Elaine had knitted for her, peeled off her gloves and piled the whole damp mess into the seat between hers and the next one, occupied by a man, alone, a man wearing a dark leather jacket. As her eyes grew accustomed to the gloom she made out a patch on the arm of his jacket, a dark shield outlined in gold with the letters GPD standing out prominently in embroidered gold thread.

Slowly raising her eyes, she caught Tony, sporting the little mustache again, smiling at her across the empty seat, across her damp clothes, across the bridge of time. Over a year since she'd seen him last and he hadn't changed a bit. He nodded, winked and turned back to the stage, settling back into his seat with an audible sigh, a contented sound, Catherine thought.

She could get up and leave or change seats, but another act was beginning and in the dark it was hard to pick out an empty seat and she didn't want to cause a commotion, but mainly she didn't think her weak knees would hold her. She stayed put, hoping that Tony couldn't hear her heart pounding and threatening to leap through her ribs any second.

When the show ended Catherine applauded with the crowd, grateful that Alyson had not been onstage, hoping her daughter wouldn't ask too many questions, she couldn't remember much about it.

The lights went up. Tony reached across the empty seat and lightly touched her arm. Weightless, but somehow intimate, and through her sweater Catherine's skin burned. She raised her arm and patted her hair. "I must look like something the cat dragged in."

"Never, Catherine." He said her name as if holding each syllable in his mouth. "You look lovely, as always."

"Oh Tony." It was a whisper, a sigh, a prayer. She'd waited so long to hear his voice, to feel him near-- Suddenly they were surrounded, caught up in a bubbling sea of giggling and bouncing girls.

"Mom, you came! I couldn't see you way back here!"

"Would I miss this, sweetheart?"

And behind her daughter, Gary Kurtz. "Detective."

Tony nodded.

Earlier, Gary had called, suggesting they take the girls out for a bite after the show. Catherine had agreed, but now... "Gary, do you think going out is a good idea, given this lousy weather?"

Before he could answer, his arm was grabbed by a miniature flapper, all silver fringe and kiss curls and kewpie doll lips. "What *is* it, Bonnie?"

"Can Aly sleep over, Dad?"

"I, um, if her mother–"

"Dad, did you see my dance?" Gina, barely visible behind Bonnie's feathers and frills.

Tony gathered her in his arms. "Yes, sweetie, I did, and you were fabulous!" Her dark eyes glowed with his praise.

"Da-ad, can Al–"

Catherine saw Gary aim a significant nod at Gina.

"Umm, you too, Gina."

Eyes fixed on Alyson, Gina whispered, "I'd like that."

A smile replaced the frown on her daughter's face. "Yeah, me too."

Catherine happily watched the three girls hug, and caught Tony's grin over their heads.

"Dad?"

"It's okay with me, long as–"

"Oh *great*, a pajama party." Brian had caught up and looked disgusted.

"Brian, put a sock in it." Bonnie turned back to her father.

Gary's eyes traveled between Catherine and Tony. "If it's okay with you two..."

You two. The implication hung in the air.

"Sure."

"Fine."

Did it seem that she and Tony answered a bit too quickly? Catherine picked up her coat. "Time for me to get on home."

Tony shrugged into his jacket. "And I have to get back to work."

Gary turned to the kids. "Who's for pizza at Vito's?"

Over the cheers of the excited chorus, Gary sent Catherine a sad little smile that plainly said, 'falling for him again, Cath?' But he quickly turned and left with his fluttering and twittering entourage.

She felt Tony's eyes on her face.

The hall was empty, yet they stood staring at each other. The janitor asked them to move along, he had to lock the doors and get on home.

She followed Tony out past the double glass doors and stopped to watch the stream of cars leaving the school. Snow fell, thicker flakes now. Perfectly formed stars settled on her coat, on Tony's dark hair, sparkling like crystal as they drifted past the lights. In the parking lot car engines roared and a ribbon of red taillights twinkled. He tugged a watch cap out of a pocket. Shivering, she pulled her scarf up over her head.

"You should have a hat."

"I look ridiculous in a hat."

"I know."

Uninvited memories of winters past flashed in her mind, and she turned to leave.

"Don't go." Tony grabbed her arm. "Feel like Chinese?"

She had to laugh. "No, thanks."

He rubbed his chin, the nervous gesture she once found endearing, quickly stuffed his hands into his pockets. "Um," clearing his throat, "now that we don't have to worry about the girls..." With the cap pulled down over his ears he looked like a little boy, big brown eyes pleading. "...Maybe we could get a coffee, or something?"

She wanted to say yes, but, "I, ah, I should go." She zipped her jacket right up to her chin, backed away. "My car is around back—"

"Mine's right here, hop in and I'll drive you to it."

Once again, zombie-like, Catherine clambered into his vehicle, the same green Explorer, quivering with the nearness of him. They crunched across the parking lot and rolled to a stop beside the majestic Lincoln, now standing alone at the back of the field under a thick coat of drifting snow. The air in the SUV was heavy with unspoken words.

"Thanks, um..." Her stiff fingers fumbled for the door handle.

Tony leaned across the console, lips formed to say— what? She never knew. He pulled her head closer and rested his forehead against hers. Kissed her eyelids, her cheeks, finally her mouth. "I've missed you so much, Catherine."

She inhaled the citrus scent of his aftershave, the scent her memory had kept alive all this time. "Oh God, Tony..." He was here, holding her, loving her, the moment she'd dreamed of for so long.

"Do you really want coffee?" He whispered the words into her scarf.

"No."

She heard the zipper slide down on her jacket and felt his hand slip inside. An electric shock went through her when his cold fingers teased her stiffened nipples. She kissed him, hard, felt his tongue dart into her mouth. She took his bottom lip between her teeth. Her body arched toward him, but she couldn't get close enough with this console–

"Tony, not here, not like this." Her voice hoarse.

He groaned.

"My place is closer." And empty, she thought. Before she changed her mind, she jumped out of his car into the Lincoln, reversing and driving off before the windows had begun to defrost, wheels spinning, spraying snow. She turned the fan up high, scrubbed a tiny space clear on the windshield with her mitten. The wipers ticked a mad little tune across the glass, *To-ny, To-ny…* She laughed out loud, knowing she had a big stupid grin on her face, but she couldn't help it. Nipples erect, belly on fire with anticipation, damp between her legs with wanting him. A mile down the highway she remembered to check if he was following her. Notwithstanding the state of the road, the big car covered the five miles as if on wings.

She slammed the car into park on the driveway and sped to her front door; Tony close behind. Inside, he took her in his arms, kissed her hair, but she pushed him away, seeing herself sprawled naked on the floor like a tramp and to hell with her upbringing. "Upstairs, Tony, not here." She kicked off her boots and raced up the stairs, dropping her hat, her coat, a trail of clothing for him to follow. He caught up at her bedroom door. She took his hand and led him inside.

Fifty-one

It's late when Catherine wakes up beside Tony on the rumpled mess of her king size bed. Across the room the fireplace glows, embers of the blaze he lit earlier. She has no idea what time it is, but what does it matter? They made love twice during the night, long and slow and satisfying, wordlessly holding each other in the interim, unable to express the joy of being together at last. Her body feels heavy, warm, loved, but her mind is restless. Questions niggle. They must clear things up before they can move on.

Beside her, Tony snores gently and she smiles, watching him sleep. If things work out, she could spend the rest of her life with him, but first… In the soft light from the fire she catches the gleam of his eyes through his thick dark eyelashes. He chuckles, reaching for her. She longs to melt into his arms, but she rolls away from him.

"What's wrong?"

"We have to talk."

"We have the rest of our lives to talk." He tries to pull her closer but she sits up, back stiff against the padded headboard, and wraps the comforter tight around herself.

He sits up next to her. "I know I have a lot of explaining to do--" His fingertips trace her mouth.

"Tony, don't–"

"I love you."

Tears start, and she swipes them away with the corner of the sheet. "If that's true, why did you stay away? Why didn't you come for me when you and Laura split up?"

"I–"

"And why, for God's sake, did you lie about us on the stand?"

"Not lies, Catherine." He scrubs at his face with both hands. "I might have fudged the truth a bit, um, to–I was trying to protect you."

"Well, it hurt." Petulant, maybe, but the wound of his denial goes deep. "A year, Tony, more than a year, and you never--"

"I was afraid, after what I did, that you wouldn't..." He turns his head away.

"Big brave cop, scared of me?" Recalling how he waffled between love for her, commitment to Laura. "No, Tony, you were afraid I would."

"I love you, Catherine, with all my heart."

"You love the thrill of being on the edge."

He fondles her ear.

"I'm serious, Tony." She pushes his hand away. "Here you are, free as a bird, no wife, no lover, no responsibilities - I bet you have a string of women--"

"I only want to be with you."

"You have a strange way of showing that." She slips out of bed. "All this time I thought I was waiting for you, needing to hear you say those words, but tonight... tonight was wonderful, Tony, but - this is hard to explain - it feels like the end of something."

His face crumples, like a little boy about to burst into tears. "Cath–"

"No, listen to me for a minute. For a long time, I lived in fear. Afraid of my husband, afraid to make a decision, afraid to do what had to be done for me and Alyson." Trailing the comforter, she slowly backs away from the bed. "You can't imagine what it's like. The threat of prison, the trial, the humiliation, then the agony of having my heart broken - no, let me finish! On my own, trying to get back to some version of normal. I had to be strong, for Alyson." She settles into the soft slipper chair beside the fireplace. "I learned that I don't need to lean on you or anyone else."

Naked, he leaves the bed and comes to her, kneeling by the chair. "But I need you!" Tears gleam in his eyes. "I thought you loved me."

Something inside closes gently as she gazes for a long moment into his handsome, tortured face. "Not enough, Tony. Not nearly enough."

Faint rosy fingers of light break through the clouds of dawn, stretch across the richly colored Persian rug and touch her bare feet. Still huddled in the little chair, she hears Tony start up the engine and turn the ugly green Explorer out of her driveway, out of her life. She has possibly just made a huge mistake, but she feels relieved, as if a burden has been lifted from her shoulders.

Wrapped in the comforter, Catherine floats down the

stairs to her gleaming new kitchen, makes herself a pot of Chai tea and curls up on the deep window seat, watching the pale wintry sun rise on a new day.

Fifty-two

Laura's career has soared in the past year. On her own she negotiated a voice-over contract for a series of television commercials for a major airline, her voice is heard coast to coast in the ads for the expanding Pop's Pizza chain, and there are other things in the works. Now in constant demand, she can ask for the moon; new friends in the business have recommended a knowledgeable contract lawyer. Agents call, hoping to represent her, wooing her with dinners at any number of fancy New York eateries, handing out tickets to anything her heart desires. She took Claudia to see *Hamilton*, on Broadway, smiling when her daughter pretended to be unimpressed with their fourth row seats, gift of a cast member Laura has come to know. This month she is in rehearsal for a little musical fantasy off-off-Broadway and after that, who knows!

She is thrilled with the possibility of appearing on the Broadway stage, but her heart is in South Carolina, held captive in a cottage not much bigger than a beach shack by the wonderful woman who saved her life. Sam; her friend... her partner.

The plane arrives an hour late, pinned to the ground at

JFK by a thunderstorm, but one step out of the terminal in Myrtle Beach, and Laura's travel woes melt away in the comforting warmth of the sun.

All summer Manhattan has been under construction; dust and grinding trucks and jack hammers pounding at all hours of the day and night. Folks who know say that is normal, just be grateful that the clean-up at the site of the World Trade Center disaster is finally finished; that had been a nightmare for years. Now, on the site where office towers once stood, reflecting pools gleam in the sun, bordered by bronze panels inscribed with the names of the 3000 people killed on that horrific day. Two of them - thank God they knew only two - were men who had served many years ago with Tony in Boston. Below ground, an impressive Museum she has yet to bring herself to visit.

But, on this glorious September day, the plane dips and turns over the bright blue Atlantic and rolls to a stop among swaying palms and sparkling white sand of Myrtle Beach. Laura digs out her sunglasses, scanning the lot for Sam's faded blue truck as she tries to balance a massive bouquet of anthurium with her carry-on bag.

Sam is parked directly under the sign for Passenger Arrivals, solid and patient in her '99 Chevy pick-up with the ancient flame-stitch afghan covering the worn seats. For her birthday Laura plans to get Sam something brand spanking new, maybe one of the small Crossover SUVs all the rage just now.

"Well, what took you, hon? I've been fightin' off these self-important airport traffic police for half an hour, you'd think they were expectin' the President today."

"Happy birthday, Sam!" Laura stretches across the seat to kiss her, dropping the flowers into her lap.

"Little boy flowers!" with a laugh, "thank you, hon."

Laura feels Sam's eyes checking her over. "You're lookin' weary, Laura." Her big warm hand brushes Laura's hair, slips over her shoulders and down her arms before settling back on the steering wheel.

"That's New York in the summer, Sam, ain't no sunshine in the City, just sticky, icky humidity." She rolls down the window to feel the breeze off the ocean. "I'll be better than new by the end of the week, you'll see. Now, did you look at the pics I posted of your new car? What did you think of the pearly pink color? I thought it looked like the inside of a seashell."

"Don't you worry yourself about a new car, sweetness. This ole buggy's been getting me around for a lotta years and I don't think it's planning to let me down yet."

"Sam, you've supported me for over a year and I've finally got me some money of my own." Giggling, Laura waves several hundred-dollar bills in the air between them. "I can pay down my credit cards and repay you and Tony." So much she wants to say. "Sam, I love you, and I want to share my good fortune with you." Shy, she ducks her head. "Last week I found an apartment in the Village, the cutest little studio with a loft overlooking a tiny handkerchief of a green park."

"Great!" Sam got the old truck started. "You're out of that smelly room on the fifth floor."

"This one is only four floors up - there are no elevators in those old apartment buildings. But Sam, you're gonna love--"

"I'm sure I will, hon, when I visit. But tell me, did you get to see your kids over the summer?"

Laura brushes a few specks of dust from her navy wool skirt. "Boy, I can't wait to get out of these stuffy New York duds."

"Laura?"

"They're not in Gilford, they're in Boston now - can you believe my loser ex-husband is living with his mother! I got the royal brushoff from that little twerp of mine."

"Gina?"

"Little miss hot shit. I offered to fly up to Boston to see them, but she's too busy to fit me in even for a burger."

She peeks into the mirror on the visor, quickly wipes smudges of mascara from under her eyes, grateful when she feels Sam's hand on hers. "I'm okay, Sam, she needs to blame someone for breaking up her home."

"She'll forgive you when she's ready, Laura."

"And Anthony? What the fuck's wrong with my son that he won't text or talk to me on the phone? Know what I think, Sam? I think Tony's got them brainwashed. Can't they see that I was suffocating? Tony had his women and Anthony had his pals and his CD's and the girls had school and dancing and boyfriends, and what did I have?" She sniffles. "The bottle, that's what." She grabs a tissue.

"Laura, we've been over this umpty-dump times. They're young, you deserted them, they need to make you pay. They'll grow up and you'll all be friends. It'll work out."

"Yeah, when I'm wrinkled and gray."

Sam runs her fingers gently along the newly tightened

line of Laura's chin. "Hon, long as there's a plastic surgeon alive you'll never be either."

Laura laughs along with her. "You always find the silver lining." She squeezes her friend's hand. "I thank the Lord every day that I found you, Sam. I love you." Still awkward admitting her feelings for the other woman. "New York's lonesome without you."

Sam shakes her head slowly from side to side as the old truck wheezes and rattles up the crushed shell driveway to the cottage. "We've had this talk before, Laura. Take me away from the Beach and I'll shrivel up and die." She turns off the engine. 'New York is where you work. This is your home."

She circles gracefully around to the front of the truck, takes Laura into her arms, kisses her full on the lips. Been wantin' to do that all day."

The screen door of the cottage next door slam shut. Their neighbor doesn't approve of gay women.

Sam takes Laura's hand. "Now, let's get you around a frosty glass of mint tea so we can talk about my new car.

Laura snuggles close to her partner and strolls with her up the steps to the sagging screen door. "It's good to be home."

Fifty-three

Tony taps his Fitbit, checks the time. Getting on for midnight, Anthony should be home soon. He's off with 'the guys', Tony hardly sees him since they moved back to the North End. He hopes the kid isn't out knocking up any broads, they'd had that talk more than enough times.

"Look at what happened to me and take my advice, son. You're with a girl, you keep your pecker in your pocket. *Capice*?"

Biggest mistake he ever made, getting Laura pregnant, letting himself get browbeat into marrying her. No balls, that was his problem. All his life he'd done everything by the book, he'd been a good boy, tried to be a good husband and father, kept his nose clean at the shop, moved out to the boonies to please Laura. And Christ, look what happened there! Now she was living the life, between her career in New York and that dyke in South Carolina!

His partner, goddam hypocrite - that weasel squealed and got the promotion that should have been his. Don fuckin' Corbett, with the mistress and the holier-than-shit attitude, suck-up to the Captain big-time. After he spread the dirt about Tony and Catherine Moore, Tony's name was crap in the department. He didn't like the cookie-cutter raised ranch, nor the snotty suburban town. In Gilford he was the 'Eyetie' with the Boston accent. When he brought up the idea of moving back to Boston to the kids, they jumped at it.

Now he sits on the cement stoop, alone in the dark, empty night. His mother's street in the North End is short, coupla blocks up to Richmond Street, two down to Boston Harbor. September in the city is hot and humid as hell, the whole neighborhood smelly with meat rotting in the dumpster behind the butcher's shop around the corner. He unbuttons his shirt and snickers, remembers his Dad sitting out here in his undershirt; wonders if they still call them wife-beaters! The muted sound of voices and laughter over on Richmond Street is a constant, white noise, except for the occasional shriek of some teenybopper, the thump of bass in a passing car.

He takes a long drag on the cigarette cupped in his palm, exhales slowly, blowing smoke rings. Like the old days. He's started smoking again because... because, hell, a guy's gotta get some enjoyment out of living. And the same old question, like a phonograph needle stuck in a groove. What the fuck did he do to deserve ending up in the shitter?

Up until Catherine, he'd done everything right and just look how that paid off! Now the only two women he'd ever loved were out of his life. One getting it on with that wuss Kurtz - oh yeah, he'd heard all about it from Gina. And the other one, swinging the other way. Ah hell, he doesn't miss them, either one. What's love anyway but a little sex and lots of responsibility!

But his luck might be turning. Sold the house for a small profit in less than a month. Listed with Remax.

All summer he's been on Gina like white on rice, but she's back in school - with the nuns! No nose ring or pot or whatever other shit she'd got herself into - in the suburbs. And she wants to teach ballet! Not tall and willowy, but a beautiful dancer and tough as nuts, she'll make a real good teacher. Claudia, a sophomore at UMass in Amhurst, with a boyfriend, Edvard. Nice guy, even if he is Danish. Tony plans to send his son to trade school, turn him into a plumber, or an electrician, they make a good living.

He grinds the half-smoked butt into the cracked sidewalk at his feet. Time to hit the hay. He must be gettin' old, learning his new job is tiring. Thanks to Gilford PD's 'glowing' recommendation, he's got a shitty desk job at his old precinct, but he won't be stuck there forever; just this morning Chief Mulvaney good as promised him the gold shield. Oh yeah, Tony Costello will rise again!

The door behind him creaks open, releasing the stink of more than a century of fried garlic into the stagnant air.

"How you doin', *figlio mio?*" A soft voice in the darkness.

"Still up, Ma?"

"I don't like to see you unhappy, my boy, seeing you like this rips my heart from my breast."

Italian women; fuckin' drama queens. "Yeah, I know, Ma, but what can you do?" He tugs the soft pack of cigarettes out of his breast pocket.

"And this smoking, *Dio mio!* Are you trying to kill yourself?"

"Ma, I'm not a kid!"   But he slips the package back into his pocket.

"Come, 'tonio, time for bed."

He's gotta get out of here, and soon.

She's moving up the stairs, still talking.   Her voice intrudes on his thoughts and he figures he'd better pay attention.

"What's that, Ma?"

"Emilia."   Puff.   "She married the Taddeo boy."   More puffing.   "Not the priest, the other one, with the short leg."

Holy-- "Angelo Romanetti's fat sister?"

She stops on the landing, turns to him.

He sees her hands, pale in the gloom of the stairwell, held out like she's measuring someone.   Oh yeah, the fat one.

And as she starts up the stairs, "Not skinny like your--"

"*Basta*, Ma, enough."

"I talk with Emilia jus' today.   Poor girl is a widow now..."

Tony laughs.   "So, Ma, when is she coming to dinner?"

He follows his mother up the well-worn steps to the comfortable old apartment on the second floor.

Soon he'll get his own place, nothin' big, a flat like this one will do, here in the North End.

Home.

Fifty-four

Late again, Catherine thinks, letting the Lincoln roll to a stop on the driveway. It's a little past six, not too late. She turns off the engine and opens the door but sits for a moment, taking in the stately old house, its new casement windows gleaming in the late day sun. Her eyes sweep the warm stone façade, inviting front porch, the flourishing landscape Gary designed and planted over a year ago.

This is a home filled with love. It would be nice to have a companion, a lover, to share her life, but Prince Charming has yet to make an appearance. For a while she hoped it might be Gary, but two lonely people do not a pair make. They are resigned to being good friends. You're only forty, friends tease, and miracles *do* happen.

If it weren't for Alyson... she might be lonely, but her bright and beautiful daughter is whole, and Catherine is content.

This evening Alyson is hosting a surprise fifteenth birthday party for Bonnie and Brian. The old house will vibrate with the music and chatter of twenty or more kids. She would never admit it, but Catherine is very pleased that

Gary will be here to help chaperone. Time to get moving, Ms. Moore, Aly's guests will be arriving any minute. Humming, Catherine collects her purse and briefcase and takes the winding flagstone path to her front door.

Home.

Hope you enjoyed *'Til Death...*

Other books by Diane E. Lock

Friends & Lovers

Picture of Love
True Love

www.DianeLock.com

Visit my author page on Amazon

or

on Facebook at
My Happy Place

Made in the USA
Columbia, SC
10 January 2020

86655889R00233